STEVEN L. KENT

THE CL4NE REBELLION

ELITE

TITAN BOOKS

THE CLONE ELITE
Print edition ISBN: 9781781167182
E-book edition ISBN: 9781781167342

Published by Titan Books
A division of Titan Publishing Group Ltd
144 Southwark Street, London SE1 0UP

First edition: May 2013
1 3 5 7 9 10 8 6 4 2

This is a work of fiction. Names, characters, places, and incidents either are the product of the author's imagination or are used fictitiously, and any resemblance to actual persons, living or dead, business establishments, events, or locales is entirely coincidental. The publisher does not have any control over and does not assume any responsibility for author or third-party websites or their content.

A CIP catalogue record for this title is available from the British Library.

Printed and bound in Great Britain by CPI Group Ltd.

Did you enjoy this book?
We love to hear from our readers. Please email us at:
readerfeedback@titanemail.com or write to us at the above address.

To receive advance information, news, competitions, and exclusive offers online, please sign up for the Titan newsletter on our website.

www.titanbooks.com

This novel is dedicated to my friend Kevin.

I wish you had had the chance to read this book, and I had had the chance to read the books that you took with you.

SPIRAL ARMS OF THE MILKY WAY GALAXY

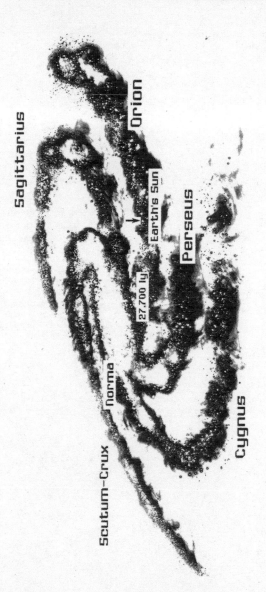

Sagittarius

Orion

Earth's Sun

Perseus

27.700 ly

Scutum–Crux

Norma

Cygnus

100.000 ly

Map by Steven J. Kent, adapted from a public domain NASA diagram

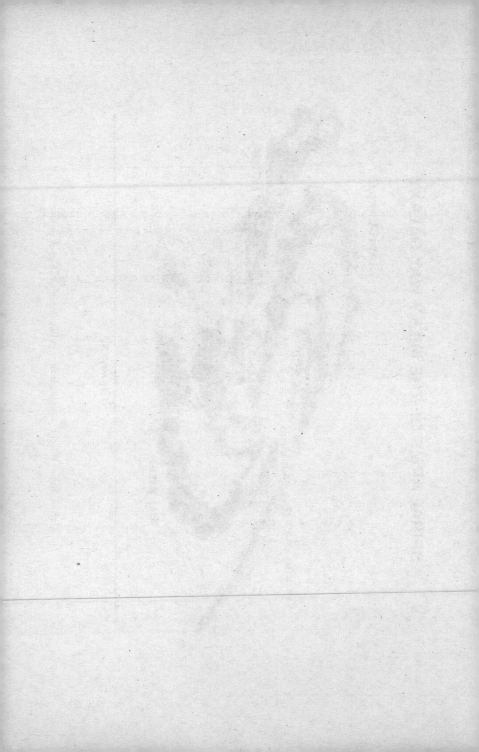

I am determined to sustain myself for as long as possible, and die like a soldier who never forgets what is due to his own honor and that of his country.

COLONEL WILLIAM BARRET TRAVIS

FIVE EVENTS THAT SHAPED HISTORY
A UNIFIED AUTHORITY TIME LINE

2010 TO 2018
DECLINE OF THE U.S. ECONOMY

Following the examples of Chevrolet, Oracle, IBM, and ConAgra Foods, Microsoft moves its headquarters from the United States to Shanghai. Microsoft executives maintain that their company has always been a global corporation and remains dedicated to the United States; but with its burgeoning economy, China has become Microsoft's most important market.

Even though Toyota and Hyundai increase manufacturing activities in the United States—because of the favorable cheap labor conditions—the U.S. economy becomes dependent on the shipping of raw materials and farm goods.

Bottoming out as the world's twelfth largest economy behind China, Korea, India, Cuba, the European Economic Community, Brazil, Mexico, Canada, Japan, South Africa, Israel, and Unincorporated France, the United States government focuses on maintaining its position as the world's only remaining military superpower.

JANUARY 3, 2026
INTRODUCTION OF BROADCAST PHYSICS

Armadillo Aerospace announces the discovery of broadcast physics, a new technology capable of translating matter into data waves that can be transmitted to any location instantaneously. This technology will open the way for pangalactic exploration without time dilation and the dangers of light-speed travel.

By the end of 2030, the United States creates the first-ever fleet of self-broadcasting ships, a scientific fleet designed to locate planets for colonization. When initial scouting reports suggest that the rest of the galaxy is uninhabited, politicians fire up public sentiment with talk about "manifest destiny" and spreading humanity across space.

The discovery of broadcast physics eventually leads to the creation of the Broadcast Network—a galactic superhighway consisting of satellite dishes that send and receive ships across the galaxy. The Broadcast Network ushers in the age of galactic expansion.

JULY 4, 2110
RUS SIA AND KOREA SIGN A PACT WITH THE UNITED STATES

With the growth of its space-based economy, the United States reclaims its spot as the wealthiest nation on Earth. Russia and Korea become the first nations to sign the IGTA (Intergalactic Trade Accord), a treaty created by the United States inviting other nations to become tribute-paying partners in the space-based economy.

In an effort to create a competing alliance, France unveils its Cousteau Oceanic Exploration program and announces plans to create undersea colonies. Only Tahiti joins the French partnership program.

After the European Economic Community, Japan, and all of Africa sign to become members of the IGTA, France dissolves its undersea exploration program and joins.

Several nations, most notably China and Afghanistan, refuse to sign the IGTA. China threatens to attack the United States and its partners if they do not share a percentage of space-earned profits, leading to a minor world war in which the final holdouts are coerced into signing the trade accord.

More than 80 percent of the world's population is eventually sent to establish colonies throughout the galaxy.

JULY 4, 2250
TRANSMOGRIFICATION OF THE UNITED STATES ANNOUNCED

Having already expanded beyond a treaty of commerce, the members of the IGTA agree to form themselves into a single nation based on U.S. law. In an effort to demonstrate that the IGTA is a unilateral organization rather than an extension of the United States, the governing body adopts the name "The Unified Authority."

Deemed inadequate for governing the galactic expansion, the U.S. Constitution is replaced by a new manifesto merging principles from the Constitution with concepts from Plato's *Republic*. In accordance with Plato's ideals, society is broken into three strata—citizenry, defense, and governance.

With forty self-sustaining colonies across the galaxy, Earth becomes the political center of the republic. The eastern seaboard of the United States becomes an ever-growing capital city populated by a political class—families appointed to run the government in perpetuity.

Earth also becomes home to the military class. After some experimentation, the Unified Authority adopts an all-clone conscription model to fulfill its growing need for soldiers. Clone farms, euphemistically known as "orphanages," are established around Earth. These orphanages produce more than one million cloned recruits per year.

Officers are drafted from the ruling class. When the children of politicians are drummed out of school or deemed unsuitable for political responsibilities, they are sent to an officer-candidate school in Australia.

2452 TO 2512
GALACTIC EYE UPRISING

On October 29, 2452, a date later known as "the new Black Tuesday," a fleet of scientific exploration ships vanishes without a trace in the inner curve of the Norma Arm—the Galactic Eye region of the Milky Way.

Fearing that the missing fleet encountered an "unknown intelligence," the U.A. Senate calls for the creation of a self-broadcasting battle fleet to enter the Norma Arm and investigate any threat to Unified Authority sovereignty.

Work on the Galactic Central Fleet is completed in 2455, and the fleet travels to the Inner Curve, where it vanishes as well.

Having authorized the development of a top secret line of cloned soldiers called "Liberators," the Linear Committee—the executive branch of the U.A. government—approves sending an invasion force into the Galactic Eye to attack all hostile threats. The Liberators discover a human colony led by Morgan Atkins, the Senate majority leader who had originally called for the creation of the Galactic Central Fleet.

The Liberators overthrow Atkins's colony, but Atkins and many of his followers escape in G.C. Fleet ships.

Over the next fifty years, a religious cult known as the Morgan Atkins Believers—"Mogats"—spreads across the 180 colonized planets, preaching independence from the Unified Authority government.

In 2510, spurred on by the growing Morgan Atkins movement, four of the six galactic arms declare independence from Unified Authority governance.

On March 28, 2512, the combined forces of the Confederate

Arms Treaty Organization and the Morgan Atkins Believers defeat the Earth Fleet and destroy the Broadcast Network, effectively cutting the government off from its loyal colonies and Navy.

Believing they have crippled the Unified Authority, the Mogats then turn on their Confederate Arms allies in an attempt to take control of the rebuilt Galactic Central Fleet. While the Confederates manage to hold on to approximately fifty ships, the Mogats take control of over four hundred ships, giving them the most powerful self-broadcasting attack force in the galaxy.

Fighting for its survival, the Confederate Arms forms an alliance with the Unified Authority. Under U.A. leadership, the combined forces stage a counterattack on the Mogat home world, destroying the entire Mogat Navy and leaving no survivors on the planet.

PROLOGUE

EARTHDATE: JANUARY 23, A.D. 2513
LOCATION: GOLAN DRY DOCKS
GALACTIC POSITION: NORMA ARM

The video record showed a subterranean city under siege, seen through the visor of a Marine combat helmet. The scene played out in tones of blue-white and gray—night-for-day vision as seen through the visor of Marine combat armor.

Suddenly a rim of light appeared above the city, raining glare down upon buildings and streets. For a moment it looked like the light came from an explosion, but it did not flash and disappear. Instead, the light expanded over the top of the city like smoke gathering over a fire. The light was bright enough to cancel out the night-for-day lens, and the visor automatically switched to a standard tactical lens. As the light came closer, tint shields formed over the visor as protection from the blinding glare.

Shit, *I thought to myself, as I felt my pulse rise.* Shit, shit, shit!

Even through the tint shields, I saw changing hues and patterns in the light as if the reds, yellows, and blues in that strange overbright light constantly kept separating themselves from the colors around them, then remixed back into the spectrum.

"Harris, you seeing this?" a voice asked me on the screen. The record was taken from my combat helmet.

I recognized the voice. It was Ray Freeman, the man who had once been my partner. "Where are you?" I asked in the record.

"One floor up," Freeman said. "You better get climbing."

I was standing in the door of an elevator station. The city in the video feed had levels; only now that we had shut down the power, I would need to climb to the next level using a rappelling cord.

"You can see that light?" I asked over the interLink—the communications system used by the military.

The light had a slow, gelatinous property to it. It seemed to seep over the city like viscous oil. As soon as I turned away from the light to run toward the open elevator shaft, the night-for-day lens in my visor resumed. The glow from that strange light had not yet reached the elevator station, but it soon would.

In the record, I ran to the shaft, attached a cord to the loop in my armor, and started up. The Marines in my platoon, at least those still breathing, had already climbed up to the top level.

The shaft looked like a gigantic tunnel turned on its end. Dozens of rappel cords dangled from the top.

"Thomer, where are you?" I called over the interLink. Thomer was one of the squad leaders in my platoon.

"In the elevator station," Thomer said.

"Can you see any transports?" I asked.

"There's a transport just outside," Thomer replied.

"I requisitioned that one," Freeman said.

"What happened to the pilot?" I asked.

Freeman did not answer, which probably meant he was dead.

The area inside this shaft would have been black as coal if not for the glow that started to pour in through the open doors. It rushed in like water from a flood, shining on the opposite wall. I had never known that a man could climb as quickly as I did when I scaled my way up that shaft.

"Load the men in the transport," I called to Thomer.

"They're in," Thomer said.

"And you're in?" I asked.

Thomer did not answer.

"Get in the transport!" I yelled.

I looked up to see how much farther I had to go. I had another twenty feet. Below me, the light in the shaft became blinding. The tint shields in my visor blocked out some of the brightness.

I looked back down. There was a creature in that viscous light—a creature nearly as bright as the light around it. It looked like a canary yellow smudge in a field of glare that had the startling silver clarity of an electrical spark. I only saw it for a moment, and I concentrated on the two black eyes. They were the size of my fists, and they seemed to be made of smoky black chrome.

The video feed froze on the image of the creature. The image was blurry and indistinct, like a picture taken by a child who can't stop jiggling his camera.

"Master Gunnery Sergeant Harris, perhaps you could give us your opinion about the nature of this creature," Admiral Brallier said, the forced calm in his voice fraying on the word "creature."

I had retired, only I wasn't allowed to stay that way. These officers would not have had any authority over a retired Marine—I was back on active duty so that they could decide whether or not they wanted to lock me up.

"I have no idea," I said. I could feel the heat rising in my blood. Brallier and I stared at each other, saying nothing.

Finally, Brallier broke the silence, asking, "Do you think it was a Space Angel?"

That video record was shot during the invasion of the planetary home of the Mogats—a religious cult that had all but overthrown the Unified Authority. In his writings, cult founder Morgan Atkins discussed meeting a radiant alien being, which he referred to as a "Space Angel." Other than Atkins, no one of any note had ever mentioned making contact with space aliens, so it was hard to take Atkins seriously.

"He fired a gun at me," I said.

"So?"

"That doesn't seem very angelic," I said.

A few people in the gallery laughed, but tensions ran high in those chambers. Most people sat mute as stone.

"No one but you saw this creature," Brallier said, turning to the screen to take another look. "I find that strange, Master Gunnery Sergeant. Don't you find that strange? From what we have been able to ascertain, the creature in this frame is nearly ten feet tall and carrying a giant rifle, but you were the only person who noticed it. How do you explain that?"

The bastard had just called me a liar. He did it in an eloquent, formal style, but he had just called me a liar, and everyone in the chamber knew it. "Do you think I made it up?" I asked.

Brallier kept blathering on about how there were thousands of Marines on the planet and how unlikely it was that I had spotted the only "bug-eyed monster" to invade the planet. "How is it, Master Gunnery Sergeant, that you were the only man who spotted the invading aliens?" The question must have been rhetorical, because instead of giving me a chance to respond, the admiral kept going.

I could not figure out why Admiral Brallier was doing so much of the talking. Yes, he was one of the highest-ranking officers in the Unified Authority Navy, but General Thomas "Tommy" Mooreland sat right beside him, a man with enough brass and braids to decorate a division. As the commandant of the Marines, General Mooreland should have had more say in my interrogation than the admiral. I was, after all, a Marine. Instead, Mooreland sat there looking stolid and angry, never uttering a single syllable.

It wasn't just the military that had turned out to watch this inquisition. "Wild Bill" Grace, the senior member of the Linear Committee, had come. He was the closest thing the Unified Authority had to a president. The other members of the

Committee came as well. So had half the Senate.

Our allies, the Confederate Arms, sent representatives as well. Gordon Hughes, the chairman of the Confederate Arms Treaty Organization, sat in the gallery. Earlier this year, the Unified Authority and the Confederate Arms were at war with each other. Now they were allies. Go figure.

"Are you saying that I lied? What would I get out of lying?" I asked.

Admiral Brallier did not respond. He stood his ground, glaring at me, sucking in his lips.

"I have no idea what to make of this," Al Smith said, putting in his two cents. Well, he was "Al Smith" to his friends. To the likes of me, he was General Alexander Smith of the U.A. Air Force, the ranking member of the Joint Chiefs of Staff. He threw up his hands. "Except for the fact that you spent two years absent without leave, you have a stellar record as a Marine, but this..."

Five more high-ranking officers sat behind the rail along with Smith, Brallier, and Mooreland, and among them was Admiral Thomas Halverson, the highest-ranking officer in the Confederate Arms Navy. There was so much brass and epaulets in the room that I half expected a marching band.

"Can you please explain to my satisfaction why you are the only Marine who reported seeing this creature? We sent sixty thousand men on that operation," Admiral Brallier said. He managed to keep his voice low, but did not bother trying to disguise the hostility toward me.

"They might have reported it," I said, "but the Navy left 59,980 of those Marines stranded on the planet, sir." I looked directly at Mooreland. As the commandant of the Marines, he might have flinched at the mention of the sixty thousand Marines betrayed and sacrificed. He did not stir.

"Watch yourself, Master Sergeant," General Smith warned me. "You are speaking to a senior officer."

As far as I was concerned, he was not my senior officer. I had resigned from the Marines fair and square.

"Okay, Master Gunnery Sergeant," Brallier said, clearly making a show of keeping his calm. "Can you think of any reason why none of the other men in your platoon saw this creature?"

I was also having trouble keeping my temper in check, but I had to hide it. He was an admiral, and I was apparently going to be a master gunnery sergeant, retired or not. *Maybe I was on the wrong side of the war,* I thought to myself. Taking a deep breath, I responded, "They were already in the kettle, sir." Marines referred to the cargo area on military transports as "the kettle." Built for durability, not comfort, kettles did not have windows. I pointed this out to the committee.

After thinking for a moment, I added, "I was the last one out. Just like it shows in the video feed, I was bringing up the rear."

"I have been in the Navy for thirty years, Master Sergeant. I am quite familiar with the layout of troop transport units," Brallier sneered, his eyes boring into mine, his face unflinching.

"Have you actually ridden in a transport?" I asked. I was being grossly insubordinate, but I really did want to know.

"I can see that I have been far too tolerant with you, Master Gunnery Sergeant," Brallier said. Sitting beside him, Smith nodded in agreement.

I wanted to tell them all to go speck themselves, but I kept quiet. I had already pushed my luck too far, and discretion is the better part of valor.

I retired from the Marines because I could no longer fight under corrupt bastards like Brallier. My platoon, what was left of my platoon, was the only platoon to make it off that planet, and only half of my men made it. Nearly sixty thousand clone Marines had been on the planet.

It wasn't the number of men who died that disturbed me; it was the way the higher-ups betrayed them. Those clones were built for war and trained to fight and die on the battlefield. On this mission, we were sent in as an advance guard and told to keep the enemy pinned down until the bulk of the invasion force arrived. The problem was, we were the bulk of the invasion. We were sent to keep the Mogats from escaping while their entire planet dissolved around them... around us.

It seemed like we had reached an impasse. Brallier thought I was lying. I did not care what Admiral Brallier thought anymore. He'd planned the invasion. Leaving those Marines to die was his idea.

"It is obvious to me that Sergeant Harris must have seen something," said Admiral Halverson, a man with no allegiance. Halverson had served with distinction in the U.A. Navy before defecting to the Confederate Arms. Under his leadership, the combined navies of the Confederates and Mogats whipped the U.A. Fleet. Now that the Confederates Arms had allied itself with the Unified Authority, Halverson was back among the officers he had defeated. Judging by the way General Smith and Admiral Brallier winced at the sound of Halverson's voice, the old wounds had not yet healed.

"It seems obvious that Harris would be the only one who saw the alien," Halverson said. "The record makes it perfectly clear that Sergeant Harris was the last man off the field. We have no way of knowing what the Marines who fell behind might have seen."

"Nothing about this seems obvious to me, Admiral," Admiral Brallier hissed. He did not look in Halverson's direction as he said this.

"Let me see if I understand this. Are you accusing the master sergeant of engineering this video feed?" Admiral Halverson asked.

I hated having Halverson on my side. I agreed with the U.A. officers—Halverson was a worm. In fact, I pretty much hated everybody in the room, except maybe General Mooreland. I did not know enough about Mooreland to hate him, at least not yet.

Everyone turned to see how Admiral Brallier would respond to Halverson's challenge. Tangible silence filled the auditorium in the moments he took to consider this question. Seconds passed, but Brallier said nothing.

"When do you think he might have engineered this feed?" Halverson asked.

"And here's another question for you: Why would he make

something like this up? Why would he do it? Why go to all that trouble?

"He didn't do it for a promotion. Hell, as I understand it, he had barely landed on the *Sakura* when he asked for his discharge from the Marines. So why bother creating a hoax like this? He didn't even want to remain in the Marines."

"That gives the sergeant and me something in common." General Mooreland, the commandant of the Marine Corps, finally spoke up. "I don't want him in the Corps. He isn't fit to be a Marine."

PART I
THE SECRET WAR

1

Until the first half of humanity was gone, all anybody wanted to talk about was the actress Ava Gardner. By then it was too late.

"She's from New Copenhagen, you know," the girl said to me.

"Who's from New Copenhagen?"

"Ava Gardner," she said. "Look, they're showing *The Barefoot Contessa* at that theater over there. Maybe we can go see it tomorrow."

I did not respond.

"Do you think Ava's a clone?" she asked. The girl's name might have been Katerina. It might have been Leanne. She had told me her name on the beach this afternoon, but I forgot it as soon as I heard it. I remembered the name of her hotel. What more did I need?

"You're not still going on about that actress?" I asked. "Who cares if she's a clone? How would I know if she's a clone?"

Katerina, or Leanne, or whatever her name was, shot me a frustrated look, and said, "I don't know. I mean, I figured you being a clone and all, you might know."

"Are you asking if they sent a memo down the clone network?" I asked.

"No, no, nothing like that. It's just... I thought maybe you, like, you know, recognized other clones when you see them." Now she sounded nervous.

"It's not like that. Most clones don't even know that they're clones. They die if they..."

"Oh, right. I heard about that. They die if they find out that they're clones. Is that for real? I heard about that, but I never believed it. How come you didn't die when you found out?"

She was so pretty. She had brown eyes, deeply tanned skin from a week's vacation spent entirely on the beach, and black hair that she pulled back into a ponytail. And she had a figure. In another few years she would probably get plump, but right now she had a tiny waist, sharp little breasts, and muscular thighs I could hardly take my eyes off of. She had reached that brief moment of physical perfection when youth gives way to womanhood.

The girl's half-moon-shaped eyes were just wide enough to give her a look of constant surprise. Her stream of stupid questions did little to change my impression of her as both pretty and pretty stupid.

Back in the Marines, we called girls like her "scrub." You enjoyed them for a night or two and moved on. This girl's vacation would end in two days. By that time I'd be glad to see her go. For that face, though, I could put up with dumb questions and conversations about movie stars for a couple of days.

"I'm not a normal clone," I said. "I'm a Liberator. Liberator clones don't have the death reflex."

Her eyes narrowed slightly. "Aren't Liberators supposed to be dangerous?"

"I make my living beating the shit out of people in an Iron Man competition," I said. "I guess that makes me dangerous."

"But you wouldn't hurt me," she said, pulling herself closer to me so that our bodies touched. She wore an ice blue bikini top and a green wrap around her tiny waist. I could feel the warmth of her body. Oh yes, I could definitely put up with stupid questions and conversations about movie stars.

We were sitting in a booth in a beachside diner. It had two benches, but she opted to cram in next to me. I noticed that a lot of girls did things like that. Maybe it made them feel like they meant something to me, like they were more than a hobby.

"Nope," I said, "I would never hurt you."

She smiled. She practically purred. If someone had told me she was still in high school, I would have believed it; but she claimed she was twenty-one years old. She may have actually been eighteen or nineteen. Two years younger than me... four years younger than me, it didn't really matter. Leanne or Katerina, whatever her name was, she was old enough to take care of herself.

"Maybe Ava's a Liberator," the girl said.

"She can't be a Liberator," I said. "All Liberators are male."

"Then how do you reproduce?" the girl asked, shock showing on her face.

She better be good, I thought to myself. "We're clones. We don't reproduce; the Department of Defense manufactures us. That's why they call us synthetics."

Now disappointment showed on her face.

"Don't worry," I said. "All the machinery works." Until that moment, I had not stopped to think that she might see me as disposable, too.

She smiled and moved in so close that she practically sat on my lap. The idea of mating with something not quite human seemed to have aroused her curiosity.

I looked at my watch. It was almost 1900. I didn't need to be at the Palace until 2030, and work didn't really start till nearly 2100. *Time enough,* I told myself as I suggested we swing by my apartment. *Time enough.*

* * *

Sad Sam's Palace...

The Palace was an old auditorium at the edge of town, a few miles west of the Waikiki tourist district and one mile inland from the harbor. It was a three-story cement-and-plaster castle surrounded by auto-repair shops, warehouses, and bars. Its light-studded marquee stood out like fireworks among the dark alleys that populated the seedier side of Honolulu.

We rolled into the parking lot at 2030. The sun had long since gone down, leaving the sky black with veins of gray clouds. The Palace's brightly lit silhouette cut an ostentatious figure against the sky. A huge marquee with flashing bulbs spelling the name "SAD SAM'S PALACE" flickered above the facade.

"That's Sad Sam's Palace?" the girl asked, as we drove toward the side gate. She seemed more confident around me now that we'd run by my pad; perhaps she thought she had impressed me.

"That's it," I said.

"Does it ever scare you, you know, fighting for a living?" she asked. "Are you ever afraid that you'll get hurt?"

The "are you afraid" question... It almost made me miss conversations about Ava Gardner. "No," I said. "I don't worry about it much."

"You must be really good," she said.

"Either that, or I just like getting the shit kicked out of me," I muttered quietly enough that she would not hear me.

"Harris," the guard said as we rolled into the lot. "Big crowd tonight. You better give 'em a show."

"That's the plan," I said as I drifted past. I parked and climbed out of the car. My date sat quietly, waiting for me to open her door for her, but I was already in fighter mode and opening a door for my date was the last thing on my mind. Seeing me headed to the back door of the Palace without so much as a backward glance, she opened the door for herself and caught up to me. She might not have been brilliant, but the girl was bright enough not to complain.

I didn't have time to think about her now. I had other things on my mind.

We went into an alley leading behind the Palace. The place was dirty, with an overflowing dumpster surrounded by a wall of garbage bags. The overly sweet smells of stale beer and old food filled the air. The alley must have made my date nervous; she stayed close to me as I knocked on the pea green metal door.

"Harris," the guard said as he made room for me to step in.

"How's the competition look?" I asked.

"Not as good as the company you're keeping," the guard said. He stared at my date and made no attempt to camouflage his interest. His fascination with my girl irritated me.

"Do I have anything to worry about?" I asked.

"You've seen this guy before. His name's Monty." The guard said this while staring at Leanne or Katerina. Whatever her name was, he was still watching her, and she didn't seem to mind the attention.

"Big guy?" I asked.

"Short. Five-eight, maybe five-ten. You trashed him bad last time. He's still missing his front teeth." The guard—I could not remember his name—was missing a few teeth of his own. I might not have been the one who extracted those teeth, but I had little doubt that he'd lost them fighting in Sad Sam's ring.

"Thanks," I said, and turned toward the locker room.

"I don't think I like this place," my date said.

"You don't think you like it here?" I asked. "Give it a little time. You'll know you don't like it."

"You don't think I'll like the fights?"

"Some girls like them, and some girls don't," I said.

The hall was long and dark with cinder-block walls and a cement floor. The Palace's auditorium was alive with bright lights, loud fans, and beer. In the tunnels and locker rooms, the atmosphere was somber, dim, and quiet. A metal bucket sat in a corner, a mop growing out of the dirty water it held. The air was humid and smelled of sweat. Somewhere not too far away, a couple of security guards, janitors, or possibly fighters were telling dirty jokes. I heard the punch line—"I told her, 'Speck you later!'"—followed by roaring laughter.

I led my date to a doorway where one of the floor waitresses stood. "Can you get her a good seat for the fight?" I asked.

The waitress gave my date a quick once-over, then said in a bored voice, "So you're the girl of the week. Pleased to meet you."

"I can't come with you?" Leanne—by this time I was pretty sure her name was Leanne—pleaded. She gave me a desperate look with those beautiful brown eyes.

"That's probably not a good idea. I'm headed to the men's locker room." I patted her hand and continued on my way. They almost never gave me a locker room to myself, and bloodied fighters were a common sight. Leanne might be all right watching the fight, but she didn't want to see the aftermath. She would have a good table near the ring, and the waitresses would warn away any guys stupid enough to approach her.

Already unbuttoning my shirt, I stepped into the locker room and did not like what I saw. Somebody had switched off the lights, and the green glow from the emergency exit sign stood out against the darkness. Pale light spilled out from the door of the shower room.

"Did you know that you are a fugitive from the law, Harris?" a familiar voice asked as I closed the door. That voice combined with the dark atmosphere sent a shiver down my spine. "Ever heard of the Elite Conscription Act?"

I had my shirt off and did not pause before unbuckling my belt and starting on my pants. If that voice belonged to the man I thought it belonged to, I preferred the lights off. "Can't say that I have," I said.

"It's brand-new; Congress just enacted it. It gives all four branches of the military the right to call men back to active duty whether they want to go back or not. The Linear Committee signed it into law without the usual fanfare. I guess 'Wild Bill' didn't want people asking questions about why the military needs to recall retired servicemen," he said.

"Nope," I said, "never heard of it."

"The ECA is not the kind of thing that the average citizen needs to know about."

"I'm an average citizen," I said. "Maybe I don't need to know about it."

"You were an average citizen. As of midnight tonight, you will be a first lieutenant in the U.A. Marines. That means you need to know about it," Illych said.

Emerson Illych was a military clone. He was not your standard government-issue military clone, the kind that had a death reflex if they found out they were synthetic; but he was not a Liberator, either. He was a Special Operations clone, a limited make minted specifically for the Navy SEALs. His kind could slip in and out of an enemy stronghold without leaving a trace other than the bodies they left in their wake. Illych and I were friendly, having fought in more than one campaign together.

"So now I'm elite?"

"Don't get too jazzed about it," Illych said. "All it takes to be 'elite' is battle experience and a pulse."

Considering the last battle I had fought in, the one where the Navy left sixty thousand Marines on a planet to die, I considered myself elite after a fashion. Illych and I stood there in a silent stalemate for a moment.

Under other circumstances I might have turned on the lights, but Illych and his brood looked better in the dark. They were built for stealth work and combat at close quarters. A thick and protective bone ridge ran along the front of their skulls, just under the eyebrows. It gave their faces a Neanderthal aspect.

The first time I came to Sad Sam's Palace, I was a naïve Marine, and I got suckered into a fight with a SEAL like Illych. The man could have killed me, but he'd slipped up and given me a break, opening the door for me to beat him to death instead. That was four years ago. I'd become less humane over the years.

"When did you SEALs start playing messenger boy?"

By this time I had stripped to my fighting trunks. It was just a question of waiting for the last fight to end so I could head out to defend my title. A moment later there was a knock on the door. "Harris, you ready?" one of the guards asked.

"I volunteered. I even took leave to come here. This is a historic event—your last fight at the Palace," Illych said.

"Just like that? They pass a new law, and poof, I'm recalled? I thought Mooreland didn't want me in his Corps."

"Mooreland isn't in charge anymore," Illych said. "He was killed in action on Hubble."

"Hubble?" I asked. I had fought there once. The Unified Authority did not maintain a settlement on that godforsaken rock.

"Hubble," Illych said. "The aliens he said didn't exist killed him and his division."

"No shit." I was stunned but not saddened. Mooreland was an asshole. The men who died with him were just clones. I was just a clone, too; but I had had the good sense to get out of the service. I closed my locker and reached for the door. "I'm coming," I yelled to the guard outside.

"You know, the aliens that you saw... the ones that don't exist, they're taking over the galaxy. At least we think it's them. No one has seen them and lived. No one but you."

"So it's begun?" My hand dropped from the door. I stood there in the dark, chilling images flashing through my brain. I saw the Mogat planet, thousands of Marines dying in the dark, and the weird light spreading over the city. I thought of the alien and about the hearing in which Brallier and Mooreland crucified me.

"Harris, you coming?" the guard called from outside.

"It's more than begun, Harris. It's in full swing."

I let those words penetrate me and felt a strange numbness. I had always known the war was coming, and now it was here. These aliens would certainly kill everyone; but from my point of view, they did not seem any more treacherous than the clone-hating officers I had served under. I had resigned myself to the idea that I would die whether I fought or not. The Unified

Authority could not stand up to this new threat. If I enlisted, I would die in battle. If I did not enlist, I would die in the civilian onslaught. Given a choice, I had originally decided that I would rather die like a sheep than give my life protecting the people who had betrayed me so many times in the past. But now that the war had become a reality, I had second thoughts.

"Harris?" the guard called from outside the door.

"Coming," I said.

"Don't get hurt," Illych said as I opened the door. "You're government property now. There are laws against damaging government property."

2

Sanity never counted for much at Sad Sam's Palace. The fighters I faced seldom scared me as much as the crowds screaming themselves hoarse from the bleachers and balconies lining the cavernous walls. Bright lights blazed down from the ceiling during interludes between fights. Once the announcer began calling the match, the crew doused the main lights and followed the fighters into the ring with spotlights.

While the main lights still cooked, I caught a glimpse around the arena. Friday night fights always attracted a crowd, but this... The audience sat so packed together they seemed to form a carpet. The loud cheering left a ringing in my ears. Scouting the tables closest to the ring, I saw Marines in Charlie service uniforms. Some wore armbands identifying them as military police.

"Ladies and gentlemen," the announcer began. I mused that neither ladies nor gentlemen would come to see this bloody spectacle.

"...Sad Sam's Palace welcomes you to our main event."

Tonight's sacrifice had already entered the ring. He stood beside the announcer, rolling his shoulders and shaking his head. The guy was short. His muscled arms hung slack by his sides, slightly bent at the elbows like parenthesis marks on either side of his body. He was barrel-chested, with a solid slab for a stomach. The guy looked vaguely familiar; I probably had given him a beating sometime back.

The air in the Palace felt hot, and the atmosphere was electric. As I stepped onto the floor, a man to my right accidentally splashed beer on me. He stood screaming at the tops of his lungs, his voice raw, and he waved his half-gallon-sized paper cup of beer in the air like a baby shaking a rattle. Two security guards walked ahead of me, clearing a path through crowds that had jumped to their feet.

"Our challenger, weighing in at 227 pounds, your Sad Sam's Iron Man champion of the evening, Thomas Monty!"

I heard screaming and pounding. Men jumped up and down like children pitching a tantrum, but no one could seriously believe this stiff stood a chance. He was just another Christian being fed to the clone lion. The lights suddenly cut out, leaving the entire arena dark except for the blazing lights above the ring and a spotlight that followed me. The floor quieted.

"And now, our defending champion, weighing in at 218 pounds, Wayson *the Liberator clone* Harris." I heard the screaming and saw the fans, but my mind was on the Elite Conscription Act. I thought about aliens that looked like they were made of light instead of matter. I thought about full-scale invasions and full-scale betrayals.

The ring was a raised platform with no ropes around it. There would be chain-link walls, but those would drop from the ceiling after I entered the ring and the referee exited it—there would be no third man in the ring in this competition.

I climbed the three-step ladder near the corner. Across the ring, Monty stood in the bright white glare, the light reflecting off the sheen of perspiration on his face. Now that I was close enough to get a good look, I saw that the guard in the parking lot had sized Monty up perfectly. He stood under six feet, maybe only five-foot-eight, but he was a bear of a man with huge shoulders. Because the bright light was directly over him, dark shadows formed over Monty's eye sockets. I could not see his eyes. No emotion showed on his face—neither hate nor anger. His lips parted, and I saw the black squares where he had once had teeth.

Sad Sam's management did not compromise the integrity of its Iron Man competition with something so foreign as a point system. The fights ended when one of the opponents was out cold or submitted. The tough guys who entered this ring seldom called uncle, though. A few people died, but no one ever asked for mercy.

The referee looked at Monty, then at me. He mouthed something. I could not hear his whispered instructions over the crowd, but I imagined it was something along the lines of "Let's put on a good show." He left the ring with the announcer, and the walls, seven-foot panels of chain-link fencing, began to lower from the rafters.

I never took my eyes off Monty. Standing this close, I saw that he had not made it through the tournament unscathed. He had a black eye, and the left side of his mouth was swollen. He also had bruises on his arms and chest. I did not feel bad for him, though; we all went through that. To become champion, you had to win the Friday Night Tournament and have enough left in you to beat the standing champ.

Cogs ground as the walls slowly lowered. Monty slid his mouthpiece over his upper teeth. I already had mine in. I stared into Monty's emotionless brown eyes. No fear showed, nor did anything resembling compassion. Perhaps he regarded me as something less than human.

The walls clanged into place. Somewhere in the darkness outside the ring, somebody rang a bell, and the fight began. Monty turned toward me and started to drift in my direction. I hit him in the mouth with a straight right, leaving a small stream of blood flowing from his already-swollen lower lip. He did not stutter or miss a step.

I took a step back. I had at least six inches of reach on this guy. I hit him along the top of his mouth with an overhand right, making sure to roll my knuckles across the point of his nose.

Monty did not so much as blink. A tough enough guy might shake off the belt across the mouth, but the knuckles to the nose would have caused anyone to wince... any normal person. If Monty had luded up before the match, the drugs would feel the pain instead of him. And if he was drugged, the chemicals would keep him demonically focused on breaking my neck. I kept my distance and long-ranged him with a few more shots.

Management supposedly tested fighters for ludes and boosters, but that was usually before their first fight. Monty might have taken something later. He might have even waited until right before this fight.

Monty lunged at me. I had no trouble dodging the attack, I simply stepped to the left, allowing him to sail on past me and charge face-first into the chain-link wall around the ring. Then I grabbed a handful of his hair with my left hand and placed my right along the nape of his neck. I rubbed his face up and down the chain-link wall like a cook grating cheese. Monty screamed like an animal, pivoted around, and broke my grip with a wild brush of his arm.

He should not have been able to break out of my grip so easily, but you can do all kinds of things with the right pharmaceuticals. Still, I had left my mark—a four-inch gash opened across his forehead. Blood rolled down his face and into his impassive eyes.

Monty stopped for just a second and smiled at me. The blood hid the outline of his lips, and red droplets speckled his teeth.

I had originally planned to carry the guy for a few minutes, maybe give the paying customers a moment to believe they were witnessing a fair fight. Now I changed my mind. Screw showmanship, I swept Monty's right knee, contacting hard at about the two o'clock angle on the poor bastard's kneecap. The leg broke easily enough, and Thomas Monty fell like a tree. He laughed as if I had told him a joke, shook his fist in the air like a man cursing his bad luck, then pushed down on the canvas mat and climbed right back to his feet. If I ever doubted my ability to put this guy away, it was at that moment.

When men are luded to the gills, they can stand up on broken legs; hell, I once saw a guy do jumping jacks on a broken leg. Thomas Monty stood on his good leg, then put weight on the broken one, which folded instantly. He took a step forward just the same, so I broke his good leg with a second kick.

Down went Monty, and this time he stayed down. He tried to get to his feet again, but the law of gravity conspired against him. He planted his feet, then leaned forward, trying to heave himself up, but tumbled on his face instead. And now he began to feel the pain.

I watched this from about six feet away, just out of his reach. I stood there with my arms folded across my chest to demonstrate to the ref that the fight was over, my opponent had nothing left.

Cursing at the top of his lungs, Monty pulled himself toward me. He reminded me of the Hollywood version of a mortally wounded soldier pulling himself heroically across the battlefield.

I took a step away. He pulled himself closer. I took another step away. He followed. The fight would not stop until he stopped chasing me, so I scooted around the recently crippled Mr. Thomas Monty and kicked one of his broken kneecaps as hard as I could.

His shriek was neither human nor animal. It reminded me of the sound of stressed metal twisting and tearing. When he swung a fist at my leg, I sidestepped his punch and kicked his leg a second time. The pain from that kick shot its way through the haze of drugs that numbed his brain, and he curled into a ball, weeping and screaming with the shrillness of an injured child.

The referee walked to the outside of the cage and yelled, "Do you submit?"

Monty screamed, rolled around on the mat, and held his legs.

The referee asked again and got the same unintelligible response, so I kicked Monty's knees to help clarify things. The lower half of his leg spun like a tetherball from below his kneecap. "Hey, asshole, the referee asked you a question."

Monty howled.

"What do you want me to do?" I asked the ref. "He's too luded to know he's beat."

"Hey, Monty!" the ref yelled.

Monty said something along the line of "Ummmmmmm! Hyummmm."

I kicked his knee again. "The guy can't defend himself."

"I can't stop the fight unless he quits," the ref said.

"Want me to kill him?" I asked. "That's what it's going to take to shut him down."

This was new territory for Sad Sam's Palace. In the past, Iron Man championships were won or lost by knockout. Seconds passed with Monty still curled on the ground, too drugged to tap out and too injured to continue the fight. Finally, the walls of the cage rose in the air, and the referee ended it.

The ref swaggered into the ring with the bravado of a sailor on leave. When he looked down at Monty, no sympathy showed on his face. Then he looked over at me. "Damn, with all the shit this guy took, I thought he would get you," he said as he raised my hand.

So ended my last fight at Sad Sam's Palace. I gave Monty's broken leg one last kick for good measure before climbing out of the ring and heading to the locker room.

3

I picked up an entourage as I stepped from the ring. MPs, both from the Navy and the Marines, fell in behind me. These boys came prepared, pistols in their belts, nightsticks in their hand. I had barely stepped to the floor when the first two fell in behind me. A few feet later, I picked up two more. By the time I reached the service hall that led to the locker room, I had my own little platoon.

I paused to look at Leanne, Bethany, whatever her name was... She sat at the table watching me. Our eyes met. I knew our eyes were the only part of our anatomy that would meet from here on out.

Other fighters and several Palace workers milled around the hall as I headed toward the locker room. They cleared out of the way as I stalked past. It might have been the line of MPs traveling behind me, but no one ever patted me on the back or told me congratulations under normal circumstances, either. It's the nature of the beast—most people don't feel sentimental about clones who beat people up for a living.

I opened the door to the locker room and found that someone had switched on the lights. My entourage did not follow me inside, nor did they leave me to my own devices. A Marine major flanked by two more MPs stood in the center of the locker room waiting for me.

"Wayson Harris, by the articles of U.A. Senate resolution 2514-353, otherwise known as the Elite Conscription Act, you have been called back to active duty in the Unified Authority Marine Corps." By the stilted way in which the major delivered this line, I could tell that he had committed it to memory.

Without saying a word, I pulled off my trunks and walked over to the bathroom. I stripped off my cup and placed it on the stand behind the sink, then strode over to a urinal. I had three prefight beers to tap, but it still took a few seconds to get started. We stood in silence, me tensing and relaxing to squeeze whatever I could out of my bladder, the major angrily watching me piss. His polished demeanor disappeared. "Lieutenant, I am talking to you."

"Go ahead."

"You will show me the proper respect, Lieutenant," the major said. "You are speaking to a superior..."

By this time I had cleared the blockage, and the old hose ran full flow. If I let go to salute, the waterworks would have flown out of control.

"I may have been out of the loop too long," I said, "but last I heard, I'm still a civilian and we don't have superiors." I gave myself a last shake and stepped away from the urinal, making a point of not washing my hands. I did grab my protective cup off the sink and toss it into a waste can, adding, "Guess I won't need that anymore."

I went to my locker and pulled out my clothes. Given the chance, the major might have had his MPs teach me a lesson about showing respect to officers, but that would not happen here. Somebody a lot more important than this major wanted me back in the Marines.

"You planning on giving me trouble, hotshot?" the major asked.

"Not me," I said. And I didn't. I stepped into my underwear and pants. I pulled on my shirt and followed the major out as meek as a lamb.

As we stepped out of the locker room, I heard the plink of hard-soled shoes running up the hall. I turned just in time to see my date.

"Wayson, what's going on?"

"I've been drafted," I said.

"Move it, Harris. You've got a plane to catch," the major said. He started to walk away. My entourage waited for me to follow him. With a hesitant sigh, I started up the hall.

"Where are you going?" she asked.

I stopped to look back at her. There she stood, with her dark hair pulled back into a ponytail, her perfect skin, and her slender figure. "Leanne," I said, "I have no idea."

"My name is Christina," she said.

"No shit?" was the last thing I said to her as one of the MPs gave me a shove. I did not expect to come back. If the aliens I saw on that Mogat planet were headed toward Earth, I wouldn't find her alive even if I did return.

"Move it, Romeo," an MP said as he gave me a careful prod with his stick.

"Get specked," I said, stopping to stare the guy down. He glared back, looking like he would have gladly dropped down one rank just to take a shot at me. I probably looked like I wanted him to try.

"Don't worry about him; he's an asshole," another MP said, nodding toward the first. That broke the ice. We left Sad Sam's.

Three jeeps waited along the road that ran behind the Palace. The major stood impatiently beside one of them. "He's an asshole, too," the MP muttered as we approached.

"He's an officer," I said. "They're all assholes."

"They're making you a lieutenant," the MP said. He led me to the first jeep, then watched from the sidewalk to make sure I climbed in.

"You haven't been paying attention," I said. "I'm an asshole, too."

4

Until recent events upended our society, the Broadcast Network was the superhighway that laced the republic together. Even flying at the speed of light, and the Navy's fastest ships did not travel at the speed of light, it would take a hundred thousand years to fly from one end of the galaxy to the other.

Broadcasting technology solved that problem. You could "broadcast" a spaceship to any spot in the galaxy instantaneously. The process involved coating the ship in highly charged particles, translating the ship and everything on it into a transmittable form, then sending it to the target location. The Broadcast Network, which was little more than a string of interlinked satellites, not only facilitated galactic travel, it also transmitted communications instantaneously. With the Network in place, man and messages could travel from the Orion Arm to the Norma Arm in less time than it would take to drive a car around the city block.

That ended two years ago, during the Civil War. A religious group called the Morgan Atkins Believers, better known as the Mogats, wanted to break up the Republic. They damn near accomplished it, too, by destroying the Mars broadcast station—

the satellite closest to Earth. By knocking out the keystone broadcast station, the Mogats cut Earth off from the rest of the Republic. With the Mars station down, the other stations lost their power supply and the galaxy "went dark."

Once the war with the Mogats ended, I had expected to hear about the government reopening the Broadcast Network or at least beginning work on a new station around Mars. If that work ever began, the news never got out. They could not have built one in secret; broadcast stations are built around mile-wide mirrors that act like focusing lenses. *Someone* would have spotted a mile-wide mirror floating around Mars. Even if the U.A. Corps of Engineers found a way to hide the damned mirror, they could never have hidden the blinding white lightning the station emitted during broadcasts.

I expected the major to drive me to Honolulu Airport—a civilian facility used mostly for servicing atmospheric transportation. The jeep rolled right on past the civilian terminal, and we drove to a small Air Force facility at the far end of the runway.

We arrived at the military hangars sometime around 2300. It was a balmy December night with a cool breeze rolling in from the sea. Though hundreds of stars glittered above, the blue-black sky reminded me of the color of bruises. No moon shone in that sky. Gauzy clouds floated slowly in from the sea.

"Is that the guy?" a guard said, as we drove up to the gate.

"That's him," our driver said.

The guard stepped back and opened the barrier blocking the entrance to the base. He watched me carefully as we drove past.

"What's he so curious about?" I asked the major. This was the first time we spoke during the twenty-minute ride from Sad Sam's.

"He wants to see if you can walk on water," the major said. "They sent ten MPs and three jeeps to bring your ass in. Normal orders are to shoot conscripts unless they come willingly."

"So you had orders to shoot me if I put up a fight?" I asked.

"Me, I wouldn't have bothered with you in the first place. I had orders to bring you in alive and in one piece."

We drove to the edge of the runway and parked beside a small military atmospheric shuttle.

"What would you have done if I said no?" I asked as I climbed out of the jeep.

"I would have shot you and said you committed suicide," the major said. "I've seen your record, Harris. As far as I'm concerned, you're worse than a deserter. You were a decorated officer, and you turned your back on the Corps."

"I was given an honorable discharge," I said.

"It's been revoked. How do you like that? You went from deserter to officer status all in one night," the major said as he loaded me on to a military shuttle, an atmospheric unit used mostly for transfers and cargo.

The commuter flew me to Salt Lake City Pangalactic Spaceport, where I boarded a C-89, a cargo hauler—a massive freighter used for both atmospheric and space hauling. Compared to the little atmospheric shuttle, this huge ship looked like a dinosaur. It could hold more cargo than a normal warehouse, but having spent years on various fighter carriers, I saw the C-89 for what it was—just another cargo jet.

The inside of the C-89 had been decked out for troop movements. Rows and rows of seats filled the cargo hold. Lockers had been built into the bulkheads for small arms and duffel bags. For reasons I did not understand, the pilot had dimmed the lights, giving the cabin a tunnel-like atmosphere. I could see heads full of gray and white hair along the tops of the seats. This wasn't a troop movement, it was a gathering of the veterans of ancient wars.

"This is the last of them," a sergeant said, as I boarded the flight. The sergeant was a clone. Until the civil war, every enlisted man in the Unified Authority was a clone.

After besting the Earth Fleet and destroying the Mars broadcast station, the Mogats launched a limited attack on Earth. They went after the orphanages in which the clone soldiers were raised. At the time, the Pentagon believed the attack on the Earth Fleet and the orphanages was in preparation for a full-scale invasion, but that invasion never materialized. Had they come, the Mogats would have won the war. Their first attack had so crippled the Unified Authority's military infrastructure that, as far as I could tell, no real attempt had yet been made to repair the damage. Even if the military had rebuilt its clone farms, it would have taken another eighteen years before the first graduates entered boot camp.

Illych had been correct when he told me that I only needed a pulse to qualify as "elite" for the Elite Conscription Act. Half the clones on this flight had white hair and wrinkled faces. The youngest man I saw had to be in his forties. I did not have any gear to stow, so I went right to the only open seat I could find.

"Can you believe we got called back?" asked the guy in the seat next to mine. He was a standard-issue clone, just under six feet tall and broad-shouldered. He had brown hair heavily threaded with strands of white. He looked a lot like me, only shorter, broader, and older. "Were you Army?"

"Marines," I said.

"Marines, eh?" the guy said. "I was Army. I heard you boys took a real shellacking at the end of the Mogat War."

"That's what I heard, too," I said.

"You must have already been out before the invasion," he said. "I heard no one made it off that planet alive."

The C-89 took off. I chose to use our launch as an excuse to ignore the comment.

C-class cargo lifts were not built with onboard broadcast engines, so I figured we would fly someplace nearby... maybe dock with one of the Confederate Arms' self-broadcasting battleships. "When's the last time you went to Mars, pal? Been years for me." Apparently the guy in the next seat and I had become pals.

"Is that where we're headed?" I asked. Nobody told me my final destination on the short flight from Honolulu.

"Off to Mars. Sheesh, the last time I was there was '95, maybe '98. Could it really be fifteen years?" He thought for a moment. "No, I passed through Mars in '07 when I went out to Olympus Kri."

48

At thirty million miles per hour, the flight from Earth to Mars could take as long as five hours depending on where each planet stood in its orbit.

"Been a couple of years for me, too," I said. All flights in and out of Earth passed through the Mars broadcast station, but nobody actually lived there. Even the soldiers and pilots guarding the planet lived on other planets. They went out and stayed in barracks for three-week shifts, then returned home.

The only populated area on Mars was the spaceport—the galaxy's biggest shopping bazaar. Since no one officially lived on Mars, everyone on the planet qualified for duty-free shopping. Merchants from every corner of the galaxy ran shops and restaurants there. The spaceport had forty-three grand hotels, six hundred restaurants, and three thousand stores. The galaxy's largest convention center was on the northern outskirts of the spaceport, and its second-largest convention center was in the eastern corner.

One of the best-known advertising slogans in the galaxy was, "Serious shoppers shop on Mars." It was probably true. Young couples used to travel to Mars from as far away as the Scutum-Crux Arm to purchase their engagement rings. The savings on the diamonds and gems more than covered the cost of the trip. Of course, back then the Broadcast Network was in operation, and you could fly from Scutum-Crux to Mars in a matter of minutes. With the Network down, I figured many of the stores must have closed.

My new buddy kept squinting to get a good look at me. He must have noticed as I sat down that I was too tall to be a standard-issue military clone; but in the darkness, he could not make out more details. Communications between clones included an interesting dance since anything that tipped clones off to their synthetic origins could have a fatal consequence. The "death reflex" was a fail-safe insisted upon by Congress to prevent clones from discovering their "nonhuman" identity and rebelling. The reflex was counterbalanced by neural programming. Clones were programmed not to know they were clones. If I asked the guy sitting next to me what he looked like, he would have said he had blond hair and blue eyes—despite both his hair and eyes being brown. Seeing his reflection in the mirror, he would have seen himself as blond-haired and blue-eyed, even if he was standing next to an identical clone whom he would recognize as having dark hair and eyes. To stop an outbreak of dead clones, that same programming prevented clones from discussing clone-related topics about each other.

"Were you living on Earth?" I asked.

"Not me. I had a small farm on Janus."

"Janus? That's not in the Orion Arm, is it?"

"It's in the Perseus Arm. I'll tell you what, when the Perseus Arm signed on to the Confederate Arms Treaty, I thought I was going to die. Me living in one of the Confederate Arms… If my parents had not died when I was a kid, that would have killed them."

Every clone raised in every orphanage was programmed to believe he was the only true orphan on the premises. Learning differently could trigger the death reflex in a standard-issue clone. As a Liberator, I discovered my true origins within a year of joining the Marines. In my case, ignorance was not blissful, and learning the truth had not set me free.

"Did the Confederate Army ask you to join up?"

"Not to fight against the Unified Authority. They knew better. As long as they knew I wasn't fighting against them, I think that was good enough. Truth is, I don't think they were worried about me. I mean, I'm fifty-six years old. I'm no spring chicken."

Hearing his age left me stunned. If the Pentagon was recalling fifty-year-old men, things were grim.

An officer came and opened a miniature movie holotorium at the front of the cabin. The compartment was four feet tall, seven feet wide, and two feet deep, a slightly curved concavity faced with a dull, snow-white finish.

"Look at that, they're going to show us something. Maybe they're going to brief us," my new pal said. He sounded excited.

I expected a propaganda film about life in the military. That's what they showed us on the way to boot camp when I was a recruit. Instead, the words "THE SUN ALSO RISES" appeared in large, three-dimensional letters that slowly revolved above the small holotorium screen.

The background of the movie was projected using old-fashioned two-dimensional technology. The foreground, the characters, the furniture, a door here or automobile there, was shown in holographic 3-D. The final product was a three-dimensional experience in which you could completely lose yourself.

"Holy speck, an Ava Gardner movie," my new pal said. "If this is how they treat the recruits, I think I'm glad I'm back in." We sat and watched our movie as the flight crew walked the aisles passing out beef noodle MREs. My pal tore his meal open, and said, "This is the life!"

I thought it a bad omen. In my experience, the services became more hospitable as the situations became worse.

"You think Ava's a clone?" the guy asked. "I saw an old film clip with the original Ava—you know, the actress from way back when. They do look an awful lot alike. It's kind of scary."

"Does it make any difference if she is a clone?" I asked.

"Sure it does. I'd be disappointed if she is. I mean, you know, then she's not the real thing."

The movie was about an ancient time in which honor seemed to mean more than victory. When men fought, they knocked each other down and walked away from the fight. Gardner looked beautiful playing a young ingénue smitten with a bullfighter in twentieth-century Spain. Looking infatuated and innocent, she reminded me of Christina. "I'd take a night with her, synthetic or not," I said, meaning both Ava and Christina.

My new friend and I traded a few more comments as we ate our MREs and watched the movie. When Gardner appeared on the screen, nobody on the flight spoke a word. Then the movie ended. As the credits scrolled, my pal looked over at me. "I'm Glen Benson. I guess it's about to become Corporal Benson. Can you believe it? A fifty-six-year-old corporal. I guess they've come up with some sort of peacetime duties for us old guys like me."

"Harris," I said, offering a hand. As we shook, the cabin lights came on. Benson looked at me, screwed his eyes into a squint, then pulled back his hand.

The way Benson now stared at me, I knew he had something he wanted to ask. I also had a pretty good idea of what that might be. I decided to make it easy on him. "You're wondering if I'm a Liberator?" I asked.

Benson's expression remained flat. "I already know what you are. I thought all the Liberators were dead," he said, sounding hostile.

"Let me guess, you were one of the soldiers they sent to Albatross Island after the prison riots." A decade before I was born, there was a riot on a penal colony called Albatross Island. The Navy dispatched Liberator clones to handle the situation.

Liberators had been designed for combat in unknown and dangerous situations. Instead of a gland with a death hormone, our physiology included a gland that released a combination of testosterone and adrenaline into our blood, giving us a combat reflex that kept our minds cool and our thoughts clear. It was a pretty good idea with one problem—most Liberators became addicted to the hormone, and the only way to keep it flowing was to keep on fighting. When the Liberators finished killing the rioting prisoners on Albatross Island, they killed the hostages, then the non-rioting prisoners, then some of the guards. The Army had to send an entire battalion to take control of the planet.

"I went to Albatross Island," Glen said. "I went to Volga, Electra, Dallas Prime, and New Prague, too. Albatross Island wasn't the worst. They only killed adults on Albatross—guards and prisoners, at least they had a shot at defending themselves."

"I wasn't involved in any of those actions," I said.

"I don't see how you could be, a young guy like you. Those massacres happened almost thirty years ago, you weren't even made yet, were you?" Glen asked.

Before I could answer, he said, "My question is why you were made at all. When did the Senate vote to bring back Liberators?"

I shook my head. "I'm one of a kind. Some factory worker made a mistake."

"A bad one," Glen said. "I was a private when all those massacres happened. General Crowley called my unit up to help with the investigations.

"You ever wonder why a decorated officer like Crowley would abandon his command to join the Mogats? I can tell you why. After seeing what the Liberators did, I wondered if the Mogats didn't have it right after all. He must have figured traitors and religious fanatics were better than Liberators.

"Now if you'll excuse me, I think I want to get some sleep before we reach Mars." Having said his piece, Glen leaned back in his chair and shut his eyes, a frown remaining on his lips. He did not speak to me again for the rest of the flight.

5

As we prepared to leave the C-89, the men around me talked excitedly about returning to active status in the military. They had created successful civilians lives, but they were clones, built and bred to be soldiers. Some of the guys talked about stopping in the duty-free stores and picking up booze before they shipped out. Others talked about buying enough cigarettes to last for their entire tour of duty. Military men love a shopping bazaar as a rule, and these retired clones were no exception.

The last time I entered Mars Spaceport, it was brightly lit and packed with civilians. Men in suits and women in smart dresses crowded the clubs and business centers. Models in tight dresses stood at the entrances of fragrance stores trying to tempt men into sniffing some new perfume. Parents took young children to play in the solariums. Everywhere you looked you saw neon signs marking some gaudy new retailer.

The men ahead of me rushed down the gangway laughing, stepped into the terminal, and fell silent. I stepped off the gangway and fell silent. Mars Spaceport had become an empty shell.

Without the crowds and the lights, the spaceport revealed

its true nature—a cavernous mausoleum. Metal gates hung like curtains over storefronts that looked as dark as deep-sea caves. Halls that had once teemed with an endless tide of humanity sat dark and silent, lit only by the plumes of red and green emergency torches.

"What happened here?" an old fellow asked as he stared along a line of dead stores. Through the darkness, I saw men with flashlights coming to meet us as we gathered in the terminal.

"Is the spaceport on lockdown?" an old recruit asked one of the soldiers as they arrived to greet us.

"Shiiit, have a look around," the soldier replied. "There ain't nothing left here to lock down, old-timer. Look around you. This place is deserted. There's nothing in the stores to steal."

"What are we doing here?" the old man asked.

"You look like you been around the block a time or two," the soldier said. "You can't possibly think I'm going to risk getting some officer on my case by spoiling the surprise." Our guides were regular government-issue Army clones. When the first two hundred of us had come down the gangway, two corporals paired off with us, leading us away from the gates and into a dim shopping arcade. The arcade floor was so wide that the storefronts on either side of us vanished into the shadows.

"Keep up," one of the corporals said as he looked back and saw slower recruits lagging behind. "Stay in a group. If one of you gets lost in here, it's our asses that will answer for it."

Unlit and empty, the spaceport transformed into a maze in which a person could easily become lost. The corporals led us down two floors to an underground railway system. Before the civil war, the spaceport maintained six separate wings, one for each arm of the galaxy. Passengers used to board these trains to get from one wing to the next.

Maybe the other wings are active, I thought.

Rumbling along at no more than ten miles per hour, we passed by boarding zones for one wing after another, the platforms were all dark. When we reached the wing for Scutum-Crux—the farthest arm of the galaxy—the train slowed and switched tracks, entering a tunnel that led us uphill and through a set of airtight doors.

"The Corps of Engineers just finished this new track a few weeks ago," said one of the corporals. He wasn't speaking to anyone in particular, just enjoying the audience of recruits.

When the outer door opened, I saw the Martian landscape. I had flown over this planet many times but never looked across the landscape at ground level. The land was flat and ugly, a featureless desert with rocks and sand and no signs of life.

"Are these cars sealed to hold air?" one of the recruits asked.

"They weren't before the Corps of Engineers got a hold of them," the soldier replied. "But don't you worry your white head over that. They're sure as shit airtight now."

Looking at the old-man recruit and corporal leading us was like looking at multiple generations of the same family. All of the men standing in this car stood just under six feet, though many of the older ones were slumped with age. Those recalled soldiers who were still young enough to have color in their hair had brown hair. I did see one or two old fellows who had tried to dye their hair with blond hair dye. Everyone had the same color of brown in their eyes, the same exact cleft in their chins, and the same bridge in their noses.

"I wouldn't worry about the poisonous air," our second corporal/guide said. "Hell, it's so cold out there you'd freeze to death."

Ah, hazing the recruits, a time-honored tradition in the military. Battle-wary veterans scaring new recruits was a tradition that might even be as ancient as the MREs they served us on the transport. On the other hand, the tradition took on a strange twist in this train car, where the veterans were in their thirties and the naïve victims were in their fifties.

The train took us thirty miles across the surface of Mars to Citadel Air Force Base. There were no roads or fences around this glowing geodesic dome, just a dun-colored building that rose out of the ground like a five-story blister. Rings of blue-white light shone about the foot and cornice of the building.

The tracks led through another air lock and into a tube that took a sharp dive under the wall of the dome. We emerged from the tube in an underground train station. Aluminum ventilation shafts snaked along the red rock wall twenty feet overhead. Bright arc lights shone down on the platform from ten feet above. The ceiling of the station was a slab of rough-hewn red rock.

The door to our train car opened, and frozen air rushed in.

"You want to hurry it up, boys," one of the corporals yelled as he pushed his way out to the platform. "The air is a few degrees south of zero." His breath formed a cloud around his mouth.

Soldiers in heated environmental suits ushered us toward the far end of the platform as we left the train. Feeling the cold air burning deep in my lungs, I trotted to the front of the herd and entered another air lock at the far end of the platform. The old men around me remained mostly quiet in the cold, though a few moaned. I suspect the men in the environmental suits enjoyed watching them suffer. I could hear muffled laughter through their masks, and why not—they wore electronically insulated jackets.

So much for Ava Gardner movies and all-you-can-eat MREs; now we were back in the real military.

"We should'a just stayed in the spaceport," one of the old men said as he stepped into the air lock. Everyone around him agreed. I could have pointed out that enormous as it was, the unshielded spaceport would collapse if hit by a single missile. The Citadel had shielded walls, batteries of defensive missiles, several cannons, and squadrons of fighters protecting it.

Warm air circulated through this tunnel. As soldiers piled in behind me, I followed the tunnel to an escalator that led upward. Two soldiers waited for us at the top.

"Well," one of them yelled, "hurry it up."

The automatic stairs took us 150 feet up at a seventy-degree angle. The soldiers that met us at the top of the stairs pointed toward yet another corridor and rushed everyone along. Finally, we passed through one last set of doors and entered the admin area.

The Citadel reminded me of office buildings everywhere. Rows of bright fluorescent light fixtures shone from the ceilings to the endless plains of white, shiny flooring spread beneath our feet. We passed cubicles and small offices, conference rooms and cafeterias.

The building was crowded with servicemen from all branches. Walking past a break room, I saw officers in blue, green, and white sitting at a table drinking coffee. The guards along the wall wore olive drab service uniforms. This was an air base, but with all the branches represented, it felt more like the Pentagon.

One of the recruits paused and asked a soldier, "Where are the billets?"

"Other side of the building," the soldier grunted, not even bothering to look at the man.

"Are we staying here tonight?" the old recruit asked.

"Not here. We'll have you back on your transport in a couple of hours."

We stopped in front of a large auditorium. A group of soldiers met us by the door and waited for us to form a group. "Anyone who served in the Army, fall in on the right. Air Force, front and center. Marines, you fall in on the left."

"What if I was Navy?" a man called from the back. There was a group of retired sailors, fifty or sixty of them.

The soldier smiled as if this was a great joke. "You're in the Army now," he said. This raised a groan from the seamen.

Of the first two hundred recruits to walk off of the transport, I was the only Marine. I stood in a one-man queue.

"You, young blood," one of the guides called to me. "What's your name?"

"Harris," I said.

He looked at his clipboard, then over to the other guide. "Yup, he's the one. Harris, we have special orders for you."

Somebody yelled, "He's a specking Liberator." I did not need to look back to know it was Glen.

The guide saluted me. "Lieutenant Harris, I've been instructed to take you to a special briefing. Would you follow me, sir?" he asked.

I nodded, and we left.

"Where are we going?" I asked.

"Officer country."

As we moved deeper into the Citadel, the base population switched from servicemen of all description to administrative airmen. Men in blue sweaters and blue pants rushed down corridors, carrying files and boxes. Men in blue uniforms sat behind desks studying computers. These men worked quietly, efficiently. They had direction.

"Who else is coming to this briefing?" I asked.

"As far as I know, you're it, sir," the corporal said.

"Aren't there any other Marines?" I asked, remembering the way we had grouped.

"Other Marines, yes; but you're the only officer," he said.

We came to a door marked "Conference Room." A small red light flashed beside the door to show that the room was in use. "This is your stop, sir," the soldier said. He saluted and left.

I let myself in.

"You're just in time, Lieutenant," the admiral said as I entered. "They're about to start."

There were no guards in the room. Admiral Alden Brocius sat at the head of a ten-foot-long table, looking frail and old. He'd lost at least fifty pounds since the last time I saw him. I could see the shape of his skull under his cheeks. Age and tension had added new wrinkles to his face.

"Admiral Brocius." I could not help but sneer as I said the name. He commanded the Central Cygnus Fleet. At some point in recent years he had become the highest-ranking man in the Navy; but as far as I knew, he never made the jump from fleet commander to Secretary of the Navy.

"You will show me proper respect, Lieutenant," Brocius said, trying to stay in command of what he knew to be a dangerous situation. He was an old man, and I was a Liberator, a class of clone designed for violence. He also knew that I had a score to settle with him. He was the one who had ordered sixty thousand

Marines to the Mogat home world and left them stranded there as the planet melted.

"I'll bet you want to kill me," Brocius said.

"More than anything I have ever wanted in my life," I said.

Brocius pulled a pistol out from under the table and pointed it at me. "I've spent the last year of my life worrying about you and your friend Freeman. I didn't even feel safe on my own damned ship, Harris; not my own damned ship. I had extra guards posted outside of my quarters, but I knew that wouldn't stop you.

"It turns out I didn't have anything to worry about after all. I got reports... Earning a living winning Iron Man competitions and screwing tourist girls in Hawaii. I wanted you euthanized, but General Mooreland said no.

"Mooreland died two months ago. I suppose you heard about that," Brocius said.

"I only heard that this evening," I admitted. "Are you planning to shoot me?" I asked.

"Quite the opposite," Brocius said. He placed his pistol flat on the table and slid it toward me.

Admiral Brocius had an antique casino on the second floor of his family mansion, but he did not play cards. He liked running games of chance, not playing them. Not a gambling man in the ordinary sense, he preferred house odds. Now, for some reason, he believed he had better-than-even odds that I would not pull the trigger. I had the gun, but he knew something I needed to know.

"Speck! Look at these pathetic bastards," a voice whispered out from a large monitor sitting in the center of the conference table. I could not see the screen; it faced away from me. "They get older with each group. These boys are decrepit. They belong in a specking old folks' home, not the damn Army."

"Given a choice, I suppose I would rather be shot than beaten to death," Brocius said, his eyes locked on mine. "If you shoot me, the military will be down one man and one bullet. Take my word on this one, Harris. We cannot afford to waste men or bullets."

I picked up the pistol but did not aim it at Brocius. "What's that?" I asked, pointing at the screen with his gun.

"It's a briefing," Brocius said. "They're briefing the recruits that came in with you."

"Gentlemen, perhaps we should get started," the man on the screen said in a loud voice. Still holding the pistol, I walked around the table to see what was happening.

From what I could tell, all of the two thousand passengers from the transport had been crammed into a large auditorium. The room was dim but not dark, and all of those old, white heads sparkled in the audience like marble grave markers. An Army major whom I did not recognize stood on a stage.

"Gentlemen, I'm going to skip the formalities and cut to the chase," the briefing officer began. "The Unified Authority is in a state of war. The war is not going so well."

The auditorium remained silent as the major paused to organize his notes. The rustling of his papers seemed almost earsplitting in that silence.

An image appeared on a screen above the major. It was battle footage. The footage showed Army men barricaded in some kind of bunker, firing M27s through ramparts at an unseen enemy. I heard the normal battlefield chatter—*There's one… Fire, fire, fry the bastard… Your left! Your left!*

Then the camera panned out over the ramparts and into the field. There, no more than thirty feet from the U.A. firing line, were creatures the likes of which I had never seen in my life. I could not tell if they were black-skinned or wearing some type of combat armor. If I had to guess, I would have put their height at somewhere between seven and eight feet. They looked bulky and powerful.

"What are those things?" I asked.

"Don't you recognize them?" Brocius returned my question with one of his own.

"I've never seen them before," I said.

The screen in the briefing room froze and closed in on one of the creatures. It looked almost human except that its entire body seemed to be made of some hard, charcoal-colored substance. I would have liked to see what happened next, but that was where the feed ended.

The alien had two eyes, which resembled shot-put balls in size and color, two ears, a very flat nose, and a mouth with no lips. Its body showed no features such as muscles or bones. Looking at the frozen frame, I tried to determine if that thing was wearing some kind of suit. I saw nothing to suggest armor, just a rounded chest and torso that were twice the size of a human's.

"Then you don't recognize it? I thought you were old friends," Brocius said at the same time the major resumed his briefing. "This guy or one of his brothers was the thing that fired on you during the Mogat invasion."

Hearing Brocius mention the invasion gave me a quick mental stab. I tightened my grip on the pistol.

We are dealing with a life-form that is not human. Your job is to kill it, the major told his audience.

"The thing I saw was made of plasma or electricity or some kind of energy," I said. "It was yellow and it glowed."

They have invaded our galaxy. They have come into our house and now they are pushing us out of the way, the major said. *We're going to give the bastards the fight of the specking century.*

"Everything they're saying in the briefing is bullshit, in case you were wondering," Brocius said. "Those things are eating us alive." He watched me for a few seconds, not saying a word, and asked, "You mind if I turn that off?" then stood up and reached over to turn off the monitor without waiting for my answer.

I shrugged. He paused, standing in mid-reach with his eyes locked on the pistol—his pistol—that I held in my right hand.

"You can forget everything Major Doolan is telling them in that briefing. It's all bullshit," Brocius said as he turned off the screen and returned to his seat.

"They have taken control of Scutum-Crux, Norma, and Perseus." Those were the three largest arms of the galaxy, but also the least populated. "They took all of that territory in under a year, and they have started to move into Cygnus and Sagittarius. If we can't slow them, they'll have control of the Orion Arm in a couple of months.

"That's why you're here, Harris. That's why they're here," Brocius said, nodding toward the blank screen. "That's why we brought back the specking Roman Legion."

"Then you have two problems, because the alien I saw glowed. I don't know what those things are, but they aren't the aliens that Atkins was calling 'Space Angels,'" I said.

"Yeah, I saw the video you captured," Brocius said dismissively. He pulled out a folder, which he opened and placed on the table. "This is from your feed." He selected a still shot and passed it to me. The shot was blurry, but the image was clear in my mind. It showed a luminous alien creature holding a broad-barreled rifle. I noticed that the rifle in the picture looked like the weapon the aliens were carrying in the video feed.

"These shots were taken on Terraneau just over a year ago." He handed me a single eight-by-ten sheet with a series of one-inch windows on it. Some of the pictures were washed out. In the first shot, a group of four luminous beings stood on one side of the frame. The rest of the picture was white. In the next frame, those same beings stood on a street.

"What is this?" I asked.

"This, Harris, is a full-scale invasion. We don't know how many troops they landed, but we had three million troops on Terraneau. They captured the planet within a couple of hours."

"What happened to the rest of these pictures?" I asked, pointing to the whited-out area.

"We think that was their landing zone," Brocius said. "They were captured by a satellite as the invasion began. We got lucky on those. Besides the video you caught, these photographs are the only images we have of these things in their transited state."

"Transited?" I asked. "Your term?"

"That's what the scientists are calling it. 'Transited.'"

"What does it mean?" I asked.

"It means they just arrived," Brocius said.

"Do you have any shots of their spaceships?"

"They don't use spaceships," Brocius said. "That was why no one believed you after the Mogat invasion. We had our entire fleet circling the planet. You said you saw aliens, but none of the ships saw anything unusual."

"How did they get to the planet?" I asked.

"You saw the bright light during the invasion... we think they came in through it," Brocius said. "It's just a theory, but it's the best we have."

I wished I could forget that light. Often as I fell asleep, my mind returned to that desperate moment as our invasion collapsed around us. I remembered the way that the strange light spread like a fog over the city and the odd glow it sent into the air. Waves of elemental colors seemed to rise out of that glow like smoke from a fire.

By the fifth frame in the series, the creatures no longer glowed. Their complexions had turned dark. I could see their massive forms clearly.

"They don't look so advanced," I said. "No vehicles, no tanks... just men on foot carrying rifles. What do you know about their battle tactics?"

"Absolutely nothing," Brocius said. "Once that phantom light you saw stretches across an area, we lose all contact with the planet. We can't transmit through it. We can't take readings through it. Those battle images Major Doolan just showed the geezers were taken from a live feed just before the light sealed off the area.

"Around the Pentagon they're calling it the 'ion curtain.'" Brocius sighed.

"What do the survivors say?"

"No survivors," Brocius said. "Once these bastards close that light curtain around a planet, there's no going back to it. We've tried reentering; nothing gets through. We've sent fighters, robot ships... nothing makes it through, and nothing ever comes out."

I placed the pistol back on the table and slid it back toward Brocius. I wasn't going to shoot him.

"You're not going to shoot me?" Brocius asked as he gathered up the gun.

"Maybe next time," I said.

"Now you know why we need every man we can get... even those old fools." It occurred to me that Brocius was older than many of those "old fools."

"So how much of what you tell me will they get to hear?" I asked.

"Not much. Then again, I'm telling you everything we know, and it's not much," Brocius admitted. "In this war, we're going to need to learn as we go along."

6

If they had asked me to accept a commission when I left Sad Sam's Palace, I would have said no. I had no choice about reporting, not with a dozen MPs breathing down my neck; but that did not mean I needed to rejoin. If I refused, the worst they could do was kill me, and I figured the aliens would kill us all in due course.

But meeting with Admiral Brocius had a strange effect on me. Here sat a man whom I had wanted to kill for over a year. I must have imagined myself snapping his neck a thousand times; but now that I saw him in person, the urge to kill Brocius slipped away.

He had come to represent everything I hated about the Unified Authority—the prejudice and abuse of clones, the deceit, the haughty attitude of its politicians and officers. U.A. officers fought wars as if they were a game of chess, an intellectual sport played on a black-and-white battlefield with pieces instead of people.

This time, though, Admiral Brocius had laid himself bare. Alone in the conference room, he could have been killed. I wouldn't need a gun to kill a dried-up old derelict like him—I could have jumped across the table and broken his neck.

Having a worm like Brocius at my mercy had an unexpected

impact on me. I won't say I forgave him, but my anger fell out of focus. Here he sat, a sheep in a stall waiting for slaughter. Looking at him now, scared and trying to look like he was still in control of the situation, I realized how I did and did not want to die. I didn't want to die at all. But if the war was on my doorstep, I preferred death on the battlefield with a gun in my hand and men that I trusted fighting beside me to dying like a sheep with a herd of civilians.

"It sounds like we can't win this one," I said.

"I suppose that depends on how you mean 'win,'" Brocius said. "We've given up on colonizing the galaxy if that's what you mean. It's theirs. At this point we're not even trying to hold on to the last of our colonies. If we can keep these bastards from reaching Earth, that will be victory enough."

Brocius slid a memory disc into the monitor. A moment later a map of the galaxy appeared before us. There it was, a whirlpool made of six spiral arms leading into a vortex dense with stars. The image showed white stars with subtle bubbles of color against a black background. The camera zoomed in on the map, showing a series of stars orbited by planets.

"The invasion started in this unpopulated section of the Scutum-Crux Arm," Brocius said.

The outer edge of the Scutum-Crux Arm, the outermost arm of the galaxy, turned red. They called this area the outer frontier. It was supposed to be unpopulated, but I knew about a very small colony of Neo-Baptists in that quadrant. I visited that colony with Ray Freeman, a mercenary and former partner. His family was among the colonists.

"There was a colony on—"

"Neo-Baptists on Little Man," Brocius interrupted. For the first time since I had arrived, he did not strike me as a scared dog trying to act ferocious. "I oversaw the evacuation personally."

"Overseeing" the evacuation, of course, did not mean that he participated in it.

"I made a deal with Freeman; we traded a life for a life. I saved the colony and he... We're square now. I don't need to worry about him." I got the feeling Brocius added that last part more to convince himself than to inform me. Ray Freeman was a large and dangerous man. Brocius had left him to die on the Mogat planet along with the Marines, and Ray was not normally the forgiving type.

"Did you have trouble getting them out?" I asked.

"You'd have to ask Freeman," Brocius said.

Ask Freeman, I thought. "Am I going to see Freeman?"

Brocius ignored the question. "I can show you what became of Little Man." Little Man was a "naturally productive" planet, meaning it was similar in size, temperature, and atmosphere to Earth. The image of the planet spun on the monitor, its blue, green, and tawny surface visible under a swirl of clouds. A small dot of light appeared on one of the continents. At first it was no more than a pinprick of light, but it spread in every direction until it flooded the entire planet.

"We placed a satellite to track the event," Brocius said. "Our scientists call the process 'sleeving.' It took about five hours for the light to spread across the planet."

"Then what happened?" I asked.

Brocius started to say something, paused, then said, "We don't know.

"The satellite did not pick up the approach of a spaceship. We learned later that the aliens don't use ships. That phantom light of theirs appears on the planet, and they come walking out of it like ghosts coming out of a fog.

"Our Navy is completely useless against them. Once that light closes around a planet... seals around the planet, we're cut off. We can't send messages in, and no messages come out. We're working under the assumption that everyone on the planet is dead.

"The aliens don't have ships, so we can't put up a blockade. We can't engage their land troops from space because the light shields them from us. Who knows what field tactics they use."

"And there's no way to send a landing force in to investigate?" I asked.

Brocius laughed. "Like I told you before, once they sleeve the planet, we're cut off. Nothing gets in or out of that ion curtain." Brocius's frustration showed. He snarled these words, then repeated them softly. "We even tried sending in a self-broadcasting ship. We programmed it to broadcast in under the curtain."

"Did it make it?" I asked.

Brocius fixed me with a patronizing grin. "You tell me. We never heard back."

I stared at the monitor. It showed a planet encased in that gleaming light. "So it's possible that people are alive down there. For all you know, they won the battle, and they just can't send a signal out."

"It seems a little more likely that they are all dead, don't you think?" Brocius asked. "We don't know anything except that as soon as the light spreads over one planet, the aliens move on to the next."

The image on the monitor panned out to a view of the Scutum-Crux Arm. This was not a photographic record shot by a satellite, like the one of Little Man. This time the screen showed a computer simulation in which entire solar systems turned dark red when they were invaded. The simulation looked a lot like a demonstration of a circulatory system with blood running through previously empty veins. The map showed the steady and unalterable progress of the invasion. On the bottom of the screen, a small window ticked off dates as the red tide covered the galaxy. It took twenty days for the invasion to reach Terraneau, the capital of the Scutum-Crux Arm, and there the simulation stopped.

"Part of the Scutum-Crux Fleet was orbiting Terraneau when the Broadcast Network went down, it's been there ever since. We lifted a scientist from the planet before it was cut off. Without the Network, we couldn't evacuate the planet."

"Why haven't you restored the Network?" I asked.

"It's too late now," Brocius said. "By the time we detected the invasion, it was too late."

He paused, brightened slightly, and added, "Of course, Scutum-

Crux is Confederate Arms territory. Even if the Network were up, we might not have activated it in their territory." Scutum-Crux was among the first arms to declare independence from the Unified Authority.

"Terraneau went just like every other battle—the light field closed the planet. After that, your guess is as good as mine," Brocius said. "The battleships were useless."

On the screen, the simulation ticked off two days with no movement, then the red portion of the galaxy began expanding. The blood-colored stream entered the Cygnus Arm, spreading slowly into the Norma Arm, then Perseus.

"Even if we could evacuate people, we just plain don't have any place to relocate them. I suppose we have time to bring a few million refugees to Earth, but it's just a matter of time."

The computer started its countdown anew. By day two hundred, the entire Scutum-Crux Arm was flooded with red, and Norma, Cygnus, and Perseus were looking pretty damn crimson.

"I don't suppose we've been able to contact them to negotiate," I said.

"We did negotiate with them, and rather successfully, too. That's the problem. Our negotiator was the late Senator Morgan Atkins."

The simulation resumed, only now it seemed to gain momentum. The calendar on the bottom of the screen did not accelerate, but the spreading of reddened territory did. Over the next fifty days, all of Scutum-Crux, Norma, and Perseus turned red. The Galactic Eye, the star-rich vortex of the galaxy, turned red in a matter of twenty days.

"That cannot be," I said.

Brocius paused the simulation.

"The Galactic Eye... there are a billion stars in that part of the galaxy."

"They move fast, the bastards," Brocius said. "The real problems are just beginning. Check the date."

The calendar at the bottom of the screen said October 23, 2514—just six weeks ago.

"We always know exactly where they are going to attack next, Harris. It's a straight march. Strategy has nothing to do with this campaign."

I looked at the map of the galaxy on the monitor and saw what he meant. The aliens had landed on the far end of the galaxy and were working their way straight across. "They might as well phone their plans in to us in advance," I said.

"They have," Brocius said. "The map you are looking at was taken from a signal they transmitted on Earth."

"They gave us this map?" I asked. "What about the calendar?"

"We added that," Brocius said. "We synchronized their attack to our calendar system. So far, it's been a perfect match." With this, he tapped the monitor, and the simulation continued up to December 18, 2514.

"That was yesterday," I said as I watched the red area marking invaded territory flood into the Orion Arm. "They sent this?"

"They're still sending it," Brocius said. "They transmit it on a continuous signal on several of our military frequencies."

"How often do they update it?" I asked.

"They don't. This is what they have been sending for over a year now. They told us exactly what they planned to do from the start, and they've gone and done it. The only explanation we can come up with is that they don't really care about killing humans; what they're really after is capturing planets."

The simulation started again. The days ticked by quickly. On March 15, the red area expanded to include the inner section of the Orion Arm, that part of the galaxy where Earth was located.

"Three months?" I asked.

"They're coming, Harris. God help us, they're coming."

7

"Have you ever heard of a planet called New Copenhagen?" Admiral Brocius asked. He looked old and broken-down. For as long as I had known Brocius, he had been a chubby old man with high corners on his hairline and a double chin. Time and stress had taken a toll. Over the last year he had grown a decade older, and he had the look of a man who had lost a lot of weight in a very little time. His mouth and eyes looked too big for his face, giving him a hungry, startled look. His hairline started higher on his head than I remembered.

"Sounds familiar," I said, remembering that I had recently heard someone mention the planet without recalling who or why.

Brocius crossed his arms and leaned back in his chair, the smirk on his face giving him an expression of mild disgust. "Been following the latest movie-star gossip, have you?"

That tipped the scales in my memory. Christina had mentioned New Copenhagen when she asked me about Ava Gardner. Now that I remembered where I heard the name, I didn't want to admit it. "Movie-star gossip?" I asked, trying to sound as innocent as I could.

Brocius didn't bite. "Yes, well, the planet is of strategic value now. It will be the aliens' last stop before they land on Earth." He tapped a stylus to the computer screen, and the image closed in on the Orion Arm. Along the arm, flags stood out marking solar systems with inhabited planets. Toward the inner curve of the Orion Arm, already covered in red, was the location of Olympus Kri. I once knew a woman from that planet. Perhaps "knew" was the right word; if everything I had heard this evening was correct, that girl might already be dead.

The map showed three inches of star-strewn space between Olympus Kri and Earth—each inch representing ten thousand light-years. The space around Olympus Kri was outlined in red. So were most of the other solar systems with inhabited planets along the way. But the red tide stopped just shy of one flagged solar system. "The Woden System?" I asked.

"That's where we have a colony called New Copenhagen, it's the closest inhabited planet to Earth. Win or lose, that's where we make our last stand. The goal is to stop the aliens on New Copenhagen. We're sending in as many soldiers, pilots, and Marines as we can get in before the action starts. We've shipped in more equipment... By the time we get through, there will be over one million troops on that planet and at least thirty guns and three hundred grenades for every man we sent in.

"We're sending our best scientists to help analyze the situation, and we'll have as many ships as we can spare orbiting the planet at all times."

"That's good coverage," I said.

"You're going in as a lieutenant. I wanted to give you a division to work with, but that was not my call. I would have restored you to colonel... maybe even made a general out of you."

"Kind of you," I said.

The sarcasm did not go unnoticed. "I put in a word for you with the Marine commandant. He said he'd give you some leeway, that's the best I could do," Brocius said.

"What happens if we lose?" I asked.

"If you lose?" Brocius repeated. "Harris, we have approximately fifty self-broadcasting Navy ships and a hundred scientific explorers. We'd be able to airlift a couple million people off Earth if we had someplace to put them, but we don't, Harris. Even if we get them off, the sad fact is that we wouldn't have anyplace to put them."

8

They made the right choice when they decided not to evacuate the planet, I thought as I stared out the window of the civilian shuttle and saw New Copenhagen. These aliens, these Space Angels, weren't just crossing the galaxy at a rate nearly one hundred thousand times faster than the speed of light; they were conquering it at that speed. The galaxy was one hundred thousand light-years from end to end, and they had captured almost all of it in a single year. Fighting an enemy that could move one hundred thousand times faster than light, why bother running?

It was just like Brocius had said, even if we could load all of humanity into some interstellar ark, we'd have no place to go. With the exception of the self-broadcasting fleet, our fastest ships could not travel as fast as light. With the galaxy under enemy control, we would need to travel to another galaxy to start again—a trip that would take thousands of years at light speed. And then what? What if the nearest habitable planet was one thousand light-years deep in that galaxy? Loading humanity into a lifeboat would mean nothing if that lifeboat had no safe harbor in which to land.

The shuttle trembled as it penetrated the planet's atmosphere. Heat and friction from the atmosphere turned the protective tiles on the shuttle's wings orange and red, then the pilot adjusted the angle of our descent and we flew over a sparkling ocean. We crossed a coast and dropped to less than a mile above the ground. Below us, the city of Valhalla spread out in every direction, a giant metropolis buried in snow. A frozen lake bordered it on one side and snowcapped forests and countryside surrounded it on another.

"Why this place? Why fight here?" the sergeant in the seat next to mine asked as our shuttle descended through ribbons of faded clouds. "Man, just looking out the window gives my ass the shivers." He was one of the really old recruits. The guy looked like he was in his sixties.

This was it, the place the human race would make its stand. The only way I would make it off this planet would be if we defeated the enemy, but could anyone defeat the Space Angels? Who knew what would happen once they sleeved New Copenhagen and that strange light cut us off from the rest of the universe. For all I knew, we might have won battles on some of the other 179 colonized worlds. All those soldiers they sent to Terraneau might be alive at this very moment, just standing around waiting for that phantom light to burn out.

I didn't believe they were alive, though. I took a cynical view. Having had a brief glimpse of the Angels in action, I believed that all hope ended once the light closed in around you.

"If we're going to die, we might as well die on a frozen wasteland," I said, joking. Judging by the sudden silence, the old fellow did not appreciate my sense of humor. As an officer, I supposed I should have come up with a more encouraging response.

According to the simulation Brocius showed me, we only

had a few hours left to dig in before the fireworks began. In the meantime, transports and commuter flights dotted the sky like lines of ants around a picnic basket. A constant stream of transports and cargo ships flew in and out of Valhalla Spaceport and the new, temporary runways the Corps of Engineers had stitched into the outskirts of town. The Navy would airlift those with the right connections to Earth. Those lucky few were mostly politicians and people from families wealthy enough to bribe their way off the planet, a brief reprieve at best.

Those who could not afford to evacuate from New Copenhagen were transported across the planet to relocation camps around the southern hemisphere. Data collected from previous battles showed that the lights always appeared first in northern latitudes, and generally near large population centers. The hope was that relocating the general population away from the fighting might buy them some time. If we won the fight, we would bring them back once the danger ended.

The Army Corps of Engineers had built several temporary bases on New Copenhagen to house the 620,000 soldiers now stationed in town. Army command, however, was located in the capitol building, in the center of Valhalla. They called it Fort Schwarzkopf.

The Air Force set up shop in a shopping mall, turning its long flat roof into multiple runways. They had a complement of three hundred Tomcat fighters. The Navy was mostly involved in the logistics of shipping in fighters and equipment; the Marines, however, would make a show of this fight. We came in four hundred thousand men strong. For the foreseeable future, the city of Valhalla was the galaxy's military base.

As for me, I had mixed emotions about joining this fight. I did not like the idea of fighting for the same specking officers who tried to leave me and my Marines stranded to die, but I didn't see much of a future in trying to make friends with the Space Angels, either. Even back when I was telling myself I'd sit this one out, I knew I didn't have it in me. I was a Marine, damn it.

I solemnly swore that I would defend the Republic against all enemies, foreign, domestic, and, I suppose, extragalactic. Besides, I was losing interest in the easy life—Friday-night fights and one-night stands were fun but not satisfying. I needed something more challenging, something to get my heart beating hard; and it did not matter whether I survived it or not. I preferred "death in battle to death like cattle," as one of my old drill instructors used to say. There just isn't anything that compares to going into battle with a platoon of willing men at your back and a loaded M27.

Semper fi, Marine.

We dropped down until we were no more than thirty feet above the skyscrapers on the way to the spaceport. Some of those buildings had ten-foot mounds of gleaming white snow piled up on roofs.

The streets below were mostly empty. Before the evacuation, Valhalla had a population of approximately three million. Only 200,000 of those residents signed up to defend their city. The rest chose the safety of a relocation camp. Populated with 620,000 soldiers, 400,000 Marines, 150,000 Airmen, and 200,000 civilians, the city was barely one-third full; but that population was compressed. From the air, some parts of Valhalla looked deserted and others looked crowded.

Looking down as we came in for a landing, I saw tanks and troop carriers. The Army sent out an enormous contraption that created waist-high bulletproof barriers by extruding plasticized blocks. The machine looked like a gigantic combine. Moving at no more than ten miles per hour, it rumbled down the middle of the highway, taking up four lanes of traffic, leaving rows of gunmetal gray barriers in its wake. The machine was officially known as a "Barrier Manufacturer," or BM. In the Corps, we unofficially called it a "Shitter." A small robotic device followed behind the BM, sanding any rough edges from the plasticized barriers. In the Corps we referred to that second unit as a "Babyshitter."

From the air, the runways looked like black straps that prevented the snowy fields from unrolling like blankets. Caravans of tractors towed carts filled with rifles and munitions into warehouses on the far side of the airfield. Off in the distance, a line of artillery rolled along the horizon. As we circled the landing strip, I spotted tanks, missile launchers, and laser cannons. The equipment blended into the landscape around it. It had all been painted white.

Then the shuttle came in to the airport, I took one last look around. We came in low over an abandoned business district with empty streets. The shuttle did not even jostle as much as a car going over a speed bump when we touched down onto the runway. As we rolled to the terminal, I told myself that a smooth landing was as good an omen as any. On the other hand, I did not believe in omens.

As I prepared to leave my seat, I had a look around the runway. Never had I seen such a buildup. A formation of Tomcats flew overhead. In the distance gunships patrolled the edge of town. They flew low to the ground, maybe just a couple hundred feet up, low enough that I almost lost track of them as they vanished behind high-rise buildings. Then the ground crew attached the gangway to our shuttle and opened the hatch.

"Welcome to Valhalla," the pilot called back as he cut the engines.

As we deplaned, a squadron of duty officers descended upon us and divided us by rank and branch. I was greeted by a Marine captain, who told me where to claim my gear and meet my ride.

The spaceport pulsed with tension as Navy and civilian transports arrived and departed every minute. Four hundred thousand Marines had flown through here over the last few days with enough field equipment and supplies to wage a war. The Navy had commandeered Valhalla Spaceport, replacing its former civilian splendor with martial sensibility. MPs and duty officers patrolled the halls, überefficient supply officers off-loaded cargo, and information desks now posted duty rosters instead of flight schedules.

Snow-brightened sunlight poured in through every wall-length window of the terminal. Officers and packs of enlisted men moved through the halls with purpose but little urgency. I saw Marine khaki wherever I looked—the floors, the gates, even on the balcony fifteen feet above me. Officers ripped past me riding carts and honking their horns to clear paths through the crowds. The natural-borns might have sat out other battles, but they could not avoid this one.

I was an officer, too... a second lieutenant. I found a head and changed into my uniform, sneering at the single gold bar on my lapel. That made me the lowest evolution of officer. No one over the rank of private took second lieutenants seriously in combat, but the bar would get me a billet in officer country. I made sure the bar was straight and went to grab my gear.

"Twenty-third Marines, Company B. If you're from Company B, grab your gear and head out!" a sergeant yelled at the old recruits as they stepped around a corner. It was a touching intergenerational scene—the sergeant, a clone in his late thirties screaming so loud that strands of spit flew from his lips, reactivated Marines in their forties, fifties, and maybe even their sixties jumping to comply.

"Move it, assholes! The captain is waiting," the sergeant yelled. "You, Grandpa, you hoping for a second retirement check?" he yelled to no recruit in particular, so far as I could tell. "Move it, move it, move it!"

"Sergeant, where do I go to gather my gear?" I asked.

He looked at me with too much mirth in his smile. Like every other clone, he thought he was a natural-born, and here was a clone in an officer's uniform asking him for a ride.

"See something amusing, Sergeant?" I asked. The smile vanished from his lips.

"No, sir," he said.

"'Cause if you see something funny, Sergeant, I'd like to be in on the specking joke."

"No, sir! The sergeant sees nothing funny, sir."

"Where are they unloading the officers' gear?" I asked.

"I have your gear, Lieutenant Harris," someone said from behind me.

The man standing behind me was a clone with the same brown

stubble and brown eyes as every other clone in the spaceport, but I recognized him nonetheless. I had no trouble identifying the men who served with me during the Mogat invasion. "Hello, Thomer," I said.

"I knew you would be here," Sergeant Kelly Thomer said, after we traded salutes. "There was no way you'd sit this one out."

"Glad you knew it," I said. "I didn't. It took an armed guard just to drag me to Mars." I was happy to see Thomer. We'd fought together, and I respected him. I could trust him under any circumstances.

"I don't see anyone guarding you now," Thomer said.

"Yeah, I shook 'em," I said.

Thomer acknowledged my joke with a grin and a nod, then said, "Come with me, sir. Philips is warming up our jeep."

"Philips? He's still around?" I asked. I liked Mark Philips; but I would not have been surprised to hear he had been shot, drummed out of the Corps, or thrown in the brig for life. He had a talent for rubbing people the wrong way, especially officers.

"Sure he's around; the Corps needs every man," Thomer said.

Thomer led the way through the terminal and out to the street. We passed a team of Marines loading gear into the backs of trucks. We passed companies waiting for rides to arrive. The snow-lined sidewalks glistened in the sunlight. The cold, fresh air stung my skin in a pleasant way. A fine powder of dry snow hung in the air.

"Any sign of the aliens yet?" I asked Thomer.

"You would know more about that than I do, sir. They've kept us completely in the dark so far," he said. "If we're fighting aliens this time, are these the same aliens you saw when we invaded the Mogats?"

"Officially?" I asked.

"Yes."

"I don't know," I said.

"How about unofficially?" Thomer asked.

"I still don't know," I said.

"Thanks, sir."

"Anytime, Sergeant."

Thomer pointed to a jeep up ahead. "That's our ride."

"Have you been on New Copenhagen long?" I asked, as we walked toward the jeep. I half expected Thomer to ask, "Officially?"

"Two days, sir. I was in the third rotation for Terraneau and Bristol Kri. If those fights had lasted another day, they would have flown me in."

"You're all right for a natural-born," I said. "At least you're up to the fight."

"Thank you, sir," Thomer said.

Kelly Thomer was a clone, of course, but like every other clone, he had been programmed to believe he was natural-born. Clones like Thomer, who had an introspective nature, tended to question the logic of their neural programming. Introspection was a self-destructive trait for a clone. If they convinced themselves they were synthetic, they would trigger the death reflex, but ignoring the questions caused them cognitive dissonance. So clones like Thomer spent a lot of time trying to convince themselves that they were clones even though they harbored deep suspicions that they weren't. It was an intellectual juggling act that might one day prove fatal.

"If it ain't the new XO," Philips said, as Thomer stowed my twin duffel bags in the back of the jeep. "Things must really be desperate if they're letting an asshole like you back in, sir."

"Philips, shouldn't you be in a brig somewhere?" I asked, climbing in the passenger's seat.

"Yeah, but they sent me here to face the alien firing squad instead," Philips said. "It's one of them opportunities to die with honor."

"And they made you a sergeant?" I asked, looking at the stripes on his uniform.

"Everyone who survived the invasion got promoted," Thomer said. "Even Philips."

"Well, I'm not surprised he got promoted, though I am

surprised he was able to hold on to it," I said. Philips, who was once the oldest buck private in the history of the Marines, had a knack for bouncing up and down in rank.

Philips laughed. "How are you doing, Harris?" he asked. "And how the hell did you end up as an officer?"

I ignored him calling me by my last name because he'd won my respect in combat. I ignored his question because I hated the gold bar on my collar.

"Thomer, how did you know I was coming in?" I asked.

"It's on the duty roster, you're our executive officer," Thomer said. "Somebody went out of their way to surround you with old friends. Your buddy Freeman is the company's civilian advisor."

"Ray Freeman is here?"

"Oh sure, he's here," Philips muttered as he put the jeep in gear. The sun was a white-gold disc in the sky. Tall buildings cast clearly defined shadows that stretched across streets and painted empty parking lots. The day was as bright as a summer day, but the air was winter crisp.

I had never seen such preparation for battle. We turned a corner and passed a team of technicians placing the final touches on a rocket launcher. A few blocks later, we saw soldiers stringing wires through a bombproof barricade.

Philips drove to the lakeshore, where a shattered layer of ice stretched into the horizon in a web of tiny white islands and steel gray water. Along the shore stood rows of trackers—motion-tracking robots that looked like barber poles. I'd seen trackers armed with everything from machine guns to missiles. These trackers had heavy-caliber machine guns and particle-beam cannons.

"I'd hate to be the alien that tries to cross that lake," Thomer said. "You'd be wide open with no place to hide."

"What if they're waterproof?" I asked. "Those things might be able to walk along the bottom of the lake."

"You wouldn't want to do that," Philips said. "The stuff they have in the water makes a machine-gun colonic look like an act of mercy. If there's so much as a tadpole alive in that pond, I'd be surprised."

"Have you ever seen a buildup like this?" Thomer asked me.

"Nope, not like this," I said.

"They must be doing ten times as much on Earth," Thomer said.

"Don't count on it," I said. "I think they sent their best men and equipment here."

"Bullshit," Philips said.

"That's not just talk?" Thomer asked.

"Look around. There are over a million well-armed troops here. We have tanks, jets, and orbital support. Thomer, if we can't pull this one out, there's no point in trying again on Earth."

"I heard they had three times this many men on Terraneau," Philips said.

"They didn't know what they were up against," I said.

"Do you know what we're up against?" Philips asked. "They haven't told us shit." He sounded angry. I didn't blame him.

"Are they trying to find someplace safe to settle?" Thomer asked.

"Not in this galaxy," I said.

Silence followed. We drove through town. Thomer and Philips took me on a circuitous route to show me all of the installations the Corps of Engineers had under way, but they had lost their enthusiasm once I said this was the final stand. Philips drove to our camp—a luxury hotel that had been converted into the most comfortable base in the history of the Marines. While he and Thomer returned the jeep to the motor pool, I reported in.

Once in my room on the twenty-third floor of the hotel, I changed into my bodysuit and armor. As I stowed away my clothes, I noticed a message on the communications console beside my bed. The base commander wanted me to report to his office ASAP.

9

"So you are the man I have heard so much about?" First Lieutenant Warren Moffat said, as I stepped out of the elevator and onto the mezzanine floor. He sat on a white leather sofa just outside the glass doors that led to what had once been the hotel's administrative offices.

"The way I hear it, you single-handedly won the Mogat War, Harris."

I did not like the way this conversation had started. He did not mean what he'd said as a compliment, he meant it as a challenge. He had just accused me of taking credit for the sacrifices of dead Marines, and the guy was clearly looking for a fight.

"I'm looking for Base Command," I said, knowing I had already found it, but hoping to derail this conversation.

"You're standing in it," Moffat said. "General Glade asked me to wait for you. Guess you're here." He rose to his feet.

I started ahead, but the lieutenant stepped in front of me.

"Let me give you a quick prebriefing, XO. I run the company. I run the show. I don't care if you are a specking Liberator. I don't care if you survived the specking Mogat invasion. I don't give a rat's ass if you turn out to be the next specking messiah, you got that?

"I am company commander, and that puts me one seat away from God Almighty as far as you are concerned. Cross that line, boy, and I will fry your ass. I will personally shove my particle-beam pistol up every hole you got, then I will shove it up the new holes I make." He stood with his face less than an inch from mine. Filaments of spit flew from his lips and splattered my cheeks.

"Will that be all?" I asked.

"I'm just getting started, Harris," Moffat said. He was in a rage, but he kept his voice low. A vein had appeared across his forehead. It started between his eyebrows and disappeared under his hairline. His face was red with rage.

Like every officer in the Marine Corps except me, Moffat was a natural-born. He was a big man. I stood six-foot-three, and he had a couple of inches on me. He had muscular arms. His biceps and triceps bulged under the sleeves of his shirt. I could see a few small scars on his scalp under the fine brown bristle of his hair. The boy had been a tough customer; probably a football star or wrestler in college.

"If General Glade thinks you're something special, that's his problem, asshole!" Moffat continued. "You got that? You may have friends in high places, but I have friends of my own, asshole. Do you hear me? You try to make yourself the hero again, and I will flatten you into a specking statistic. I will turn you into K.I.A. roadkill so fast you won't have time to wet yourself." As he said this, he placed a hand on my shoulder.

He should not have put his hand on me. Now I found myself angered to the point that I began to have a Liberator combat reflex. The hormone was beginning to flow through my blood, soothing me and pushing me to attack at the same time. Struggling to keep my temper in check, I brushed Moffat's hand from my sleeve. "I'll keep that in mind," I growled, still hoping to keep my growing need for violence in check.

Huuuuhhh Huhhhh. General James Ptolemeus Glade stood

at the door behind Moffat clearing his throat. At that moment, I thought his throat-clearing ceremony was meant to catch our attention. It wasn't. I soon learned that he made the same noise during speeches, meals, and probably in his sleep.

"Is this our new man, Lieutenant?" he asked Moffat.

"Yes, sir," Moffat said, taking a step back from me. "This is the famous Lieutenant Harris."

"Out of my way. Moffat. Out of my way. Let's have a look at him," Glade said. He gave me a quick inspection, then invited Moffat and me to follow him into the admin offices. "Lieutenant Harris, I've read your record. It's a pleasure to have a Marine of your caliber under my command."

"Thank you, sir," I said, feeling more than a little off balance. Generals did not, as a rule, pay attention to the lieutenants under their command, let alone greet them.

"I hear you fought on Little Man and in the Mogat invasion. You've been in on the big ones, haven't you, Lieutenant." Then his smile tightened. "Scuttlebutt around command is that you once shot a colonel in the line of duty. Is that true, Harris?"

"I've heard the rumor," I said.

"The way I hear it, it's not just a rumor. I heard you shot Aldus Grayson," General Glade said. "Now, I knew Grayson."

Oh shit, I thought to myself.

Glade put on a good "plain folks" persona, but looking into his eyes, I could tell that he was shrewd and keenly aware of everything around him. "I went through Annapolis in the same class as Grayson. We graduated from the academy the same year, he and I and about ten thousand other cadets.

"I'm not sure Annapolis ever saw a more pompous, self-aggrandizing, useless cadet than Aldus Grayson, if you know what I mean—but I hate to think he was shot by one of his own."

"Yes, sir," I said.

As I watched Glade, I realized that he had not said this for my benefit. He was delivering a message to Moffat. His eyes bored into the first lieutenant's, expressly driving home the message with one last phrase, "Though I suppose it's sensible to shoot dogs and officers when they go rabid."

Only a ten-man staff worked in Glade's administrative office. The generals and admirals I had met prior to Glade all insulated themselves with bloated staffs. Glade, who rose through the ranks on the battlefield, kept as small an entourage as possible.

"Like my offices?" Glade asked me.

"Very elegant, sir," I said.

"Seems like a waste of space to me," Glade said. "Now if you want to see something really impressive, you should see what the Army has done with the capitol building. They have turned that place into a world-class command center. That's where all the real work gets done.

"This here is my office," he added as he opened the wood-paneled door. "I spent six years assigned to the Pentagon before the Civil War broke out. I visited the offices of each of the Joint Chiefs; none of them had an office like this."

Glade's office was thirty feet long and thirty feet wide. He had a glass-and-pewter desk, glass shelves with recessed lighting, a white marble crown below the ceiling, and hand-annotated battle maps taped to the wood-paneled walls. Rows of leather-bound books stood in the bookshelves, and a line of fancy liqueurs rested on the ledge over the wet bar. The rug was burgundy red and more than an inch thick; the soles of my shoes sank into its cut-pile depths.

"Do you know where they got the name 'Valhalla'?" Glade asked.

"That was Viking heaven," Moffat said. "That was the home of the Norse gods." He had a smirk on his face that said, "You don't get an education like that in clone orphanages."

"Good, Moffat. Did you take humanities in the academy?" Glade asked.

"Yes, sir," Moffat said.

I, too, had read a little Norse mythology. Unlike the gods of the Greek and Roman eras, the Norse gods could die. They expected to ultimately lose the battle of good and evil. I did not volunteer that information.

Huuuuh. Huuuuh. "Lieutenant Harris, I had a chat with Admiral Brocius before you arrived. He speaks very highly of you. He recommended that I provide you with anything you want and stay out of your way. I must say, Lieutenant, I am not used to giving my junior officers that kind of latitude." He looked at me for a response.

I did not know what to say, so I remained silent.

"Do you have any questions, Lieutenant?" Glade asked.

"No, sir," I said.

"As I understand it, Admiral Brocius briefed you about our situation, is that right?"

I looked over at Moffat. He tried to give me a threatening glare, but it looked more imploring than menacing. "I understand a friend of mine has been sent here as a civilian advisor."

"You mean Freeman," Glade said. "Admiral Brocius tells me that you've worked with him before."

"He's a friend of yours?" Moffat said. "Interesting piece of work... I thought his kind was extinct."

Glade glared at Moffat. "What do you mean, Lieutenant?"

"Have you seen him? He's a black man. An African. There aren't supposed to be races anymore, but Freeman, his skin is black as tar."

The room went silent for several seconds before Glade spoke up. "Is there a point you wish to make, Lieutenant Moffat?"

"No, sir," Moffat said. Thickheaded as he was, he was bright enough to know that he had just stepped on a land mine.

"Ever heard of Shin Nippon?" Glade asked. Everybody knew about Shin Nippon, the all-Japanese colony. After the role Shin Nippon played in ending the Civil War, the U.A. Senate allowed the racially pure people of Shin Nippon to form a nation within a nation and settle the Japanese islands on Earth. "Welcome to the twenty-sixth century, Marine. Races still exist, and will exist as long as there are humans to preserve them."

"Yes, sir," Moffat said. "I don't trust Freeman."

Not trusting Ray Freeman was another story. He and I had been partners for two years, and he still made me nervous. He was smart, dangerous, and silent, a man who radiated intensity and seldom spoke. I had seen him kill enemies for money and revenge... and maybe for the fun of it. I once saw him glue a live grenade to a man's hand and pull the pin. When I first met Freeman, I thought he had no allegiance to anyone but himself; but I was wrong. He never fought against the Unified Authority.

"What do you think of Freeman?" Glade asked me. He cleared his throat again.

"I'd trust him with my life," I said.

"Just you keep that bastard out of my line of sight," Lieutenant Moffat warned.

"You know, Moffat, I've been trying to play nice with you," Glade said. "I came out and caught you browbeating your XO for no apparent reason, and I tried to warn you that Lieutenant Harris is not an officer to be pushed around—but here you are, doing it again.

"I tried to be diplomatic with you, but now I think I'll just be frank. I would put you on permanent KP duty till this war is over, but I don't want to risk you poisoning my men. That leaves me very few other options.

"Against my better judgment, I am going to trust you to conduct yourself in a manner befitting an officer in the Marines. If you do not live up to my expectations, I will be forced to either bust you down to private, put you in the brig, or have you shot. Any one of those options would be fine by me." He cleared his throat again; this time I was almost sure it was for emphasis. "Do I make myself clear, Lieutenant Moffat?"

"Yes, sir," Moffat said.

"Harris, Brocius says to let you and your platoon prosecute this war any way you see fit. You want tanks or air support, I'm supposed to provide it, no questions asked. I can't make many promises, but I do promise to protect you from hotheaded officers;

and I will give you whatever support that I can.

"Don't expect me to dig you out if you speck up. You do what you think is best, but if you get yourself captured, don't expect me to risk men pulling your ass out of the fire."

"No, sir," I said.

"Last I heard, the boys in Intelligence think we still have a few hours before this shooting match begins. Do you have any plans?" Glade asked.

"I want to run some recon, sir," I said.

Glade nodded. "Recon? We have every inch of this planet mapped, scaled, and under electronic surveillance. We have this planet so wired that the rabbits in the woods can't so much as fart without us listening in. What can you possibly hope to accomplish?"

"Sir, if I can locate the enemy's launch point, I may be able to determine numbers, logistical clusters, maybe vulnerabilities..." I said. "I want to see if I can come in behind the enemy."

"I believe the general just warned you not to get caught," Moffat scowled, a grin on his lips.

"Excuse me, sir, but I believe he said he would not pull my ass out of the fire if I did get caught. I don't intend to get caught."

"No one intends to get caught," said Moffat.

"We could get some good intel if this works. And if I do get caught, at least we'll know we're dealing with an alert and dangerous enemy," I said.

"Not bad, Harris. Not bad," Moffat said with transparent respect.

"Tell you what, Harris. The Navy set up a full-scale Science Lab just a few miles from here at the University of Valhalla. You go out there and do what you need to do, and you bring in one of those bastards. You bring one in alive." Glade cleared his throat. "You bring us a live one, so the boys in the lab have something to play with.

"You do that, Harris, and I'll put every man in your platoon down for a chestful of medals when this is over. I'll tell you what, you bring me one of those bastards, and my wife and I will have your whole platoon out to the house for a barbecue." Glade sounded excited. I got the feeling that he liked the idea of the Marine Corps bringing in the first prisoner.

"Your house? Are you from Valhalla originally?" I asked. With few exceptions, officers—the black-sheep children of politicians and bureaucrats who either could not cut it in school or in the political arena—came from Earth families.

"They set up housing for officers' families. They're calling it the 'Hen House.'" Glade sounded somber. "Moffat, you're a married man."

"Yes, sir," Moffat said.

"You brought your wife?"

"Yes, sir," Moffat said.

I saw a chilling implication. Why shouldn't the officers bring their families? If we lost here, their families would be as good as dead on Earth.

Glade cleared his throat once more, softly this time, the sound mostly muffled. "I guess that's all I have to say." He saluted, and said, "Good luck, Harris."

Moffat and I left the admin area without speaking a word. Originally I had hated this man, now I found some form of sympathy for him. He was fighting to save his wife, not just to advance his career.

As the glass doors closed behind us, Moffat said, "Just keep out of my way, Harris. I've dealt with assholes like you before."

"No, you haven't," I said. "Not like me."

10

Since the early days of the Unified Authority, the colonies had always been a great melting pot. In an effort to prevent boundaries being drawn along racial lines, the U.A. government forcibly mixed peoples of all nationalities in the various colonies. As the government got to decide who went to which planet, racial division was virtually eliminated by fiat.

The government, however, allowed a few churches to establish colonies as well. These colonies were not as closely regulated as the ones founded by the government. If the rumors were true, the Catholic Church still had priests of purely Italian descent. Unless they were clones, those priests had to have come from Italian parents. The government did not need to worry about the priests extending their race, however, since they had all taken an oath of celibacy.

Ray Freeman descended from a long line of Neo-Baptist colonists, men and women of African-American descent. Freeman's dark skin and huge size intimidated people. He stood a hulking seven feet tall with a heavy and powerful physique, the build of a blacksmith, not an athlete. He had so many scars along the back of his head that hair could no longer grow there even if he did not shave his head bald.

Freeman's eyes were clear and white and set far apart. His irises were as black as a starless sky; they were the only truly black part of his body. His skin was the dark brown of ebony.

Freeman was brilliant, deadly in battle, and utterly ruthless.

Despite his Neo-Baptist upbringing, he never showed remorse.

"It's about time you got here," Freeman said, as I climbed from the back of the truck.

"You knew I was coming?" I asked.

"Philips told me."

I was the last man off the truck. Freeman and I watched as Philips and Thomer led the rest of the platoon across the landing strip, where three helicopters waited—two personnel carriers and a gunship escort. The men formed a line and waited for my orders.

"I didn't know you and Sergeant Philips were friends," I said.

Freeman ignored this comment. He probably did not like the connotation of the word "friend." His life had room for allies, partners, and people who employed him, but no one came any closer than that.

Before leaving base, we were issued white-coated combat armor instead of the dark green we normally wore. In the snowy forests, the white armor would provide better camouflage. Around the plowed streets of Valhalla, however, the armor could not have been more visible if it had been painted red and dotted with a bull's-eye.

The three aircraft were also painted white. They also stood out when environed by the city.

"I saw Admiral Brocius," I said. "He says you made a deal with him to get your family off Little Man."

Freeman nodded. "He and I are square."

"Where are they now?" I asked, as we headed toward the helicopters. "Are they safe?"

I felt a strange pang in my gut when I thought of Freeman's

family. The only time I had ever felt something that might have been love was for Freeman's sister, a single mother with a teenaged son. Her name was Marianne. Her son was Caleb. Marianne and I might have had a romance, but our relationship ended prematurely. I still thought about her from time to time.

"They're as safe as they can be in this galaxy. Brocius relocated them here."

"New Copenhagen?" I asked.

"It was the best Brocius had to offer," Freeman said, as we reached my men.

"Sergeant Thomer, what is the status of the platoon?" I asked, when we reached the helicopters.

Standing at attention, Thomer yelled, "All men are present and accounted for, sir." It was formal, the Marine Corps answer to a minister welcoming his congregation to church, but discipline was a facet of Marine life that could not be ignored. I had fought with some of these men, but others were new to me. If we went into battle without going through the formalities, the new ones might get the wrong idea and think I did not care much about discipline.

"Very good, Sergeant," I said. "Load the men on the choppers."

"Aye, aye, sir," Thomer yelled. He was a quiet man but also a by-the-book Marine. Freeman and I waited for Philips and Thomer to direct the platoon onto the choppers, then we climbed in. Including Freeman and me, we had forty-four men.

Assuming Naval Intelligence interpreted the aliens' simulation correctly, the invasion would take place today. Data from past attacks suggested the lights would appear in the early evening. That was the Pentagon's best estimate. What we gleaned from our long string of losses was that the lights generally started near the largest city on the planet and almost always in a northern region of that planet. The brains at the Pentagon might not have the slightest clue about what would happen next; but when it came to where and when the invasion would begin, they had it down.

I wanted to see when and where the enemy landed and watch for any vulnerable moments. Would they have their weapons drawn when they first appeared? Would they arrive in formation? Did they have protection when they landed, however they landed? I wanted to see if we could surprise them behind their lines and maybe end this fight early with a well-timed bomb. If we managed to hold out against the first wave of their attack, maybe we could bring a division out to greet them the next time they arrived.

For this little field trip we would travel in helicopters. No bulky transports for us, just sleek atmospheric vessels. The rotary blades on the top of the choppers made a suppressed *tock-tock-tock* noise as they began to spin, and we lifted into the air.

As we took off, I looked around the well-fortified city of Valhalla. Even from here I could see batteries of rocket launchers, gun emplacements, and troops... lots and lots of troops. It was late afternoon. The sky no longer looked white as paper. It had turned blue and orange as the sun slid toward the horizon. I had my armor on, but not my helmet, and the cold air stabbed imaginary needles into my cheeks.

"We'll put up a good fight," I said as I watched an armored column roving outside the landing-field gate.

Freeman did not respond.

The three helicopters formed a caravan, the gunship leading the way, with the two choppers remaining side by side behind it. Some of my men sat quietly, staring out the portholes, studying the landscape below. The forests ahead were cold and full of shadows.

I donned my helmet and checked the ocular controls. From here on out, I would see everything through the lenses of my visor. Marine combat armor had night-for-day lenses, heat-vision lenses, automatic tint shields that protected against blinding light, and farseeing telescopic lenses. The equipment also included sonic locators, smart tags for identifying personnel, and interLink communications gear. General-issue armor would not stop a bullet or absorb a particle beam, but the bodysuit would keep me comfortable even on a long march through the snowy woods.

Though he was not a Marine, Freeman had been fitted for armor as well. Where they found a suit that could fit him, I had no idea. His chest and shoulders had to be eighty inches around; his biceps might have been a full twenty-five inches.

"What's the plan?" the pilot asked me over the interLink, as I settled in.

"First, we're going to kill time until we know where to go," I said. "It might be an hour, maybe more. You see that forest? In a little while some bright lights are going to appear out there."

"And there's going to be an army of aliens out there, too," the pilot commented.

"First the lights, then the aliens. Take my word for it. The Marine Corps has experience with these things," I said. The pilot was Navy. Navy chopper pilots tended to be a bit more skittish than Marine Corps pilots in these situations.

"So we're looking for the light?" the pilot asked.

"I need you to drop us as close to the lights as you can, then head back for base. Our goal is to slip in unannounced; having choppers thumping overhead isn't going to help with the mission."

"Understood." The pilot sounded relieved.

We had reached altitude and were now flying across an outer suburb. Below us, Valhalla was a grid of plowed streets and houses with an occasional park or school or shopping center.

"You interested in heading anyplace in particular while we wait?" the pilot asked. We were speaking on an open frequency. Every man in the platoon could hear us. So could Freeman. As a civilian advisor, he was not technically a member of the platoon.

"Freeman, got any ideas?" I asked.

Because of his huge size and icy demeanor, Freeman's intelligence often went unnoticed. He did not stumble into situations. He considered the angles, studied whatever information he could, and had a keen eye for any advantages to be had. With Freeman, I never needed to worry about uninformed opinions blending in with the facts. Since he did not know any more than me, he simply shook his head.

"What's it look like beyond those hills?" I asked the pilot, pointing to hills to the west.

"It looks dark; that's how it looks," the pilot said. I got the feeling he did not want to stray any farther from town than necessary.

"I can see that," I said. "What is the terrain like?"

"Forest, mostly. It's pretty dense."

"Use your radar; see if you locate a clearing. You may need to drop us off out there," I said.

"Yes, sir," the pilot said.

The sun set quickly during the New Copenhagen winter. First the horizon became red and gold and orange—a molten copper sun sinking behind clouds that looked inflamed and infected. Then the sky was purple with gray clouds. As the last streaks of light slowly drained from the sky, the horizon went from indigo to black. Snow-covered trees formed a carpet below us, and mountains looked like phantom shapes in the distance.

"How far out do you want to go?" the pilot asked.

I glanced at Freeman, then said, "Ten, fifteen miles, not any farther than a half day's hike back to town."

The pilot headed out over the woodlands, cruising quickly while remaining no more than ten feet from the tops of the trees, a tactic called Earth mapping. The pilot kept us low enough to pass under most tracking technologies. It was a wise precaution.

It only took a couple of minutes to reach our target area. On the off chance that the aliens came late, we had fifteen hours of fuel. We circled and evaluated the terrain, and looked for places where we could set up an ambush. We looked for paths and hollows, places where we could hide should we need to retreat.

We flew for over an hour, cruising over rivers, lakes, and endless woodlands. We skimmed over hills and saw no phantom lights. The moon appeared in the sky, and the first stars began to show. In the distance, we could see the low glow of city lights generating over Valhalla.

"Maybe they aren't coming," Thomer said over the interLink.

That thought had occurred to me as well, but I knew better. "Maybe," I said.

"They're coming," Freeman said.

"How do you know?" I asked over a discrete connection that the other men in my platoon would not hear.

"I saw their damned battle plan," Freeman answered over that same connection.

"You mean the battle simulation they broadcast? Maybe we misunderstood it," I said. "Maybe they changed their minds."

A few minutes later the pilot radioed to tell me that he'd spotted the phantom light. I moved to the front of the helicopter to ask where, but didn't bother asking the question. I could see it clearly myself.

A small dome of light had started to grow out of the forest about twenty miles from us. Its glare shone through the trees like twisted spokes, and the top of the dome rose above the trees, casting alternating waves of red, blue, and yellow into the black sky. The stars above the scene vanished, canceled out by the glare from that dome.

"We need to come in behind it," I told the pilot.

"Which side is the front?" the pilot asked.

"Let's come in from the west, the side facing away from town."

"We're on our way," the pilot said. A moment later, however, he signaled me again. "Lieutenant, I ran a satellite sweep of the position. The trees are too thick for us to land around that light source. The closest spot I can drop you is about four miles back."

"How about to the north?" I asked.

"About the same," the pilot said. "The closest spot I've got is about three miles from their point of origin, but it's southeast of the light. That will place you between the light and town."

Not knowing anything about the enemy, I did not want to risk being caught in the open. All I had to go by was my briefing with Admiral Brocius and the Space Angel I had seen on the Mogat planet. If an alien like that caught us in the open, we would be as good as dead. "Got any other options?" I asked.

"No, sir."

"Okay, get us there quickly. I have a feeling we're going to need to dig in."

"Yes, sir," the pilot said.

"Listen up," I said over an open frequency that my men would hear in both helicopters. "We're headed in. The choppers are not here for air support. Once we reach the drop zone, we're on our own."

Now came the part I always hated about briefings, the pep talk. "So what's the latest rumor around base? What have you boys heard about the enemy?" I asked.

Thomer and Philips, veterans of the Mogat invasion, had to have a pretty good idea about what was going on. They were under orders to keep that opinion to themselves, and the clone programming in their brains meant they obeyed orders.

"They showed us a video feed from Terraneau, sir," one of the men said. The interLink marked the message as coming from Private First Class Scott Huish. "And I heard some officers call them 'Space Angels.'"

"Those officers were full of shit," I said. "I've seen one these speckers up close, and it wasn't an angel."

"Are we really fighting aliens, sir?" It was Huish again. "I always thought that only humans lived in this galaxy."

"I guess that means they came from outside the galaxy," I said.

"We're approaching the site," the pilot told me.

In the distance, the light had grown from a dome to a mountain. It reached high into the sky and continued to spread until it was already more than two miles in diameter. The light was like a clear, bright gel that oozed out, engulfing everything it touched.

As the dome expanded, it spread in every direction. Our gunship escort swept the area first for any sign of the enemy. With its antenna array, the gunship could detect a noise as soft as a heartbeat. Its motion-tracking sensors would scan for movement, then remove interference such as leaves rustling in the wind. Even with the noise produced by chopper blades and wind, the sensors would be able to sort out the sound of a twig snapping or the slight movements of an assassin hiding in the trees.

"I can give you the complete lowdown we have on these aliens before we land. You see that light out there? That light is going to close in around the planet. Those mother-specking aliens travel inside the light. Got that? That is all we know."

"The drop zone is clear," the pilot said over a direct frequency.

"Circle it a couple of times," I said on the same frequency. "I'm not done building their self-esteem."

"It might be nice if we knew how to communicate with them," one of my Marines said.

"If we know how to kill 'em, that's enough for me," Sergeant Philips said in his distinctive drawl.

"Damned specking right, and that is the only thing we need to know," I said. "I don't care what they eat, how they talk, or how they specking reproduce. You boys got that? This is Marines Biology 101; we study how to kill the bastards and leave everything else to the other sciences."

Then, still using the open frequency, I told the pilot to take us down.

The gunship took one last sweep of the clearing, the searchlights under its belly casting a crisp white beam onto the snowy circle below. Along the edges of the light, the trees around the clearing looked half-bleached and half-etched in shadow. The other chopper went in first, lowering slowly, then hovering about six feet off the ground. The door rolled open and twenty-three Marines in white combat armor jumped to the ground.

Having delivered its cargo, the chopper rose sharply and slid out of the way to make room for us. Armor or no armor, I felt my stomach drop along with our chopper as the pilot lowered us into position. The chopper doors slid open on either side of the cabin. The men nearest the doors swung their legs over the edge and jumped out. As the commanding officer, I jumped last.

"Good luck, Lieutenant," the pilot said, as I prepared to jump. There was a different camaraderie to this mission than I had ever experienced in past missions. In the past, I had always sensed a certain distance between me and the pilots who flew me into battle. They were dropping me off and rushing to safety. If we made it out, that was good. If we died, well, that was part of the game. Not this time, though. This time we were all in it together.

He watched me from the cockpit. He saluted, and I returned his salute, then leaped. I fell for a moment, then plunged into a four-foot snowdrift. Above my head, the chopper rose straight up toward the sky. The gunship performed one last security sweep of the area, and our convoy left.

11

For logistical reasons, the smart gear in our visors included an absolute compass—a device that affixed the geographical directions north, south, east, and west to our visual display. They were not true compass points based on magnetic poles, but because our gear gave each of us the exact same reference points, it helped us coordinate our movements.

The gunship and helicopters flew east toward town. In the sky above them I saw a three-quarter moon. I saw clouds and stars, heavens that would soon vanish behind the false ceiling that the aliens were spreading across the sky. The light from their ion curtain did not dissolve into the darkness like other light. Instead, it remained condensed.

Before switching tonight-for-day vision, I surveyed the drop zone through my default tactical lens. Our armor was the exact white of fresh-fallen snow, and it diffracted ambient light the same way the snow did. If we lay flat on our stomachs, we would fully blend in with the landscape around us.

When I switched to my night-for-day lenses, which displayed the world in blue-white-on-black images, my men completely disappeared into the landscape around them. Night-for-day vision tended to compress the world into two-dimensional images, blurring the white armor into the snow. No matter. I would not need the night-for-day lenses much longer, not once that phantom light spread over us.

"Thomer, report," I said.

"Every man accounted for, sir," Thomer said.

I ordered the platoon to form into fire teams, then told them to look for a good place to hide.

"How about town?" Philips asked.

Borrowing a page from Ray Freeman's playbook, I pretended I did not hear the comment. "Philips, take a fire team and flank our movements."

Philips could hit the bull's-eye sixty out of sixty from a hundred yards. I liked the idea of having him cover us if it came to a firefight. If we ran into resistance, the rest of the platoon would keep the enemy pinned while Philips's squad flanked them and shot them—a time-honored Marine tactic.

"Aye, aye, Kap-y-tan," said Philips. He was great in combat and an asshole in every other situation. If anyone else in the platoon called me anything but "Lieutenant" or "sir," I would have corrected him. With Philips, I wanted that layer of irreverence. The few times he showed officers proper respect, I generally worried about him losing his edge.

We left the clearing and entered the forest. The snow was not as heavy under the trees. In some spots the trunks grew so thick that their branches seemed to form a solid roof over our heads and I only found patches of mud on the ground. I saw everything in the blue-white imagery of night-for-day vision crystal clear and devoid of depth. The world under the trees was dark and shadowy, but it was far less confusing than standing out in the snow where my men and their surroundings blended into a single blue-white sheet. Here I could see my men against the contours in the forest floor.

As we walked, I tried to imagine what this forest might look like during the day. Sunlight would penetrate the branches, a silvery ray slanting here and there toward the forest floor. Some light would filter in from the clearings. I could find no trace of the moon or stars through the branches above.

"You know that attack simulation the aliens sent out... how do we know they meant for us to receive it? Maybe they just use the same frequencies we do," I said over a private channel between me and Freeman. "Maybe we intercepted a battle plan they meant for their generals."

"The signal originated on Earth," Freeman said.

"On Earth?" I asked. "Do we know where on Earth?"

"It came from their embassy," Freeman said.

I wanted to laugh. It sounded like a joke, a bit on the sarcastic side, but funny nonetheless. The problem was, Ray Freeman had absolutely no sense of humor. He lacked the capacity to tell jokes, even "Why did the chicken cross the reactor" jokes.

"They have an embassy?" I asked.

"Remember the building I staked out just outside DC?"

"You said it was a Mogat base," I said. In the weeks before the Mogat invasion, Freeman located a building on the outskirts of Washington, DC, that employed the same advanced shielding technology that the Mogats used to protect their ships.

"I was wrong," Freeman said. "The shields around that building did not shut down when we attacked the home planet."

"Brocius says they want us to evacuate planets before they arrive," I said. "He believes that is the reason they sent us their plan. Think he's right?"

I was sure he did not know the answer, but I hoped he would guess.

Guessing, however, was no more a part of Freeman's nature than telling jokes or showing mercy. "I don't know," he said.

"Lieutenant Harris, you'd better have a look at this," Thomer called to me over the interLink. He and several of the men from the platoon had gathered around the edge of a small clearing. They stood in a thirty-man semicircle, M27s in hand. Freeman and I came to join them.

Not expecting to hear much more than standard patrol chat, I switched to the platoon-wide frequency to eavesdrop on what the men had to say. I was doing more than snooping, though—this gave me a chance to gauge their morale. As their voices came labeled inside my helmet, I knew that the first conversation I locked in on was Thomer contacting Philips.

Can you guys see what's going on? Thomer asked Philips, whose fire team was flanking the platoon somewhere twenty or thirty yards away.

It's all trees and branches around here. What you got? Philips responded.

The sky is full of light. It's just like Mogatopolis all over again. Thomer sounded depressed as he said this.

At least the planet isn't on self-destruct this time, Philips said. *I still have nightmares about that specking invasion.*

Yeah, me too, Thomer said, still sounding down.

There it was, the phenomenon that Admiral Brocius had called the "ion curtain." During the invasion I had mistaken it for some kind of benign glare; now I knew that it was a luminous barrier, a wall of light designed to cut planets off from the rest of the galaxy.

Staring at the edge of that light, which loomed high above the trees, was like gazing into the spark made by an arc-welding machine. The light was beyond white, platinum—white with a gold tint hidden deep within its translucence. As I stood there staring into it, the lenses in my visor switched from night-for-day to tactical view with tint shields to protect my eyes.

The dome had spread more quickly than I expected. It was only a mile away at best.

What's it like once the light spreads over you? Corporal Trevor Boll, who was not with us during the Mogat invasion, asked Thomer.

It's nothing. It's just a bright light; don't worry about it, Thomer answered. He tried to hide the concern in his voice but failed.

Ah, speck. I didn't ever want to go through this again, Philips said.

I'm sending you an image, Thomer said to Philips. Our helmets had imaging equipment that not only allowed us to view the world through different lenses, it let us record and transmit what we saw. Corporals and up could control the gear to capture video and send it over the interLink. *You don't have to open it if you don't want to.*

Oh, hell no. I don't want to see it. A moment later. *Ah, shit, Thomer. I didn't want to see that. I still have nightmares from last time.*

Brocius called this "sleeving" the planet. That was what it felt like—as if some sort of material closed around us. It certainly did not act like light. The leading edge of the brightly lit curtain did not shine into the sky around it. Where the curtain had spread was bright, while the sky just beyond was still dark. Shimmering waves of elemental colors—pure hues of red, yellow, and blue—showed in the light like an aurora borealis.

Is it radioactive? one of the men asked over the general frequency. He sounded nervous.

No, several voices answered at once. We had a rudimentary Geiger counter in our visors as well.

The light won't hurt you. That was Thomer.

The light won't hurt you, but whatever's inside of it might specking eat you for lunch, Philips, always the charmer, said. At least he had the good sense to say it over a private frequency that only sergeants and higher would hear.

"Well, boys, it's safe to assume that the enemy is at hand," I said. "Any suggestions on a good hiding spot?"

"There's a nice ridge over here. Might make a good place to dig in." The message came from Private First Class Steven White, one of Philips's men.

"We'd have the high-ground advantage," Philips added.

"Set a beacon," I said. Philips created a virtual beacon—a red spot that appeared in all of our visors showing us the direction to follow, and I ordered the rest of the platoon to follow. As we headed toward the beacon, I spoke to my men. "The light will not hurt you, but we don't know what else it might be able to do. It might have some kind of sensor ability, like a radar. It might be able to detect our body heat or our breathing or the chemicals in our bodies or the electrical impulses in our brains."

"Want me to stop thinking?" Philips asked over a private channel.

"I'd be glad enough if you'd stop talking for a change," I said.

"Sorry, sir," Philips said in a slow drawl that told me he was not.

We reached the beacon. It marked a low-slung hill. The trees did not grow as close together on this hill, opening the way for a thick layer of snow on the ground.

The dome of light was closing in. At this rate it would spread over us in another minute. So long as the light did not have some sort of radar or sonar to detect us, I thought we might be able to hide. With our white armor, we would be nearly invisible in the snow, and our armor would shield the heat from our bodies.

"Man, this shit is blinding," one of my Marines said.

"Things are going to be bright for a while, so you might as well get used it," Philips said.

"Stow it, you two," I said. We didn't have time for a philosophical discussion about alien lights. "Gentlemen, the fun is about to begin, you better find a good place to hide and dig in."

12

I did not know much about physics, but I knew enough to see that the light around the alien landing did not behave like natural light. It didn't move, it spread like a viscous fluid, slowly flooding the forest and engulfing everything it touched in a bright silvery blanket. Light shining from a source like a star or a bulb casts shadows. This light seemed to turn the very air into a light source so that there were no shadows anywhere.

The light mesmerized my men. Private First Class Harold Messman summed it up best when he said, "Holy specking shit."

Burrowing through a three-foot mound of snow on the side of the hill, I tried to forget about the phantom light and concentrate on the aliens. We were directly between the origin of the light and Valhalla. Somewhere in that light, an alien army was headed our way.

Most of my men hid behind trees. Up the slope from me, an entire fire team crouched behind a stand of fallen logs. A few feet ahead of me, Ray Freeman concealed himself behind a boulder that was about the size of a large dog. Big as he was, he had to lie chest down in the snow to keep from showing, and even then it was a tight fit. At least his combat armor protected him from the cold.

My own situation wasn't much better. As I was lying facedown in the snow, my body was pressed against the joints in my armor. The creases in my shoulder guards were wreaking havoc on my neck and chest. Because of the shape of my helmet, I could not lie flat on my stomach, it cocked my neck back. We had to keep our M27s hidden, too. Their black stocks and barrels would be a dead giveaway. I buried mine in the snow. Good thing it was not the kind of gun that jams up when a little mud splashes into the barrel.

I had no idea how many soldiers the enemy might bring, but it seemed likely that an intergalactic army might rely on overwhelming force to secure new territories, wipe their enemies out entirely, then move on to the next conquest. Over the next while, a million soldiers might pass this glade.

"Get comfortable, boys," I said over the interLink. "We may be here for a long, long time." *Hours,* I thought. Then I added, "Keep your eyes open, but hold your fire. We do not want to engage.

Repeat, we do not want to engage."

"What if they spot us?" asked one of my privates.

"Just sit tight, Messman," I said. "Don't start shooting until I give you the order."

"Yes, sir." He sounded nervous. I needed him to hold tight. All it would take was one loose cannon to give us away.

Now that the flood of light had spread over us, my visor automatically switched to tactical lenses with moderate tinting to protect my eyes from the glare. The trees and moss were awash with color—dark green needles, lime green moss, stones the color of iron, trunks with gray bark, ferns with red leaves.

The light had enveloped the forest for as far as I could see. Everything was drowned in liquid light. During the Mogat invasion, I managed to escape before the light closed in around me. Our transport took off just in time to avoid it. This time, there was no escape.

Using the Geiger counter in my visor, I checked for radiation and found nothing. The environmental equipment showed no change in air temperature, and I could see that the light did not melt the snow, which glistened like a blanket of diamond fragments along the ridge.

"Holy shit! Look at that ugly specker." Philips spotted the Angels first. "I saw the video feed, but I didn't believe it."

The creatures looked like they were made out of light, but not the same light that now flooded the forest. The liquid light pouring across the forest was silver-white, like raw electricity. The creatures were bright yellow.

The first Space Angels around the bend looked like statues sculpted from yellow neon light. Their movements were stiff and stilted, as if their limbs had somehow become locked by the snow. Made of light or glass, they marched along the ground. No floating, no flying, no vehicles. Instead, column after column of eight-foot-tall soldiers that looked no more substantial than a smear of light marched along the ground below us. They had heads, arms, and legs, all with fairly human proportions only larger. They carried enormous chrome rifles cross chest. The aliens might have looked like they were made out of energy, but those damn rifles seemed pretty specking real. I remembered how one of those bastards had fired a bolt at me as I tried to escape up an elevator shaft on the Mogat home world.

Marching past us, the Angels never spared so much as a sideways glance. If I'd had more men, guns, and guts, I might have tried to end the war right then and there. The minutes passed by slowly as we lay hidden watching the alien army parade past. *If there are a million of them, we may be trapped here for days*, I thought to myself. I also berated myself for not arranging a more comfortable hiding place.

At some point one of my men started to panic. "Oh God! Look at them! Look at them! What are we going to do?" he whimpered to himself, and the interLink equipment in his helmet dutifully broadcast it out to every man in the platoon.

Thomer took care of it. "Quiet down, Anderson," he said. "They don't even know we're here."

"Thomer, is he going to be okay?" I asked over a discrete link.

"He'll hold up," Thomer said. "They'll all hold up."

"Good thing we don't have any kids fresh out of boot camp," I said.

"I'd take a dozen kids over those fossils the Army brought in," Thomer said.

Thank God for Kelly Thomer, I thought to myself. The men trusted him; he commanded their respect. Something in the way he addressed Private Anderson calmed the man down. It was lucky Thomer was able to do that. Freeman would have slipped in behind Anderson and snapped his neck before he'd risk the kid giving away our position.

Zooming in with the telescopic lenses in my visor, I studied the faces of some of the creatures. At first glance they all looked alike to me, like ants or fish. They all had the same big eyes and jutting lower jaws. Their size, about eight feet tall and broad as bears, seemed uniform. Their size and shape was the only constant.

The first Space Angels looked more like body-shaped auras than living creatures. As more passed, however, the aliens started to take on a sand-colored look. Their bodies began to look like they were made out of substance instead of light, as if some kind of crust was forming around them. They continued to get darker as they marched past us. Bulky, statuesque soldiers with an iron gray patina on their skin replaced the sleek creatures with the golden translucence.

These aliens had huge, featureless bodies. I saw no seams or edges to suggest they were wearing clothes or armor, nor cavities or lines to suggest they were naked. Aside from arms, limbs, and heads, the bodies had no features at all. They had nothing even remotely resembling hair on their limbs or pumpkin-shaped heads. I did notice that a few of the creatures had cracks in the outer crust that had formed on their bodies. I could see yellow-colored light shining through those cracks. When I used my heat-vision lens to take a reading of the aliens' heat signature, I saw that they still generated no heat whatsoever.

The seemingly endless procession of aliens continued to file past us. At one point I realized that their numbers were in the tens of thousands. Not long after that, the column ended abruptly.

"They're gone," Philips said over the interLink.

"Stay where you are," I said. "That might have only been the scouts." We remained hidden in our snowy camouflage for several more minutes, but no additional aliens materialized.

"I'm open to suggestions," I said over the command line so that only Thomer, Philips, and Freeman heard me.

"It didn't seem like there were enough of them to take over a planet," Philips said.

"He's right, sir. That can't be all of them," Thomer said.

"I suppose it depends on what each of them can do. If those guns fire nukes, they'll toast us in an afternoon," I said. "What do you think, Ray? Do you think they landed more troops somewhere else?"

"One landing site," Freeman said. "That's all we've ever seen."

"If that's all they need to capture a planet, those are going to be some pretty damn tough mother speckers," Philips said. "Either that, or we're going to carve those boys new assholes when they reach Valhalla."

"Maybe we should get back to Valhalla," Thomer said. "They may need all the help they can get."

"Thomer, there are four hundred thousand Marines, six hundred thousand soldiers, and about a trillion surface-to-surface missiles waiting down there," Philips said. "You can't possibly think the forty of us are going to make a difference."

I considered our options. The aliens would not reach Valhalla for another hour. Philips was right. Even if we found a way to reach the city before them, there was nothing we could do. Using the interLink, I tried to reach General Glade. When that failed, I forwarded him the video-feed file of everything I'd seen and labeled it "urgent."

"There's no point heading back to Valhalla," I said on the command line, then switched to the open frequency and spoke to the entire platoon. "We're going to follow the bastards' tracks and see where they came from. If we find their base, maybe we can speck with it. Now move out."

If we found an alien base, I planned to place some charges around it, but what I really wanted to find was a scout or a guard or a straggler who we could capture. I wanted to bring a trophy back to General Glade.

Using the gear in my helmet, I tested the ground for traces of radiation. The forest was clean. "Freeman, you picking up anything I should be concerned about?" I asked.

Freeman surprised me by removing his helmet. The temperature had dropped to below freezing, and steam formed when he breathed. He reached into one of his utility pockets and removed a small laser scope, which he pointed into the sky. "Did you get a good look at the sky?" Freeman asked.

"You mean the colors?" I asked.

He looked back at me and nodded. "Take a look through this."

I pulled off my helmet and aimed the scope into the sky. Sensors within its housing ran an instant retinal diagnostic, then projected a hairline laser as a direct extension of the angle of my vision. Markings along the edges of the scope displayed the distance between my eye and the target. As I looked across the forest, I marked 37' 3.5" between me and a tree. I marked 4' 1.8" between me and Freeman. When I looked up into the sky, both the end of the laser beam and the numbers vanished.

"Something's wrong with your scope," I said as I tested it on a tree that was precisely 43' 7" away. I sighted the sky again. Once again the beam and numbers vanished.

Freeman replaced his helmet over his head. I did the same, glad to feel the warmth around my face.

"There is something in this light that disassembles waves," Freeman said.

I could still see shimmering strokes of blue, red, and yellow above us. It never occurred to me that they might be the frayed edges of the light around us. If no waves could penetrate this light field, we were cut off from the rest of the galaxy. And that made sense. Once the planets were sleeved, they were cut off... we were cut off. The aliens had effectively placed a wall between New Copenhagen and the ships orbiting the planet. Back on Earth, the brass would see the sleeve and write us off before the battle even began. Could that be what had happened on all of the other planets?

"Thomer, Philips, have your men run an equipment check," I said as I toyed with the idea that mankind might have kicked these aliens' asses on all of the other 179 populated worlds, and we wouldn't know it. But I knew that these guys would not have been able to cross a hundred thousand light-years of space, sleeving every planet they passed, unless they had something going for them. There had to be something more, something we were overlooking.

"Sir," Thomer said, interrupting my thoughts. "Lieutenant, all of the equipment checks out."

"Thank you, Sergeant," I said. I switched to the open-frequency channel, and said, "Listen up. I want to take one of those bastards home alive. You got that?

"Break into fire teams, we're going to sweep the woods. I want to find some scouts. If you see a column heading your way, dig in and radio me. If you see some stragglers, I don't care if they are watching birds, eating babies, or building a memorial to peace in the universe; you will not, repeat, *not* attack. You contact me, and the entire platoon will converge before you make a move.

"Do you read me, Marines?"

"Aye, aye, sir," came back.

"Head north and west toward their original position. Platoon leader, fan 'em out," I said. Thomer, my platoon leader, took over from there.

Leaving the hill, I took one last look around the scene. The way the Space Angels had lit this thick forest fascinated me. There were no shadows. The light came from every direction instead of one. They really had flooded the place with some sort of illumination that behaved like liquid.

13

"Lieutenant, we found the place where the aliens landed," Philips said over the interLink.

"Any unfriendlies?"

"Nah. Not an alien soul in sight."

"Do they have buildings? Is there any kind of fortification?" I asked.

"Nope, but they've got some awful big balls."

"What are you talking about?" Philips probably thought he was being cryptic; I thought he was being a pain in the ass. "Put up a beacon and stay hidden," I said.

On my visor, Philips's virtual beacon looked like a translucent red fence that ran through the forest. The same line would appear on every man's visor. You could see through it; no point blinding the troops, but it was bright and impossible to overlook. I ordered the entire platoon to converge on that beacon.

The path Philips had taken led through trees, over a creek, and around several clearings. By this time the entire forest was as bright as a desert under a midday sun. As I climbed over a gentle rise, I found Philips sitting on a log "supervising" as his men searched the area.

There, partially hidden by a pocket of trees, sat a perfectly round sphere of light. It was approximately ten feet in diameter and appeared to be constructed of nothing but light. Until the moment I saw that sphere, I had thought that nothing could be as pure and bright as the light filling the forest, but the sphere proved me wrong. The tint shields in my visor doubled themselves to protect my eyes as I stared into the ball of light.

I stood there, staring into that odd bubble of light. It might have been some sort of hologram, but how did they get the light to confine itself? As I examined it, Ray Freeman came up beside me. I did not need to see Freeman's virtual dog tag to recognize him.

"Is that some kind of portal?" I asked him over an open frequency, not even caring if the rest of the platoon heard me.

The sphere was as transparent as glass and completely empty. By this time the rest of the platoon had gathered around it, and I could see men clearly through its walls.

Until that moment, I had not yet grasped the significance of these aliens traveling across space without a ship. They had somehow ridden in on this light. We were still tramping around the galaxy in specking spaceships while these aliens simply materialized wherever they wanted. Our technology was primitive compared to theirs.

"Are you sure this is how they got here?" I asked Philips.

He pointed to the ground around the sphere. On one side of the sphere the snow remained fresh and white, on the other the aliens had stomped it into soupy mud dotted with footprints.

"Their footsteps start right there," Philips said. "I figure they must have come out of that thing when they started their march."

"Why didn't they leave some sort of guard?" Thomer asked as he came and joined us.

"To guard what?" Philips asked. "What are we going to do, cut the power? It's a specking ball of light." He picked up a pebble and tossed it through the sphere.

"Leaving it unguarded doesn't seem very military," said Thomer.

I checked the sphere for heat and radiation and found nothing.

"It's so clean it's practically not there," I told Freeman.

Freeman removed his helmet and shined his laser scope into the sphere. He replaced the scope in its pouch and put on his helmet.

"Well?" I asked. When Freeman did not respond, I rephrased the question. "Did the beam get through?"

"Yes," was all Freeman answered.

I was about to ask more when I got a signal from Base Command, and General Glade addressed me. "Lieutenant Harris, I just viewed your report." Glade's voice betrayed tension.

"Have they reached the city yet?" I asked.

Huhhhh Huuuhhhh. He cleared his throat. "They're not here yet, Lieutenant, but it won't be long now. Do you have anything new to report? Any luck catching one of those bastards?"

"No, sir," I said. Even as I said this, I noticed something strange. The light in the sphere had begun pulsing. "Fall back!" I yelled.

"Take cover!" Thomer and Philips yelled. They must have noticed the change in the sphere at the same moment I did.

"What's happening out there?" Glade asked.

"I'll send you what I'm seeing," I said as I backed behind a tree and crouched. Using optical commands, I forwarded the images in my visor to Glade, then I forgot about him entirely.

The sphere stretched as if it were made out of rubber. It doubled in size until it was twenty feet tall, then expanded again so that it was now as tall as the trees around it. As it stretched to an oval shape, I saw that there were more Space Angels inside it—hundreds of them.

"Harris, get your men out of there!" Glade ordered. "Harris—"

"General, I need to go," I said, knowing that he had just given me about the worst advice he could have. We might have done better attacking the aliens than showing them our backs. We needed to stay calm, and we needed to stay hidden.

"Steady, boys," I said. "Get comfortable. It looks like we might be here for a while."

The figures inside the sphere had a gold cast to them, otherwise, they might have been completely invisible. Space Angels, monsters, alien invaders, whatever you called them, here they were. They sort of congealed in the light and strode right out of that sphere without a moment's pause.

"You seeing this?" I asked Freeman.

"Good God," Glade answered. His frequency overrode any other communications. "How the speck are we supposed to fight something like that?"

Freeman did not respond.

The way they glowed as they stepped out of that sphere, the creatures could not possibly have been made of solid matter. They looked like gold extensions of the white-gold light inside the sphere and nothing more. The creatures carried those oversized rifles; but inside the sphere, even the rifles looked like they were made out of light.

14

More aliens came, but not in the large numbers they had before. We hid behind trees, rocks, and ferns, watching them stroll out of that sphere for forty minutes. This time no more than a thousand aliens materialized. If this was the second wave of the invasion, it was even more pathetic than the first wave. The aliens did not bother themselves with such details as securing the area when they emerged from the sphere. They formed into loose ranks and disappeared into the brightly lit folds of the forest.

As I crouched down behind a rock, I noticed that the Angels did not speak to each other. Having just materialized as little more than light, they might not have had the organs needed to speak to each other even if they'd wanted to.

I assumed that this sphere employed some variant of the broadcast technology we used to transport ships. The aliens coming out of the sphere, having had their molecular structure hyperaccelerated, seemed more like they were made out of energy than matter. Maybe that was what gave them that radiant appearance. As we had seen when their army passed us before, they cooled down into matter with time. Even in this energy form, they did have weight. Their feet sank into the squishy mud around the sphere. When they stepped forward, mud stuck to their feet.

The sphere began compressing into itself, but even as it shrank, three final figures emerged from it. Two of these last aliens carried rifles, the third appeared to be empty-handed. They stepped out of the light, stood still for a moment, and followed the rest of their ranks into the forest.

Watching the aliens vanish into the trees, I felt relief. This was not the innumerable army I had expected. Nor were these the nightmarish battle conditions of the Mogat invasion, not with the forest filled with light.

Sergeant Thomer signaled me. "Want me to go after those last ones, sir? I can take a squad."

"Send Philips after them," I said. "Tell him to track them down but not to engage. I want to be there when the shooting starts."

"Aye, aye," Thomer said.

"And Thomer, make sure he knows his ass is on the line."

Moments later, five men split off from us. For some reason I had the feeling that I would never see these men again, and I noted each of their names in my head. Philips took the lead; he always took point when he was in charge. The four men in his fire team were Corporal Trevor Boll as grenadier, Corporal Lewis Herrington as rifleman, Private First Class Scott Huish as automatic rifleman, and PFC Steven White as second rifle. I noted the care they showed as they cut through woods, using trees for cover, moving quickly enough to catch up to the aliens and silently enough not to get caught.

The big question was what they would do once they spotted the trio of aliens. Of all the men in this platoon, Mark Philips was the one with the right skills for sneaking up on the enemy and setting an ambush, despite his lack of discipline.

And then there were the questions about the aliens. Had I underestimated the bastards just because of their numbers? Had I sent these men, my men, to an unnecessary death?

Philips jumped a small ledge and juked behind a tree, keeping his M27 out and ready. Other Marines preferred to use their M27s in their pistol configuration for maneuverability, but Philips almost always mounted the rifle stock. He crouched, checked to the left, then the right, then dashed out of sight. Boll followed, then Herrington and Huish, followed by White in the rear. *Good men,* I thought. *Maybe among the best the Corps had to offer. Semper fi, Marines.*

The chatter among the men of the platoon was nervous but controlled. I gave a quick scan on the interLink and heard:

Tell me how the speck you kill a specking beam of light?

There weren't very many of them. That's something.

Not if we can't kill them.

How do we know that was all of them? There might be a billion more on the other side of town.

Tuning out the chatter, I turned to survey the area and saw Freeman approaching the sphere. "What are you doing?" I asked.

He pulled a pistol from his armor. As a civilian, Freeman could carry whatever equipment he saw fit. When it came to battle arms, we government-issue types carried M27s and particle-beam pistols, and that was about it. Knives were optional.

Freeman stood about twenty feet from the sphere, leveled his pistol, and fired three shots through it. The bullets struck a tree on the other side.

"Basic physics," I said. "Light and bullets don't mess with each other."

"Ever fired a bullet through a laser stream?" Freeman asked.

As a matter of fact, I had. That was the kind of mischief we pulled back in the orphanage. For young military clones, firing guns and experimenting with battle lasers was a wild time. We'd sneak off to the range and "cross-fire" bullets through a laser beam. The bullets ended up as formless blobs. Remembering the turd-shaped blobs, I asked, "Do you think this thing is a laser of some sort?"

After pocketing the pistol, Freeman pulled out a particle-beam pistol. He walked around the sphere until he had a straight shot at the tree he had hit with his bullets. It was a big tree, maybe fifty feet tall, with a trunk that was easily three feet across. That tree might have been a hundred years old, but it would not see another winter night. Freeman held his pistol a few inches from the trunk and fired. The spot that the sparkling green particle beam struck exploded in a flash of bark and splinters. The tree toppled, leaving a five-foot stump with a jagged crown.

"What the hell are you doing?" I asked.

"Running a scientific experiment," Freeman said. He put the particle-beam pistol away and produced a combat knife with an eight-inch serrated blade. Then he went to the trunk and began digging out his bullets. By this time, most of my Marines had come to see what the giant in the combat armor was up to. Big, silent, and scary, Freeman was just as enigmatic as the aliens.

After prying the first of the bullets out of the stump with his knife, Freeman held it up for me to see. The bullet glowed as if he had just pulled it out of a furnace. I switched the lenses in my visor to heat vision, but the shell was not hot, it simply glowed.

"I wouldn't touch that; it might be radioactive," I said.

"I already checked," Freeman said as he dropped the bullet into a bag. He dug out a second shell and placed it in his bag with the first bullet.

"Thomer," I said, "send some men out to sweep the area. I want to know if there are any more of these light spheres out here."

"Aye, aye," Thomer said.

I walked closer to the sphere. As I approached, the tint shields in my visor increased. The sphere did not become brighter, so it must have been the proximity that set off the tint shield.

"Harris, the aliens have begun their attack." It was not General Glade but Lieutenant Moffat who contacted me. He sounded strangely calm. "Intel is estimating their forces at approximately fifty thousand troops. How the speck do they expect to invade us with fifty thousand troops?"

"Are they putting up much of a fight?" I asked.

"We were a lot more scared of these guys before they got

here," Moffat said. "They beat the shit out of our gunships, but our ground troops are holding their own. So far they don't look all that specking dangerous."

I took a moment to process this information. "Have you been up to the front line?" I asked.

"The Army is taking this one," Moffat said. "How about you? Any luck capturing a live one?"

"Not yet. We found where they landed, if you can call it a landing. It looks more like they broadcast in."

"Broadcast in? Nice, very nice. What's the ETA on your return?"

"I was hoping to look around a bit longer," I said.

"There's no rush, Harris. Dig up what you can and get back here when you're done," Moffat said before signing off.

I stood there thinking about the aliens. The Unified Authority had just survived a civil war with the Mogats, an enemy with next to no military experience and no ground troops. Survived was the optimal term. The Mogats won too many battles before we finally tracked them down and eviscerated them. Now we were fighting an alien invader that telegraphed its battle plans and sent fifty thousand troops to battle our million. *Maybe our luck is holding up. Maybe the entire universe is incompetent,* I thought.

Thomer woke me from my thoughts. "Lieutenant Harris, we found nine more of those chambers."

"Chambers?" I asked. I had already labeled them "spheres" and subconsciously assumed that everyone else had as well.

"The glowing balls," Thomer said. "We found nine more of them just north of here."

I gave the sphere another glance to make sure it wasn't growing. It seemed stable. "Good work, Thomer. Bring your men back," I said. "I just got a report from Moffat—the fireworks have started."

Impossible as it sounded, I thought the war for New Copenhagen might end as suddenly as it had started. The aliens would probably send in more reinforcements, but maybe they were having the same problems on every planet. How big an army would you need to conquer an entire galaxy? Sooner or later they had to run out of soldiers. Maybe they were running out now. With only ten spheres for landing more soldiers, they would never be able to land a large enough army in time to save this campaign. I was beginning to feel like we had just dodged an apocalyptic bullet.

"Freeman, what do you think about setting up a line of trackers to guard the area?" I asked. "If the bastards send in reinforcements, maybe we can pop them as quick as they appear."

I imagined a line of the motion-tracking robots—little more than poles with radars and trigger fingers—surrounding each sphere. Bullets passing through the spheres might get irradiated, but they did pass through the spheres. And if the bullets did not kill aliens, we could equip the trackers with particle beams, lasers, gas canisters filled with noxium gas, or rockets.

At that moment it all seemed so easy. If our lines could just hold outside Valhalla, these alien bastards could be killed. The once-impossible war now seemed so winnable. For the first time since my meeting with Admiral Brocius, I could close my eyes and see the end of the war. The possibilities seemed endless.

15

"We found their scouts," Philips said. He and his fire team had been tracking the aliens for most of an hour.

"Are they still a party of three?" I asked.

"If you still want to take one alive, Kap-y-tan, the odds aren't going to get any better. Want me to take 'em?"

"How close can you get?" I asked.

"How close do you want me to get? It's like tracking stiffs. I bet I can get close enough to piss on them." Philips sounded brash. That was good.

"Close enough to piss on them?" I asked.

"Well, maybe not against the wind. I don't know if these boys are fresh out of alien boot or just plain stupid, but they sure as hell don't act like galaxy conquerors."

"They might still have something up their sleeve," I reminded Philips.

"So can I move in?" Philips asked.

"Send up a beacon," I said. "Don't move till I get there."

"Yes, sir," Philips said, sounding so wooden I wanted to shoot him.

"Do not engage them, Sergeant. If I hear shots, you better hope they kill you first," I said. "I'm on my way."

"Got it, sir." I heard the annoyance in Philips's voice. Not that it would matter to someone like Philips, but I understood his frustration. He was a resourceful Marine, a veteran on the battlefield who had earned and lost his first stripes by the time I learned to walk.

I ordered Thomer to herd the rest of the platoon back to town while I headed north after Philips's beacon. Freeman went with the platoon so he could deliver his bullets to the Science Lab for analysis.

By this time, nearly four hours had passed since we first sighted the phantom lights. The ion curtain had long since closed around New Copenhagen, cutting us off from the rest of mankind. Cutting across a clearing, I looked into the sky for signs that the light field was fading, but it was as solid as ever. The woodland around me was unnaturally bright. Even under the trees and in the deepest thickets, I could see patches of mossy ground that sunshine would never have reached under normal circumstances. Light sparkled off distant snowdrifts.

"You're not going to believe this, Harris," Moffat called in. "The fight's over, we routed the bastards." He sounded jubilant.

"It's over?" I asked.

"They folded; the specking jokers just plain folded."

"Any signs that there might be more of them on the way?" I asked.

"I was going to ask you the same question," Moffat said. "If this was the whole damned war…"

"One of my fire teams is tracking some scouts," I said. "We're going to bring one in."

"You might want to hurry back. The party's already started," said Moffat.

"Just make sure you don't drink Valhalla dry before we get there," I said, trying to forget how much I hated this prick.

"Tell you what, Harris, you bring back a live one, and I'll find the best bottle in the whole specking city for you," Moffat said, before signing off. He'd pulled a Jekyll and Hyde. I could not believe this was the same power-hungry asshole who tried to threaten me a few hours back.

I wanted to feel excited by his news, but I knew better. It was beginning to feel as if we could win the war, but it could not possibly happen this easily and this quickly. Using a platoon-wide frequency, I said, "I just heard from base. The Army has routed the enemy."

"Routed them where?" one Marine asked.

"They won the battle," I said.

Silence.

"The Space Angels, the aliens, the speckers we watched head into town... they're dead. I just got a report from Base Command—the Army annihilated them."

The silence lasted another moment, then I heard excited chatter, which instantly silenced when Sergeant Philips asked me, "Are you saying that the war's over?"

I had to think about this for a second. That was what they were celebrating in town. I knew it could not be over. No one would send a mere fifty thousand troops to capture a planet. You couldn't even hold a city with fifty thousand troops. Their ion curtain still had us in its sleeve. There simply had to be more aliens on the way. I did not want to say that, however. I did not want to crush the morale. "No, it's not over," I said. "But the first round went better than we could have hoped for."

The shouts, the cheers, and the rapturous cursings restarted spontaneously, but Philips did not join in. "If it's not all over, sir, can we get back to capturing this alien?" he asked. When everyone else was serious, Philips bucked discipline and flaunted authority. Now that everyone else celebrated, Sergeant Mark Philips was all business.

"I'm on my way," I said.

Philips's beacon led through well-trafficked territory where snow, ferns, and small trees had been tromped into the mud. Soon, though, the beacon took me into a less-traveled glen. Virgin snow with a few footprint trails gleamed in the bright light. The aliens followed a natural pathway that led through thin growth while Philips and his men had stuck to the trees. I recognized their boot prints.

The aliens' feet left rectangular prints in the shallow snow. When they reached drifts, the bastards sloshed through without lifting their feet out of the snow. Instead of leaving a line of individual prints, they dragged their feet and left ruts in their wake.

I spotted Huish before I saw the others. He was kneeling in a small gully, his gun trained on the enemy and his finger on the trigger waiting for the order to shoot. I identified him by the virtual dog tag over his helmet.

"What is the situation?" I asked Huish over a direct link.

"They're just over that rise, about thirty yards out. Philips and Herrington are moving in for a better angle," he said, pointing with his rifle.

I hid behind a tree and surveyed the scene. Looking along the edge of the gully, I spotted White and Boll. Philips and Herrington lay flat on the ground in a patch of ferns. I don't know how well concealed they were from the aliens, but it took me a few moments to spot them.

"Do you have a good line on them?" I asked Philips on a direct channel.

"All three of 'em," Philips said. "Can we get this show under way, sir... now that you're here to help?"

I stole up the rise, cutting through the ferns at a crouch and making as little noise as possible. Below us, the ground seemed to form a bowl, offering the aliens no protection. One of the aliens knelt and played with some sort of scientific instrument while two others stood guard. The one with the instrument was poking a four-inch needle into the ground.

"Maybe they're a science team," I said.

"Bet you're right. Can we cap 'em now?" Philips asked, not bothering to hide his annoyance.

"I want to take the one checking the soil home with us... alive," I said.

"Got it," Philips purred. He signaled Huish and Herrington to flank the aliens from behind. I sighted in on one of the guards as Philips assigned targets to his men. The creature's eyes were the same color as the rest of his face. They looked no more lifelike than the eyes on a marble statue. The face had a more or less human-looking mouth and nose.

There was that one brief moment of anticipation as every man took his place and homed in on his target. A breeze whistled through the trees, shaking branches just hard enough to dislodge the snow from some distant tree. I saw a blue-and-red bird hopping on a limb a few feet above one of the aliens.

On my visor, the names Tom, Dick, and Hairy appeared above the three aliens. Tom and Dick were the guards; Hairy was the scientist. Philips had placed these designations so that we all knew what we were doing. "Lieutenant Harris wants us to take Hairy home with him," Philips said.

"Boll, Herrington, you guys smack Tom. Take him out fast," Philips whispered. He sounded completely calm. "Huish, you and I get Dick."

Boll and Herrington laughed. I got the feeling Huish would take grief about getting "Dick" for some time to come.

"What about me?" White asked.

"Make sure Hairy doesn't get away. Lieutenant Harris has a thing for him."

Now everyone was laughing. If this did not go well, Philips and I would have a conversation when we got back to base.

"Take 'em out!" Philips yelled.

I fired a three-shot burst. The bullets struck Dick on the side of his head, just above the tiny nubs that looked like ears. Sparks flashed where the first bullet struck, as if it had glanced off a rock. The second and third chipped at the head, producing a shallow gash.

Dick spun to face me. Its face was impassive. Its eyes seemed as fixed as flint stones. It must have been searching for me, but I could not tell by looking at those eyes. I aimed at its forehead and fired off three more shots, making the alien stumble backward. I wasn't the only one shooting the bastard. More chips spattered off its back and shoulders.

"What do I have to do to kill this specker?" one of the men yelled.

I aimed at one of its eyes and fired again. The eye chipped, but it was the same color under the surface, and nothing leaked from the hole, as if the alien had been carved out of stone.

"Speck!" Philips yelled, sounding nearly out of control. "I hit that bastard in the nuts. Go down, asshole! Your nuts are busted!"

Hairy, the scientist alien, stopped taking readings and ran to join the guards. Dick's rifle fired, making a cooing noise as a yard-long bolt of white light flared from its muzzle. The bolt traveled through the air at the absolute speed limit of what a man can track with his eyes. I perceived that bolt as much as saw it, watching where it started and where it struck while my mind filled in the holes. The light bolt struck a thick mound of dirt to my right, cut through the mound, and continued through the air. A plume of smoke rose from the hole it left in the ground behind it.

"Fall back," Philips told his men.

I agreed with that order, but I did not follow. Aiming my M27 at Dick's right shoulder, I held the trigger down. I must have fired twenty rounds within a two-inch spread before the alien stumbled backward. I continued shooting as the shoulder dented, fractured, then splintered. Dick's right arm fell to the ground, and his rifle fell with it.

Boll, a grenadier, popped out from a ditch and fired a rocket that hit the ground somewhere between Tom and Hairy. The ground shook on impact. Mud and bits of rock sprayed through the air. The heat from the explosion filled the air with steam that evaporated as quickly as it appeared. The report of the explosion echoed off distant trees.

The explosion sent the aliens flying in opposite directions. One crashed into a tree, spun part way around its trunk, then landed twenty feet farther on. Had it been human, it would have been torn in half against that trunk. Even in combat armor, a man would have been ripped in half. I did not see where the other alien landed. By this time, capturing prisoners was the last thing on my mind. All I cared about was getting my men out of this skirmish alive.

When Dick rose to his feet and picked up the rifle with his remaining arm, Boll fired a rocket at the bastard. That rocket could have blown an entire platoon into an unrecognizable pile of limbs and parts. It might have knocked a tank on its side or caved in a small building. In this case it simply split Dick in half. His body broke. Boll fired another rocket, striking Hairy in the chest and blowing him apart while Philips and Herrington continued firing at him.

It was not until the shooting stopped that I noticed that both Huish and White had been hit.

White lay flat on the ground, a fist-sized hole seared through the back of his armor. One of the alien bolts had passed through ten feet of ground, through Private First Class Steven White, armor and all, and continued on into the trees beyond. The wound was clean, cauterized, and probably instantly fatal. A wisp of steam rose from that hole. Heat from the bolt had melted his armor, leaving a stream of polymerized metal dribbling into the hole in his back. If I had chosen to place my hand in that hole, it would have come out clean. There was no blood.

Huish was not so lucky. The bolt had passed through his right shoulder, taking a small and clean chunk with it. The wound might not have killed him had he not gone into severe shock. He lay on his back, shivering convulsively like a man in an icebox. The plates in his armor rattled against each other.

Philips and I stayed with Huish while Herrington and Boll went out to gather the body parts and equipment the aliens left behind. Philips pulled off Huish's helmet and loosened his chest plate. He could not pull the plate off because much of it had fused into the wound. He tried to talk to Huish, but he never responded. By the time Herrington and Boll returned with alien body parts, a rifle, and the meter that Hairy had been using, PFC Huish had quietly died.

16

"We're coming in," I radioed Moffat. "Has the rest of the platoon arrived?"

"Present and accounted for," he said. "Sergeant Thomer says you stayed back to catch a prisoner. How did it go?"

"I've got some body parts and a weapon."

"General Glade wanted a live one. We don't need more body parts or weapons," Moffat said. I knew he was right. The Army had just used fifty thousand aliens for target practice—alien body parts would be in plentiful supply.

"We captured some of their scientific equipment. I think they were taking soil samples," I said.

"Scientific equipment? Not bad, Harris," Moffat conceded. "Not bad. It doesn't earn you the best bottle of booze in Valhalla, but I'll spot your first round in the officers' lounge." That was a tired old wartime chestnut—our drinks were free.

Moffat struck me as a man who appreciated platitudes. I had only met him that day, and this was the third time I had heard him say that bit about "Not bad, Harris. Not bad." It already meant less than nothing to me.

"We lost two men," I reported.

"Noncoms?" Moffat asked.

Stupid question. I was the only officer who went on the mission. "White and Huish... both privates."

"Good men, I'm sure," he said, sounding about as unmoved as a man can get. We signed off, each of us glad to be rid of the other.

While Boll cut down branches and built a travois for carrying back our dead, Herrington brought me one of the alien's rifles. Its stock was featureless and lacked even a trigger. It looked like a nickel-plated pipe and weighed well over fifty pounds. How any creature could carry and use such a weapon I did not understand. Herrington lifted the rifle to his chest and tried to sight down its barrel, but he could not hold it steady.

Herrington also brought in a head and a long section of back. Looking over these parts, I saw no signs of muscles, veins, tissue, or bone. The limbs we found were solid and unmalleable. There was no tissue, the body parts had the same composition inside and out. As I rolled one of the heads we collected with the toe of my boot, I realized this thing had no more brains than the head of Michelangelo's statue of David.

"Do we want to haul this shit home with us?" Herrington asked.

"Only the meter," I said. "Moffat says they've got all the body parts they can handle," I added. So Herrington helped Boll load the bodies onto the travois. I watched them lift and lower the bodies as they lashed them into place. They strapped Huish on the travois first. Watching the scene, I noticed how his armor was stiff but his limbs hung limp.

"So we attacked them for nothing?" Philips asked. He had ambled over toward me unnoticed.

"We got this," I said, holding up the soil-reading tool that Boll retrieved. The unit was about the size of a shoe box. There was no visible way to read the damn thing, it didn't have any window, meters, or dials.

"Well, that makes me feel a whole specking lot better," Philips said. "As long as we aren't leaving this specked-up mission empty-handed."

"Watch it, Sergeant," I said, though I agreed with him.

Moffat called in a couple of hours after we started back to town.

"Where are you?"

I had precise coordinates from the equipment in my visor. But rather than give him the specifics, I simply said, "We're headed toward town."

"As far as we can tell, the woods around the city are clear. Maybe I should send a patrol to bring you in, just in case."

"I appreciate it," I said, but I was just playing along. He wasn't trying to bring us in safely. He wanted a hand in the delivery. If the stuff we captured proved valuable, Moffat would try to take credit for finding it.

We broke off our transmission, and I took a moment to stare out into the diamond-bright sky. It looked like midday with direct sunlight coming down from every direction. I could not see Valhalla itself—we were too far from town—but I could see smoke rising from that direction. Several tails of smoke twisted and curled into the sky. Most of it was of the white-artillery variety, but some of the smoke was the greasy black you get from machine and fuel fires.

Philips, who was scouting up ahead, radioed me to say, "The area's clear."

"Base Command says the woods are clear all the way to town," I said.

"If Lieutenant Moffat is so specking sure it's safe, why the hell doesn't he come get us?"

"He is," I said.

"Harris, did you see those bastards, goddamn it? Those sons of bitches are bulletproof. They're damned near rocketproof." I could hear pain and anger in Philips's voice. He sounded frantic, but I knew it was with regret rather than fear. A man who had spent so much of his career as a private, Philips had never lost Marines under his command before. Once we got back to base, he'd start looking for some way to get himself busted down to private again. He might pick a fight with an officer or simply spend a day absent without leave. He would do whatever it took to get himself relieved of command. I could hear it in his voice.

"What are we doing out here, Harris?" Philips asked. "What the speck did we accomplish?"

"We killed three of theirs," I pointed out, ignoring his calling me by my last name.

"Yeah, and they killed two of ours. We had the specking drop on them, and they still nailed us." There was no fear in his voice, just anger and frustration.

We continued toward town, Philips and I moving ahead in silence, Boll and Herrington keeping up a running commentary. Another hour passed. I never saw Philips. I could tell he was somewhere ahead of us, but he kept himself hidden in the trees. When we reached a clearing in which a three-hundred-foot radio tower stood, I found Philips resting at the edge of the trees—a good sign, I thought. At least he wasn't trying to run himself to death.

As I approached, Philips said, "We didn't kill them. We specking broke them. They're like chunks of metal or something. Who the speck cares if we nail them, they're just specking statues!"

I agreed, but I was not going to say so. Philips was speaking on an open frequency. Boll and Herrington could listen in. As an officer, I had to sound authoritative and in control in all situations. I came up with the best answer that I could manage. "There are a lot more of us than there are of them," I said.

"What?" Philips asked.

"We have over a million troops defending Valhalla, they're going to run out of men before we do," I said. It was a poor attempt at humor, but it was also the truth.

We crossed the clearing, passing under that radio tower. There was something humbling about walking past a skeletal structure that was fifty times taller than me.

"You want someone else to scout for a while?" I asked. I knew Philips would turn down the offer. With so much tension running through him, he probably welcomed the chance to be alone.

"We're almost back," Philips said. He sped on ahead, vanishing behind the first row of trees. It was disorienting to see a man disappear into a well-lit forest. You expected him to disappear into shadows when he stepped under a tree. Now that the invaders had spread their ion curtain across our planet, the grounds under the trees were no darker than the grounds in the open.

"How are you two doing?" I asked, turning to Herrington and Boll. They had the hard job, dragging a 350-pound load on a travois through the snow. They didn't complain, though, and when I offered to take my turn pulling, they turned me down. All Herrington would say was, "With all due respect, sir, I could use a shower and some rack time."

Boll was even more circumspect. He grunted an unintelligible answer that ended with "sir."

Five minutes later, Philips radioed in to say that he had rendezvoused with Moffat and his welcoming party. They escorted us back to town.

17

The Hotel Valhalla was quite the billet. Officers had rooms to themselves. Enlisted men stayed in the convention center, where barracks had been set up in the enormous ballrooms. Before heading in for a debriefing with General Glade, I swung through the Valkyrie Ballroom to look in on my men.

Entering the cavernous room, I discovered that despite the elegant setting, inside the ballroom/barracks the life of enlisted men remained unchanged. Men lounged around in their skivvies speculating about who was scared and who nearly wet their pants. Including a support platoon, which mainly pushed papers and hauled supplies, our company had four platoons. Company command held the first platoon in reserve in case the battle went wrong. Second Platoon spent three hours posted just north of the front line, in case the aliens tried to flank the Army's perimeter. Kelly Thomer and the Third Platoon spent the battle scouting enemy territory with me.

Now that the fighting was over, members from the various platoons sat around swapping exaggerated stories. To hear some of Thomer's men talking, you would have thought we took on the whole alien army instead of hiding in the snow and watching them pass. The guys from the Second Platoon spun a good yarn about guarding the walls of the city. Sergeant Shepherd never once mentioned the rocket launchers and laser cannons, let alone the 150,000 soldiers on the bleeding edge of the battle. The way he told the story, it sounded like he and his men engaged in hand-to-hand combat.

Off in the distance, I saw Mark Philips, dressed in his government-issue boxers and tank top, sitting on his rack playing his harmonica. He could play a lively tune when he wanted, but now he played softly to himself. He slid the silver harmonica slowly back and forth across his mouth, and his eyes stared off in the distance.

"Sergeant Thomer," I called. The entire pack of men stood, turned, and saluted. "Can I have a moment?"

Thomer joined me. I led him to an empty corner of the ballroom, far away from Philips, and still I spoke in a whisper. Under normal circumstances he did not care what people said about him; but Philips blamed himself for the deaths of White and Huish, and he might have developed a new sensitivity.

"How is Philips?" I asked.

Thomer was the only Marine that Philips actually considered a friend. They had served together for years.

"He isn't talking. What happened out there?"

"His fire team ambushed an alien scouting party," I said. "It went bad."

"He says he got White and Huish killed," Thomer said. "You were there. Did he do anything wrong?"

"It looked like a perfect op. Philips slipped in behind them without being seen. He waited for the order, then he opened fire."

"So what happened?" Thomer asked.

"Those speckers are damn near bulletproof," I said. "Their guns shot right through the ground. White was dead by the time the shooting stopped. Huish... he hung on for a while."

Thomer nodded.

"Keep an eye on Philips. I don't want him doing anything stupid," I said.

"We're talking about Mark Philips," Thomer said. "When he gets like this, there's no stopping him."

"Well, do what you can," I said. Thomer saluted and I saluted, and I headed to Base Command.

"Leave your helmet with my staff," General Glade said. "We'll download whatever you've got and let the boys in the Science Lab have a look at it."

I always considered men to be out of uniform when they wore their combat armor without their helmets, but I knew better than to argue with a general. I took off my helmet and handed it to the major standing beside General Glade's desk. The man showed no pleasure in accepting it. He turned to salute the general, then left the office.

Glade watched the man leave, then said, "Makes a great secretary, doesn't he? He's a piss-poor excuse for a Marine, but he does okay as a secretary. I hate having assholes like him on my staff."

We stood in silence for a moment, then Glade said, "There's something I want to show you. Let's go for a ride, Harris."

We left the offices, walked down to the lobby, and headed out of the hotel. A fancy black limousine awaited us in the hotel parking lot, the engine running, the driver waiting inside. "Head over to Vista," Glade said as he climbed in behind the passenger's seat. I sat behind the driver.

"Aye, aye, sir," the driver said.

"Vista's on the edge of town. You probably drove down it on your way in from the spaceport. Beyond that is Odin Street, but we don't want to drive on Odin right now." *Huuhhhh huhhhhh.* He cleared his throat. "Odin is the kill zone. There are trackers, rocket launchers, and a hellhole of mines waiting for anyone who so much as taps a toe on Odin Street.

"The way things stand now, Mo Newcastle's Army boys are

guarding Vista Street. Assuming those alien bastards come back, taking the battle to them is going to be our job."

Mo Newcastle was General Morris Newcastle, the highest-ranking officer on New Copenhagen. I had never met him before, but I knew the name.

The miles of city we passed between the hotel and Vista were completely unchanged except for the unflinching light that now blanketed the city. The buildings were untouched. Tall skyscrapers lined the streets, their windows reflecting the light in blazing white squares.

Sixteen hours had passed since I'd led my platoon into the forest. We had left in the late afternoon, spent the night chasing aliens in the forest, and now it was nearly noon. There was something unnerving about living in an endless day, and I had not yet come to grips with it.

The closer we came to the city's edge, the more apparent it became that we had entered a military zone. Soldiers patrolled the sidewalks. Lines of trucks ferried weapons and supplies ahead. Troop carriers and armored vehicles choked the streets, and the traffic crawled.

"Near as we can tell, they underestimated our numbers," Glade said. "The Mudders came in about fifty thousand strong. We know that because we placed sensors outside the city."

"The Mudders?" I asked.

"That seems to be the popular name for them around the ranks," Glade said.

"Is that mudder as in you mudder-specking son of—"

Hhhhuhhh. Huhhhhh. Glade interrupted me by clearing his throat. "The term is 'mud,' as in the stuff you get when you mix water and dirt."

He thought for a moment, and said, "Juvenile, I know. But what do you expect? The Army came up with it. I think Newcastle likes it, says giving the enemy demoralizing names is good for morale." He cleared his throat, only this time more softly.

"The enemy does not appear to have tanks, jets, or vehicles of any sort, and they all carry the same weapon, some kind of light rifle. Frankly, I wish they had something else. Those rifles gave our troops a fit yesterday."

"Maybe we can replicate their technology," I said.

"Did you get a close look at one?" Glade asked. "The damned things weigh a ton."

"Yes, sir," I said.

"You didn't happen to fire one, did you?"

"No, sir," I said. "I couldn't find the trigger."

"We had the same problem. I'm sure the boys in the Science Lab will know what to do with it," Glade mumbled, not sounding confident at all.

The traffic sped up as three trucks pulled onto the sidewalk and began off-loading surface-to-surface rockets—non-radiation-bearing rockets, each of which packed enough explosives to destroy a city block.

"You've been firing STS rockets at them?" I asked. It seemed like overkill. Normally, the U.A. Military tried to win battles as decisively as possible with as little force as possible.

I watched soldiers carefully unloading the rockets from the trucks as we drove by. Crews had formed around each of the trucks.

"We used smaller ordnance last time, but we'll switch to STSs if the bastards come back. That was Colonel Mooreland's idea. You remember General Tommy Mooreland, the colonel is his son. His daddy died fighting in the Scutum-Crux Arm; he's got a score to settle with them, says he wants to end this one quickly. Can't say that I blame him."

We arrived at the Vista Street bunker, an enormous structure that stretched twenty miles along the western edge of the city. Similar bunkers lined the northern edge of town. These were the sides of town that faced the forest. Having decided that the southern suburbs offered no strategic value, the Army seeded them with mines and tracker robots, then left them unmanned. The eastern edge of Valhalla fronted a great lake that was laced with all sorts of automated defenses. Philips and Thomer pointed the lake out to me on the way from the spaceport to the Hotel Valhalla.

The car pulled to a stop, and we climbed out. "Wait here for us," Glade told the driver. "We shouldn't be more than an hour."

The outer wall of the bunker was a 50-foot-tall structure made of three-foot-thick steel alloy protected by electrical shields. Like every other piece of equipment that we had on New Copenhagen, this was the best and the latest technology, able to withstand an atomic explosion. The heat from an explosion would not melt this structure, and the force from the explosion would not blow it down. The men inside the bunker might be incinerated, but the bunker itself would survive.

"How long did it take to build this?" I asked, looking down the length of the great wall.

"About a month," Glade said. "The Army Corps of Engineers rigged a temporary broadcast station just for bringing materials in on special barges. It's amazing how the red tape gets cut when people are fighting for their lives."

The bunkers were the same lifeless gray color inside and out. The light from the ion curtain did not penetrate their gloomy depths. Bare bulbs hung from wires in the ceiling.

As General Glade led me up some stairs, I saw a scattering of bright spots that looked like searchlights shining through the wall. It was not until we came closer that I realized the beams were coming from outside; they were holes through the yard-thick walls. The areas around the holes had the wilted-flower look of molten metal. I knelt and looked inside one.

"Pretty impressive, isn't it?" General Glade asked.

"What happened?" I asked.

"The Mudders' rifles shoot right through our shields, Lieutenant," Glade said. "We were able to kill most of their troops out in the forest, but a couple hundred of them got through."

"And their guns did this?" I asked, my mind on Private Huish lying on the snowy ground, shaking to death.

"And that," Glade said, pointing to a matching hole in the opposite wall. The bolts had shot clean through both shielded walls.

After that, the tenor of the tour became more somber. General Glade led me through the second-level corridor, an endless lane pinched between charcoal-colored walls lit more by the beams of glare shining through the occasional hole than the lights hanging from the ceiling. We passed through a hatch and entered a metal catwalk that ran the length of the bunker. When I looked down from the catwalk, I saw barracks below us.

When it came to accommodations, the Marines got the better end of the stick for a change. The Valkyrie Ballroom was crowded, but our boys had enough light to read and space to breathe.

Billeted along the bottom floor of this bunker, these soldiers must have felt like they were living in a mausoleum. I heard a few men snoring in the shadows below me. There were none of the spontaneous card games that I would have found back at the Hotel Valhalla. We had bars, gymnasiums, and a pool—the soldiers in this installation were lucky to have running water in their latrines.

"These are pretty shitty accommodations," I said.

"Frontline accommodations, Harris," General Glade said. "Soldiers not posted on the front line are billeted in buildings downtown."

As my eyes adjusted to the darkness, I saw that many of the soldiers were old. Glen Benson, the fifty-six-year-old corporal who had sat next to me on the trip from Earth to Mars, was probably down there... if he had survived the fight. Maybe there were thousands of Glen Bensons down there, all sleeping cozy in their cots waiting for the next attack.

As we cut across the bunker, we passed technicians working on wall-mounted cannons. We passed a radar station. We passed gunnery stations. After confirming that the area was still clear, Glade led me onto the roof of the bunker.

When I had flown into Valhalla, I saw an orderly city surrounded on two sides by pristine forests that were buried in snow. Everywhere I looked, I saw green and white under an ice blue sky. The outskirts were virgin, and the city was clean. That was all gone now.

There had once been a tidy suburb beyond the Vista Street bunker, an upper-class community with large homes and upscale shopping malls. I could tell that much by examining the smoldering battlefield that spread out before me. The enemy had been beaten back, but the battle had not been won as easily as I had been led to believe.

We had a term in the Marines—FOCPIG, which stood for Fire, Observed, Concealed, Protected, Integrated, non-Geometric. It described the obstacle courses you built to guide enemies into heavy fire. That was the benefit of being the home team when unfriendlies came to visit—they had to make their way through a landscape created to speck them over once and for all.

Acres of homes, stores, and churches had been leveled long before the aliens ever arrived, but the ruins of those structures remained. To get through these ruins, the enemy would need to follow paths designed to bring them into our sights. FOCPIG— limit the places your enemy can enter, then point your guns at the places that are left.

The grounds below the Vista Street bunker were covered with the broken bodies of dead aliens. Now I understood why Lieutenant Moffat advised me not to waste my time bringing back alien parts. From where I stood, I could see the wreckage of a dozen gunships lying about like insects both enormous and dead. A small fire still flickered in one or two of the wrecks.

The real carnage, however, lay about one mile out, where our intermediate defenses had battered the aliens. These aliens were killed by our heavy ordnance—rockets and laser cannons capable of destroying a building or sinking a ship. From the top of the bunker, I could see smoke rising from burned-over craters left by rockets and heaps of brick, steel, and dirt where buildings had once stood.

"We lost 137 gunships," General Glade said. "The Army lost better than 20,000 troops.

"I'll say one thing for those bastards—they came right at us. I don't think a single one of them ever turned back. It didn't matter if we hit them with machine guns, grenades, or cannon fire, those bastards marched right into it, Harris. They fought to the last. We got every last one of them."

That sounded good.

Glade paused for dramatic effect, then delivered the bad news. "If they come back this week, the Marines take point. We have to beat them out there"—he pointed to the forest—"stop them in the woods so the Army can rebuild its perimeter." *Huuhhhh huhhhh.* He cleared his throat.

The general delivered most of his meaning unsaid. Next time we would meet the enemy out there without the benefit of rocket launchers and shielded bunkers. I thought about the yard-long bolts of light that flew through the air like javelins, cutting through any embankments, trees, and combat armor that happened to get in the way. I thought about Private Huish shivering as he died.

Twists of smoke still rose from the wreckage beyond the bunker. FOCPIG, indeed.

18

The only stores still operating in Valhalla were the ones that catered to the GI crowd. Crews stayed to open liquor shops, cigar stores, bars, and movie houses while grocery stores, bookstores, and clothiers remained empty and closed. It didn't matter whether you entered a coffee shop or a fine grill; so many military types were crammed around the tables that every restaurant felt like a mess hall. With most of its civilian population in a relocation camp and nearly a million servicemen walking the streets, Valhalla felt like an extended military base.

Among the hundred thousand men who formed the local militia, there were hundreds of devoted capitalists who owned bars, and they willingly opened their establishments between battles, God bless them. Large pockets of Valhalla's low-rent entertainment district ran round-the-clock operations, and some of the finer establishments opened their doors as well. The day after that first battle, more than five hundred bars opened for business. Restaurants, movie theaters, and arcades opened. Most of the Marines I knew would have preferred to have waitresses working the tables instead of off-duty militiamen, but I never saw anyone refuse a drink.

We were on call, of course. If something happened at the front, we would hear sirens and report for duty in an instant. With the entire city on continuous alert, our commanders could muster their scattered platoons and report in a matter of minutes.

Approximately one-tenth of the men could go on leave at a time now that the shooting had ended. With the exception of Philips, who spent the day on his rack staring into space, the entire platoon headed into town for the night. Thomer offered to hang back with Philips, but I didn't think it would matter. He was somewhere between grieving and guilt-stricken, territory most Marines prefer to travel alone. Philips might come out of this funk in a day, or it might take a month, but his wild nature would pull him through. Until then, the best thing we could do for Sergeant Mark Philips was to give him space to work things out while watching him closely enough to make sure he did not hurt himself.

I headed into town with five guys from my company, all enlisted men. Officers and enlisted men did not pal around together as a rule, but I was also a clone. In the hierarchy of U.A. Marine Corps society, the gap between officers and enlisted men was not nearly as pronounced as the separation of natural-borns and synthetics.

We borrowed a jeep and drove deep into town. Driving the streets of Valhalla, it was easy to forget we were fighting a war.

The entertainment district was alive. Marines, soldiers, and civilians crowded the streets. The dance clubs were closed, but crowds packed the movie theaters and bars. The MPs turned out in force, too. Walking around with their armbands and nightsticks, they scowled at every man they passed.

What downtown Valhalla really needed was a dog catcher. Packs of stray dogs roamed the alleys, looking for food. They posed no threat to humans, especially in a community in which most pedestrians carried M27s, but the dog shit was turning alleyways into minefields.

People's pets became the first victims of the mass relocation. In the rush to relocate the human population, house pets were left to fend for themselves. The dogs and cats seemed to adapt, but I suspected that the domesticated fish, bird, and hamster populations were on their way to extinction.

There were so many jeeps parked along the sidewalks downtown that the place looked like a motor pool. We ended up parking in a residential area and walking eight blocks back. As we walked, Private Skittles made a snide remark about all of the old, white-haired soldiers we passed. "I don't know about you guys, but seeing all these old guys around gives me the creeps."

"Philips calls them the 'Prune Juice Brigade,'" Thomer said. Philips's quotes were always good for a laugh.

Then Corporal Thorpe asked the question of the day, "What happened out there with Sergeant Philips?"

"I heard you capped one of those things with a rocket," Skittles said to Corporal Boll. "A rocket... Man, you must have blown that bastard to bits."

Neither Herrington nor Boll seemed interested in talking about the skirmish. Herrington ignored the comment. Boll gave Skittles a tight smile, and grunted, "Something like that," in a voice just above a whisper.

"Think there's anyplace around here that serves Crash?" I asked, hoping to change the subject. Crash was a hard liquor made out of potatoes grown in toxic soil. The U.A. Senate had recently banned the stuff due to a rash of fatalities, but Marines loved it because it was cheap and got them drunk fast.

"They don't serve that anymore," said Thorpe, taking the bait. "It's been banned."

"Banned?" I asked, pretending I had never heard about the ban. As I looked over at Thomer, I could tell he saw through me. He smiled but did not say a word.

"A bunch of college kids died after drinking it in a frathouse initiation," Skittles said.

"No shit?" I asked. "Curbing the frat-boy population. I never thought of using it for that."

Wherever we went, we ran into crowds. The restaurants and bars had lines that stretched half a block, so we wandered off the main drag and began searching smaller streets and back alleys. There was dog shit everywhere, but the ion curtain provided enough light for us to avoid stepping in it.

Five blocks off Main Street, we finally found a small pub that only looked mildly overcrowded. When the guy serving the drinks said he would be able to seat us within the hour, we decided we were not going to get a better offer. It actually took two hours, but that was okay.

Herrington pointed out the window, and said, "Hey, look, an Ava movie's showing in the theater over there." It was an Ava Gardner double feature—*The Sun Also Rises* and *On the Beach*. What red-blooded Marine could resist?

Among the vices that appealed to enlisted men, drinking was the uncontested champion, with sex coming in a strong second. Movies did not figure into the top ten, at least not before Ava and her lovely face.

"I bet Ava does some naughty stuff 'on the beach,'" Skittles said.

"No, man, it's not like that," Thomer said. "I saw it. It's an end-of-the-world flick. She's stuck on a planet with radiation problems, waiting to die."

"C'mon, it's got to have some good visuals; it's an Ava flick," said Herrington.

"She does look good," Thomer agreed.

"Think she really is a clone?" Herrington asked.

Thomer shook his head. "I hope not," he said.

"Would it make a difference?" I asked.

"Well, I hope she is a clone," said Skittles. I first met Private Timothy H. Skittles as we rode the helicopter out to the forest, and I already liked him. The kid was nuts.

"You hope she's a clone?" Thorpe asked.

Before Skittles could answer, one of the two guys running the bar showed us to a table. We carried on the conversation as we headed across the floor. The six of us sat around a small, square table that was meant for two people.

"Sure I hope she's a clone," Skittles said as he scooted his chair toward the table. "If she's a clone, they can make more of her. I'd take one."

This got a laugh, but Thomer did not join in. The conversation had strayed far too close to a discussion of cloning and identity for an introspective clone like Thomer, who suspected he might be synthetic.

After that, things became quiet as we watched soldiers and Marines come and go. Herrington and Skittles continued to opine about Ava Gardner. Boll and Thorpe argued about the virtues of Earth-brewed beer over the outgrown stuff.

I let my mind wander, until I heard Thorpe ask, "Lieutenant, what happened with Philips?" The weight of that question smothered all other conversation.

"What happened?" I repeated. I sighed. I looked at the waiter, hoping he would come and take our order. I looked out the window, hoping to see some distraction on the street. Thorpe, who was always earnest, waited patiently until I answered. "What did he tell you?"

"He wouldn't talk about it," Thorpe said.

"You know what they were doing. I sent them to capture an alien," I said.

"You went with them," Thorpe added.

"Yes, I went too. I didn't want to miss out on all the fun," I said. "Three of the aliens split off, and Philips followed them. We set up an ambush. We had the drop on them, so what could happen, right?"

"Those sons of bitches are bulletproof," Herrington said.

"Damn straight they're bulletproof," I said.

"One of them was doing some kind of science experiment when I got there. The other two were standing guard, but the one doing the experiment wasn't even holding a gun.

"It was all perfect. We were on a hill overlooking the bastards, and we opened fire.

"Just like Herrington said, the bastards were bulletproof. I emptied an entire magazine on one of the guards, but the specker didn't die. And their weapons... they shot right through the embankment."

I had not realized how much that skirmish had bothered me. Once I opened up and started talking, the words just kept pouring out. "Boll nailed them with his grenades, but they hit White and Huish during the firefight. White died right away. Huish, though... he went into shock. I'm no doctor, but I don't think it was the wound that killed him; I think it was the pain that did it."

The waiter finally came to ask for our order, but now he was an unwanted distraction. We asked for a round of beers and sent him away.

"So why is Philips taking this so hard? You'd think he would blame you if he had to blame somebody," Thorpe said. He did not mean this as a challenge. As I thought about it, he made a good point.

"You've never had your own command," I said. "I sent them out, but he told them where to go and when to shoot. A guy like him, when things go wrong, he's not looking to cover his ass, he just thinks about the men he lost."

"That's the shits," said Skittles.

After that, we sat without speaking until the waiter brought us two pitchers of beer, and we all drank, glad to keep our thoughts to ourselves. The taste of beer improved my mood. It probably had the same effect on everybody else.

"Wish there were women around here," Skittles said. "It's kind of weird being in a town with all men."

"It kind of reminds me of being on base," said Boll.

We all would have preferred having a woman slinging our beers, but that did not stop anyone from downing them. The first two pitchers went dry in an instant. Seeing this, the waiter brought two more. And another two, and two more after that.

I was glad that the beer distracted the other guys, but it did not erase the image of Huish from my mind. I would have liked to get drunk, but I was no more likely to get drunk from beer than from soda. Nothing short of Sagittarian Crash ever plowed me under.

The other guys, though… A few of them could barely sit straight after the third round of pitchers.

We asked about food, and the waiter informed us the cook was gone. After Skittles begged for grub and Herrington all but threatened the man's life, he said he could bring us sandwiches and chips. Thomer told him to make enough for ten people and offered to pick up the tab.

When the sandwiches arrived, I saw that the bread was stale and the meat was stiff and unidentifiable. Boll and Herrington said they tasted fine, but I thought I would rather eat back on base. I told them I was leaving because I didn't want to see Skittles puke, but that was a lie. The truth was that I felt morose and wanted to be alone.

Handing Thomer the keys to the jeep, I went out to the street and turned west. The night was brighter than noonday. I would have no trouble finding my own way home.

19

Like most of the planets the Unified Authority chose to colonize, New Copenhagen was almost exactly the same size as Earth. It orbited its star from approximately the same distance that Earth orbited the sun, and both planets rotated at nearly the same speed. The term "day" on New Copenhagen meant just about the same thing that it meant on Earth—at least it did until the aliens "sleeved" the planet in a curtain of light.

It does not matter if there are people in the forest when a tree falls, the event still produces the vibrations that humans, animals, and audio equipment register as "sound." It did not matter that the ion curtain made the sky so bright that we could not see beyond the atmosphere, the sun still shone.

Three days after their first attack, the Mudders returned.

The scream of klaxons woke me out of a largely dreamless sleep. I leaped out of bed, pulled on my bodysuit, then clapped on my combat armor, the whole process taking less than a minute.

I grabbed my M27 as a matter of course. That was the default weapon of a U.A. Marine, sturdy, durable, and accurate. As I headed out the door, though, I saw my particle-beam pistol lying on the writing desk beside my bed. Wanting to travel light, I had not taken that weapon on the last mission. We generally did not use particle-beam weapons in a normally breathable atmosphere, they were a high-maintenance nightmare. If you accidentally closed the outtake valve, they overcharged and exploded in your hands. If you jostled the lenses and they fell out of alignment, the gun would simply refuse to shoot. Bullets had always been effective enough when the enemy was human, but battering the Space Angels with bullets had proven ineffective in our first meeting. A particle-beam weapon, which disrupted the target at an atomic level, seemed like less of a gamble. I grabbed the pistol but still held on to my M27 for good measure.

As I left my room, I joined a stream of men racing through the halls. We all knew the pecking order. Majors and up, heading to command shelters and wearing service uniforms instead of armor, went for the elevators. Mere lieutenants, like me, did not need to be told where we fitted into the hierarchy. I joined the mass of armor-wearing junior officers sprinting down the stairs to the lobby.

As I entered the stairwell, I saw one of the klaxons that Command had installed near the door. The little specker was no bigger than a saltshaker, but it screamed loud enough to shake the walls, and the engineers had placed one at the top of each flight of stairs. If not for the protection of my helmet, I might have gone deaf running down the stairs.

A cavalcade of men in combat armor poured down the stairwell, not stopping for oncoming traffic, their boots clanking against the concrete steps, the joints in their armor rattling. *Yaaaayyyeeeeeeeee,* the klaxons wailed nonstop, their unceasing screech boring through our helmets until our heads felt like they might split in two. I tried to use the noise-canceling filters in my helmet to screen the sound out. I turned off the ambient audio receiver and still heard the shriek of the klaxons through the supposedly soundproofed shell around my head.

We trampled down the stairs and out into the plush hotel lobby. As I entered the lobby, I received the same instructions issued to every Marine in the hotel. "This is not a drill! Companies, form up in the parking lot. This is not a drill!"

The lobby of Hotel Valhalla was jammed as multiple regiments of Marines rushed through. All told, nearly twenty thousand men were billeted in that hotel.

Long lines of trucks formed in the parking lot. Officers in service uniforms segregated us into battalions as we ran, directing one battalion this way and another battalion that way. By the time we reached the trucks, they were breaking us down into companies. Our briefing—whatever briefing we would receive—would come as we drove to the front.

As I headed for the trucks, I saw Ray Freeman running with a field bag dangling over one of his shoulders. Being a full foot taller than any of the clones around him, he stood out.

"You have any idea what's going on?" I asked Freeman, as he got into the back of a truck. Other men climbed into trucks, Freeman simply stepped onto the bed.

"Nobody's talking," Freeman said. His voice was so low I felt it as much as I heard it.

I climbed in behind him. Across the bed of the truck sat Lieutenant Moffat, our intrepid company commander. As his executive officer, I took the seat across from him and waited for orders. Freeman sat beside me.

"Harris, get me a head count," Moffat ordered.

They'd squeezed an entire platoon into the back of the truck—forty-five men, including Moffat, Freeman, and me. As I scanned the men crammed in around me, I was relieved to see Philips among them. I radioed to our other trucks and asked for a head count.

"Is every man accounted for?" I asked my platoon leaders. Once all three combat platoons radioed in the affirmative, I relayed that message to Moffat and the briefing began.

"Listen up," Moffat, the kind of CO who enjoys reminding his men who is in charge, shouted as if we were not wearing equipment which automatically controlled the audio volume in our helmets. "The Mudders are back. An Army tracking station picked them up seven miles west of town. They're headed northeast toward Valhalla. From what we can tell, the dumb bastards plan to hit the exact spot they attacked three days ago."

They could have gotten us to the battle more quickly in helicopters, I thought. Then I remembered the ruined gunships on the battlefield and decided that the trucks seemed like a good idea.

"We're going to try to come in behind them," Moffat said. "Command is sending two light infantry divisions to keep the Mudders pinned down while we flank them from the west. When we are in position, we will launch a counterattack, dividing their line in two.

"Once we have broken their lines, our objective is to finish the bastards off before they can retreat. That is all."

Not a very inspiring briefing, I thought to myself as the battle plans slowly took shape in my head. I thought about that deep forest with its dense growth and slow rises. There would be no point in taking cover behind hills and rocks in this battle when the enemy could shoot through anything.

I looked over at Freeman. He sat, his helmet on, leaning back against the wall of the truck, his huge body rolling along with the truck's bumps and jounces. "You think they're going to bring more men this time?" I asked.

"Fifty thousand," Freeman said.

"Fifty thousand?" I asked.

"Fifty thousand, just like last time," Freeman said.

"How do you know that?" I asked.

"I just heard from the Science Lab," Freeman said.

"You're in touch with the Science Lab?" I asked. Freeman did not bother answering.

The trucks rolled fast. We took a main artery out of Valhalla, then followed a highway deep into the forest. Somewhere out there, the fighting had begun. I could hear the rumble of handheld rockets in the distance. We were too far away to hear the rifles.

We drove for less than an hour before the trucks pulled off to the side, and everybody got out and fell into ranks. I did not realize the sheer size of our convoy until I climbed out the back of the truck. A line of two hundred trucks stretched out behind us, each carrying a platoon with forty-two men. Bringing tanks into this battle would have done us no good because the forest terrain was too overgrown for heavy equipment. I did see smaller vehicles—missile-bearing ATVs and Jackal attack vehicles.

We formed into companies and headed away from the road.

The grounds around us were virginal. We trudged through deep drifts and air powdered with miniscule flakes of snow. A layer of clouds floated below the ion curtain, but the clouds cast no shadows. Just as the air was bright under the trees of the forest, the space under the clouds had its own illumination.

We marched into the trees, ten thousand men strong. My company belonged to the Second Expeditionary Marine Brigade. The first brigade and several other units would pour into the forest from other directions. Our heavy-artillery units would act as a hedge to keep the enemy from reaching the city limits while we flanked the aliens. If everything went according to plan, we would break their lines and cut off their retreat. Everything hinged on the numbers. The Army reported the enemy force at a mere fifty thousand troops. If their report held true and the aliens returned as understaffed as they arrived the first time, the battle would end quickly.

While the rest of us prepped our M27s, Freeman brought out his sniper rifle and loaded a magazine into it.

"You're shooting bullets?" I asked. "I expected you to have something… I don't know… bigger. Maybe shoulder-fired nuclear-tipped rockets or something."

"These will do," Freeman said.

"Powerful?" I asked.

Freeman pointed out a tree on a distant hill. The crack of his rifle attracted the attention of the men milling around us.

Up on the hill, the upper half of a very large pine tree hopped in the air and fell like a bowling pin. Freeman slung the rifle over his shoulder. "I'll meet you back in town," he said.

"Where are you going?" I asked.

"I want to get to their drop zone," Freeman said.

"Why?" I asked.

"I have a package to deliver," he said.

"Something that makes a loud bang?" I asked.

"Something more scientific," Freeman said. With this, he bounded a wide drift and headed off.

"Where does your buddy think he's going?" Lieutenant Moffat asked.

"He didn't say," I said. Lying to officers like Moffat was easier than telling them the truth.

20

In all the battles I'd fought, this was the first time I had ever seen Jackals in action. Jackals were jeeps with enhanced engines and armor. They had ten small, independent wheels along their chassis instead of the standard four—four wheels up front and six in the back. Each had shielded tank armor along the sides and front and a machine-gun turret up top. The machine gun fired variable loads.

The military categorized Jackals as a "dated, but not obsolete" combat vehicle. The design of this venerable old battle-ax had not changed for eighty years. Fast and maneuverable, Jackals were an especially useful unit for lightning attacks in tightly confined areas.

I watched the Jackals weave in and out of trees at speeds nearing forty miles per hour. They leaped over ledges, sliced through snowdrifts, and splashed across creeks. I suppose a Jackal would make an easy target in an open field, but traveling at those speeds through trees, they looked impossible to hit.

We marched five miles into the forest, moving east toward town. Our battalion would be the spearhead, the wedge that would snap the enemy column in two. We would sweep down from the north. If everything went according to plan, we would leave the bastards with only a token force to attack the city while other battalions dissected the rest of their force in the woods. There would be no quarter given. We would pound the Mudders until we destroyed every last one of them.

As we pushed through the forest, the echoing thunder of rockets became louder. Occasionally we would pass some break in the trees and see tails of smoke rising in the distance. Then we crossed the invisible line bordering the battlefield, and the explosions became something we felt as well as heard. The ground trembled slightly when rockets were fired, and branches rattled above us.

The ATVs and Jackals continued streaking ahead, then channeling back, running along our flanks, then clearing new paths. At one point, an ATV leaped over a ridge, and exploded into a fireball. Through the flames and smoke and the glare of the ion curtain, I saw the bolt that speared the vehicle.

Flames trailing behind it like a wild mane, the ATV finished its arc and landed smoothly before skidding sideways into a tree. Medics ran to check the two-man crew, but they did not need to bother. Already twisted around the trunk of the tree, the ATV exploded, and the passenger tube broke open to reveal the driver and gunner, covered in flame, skin charred black, and motionless.

I saw this as I ducked behind a tree and prepared to fire. We had not run into the alien army itself, just a couple of scouts. The nearest platoon tried to pin the enemy with suppressing fire as a second platoon flanked them and cut them down. But you cannot pin an enemy that has no fear of being shot. The two aliens marched forward and returned fire as an entire platoon shredded them with an endless stream of M27 fire.

As if attracted to the gunfire, the next wave of aliens came pounding through the trees. Had it not been for the glare of the ion curtain, the Mudders would have blended into the forest. Their dark skin would have worked like camouflage had there been shadows.

An ATV streaked past, presenting a diversion. The Mudders

did not take cover but simply marched ahead, firing spears of light that bored through trees, rocks, and anything else they hit.

We were not entirely ready for them, but the Mudders did not catch us by surprise, either. We would have had a better position if we had had more time to dig in. Many of our men found cover behind trees and fallen logs. Others had no choice and simply knelt in the open. Our entire company showered a continuous stream of M27 fire, battering the Mudders and everything around them. Shreds of bark and wood flew through the air; branches fell, then danced along the ground.

Moffat radioed me to say that another large force of Mudders was headed in from the north. Our company was assigned to form a skirmishing line with three other companies. The objective was to maintain a hundred-foot buffer between us and the aliens while the rest of the regiment dug in.

"Spread out, spread out," I radioed as I moved up and down the line. "Thomer, take your platoon and cover that rise." Moffat moved among the men, doing the same. We only had a few moments before the aliens arrived. The first of them walked out from a stand of trees. More followed.

The Mudders' absolute disregard for our firepower made holding our position nearly impossible. They just did not care if we hit them. I'd seen Marines spend more time bracing themselves to step into a cold shower than these aliens spent before preparing to walk into our fusillade. Our gunfire chipped away their bodies, slowly splintering their broad chests and heads.

Looking across our line, I saw Philips out in the open, firing three-shot bursts from his M27. White bolts struck the tree behind him and sailed through the air around him.

As a survivor of the previous skirmish, Philips knew what would happen if he got hit. But there he was, not even trying to take cover.

I set up an interLink connection between me and Philips and heard nothing but his breathing. He wasn't even talking to himself. Normally he was the noisiest Marine I had ever known, maintaining nonstop commentary with himself when he could not find another audience.

"Philips, fall back," I ordered. He did not respond.

Thomer, always the guardian angel, climbed out from good cover so he could pull Philips to safety. "Leave him," I yelled.

"He'll get hit," yelled Thomer.

But Philips had angels looking out for him. An alien light bolt drilled through the tree directly behind Philips's head. The trunk caught on fire. Philips seemed not to notice any of this. More bolts speared the ground near his feet and the bushes around him, but nothing hit him.

"Harris, take your platoon and fall in around my beacon," Moffat ordered. Had I been a general-issue clone, I would have called up a platoon and started toward the beacon before sizing up the situation. Automatic order response was programmed into their DNA. As I followed the beacon signal, I saw that it led to an indefensible knoll with no trees or rocks for cover and no strategic value.

"We can't hold that area. It's in their path, sir," I yelled.

"I gave you an order, Harris."

Following that beacon would expose our flank to the aliens. Moffat had a point, though. If we could hold that area, we might turn the tide of the battle. I wanted to get to that knoll but following a different path.

I switched to a private frequency so I could speak with Thomer. "You got Moffat's beacon?" I asked.

"Yeah. Is that for us?" Thomer asked.

"No," I lied. If I had told him the truth, his reaction would have been to follow orders. "Take the platoon in from behind the hill, and don't take any chances. Those bastards can shoot through rock."

I watched Philips, expecting him to ignore the order, but his programming won out. He stayed with Thomer and the rest of the platoon as they fell back, then moved up to take point as they circled the hill.

"I told you to secure that hill," Moffat called to me. He was screaming like a lunatic now. I imagined more than a little spit flying inside his helmet.

"We're on our way, sir," I said.

A Jackal skidded to a stop to the left of the beacon. The Marine in the turret sprayed heavy-caliber shells into the growing bank of Mudders as they came swarming out of the woods. The three-inch shells tore through trees and Mudders alike. One alien tried to charge the Jackal, wading into the heavy fire. The bullets slowly ground the crazy bastard into mulch, shredding it even as it continued its charge. The Mudder managed to get about twenty feet in that barrage before falling in a heap of pieces.

A line of five Jackals sped in from another direction, firing into the enemy line while weaving through the trees. Moments later they emerged for another pass, their tires kicking up mud and twigs as they skidded past.

The Mudders fired back. When three bolts struck the first of the Jackals, the driver lost control, and the vehicle flipped. More bolts hit the chassis as it burst into flames. The Jackal spun through the air and settled roof down.

The Mudders opened fire on the other Jackals. Two made it to safety; two more crashed.

"Heads up!" Thomer yelled, as hundreds of Mudders crested a distant ridge and opened fire.

Grenadiers standing near the top of the hill fired rockets into the Mudders' ranks, then dropped back. The ground around the aliens seemed to boil as the rockets kicked up a veil of steam, mud, and leaves.

We could not let the Mudders drive us back, but a single platoon could not hold this hill. At least a hundred Mudders had gathered on a nearby ridge. Hiding proved useless when the aliens returned our fire; the bolts from their weapons cut through the ground like needles through a sheet. I saw a bolt pass through a boulder and hit one of my men in the face. The bolt continued on through the back of his helmet as the Marine fell to the ground, his dead body still trembling as the muscles in his arms and legs exerted their last impulses of life.

Thomer sent three grenadiers to scatter the Mudders, but the grenadiers attracted too much attention. When they appeared at the top of the knoll, the Mudders fired at them and continued firing at them even after they dropped back behind cover.

Another squadron of Jackals skidded into range, fired a hailstorm into the Mudder line, then vanished. Under the cover of the chaos created by the Jackals, platoons crowded in beside us. Another force attacked the Mudders from the right, and it looked, for a moment, like we would hold. The enemy line seemed to crumble in disarray, but then a small herd of Mudders charged into our fire. The platoons on either side of us gave way, and my platoon suddenly became the point of the spearhead.

"We need to hold this area!" the regimental colonel yelled over an open frequency, and a virtual beacon appeared around us.

Now the battle hinged on our little hill as the entire specking regiment followed the colonel's beacon. Ten thousand Marines headed in our direction as hundreds of Mudders, looking like three-dimensional shadows, aimed their guns in our direction. Jackals streaked by and fired into them, but the crazy bastards did not fall back.

I would have given a year's pay for air support, but that was not going to happen in this battle. The Mudders had destroyed two-thirds of our gunships during the last battle, and whatever gunships were left would be in effective in this heavily forested terrain.

ATVs poured in from every direction, firing rockets into the enemy line, then charging through it, weaving in and out around the trees as if they were running a slalom course. One leaped over a ridge, firing two rockets in midair. The rockets pummeled the enemy line, leaving a gap in it, but when the driver tried to thread that gap, a Mudder stepped in the way. That alien must have weighed one thousand five hundred pounds, maybe even a full ton. When the light-armor ATV struck it, the Mudder only spun and fell backward as if it tripped.

And still the Mudders did not drop behind cover or halt their disorganized march in our direction. Thousands of bolts of light rained down on the ATVs. But the ATVs were fast and low to the ground, difficult targets to hit.

The rest of the regiment arrived en masse. Grenadiers launched rockets over the ATVs, and automatic riflemen fired an endless hail of M27 fire into the enemy line. The Mudders continued to fire at the ATVs—a wasted effort. They hit a few of the fast vehicles but left themselves open to our grenadiers and fire teams. A gap had formed in the enemy line, and in came the Jackals.

I could feel it. I could taste it. The battle had swung in our direction, and in another moment the Unified Authority Marines would begin another charge. Tension built as I waited for the order. When the regimental colonel finally gave the order to advance, it came as a relief. I allowed the momentum of the regiment to draw me forward. This was not a wild charge. It began slowly and methodically, but it was also unrelenting. There were men in front of me and behind me. We pushed over a rise, beyond a line of trees.

As I left the protection of the trees, I experienced that pleasant stinging in my veins, the combat reflex. A mixture of adrenaline and testosterone flowed through my blood. It was like the return of an old friend, maybe more pronounced on this occasion than ever before. I felt both calm and excited at the same time. It left me peaceful, almost blissful, and ready to kill. I did not become part of the mob; my thoughts remained my own. But I shared its purpose—we had come to kill.

By this time I had lost track of which men belonged to which company. With so many Marines pushing in around me, I simply ignored their virtual dog tags as they appeared in my visor. There comes a time when chaos takes over, and all strategy is lost on the field. We had reached that point.

When I saw Mudders, I aimed and fired. I no longer entertained any objectives other than to kill. It was hard to shoot with men jostling around me, bumping me, constantly forcing me forward.

When I shot at enemies, I never shot alone. We were ten thousand men moving in unison, and we fired at every Mudder we saw. When small groups of aliens stepped over a ridge or out from behind the trees, so many bullets ripped into them that they simply shredded before our eyes.

As I reached the top of the rise, I saw a Mudder no more than fifty feet away and fired over the helmets of several Marines. Hundreds of bullets bounced off the alien's hide. I did not see if it fell. The momentum of the regiment shoved me on, and I lost sight of it.

A knee-deep stream ran across our path. I splashed into the water, high-stepping my way across, afraid to fall because I knew I'd be trampled. It was not until I emerged on the other side of that stream, slipping on the rocks along the shore, that I looked back and saw the extent of our casualties. As we crossed the far bank and stepped over a rise, all of our cover had fallen away. The slippery rocks I'd stumbled over as I crossed the river were dead Marines. Dozens of them lay facedown in the water.

A thousand Marines now funneled in through a bottleneck no more than three hundred feet across. The aliens fired into our ranks, and we fired into theirs. Still we pushed ahead. When I crested another ridge, I saw that the ground that I had first thought was a snow-covered forest was really piled with dead Marines in white combat armor. Yard-long bolts of light soared through the air at speeds we could see but not dodge. Men around me were hit in the head, the chest, the arms, the legs.

Had I not been part of the herd, I would have found cover and dug in. But this was not a battle in which men dug in and fought— this was a charge. Marines pushed at my back. Marines ran ahead of me. We splashed over the banks of the creek, stormed across the field of fallen men, and crashed headlong into enemy fire.

A few feet ahead of me, a bolt seared through a Marine, and the Marine behind him, then a third Marine. The bolt pierced the first man in the head, the next through the chest, and barely grazed the final man in the arm, but all three would die. Whenever those bolts connected, it caused such trauma that a shot through the arm was every bit as lethal as a shot through the head.

We continued our rush, all the time hearing officers taunting us, coaxing us, their voices ringing in our helmets and merging with our thoughts. "Run!" "Get going!" "Move it! Move it! Move it!"

An ATV skidded around a hollow, catching three Mudders from behind. It fired a missile that blew the Mudders apart, and the ATV rumbled over their bodies as if they were no more deadly than overgrown roots.

Switching from my M27 to a particle-beam pistol, I continued to run in the stampede. My pistol was made for close-combat situations, and that phase of the battle was about to begin. The aliens were all around us now, their massive single-colored bodies blending in with the landscape.

The men to the right and left of me fell a few moments apart. The one on my right was hit in the gut, and his legs crumpled beneath him. The one on my left was hit in the face—I saw the bolt coming and turned in time to see it strike his visor and tear through it. The plasticized glass in his visor had already melted as he fell backward and was trampled.

I did not know the man's name and did not bother reading his virtual dog tag. I got a quick glimpse of him as he fell, and then the momentum of the pack forced me on.

"Move it, you specking sons of bitches!" some officer yelled at us. The interLink seemed to fuse with my brain.

Once we reached the next ridge, the momentum slowed to a crawl. With every step I pushed off the back or head of a fallen Marine. In this situation, I had no time to worry about stepping on fallen Marines, but the footing was terrible the way the bodies slid under my weight. As I stumbled forward, I began to run into broken Mudders as well. A hundred yards more, and the white of Marine combat armor gave way to charcoal as the battlefield became a junkyard of alien body parts.

At some point, I felt one of my legs pulled out from under me, and I fell on my face. I swerved around and saw that one of the dying Mudders had grabbed my ankle. The creature had been blown in half. Its chest, arms, and head were still intact, its eyes looked to me as if they had been carved out of iron or stone. I wondered if the thing could see me as I swung my pistol into its face and fired the sparkling green beam. I held the trigger down for several seconds, though it had already released me.

The eyes never flinched. I continued to fire. The head stuttered, then exploded like a skeet. Bits of some material that might have been clay or metal or both burst out of its face, then I was back on my feet.

Our regiment slammed into the Mudders from the south and east. We continued to pour into them in a column, but they would not retreat. They tried to push back against us, but by that time, their attack had no teeth.

We started out ten thousand troops strong but had lost a lot of men. Our objective had been to cut the Mudders' line and stall their advance toward Valhalla. We succeeded at breaking their lines, but we did not stall their attack. Nothing could stall their attack. The aliens we did not kill continued on toward the city. To a man, these bastards knew nothing of retreat.

Perhaps Glade had foreseen this. His Twenty-third Regiment came in from the north and east, creating an additional buffer across the city lines. They slashed into the enemy, creating a second front. Other regiments circled in behind the aliens, coming in from the south and west. Even then, the Mudders did not yield; they simply broke into groups and continued the fight until we struck down their last men.

The report that day was good.

The Fifteenth Regiment, my unit, struck first. We broke their line, trapping the aliens between ourselves and the Twenty-third Regiment. Between our two regiments we killed over fifteen thousand aliens and lost only three thousand five hundred men— by far the lowest casualty rate in the campaign.

After we snapped their lines, thirty-five thousand Mudders headed south and west, but the trap had been sprung. They ran headlong into the Eighth, Tenth, and Sixteenth Regiments. The battle lasted several hours with the Mudders fighting the Marines to a stalemate until the Ninth and Twelfth Regiments arrived from the west.

When the Seventeenth, Twenty-ninth, and Thirty-third came in from the east, trapping the aliens on yet another flank, the battle finally came to a close. Though they were shamefully outnumbered, the Mudders stood and fought.

Opting for aggression over caution, Glade poured more men into the fire—officers and enlisted men alike. When the stakes are too high to rely on a surgical strike, you need to rely on your numbers. Against an alien force of fifty thousand troops, General Glade sent over one hundred thousand Marines. Only twenty-four thousand of those Marines returned.

By day's end, we had lost over seventy-five thousand men, but we had won the war!

That was what we all kept telling ourselves, that we had won the war.

21

When we left the hotel for the battle that morning, we needed 250 trucks to transport the troops. We returned in 121, what was left of us at least. On balance, things seemed hopeful.

Other regiments continued to fight as we turned to leave the field, but our part of the battle had ended. All we knew as we loaded into the trucks and headed back to the hotel was that we had lost nearly one-third of our men. We were exhausted both physically and emotionally, but mostly I think we were nervous about how the other regiments would fare. No one spoke as the trucks rumbled back toward town.

The trucks dropped us in front of the lobby. As I climbed out, I felt the eyes of my men resting on me. "We sent those speckers packing. Now go clean up," I said, then I brooded as I wandered up to my room and changed out of my armor. There was tension in the air. I took a bath and a nap and ignored the noise when somebody knocked on my door. I kept the curtains closed and the lights off, creating my own personal nightfall.

A few minutes later the first reports leaked. I heard shouting outside my door and stuck my head out. I saw a group of officers celebrating in the hall and asked what happened. One of the officers turned toward me long enough to say, "It's another massacre, just like last time. Better!" The officer said he was on his way to Valhalla Skyline, the restaurant and bar that occupied the top two floors of the hotel, and asked if I wanted to come. I thanked him and went back to bed. I tried to sleep, but I was too keyed up, so I dressed in my Charlie service uniform and took the elevator up the Skyline. The bar was packed with officers, hundreds of them. Rings of officers swapped battlefield stories in the open area that was intended to be the dance floor. I wrestled my way into the crowd and felt the excitement.

Moments later, an officer made his way to the stage and gave the first official update. The Eighth, Tenth, and Sixteenth Regiments successfully engaged the aliens, sweeping in from the south. He did not release casualty numbers but could confirm that the attack had been entirely successful. A few minutes later, the officer returned with more information—the Ninth Infantry Regiment and the Twelfth Light Artillery Regiment had flanked the aliens from the west while three more regiments surprised the enemy on their eastern flank.

Thousands of officers shouted at the tops of their lungs.

Forty minutes later, the briefing officer appeared again, and this time he made it official, announcing complete and total victory. Moments later, the message was repeated over the hotel speaker system.

A trio of colonels climbed onto the bar and began tossing bottles of booze into the sea of officers. Arms waved in anticipation, and feeding frenzies flared wherever the bottles landed.

I never stopped to wonder why this victory should be more permanent than the one we had three days earlier. Nothing had changed, the Mudders had come at us with an army exactly like the one we just routed. But that first victory seemed insignificant, like an opening act. This one had finality about it; this time the bastards knew what we had, and we still sent them packing.

The elevator doors opened, and a new tide of Marines poured onto the floor. Officers crowded around each other like bullets in a box. By now hundreds and hundreds of officers had packed into the bar, drinking, boasting, yelling at the tops of their lungs.

Bottles of beer slowly trickled across the room. No one could talk above the crowd, you needed to shout as loud as you could if you wanted to speak to the man standing next to you. The more each man shouted, the louder the aggregate noise became.

In one corner of the room, a ring of twenty or maybe thirty officers sang a drunken version of "The Halls of Montezuma," the anthem of the Unified Authority Marines. All of them held glasses of beer, which they waved and clanked together as they sang. Beer and suds flew everywhere. Nobody cared.

Then a man sitting near the big observation window spotted a convoy of trucks driving into town. The caravan should have been endless. But it was not endless, not endless at all. There might have been a thousand trucks, but not much more than that. Watching them roll into town from way up at the top of the hotel, we could see the end of the procession.

Slowly, as if someone was turning down the volume, the entire bar went silent. The sight of those trucks was like a dirge. Then Base Command ordered all officers down to the enlisted men's barracks to prepare for debriefing. I took one last look at the end of the line of trucks and headed for the stairs.

Downcast officers stumbled out of the bar. I caught brief snatches of several conversations.

"Weren't there a lot more trucks this morning? I could have…"

"…damn it. It's over, right? I mean, we crushed the bastards…"

The celebration had gone out of all of us. Everybody's mood had changed, including mine. For no reason at all, I had come to believe we had won the war and not just a battle; and though I had no new information, I now knew that something had changed.

As I reached the Valkyrie Ballroom—the barracks my battalion called home—a young major approached me. "Lieutenant Harris?" he asked.

I saluted.

"General Glade would like a word with you."

* * *

"Harris, glad they found you," General Glade said. We traded salutes.

He looked tired. He was a skinny man with a weak chin, a long, hooked nose, and a round, balding head. Looking at his face and head made me think of a parakeet.

"Congratulations, General," I said.

Huuuuhh. He cleared his throat. "Not much of a victory, Lieutenant. We lost a lot of men. I'm not so sure congratulations are in order."

I did not know how to respond, so I said nothing.

"We can talk on the way, Harris. We have a briefing at the Science Lab, and they asked me to bring you along."

I was a second lieutenant. For me to attend the same briefing with a general was beyond unusual, it was downright bizarre. Then I remembered Freeman mentioning the Science Lab and realized that he might well have mentioned my name to the scientists holding the briefing.

Two staff officers met us as we left the office. They led us through the lobby, a plush indoor palace with burgundy carpeting and crystal chandeliers. The area was abandoned. Briefings had already begun in the ballrooms; every Marine on the premises was required to attend.

Almost every Marine. Since I was traveling with a general, I was excused. The two staff officers led us out to the main entrance, where a sedan waited under the portico. Glade and I climbed into the back. The staff officers, both of whom outranked me, sat in the front.

News of the victory had already spread through Valhalla. With the Marines and Army holding mass briefings, most parts of the city lay empty; but hysteria had erupted in the areas occupied by the civilian militia. We passed neighborhoods in which rapturous mobs filled the streets—men dancing and drinking and celebrating. *Valhalla has got to be the galaxy's happiest ghost town,* I thought to myself. Loud music rang in the air. I saw a man in a heavy jacket carrying four bottles of whiskey, two under each arm, while waving a fifth bottle in the air.

Glade cleared his throat. "It's a bit early to celebrate," he grumbled. The officers in the front seat heard him and nodded. One sighed, and said, "Civilians."

We drove to the University of Valhalla, a sprawling campus that reminded me of just about every other university I had ever seen. We passed a large fountain that had become the domicile of hundreds of ducks. We passed walkways lined by trees that had long since shed their leaves for the winter. Except for the military supply trucks and security stops, I might have guessed that the university had closed for the season.

The university campus sat serene. Fresh white snow had built up on the lawn areas. Melting snow covered the streets and walkways. The air was clean. The weather had washed this part of the city clean, and there were no occupants to mess it up again.

We parked near what had been the university's School of Science and now served as the military's scientific laboratory. The outside of the building had a glass entryway and an old gray brick facade. The benches outside the main entrance were buried in snow. The building itself went three stories up and three stories down. On this day, the debriefing took place on the bottom floor.

Apparently the four of us—General Glade, his two staff officers, and me—were the last of the elect group to arrive. We passed through a security station at the door and another, larger, station by the elevators. An MP took us down to Basement 3, where we were met by an armed escort that led us through the halls. As we entered the auditorium in which the briefing would be held, I saw a lot of brass. The meeting was for generals and their staffs, an elite circle in which I was the token clone.

Glade and his two staff officers found a row with three open seats and filled them. I sat alone on the next row. It didn't bother me.

There was a stage at the front of the auditorium, but the scientist running the show did not use it. He stood beside a table, the objects he placed on display along the table magnified on the screen above his head.

"I understand we are all here now," said the old scientist conducting the meeting. He was an odd-looking man—tall and skinny, built like the human version of a cotton-tipped swab, only bald. He had thick glasses, an unkempt ring of cotton-fluff hair, and a lab coat draped over his skeletal body. The guy probably stood a good six-foot-four, but if he weighed more than 140 pounds, I did not see where he packed it. He had a low, jittery voice giving the impression that his mouth had trouble keeping up with his brain.

"Um, we have made some significant discoveries over the last twenty-four hours," the scientist began. "I'm not really sure where to begin. Under normal circumstances I would publish my results and present them in a conference. Under these circumstances, I will present our findings directly to you."

"Can we get on with this?" someone asked from the front row. All the officers on the far end of the auditorium wore Army green. When push came to shove, the Army headed this operation.

"Yes, yes, of course," the scientist muttered nervously. "Over the last three days, we have explored the anatomy of the aliens you refer to as the Mudders." His mentioning the term "Mudders" brought a snicker from the officers, making the scientist all the more nervous. "We have been unable to secure a complete cadaver for examination, so we have had to work on, um, how can I put this, the various parts that have been delivered. I have brought a head and some other samples of alien anatomy with me today." The scientist pointed a trembling finger at the table.

"Yes, yes, we see that." The voice came from the Army section again. That kind of open disrespect would only come from the highest-ranking general.

"When... when... when we received these parts three days ago, they were solid. We cataloged their weights at that time. Depending on the damage, heads generally weighed 98 pounds and 3.2 ounces. Arms weighed 133 pounds and 2.2 ounces. Legs weighed 268 pounds, 5.1 ounces. We received portions of torsos, though these were generally badly damaged."

"The only good alien is a dead alien," said a member of General Glade's staff. This brought a round of subdued applause. These old officers were behaving like a bunch of rowdy enlisted men.

"Upon examination, we… we found that the aliens had a precisely uniform body weight of 3 pounds, 6.3 ounces per cubic inch."

"A uniform body weight per cubic inch? Is that any part of the body? Do humans have a pound-per-inch weight, too?" This question came from the Air Force section. The general asking sounded interested.

"No, no, sir," the scientist stuttered. He looked so uncomfortable in front of these officers. "No, sir. Human bone, fat, muscle mass, organs, and hair all have unique weights and densities.

"The aliens do not have bones or muscles. They seem to be made out of a metal-clay polymer that is foreign to our understanding. We've tried to analyze the material. I'm afraid we could not find an equivalent material on our known periodic table of elements." The question from the Air Force section seemed to relax the old goat.

The scientist prattled on for another five minutes, comparing the polymer to various known elements and explaining how it differed. I heard whispered conversations starting around the room. No one listened until he said, "The parts we have collected are rapidly degenerating."

"They're doing what?" the Army general asked.

"The material is degenerating," the scientist repeated. "These alien sections were solid when we received them. They contained a solid mass of the new element that Dr. Sweetwater has labeled 'MBC,' or more properly, 'Mudder Brown Carbon.' When they first arrived, these alien sections were highly concentrated; we could only obtain samples for spectral and elemental analysis using a laser scalpel.

"Even so, we were able to determine that they were not composed of living tissue. Upon early examination, we, um, we found that there were no signs of entrails for analysis."

"Entrails? You mean guts?" someone called out.

"We, uh, tried several experiments to see if we could break this material down to its most elemental form. We superradiated samples with three hundred thousand grays. This material does not absorb radiation." As he became nervous again, the scientist's stuttering returned.

"Are you saying they can't be nuked?" an Army general asked. This time I saw the man asking the question—a pudgy little man with a flattop of white hair. I didn't recognize him.

"N-no, sir. The trauma caused by the explosion might destroy the avatar, but the radiation would not bother it."

"Avatar?" the general asked. "What the speck is an avatar?"

"Um… ah, it's a representation."

"A representation?" the general asked. "Somebody help me out here."

"Avatar? You mean like the characters in computer games?" somebody asked from the Air Force section of the room.

"Computer games?" the Army general asked. "Games!"

"I understand you use computerized combat simulations to train your men," the scientist said.

"Oh… battle simulations," the general said, sounding somewhat appeased. "What do the Mudders have to do with combat sims?"

"These are not living creatures," the scientist said. "These are physical representations of creatures that are controlled by the creatures they represent.

"The samples we received contain no semblance of living tissue. As you can see," he said, pointing with a foot-long metal stick, "the material is uniform. There is no muscle or bone. It's almost as if this creature w-were a living statue."

"What about their guns?" This time it was one of the staff members Glade brought. "Those are real."

"Oh, the weapons, now that was fascinating," the scientist said. "The weapons degraded even faster than the aliens themselves."

"Degraded?" The Army general clearly wanted to turn the

briefing into an interrogation. "You said that before. What do you mean by degraded?"

"Th-this creature and his weapon are… are… are made out of the exact same material. They are made out of the element we refer to as MBC. Also, um, the illumination shield that has enveloped New Copenhagen appears to be made out of that same element."

Spontaneous arguments broke out. The soft-spoken scientist tried several times to restart his briefing, but his bullheaded audience paid him no mind. He watched nervously, slicking back his cotton-fluff hair.

Finally, the chubby Army general took control of the meeting. "Just to make sure I have got this straight." He waited for the auditorium to become quiet and started again. "Just to be sure I have this straight, you claim that the Mudders and their guns are nothing more than computer characters made out of light? Is that what you are saying, because if it is, we may need to find some better scientists. Those Mudder bastards were alive enough to kill eighty thousand Marines today. Those were flesh-and-blood clones they killed out there. This was not some bullshit computer simulation."

The general stood and took a step toward the stage. Now that he was out of his seat, I saw that the general was short as well as chubby and old. But compared to the scientist, he looked like a green beret.

"No one is calling this a computer game," Ray Freeman said as he stepped in from the wings. Ray stood nearly two feet taller than the general and weighed more than the general and the scientist combined. He had been hiding somewhere, and he now came downstairs along the front of the stage.

The general spun around to look at Freeman, then paused. I don't know if he recognized Freeman or was simply put off by the sheer size of the man. "I see," was all the general managed to squeak out. "I, uh, just wanted to clarify the point," the general said as he returned to his seat.

"Thank you, Raymond," the scientist said, turning and smiling up at Freeman. Freeman walked to the edge of the stage and sat, watching over the scientist like a bodyguard.

With Freeman watching over him, the scientist gained confidence. For a moment, he and his audience looked at each other in silence, no one quite knowing where to pick up. Finally, a general from the Air Force asked, "What did you mean by degrading?"

"Oh... oh yes," the scientist said. He surprised me by lifting the specimen of an alien arm with one hand. "When we received this limb, it weighed 133 pounds. Compared to a human arm, that would be about—"

"Can you please get on with this?" the Army general asked. Some of the other officers in the room sounded a note of agreement.

"This limb was too heavy for me to lift," the scientist said.

"Within an hour of our receiving it, we realized it had begun to degrade."

The scientist carefully replaced the arm on the table, then took hold of the forearm with both his hands like a man breaking a stick. He snapped the forearm in two and held up the wrist and hand. "Three days ago I could not lift this limb, let alone break it in two. Over the last 72 hours, the weight of this arm has dropped from 133 pounds to 27 pounds. The limb has become hollow and brittle. It is as if the MBC particles are evaporating."

"Can you explain how that could happen?" an Air Force officer asked.

"I cannot explain it at this juncture. Dr. Sweetwater has a hypothesis, but we need to put it to the test before we discuss it," the scientist said.

"And you said that their guns are made out of the same stuff?" the Air Force general asked. By this time, the briefing had reached a low level of pandemonium.

The scientist bent over and picked up a box that sat beside the table. He looked into the box, shaking his head as if trying to steel himself for a difficult task, then brought out something that looked like a two-foot-long mud clod.

"This is one of their guns," the scientist said.

That could not possibly have been one of the guns, I thought. It was the right basic shape, but it looked old and dirty, like something you might find rusting on the bottom of a lake. There was no hint of the nickel plating.

"What happened to it?" someone asked.

"It is degrading to its tachyonic form." The scientist turned the box over and poured out a small pile of dust.

"It all turns into dust?" somebody asked in a voice loud enough to be heard above the chaotic chatter.

"This is all that we have left from the scientific instrument that was captured three days ago. As you can see, the instrument has nearly completed the entropic cycle." The rectangular stone he held up looked like an oversized brick. "Everything the aliens create ultimately reverts back to tachyons and evaporates."

"And what are tachyons?" the Army general asked.

"Tachyons? Why, tachyons are one of the great mysteries of science. They are a class of particle that is too small and fast for us to detect. We have no way of proving tachyons exist, but all of the data we have collected from the aliens are consistent with our understanding about the properties of tachyons."

"Wait. Wait a moment, Doctor," the little Army general shouted, once again leaping to his feet. "So you do not know if anything you have told us is accurate? It's all your opinion? Is that right?"

"The… the data supports our theory," the scientist said.

"Subatomic particles?" the Air Force general asked. "Tachyons are subatomic particles?"

"Yes, sir. Tachyons are particles that move at a speed greater than the speed of light. Theoretically, it takes a great deal of energy to bond these particles in place. We have been able to measure enormous amounts of energy released by these body parts and this weapon as they degrade.

"I can try to explain the mechanics of this, but—"

"I'll take your word for it," the general said. "It doesn't matter anyway. We defeated them. Killed them, broke them… it really doesn't matter." Taking a moment to look back at the officers around him, the Army general smirked and said, "My colleagues in the Marine Corps degraded a lot of tachyons this afternoon."

The audience laughed.

"If our theory is correct, General, over the next seventy-two hours the avatars will simply reassemble," the scientist said.

The laughter stopped.

22

The picture on the screen was a familiar one. It showed three Mudders in their glowing form—the form that Morgan Atkins had labeled "Space Angels"—as they emerged from one of those light spheres in the forest. The picture might have been downloaded off any of my men's visors, but I suspected it was taken from mine.

"From what we can tell, the illuminated fields shown in this feed act as incubation chambers. We were initially stymied as to how the fields functioned, then Raymond provided the missing pieces for us to form a theory." The scientist paused to smile at Freeman, who, of course, did not respond.

The picture of the Mudders vanished from the screen, replaced by a close-up view of the glass dish with the bullets on the table. "These bullets passed through the alien incubation field," said the scientist.

Passed through? I thought. It made it sound like Freeman tossed them through the sphere instead of firing them into a nearby tree.

"The energy inside this field was so intense that it altered the composition of the bullets. Before entering the field, they were composed of a lead-and-steel alloy coated with Teflon. After passing through the field, the Teflon fused with the steel.

"When the spent bullets were first retrieved, they glowed almost exactly the way that the avatars glowed when they emerged from the field. Over the next few hours, the bullets attracted trillions of tachyon particles out of the atmosphere. By the time Raymond delivered the bullets to us, the tachyons had formed a cylindrical crust around them.

"Because the bullets passed through the field in a matter of milliseconds, they did not receive the prolonged charge necessary to form a lasting bond."

The scientist looked up at the screen again. He ran the video feed of the three glowing aliens a second time. As the last alien stepped out of the sphere, he froze the feed.

"If our hypothesis is correct, the avatars leave the field as a mass of energy so powerful it is able to attract tachyon particles out of the atmosphere and bond them together."

"So the particles, these tachyons things, are forming a skin around a creature made of energy? Is that your point?" one of the generals asked.

"Not a creature—a signal," the scientist said. "Remember, the beings you have encountered are only avatars, representations of creatures in another location." He smiled nervously, exposing enormous teeth that might have looked more at home in the mouth of a horse.

"But you said these same particles are what make their guns? That doesn't make sense to me. Their guns are too complex. How can they come together to make the working parts of a light rifle?" This question came from the Air Force section. I heard no sarcasm in the tone.

"These creatures appear to have the ability to manipulate tachyon particles on a fundamental level. From what we have been able to determine, it appears the particulate matter that is attracted to the avatars remains constant while the particles that arrange themselves into the weapon re-form themselves into a wide array of materials."

"Come again?" one of the generals asked.

The scientist thought for a moment, then said, "The tachyons arrange themselves into wires, prisms, or whatever materials are needed to create those guns."

"So you know what's inside those rifles? Can we duplicate them?" the Army general asked.

"No, the rifles had degraded to mostly dust by the time we received them," said the scientist.

"Just to be sure I understand this, you have no idea how they work?" the general asked.

"No, sir," said the scientist.

This caused yet another chaotic outburst, generals not so much arguing as agreeing with each other that the information in this briefing had re-formed itself into a colossal waste of time.

The briefing lasted another twenty minutes. When it ended, the officers filed out of the room. "Well, gentlemen, you have just seen your tax dollars at work," General Glade said in a wry voice as he passed the Army contingent. "An hour wasted and millions of dollars spent just so some egghead scientist could tell us what Lieutenant Harris discovered three days ago—that we have to break these, these, Avatar bastards instead of killing them. There's a breakthrough for the history books."

Glade's reference to the "Avatar bastards" was the first time anyone used the term "Avatar" as if it referred to a race. I liked it; it sounded a hell of a lot better than Mudder. Hearing his comment, the Army brass laughed.

For once the Army and Marines seemed to agree about something. I didn't laugh, though. I didn't mind Glade, he was more respectful than most of the officers I had served under; but he had to be pretty thick if he didn't understand the implications. If we really were fighting avatars of aliens instead of the aliens themselves, Glade had just lost one-fifth of his command without so much as denting the enemy.

We walked out of the science building and into the blinding glare of the ion curtain, which, according to that scientist, was also composed of tachyon particles. The auditorium had been dark and warm. Out here, the frosty air braced my skin, and I had to shade my eyes to see in the tachyon-charged atmosphere. It looked more like 1300 hours than 2200.

Could all of the brass have been that obtuse, I wondered. None of them seemed to understand. The generals chatted on the university lawn for another ten minutes, then Glade took his entourage and climbed into his car.

"Hey, maybe if the Mudders are like representations of creatures... What if...? What if the real aliens are so wrapped up in their avatars that they die when we kill the avatar off?" Glade's aide/driver asked as he started up the car.

Glade, who had clearly lapsed into a foul mood, grimaced. "What kind of stupid idea is that?" he asked.

"I don't know," the man said, sounding a bit embarrassed. "I'm just trying to expand the matrix."

"Did you see the look on General Newcastle's face when that Freeman came down from the stage?" another staffer asked. The question sounded pandering, as if he wanted to change the subject and maybe flatter Glade by making fun of a rival general. "I thought he was going to piss his pants right on the spot."

"Freeman, he's a piece of work," said the first staffer. "I hear he ran for the hills the moment the shooting started this morning."

I could feel myself tensing. The asshole had fought the war from behind the guarded walls of Base Command; he had no right to judge men who went to the field. He was my superior, but he was full of shit. I was about to tell him what I thought, but General Glade spoke first, "You know, son, when you don't know what you're talking about, you really should keep quiet. That way you won't make such an ass of yourself."

The mood around the hotel was somber when we returned. My men had not been told about Avatars or tachyons in their briefing—that was highly classified information for a highly privileged few—but they had heard numbers. Marines judge battles by results. When my men heard that eighty thousand men died killing fifty thousand aliens, it sent a chill through the company.

There were a few wounded—men who broke an arm or a leg in the charge. But every Marine who got shot by the aliens died. It was the shock that killed them—whether they were shot in the head or the foot, the shock killed them as surely as it had killed Huish.

"Where were you?" Moffat asked me, as I left the company's barracks on my way to my quarters.

"I attended a different briefing," I said.

"You had orders to attend the briefing with your company," Moffat said. He had not raised his voice yet, but I could tell his blood was up.

"No, sir, you had orders to attend the briefing with the company. General Glade gave me different orders," I said. "Perhaps you should take it up with him."

"General Glade?" he asked. "Why wasn't I invited?"

"I have a better question," I said. "Why was I invited? From what I could tell, the briefing was for generals and their staffs."

Moffat thought about this for a moment. Though I tried to downplay it, there was an implicit threat in what I said. If I was invited to that meeting, it meant that at least one of those generals wanted me around. Since Moffat was not invited, it meant that none of the generals knew he existed. As he considered this, he took a step back, and the muscles along his jaw relaxed.

"Care to share anything that you learned?" he asked.

I shook my head. "I wish I could, sir," I said. For what it was worth, I sincerely did wish I could discuss the briefing with Moffat and every man in the company. I did not like it when officers kept potentially important information from the men who needed it most, the ones who put their lives on the line.

"You will tell me what you can, when you can?" Moffat asked. His belligerence had melted away. I think he recognized that I had heard something that genuinely rocked me—something even more disturbing than the casualty figures.

I nodded.

"I need you to rearrange the roster; Command wants volunteers to guard the Hen House," Moffat said. "The paperwork is in the company office. They want our roster within the hour." We traded salutes, and Moffat walked off, still a prick, but a prick who knew when to back down.

Most of the company was out for the night. With so many Marines dead, they would keep the celebrations subdued, but as far as they knew, they had not only just won a battle, they might have won the war. Heavy losses or not, they had the right to celebrate. I could have gone into town and joined them, but I knew the truth—we were in worse trouble than ever, and, at the moment, I could not bring myself to drink with guys whom I might shortly betray. When the Avatars regenerated, I would send the men out thinking they were engaged in a fair fight against an enemy who could be killed. I was keeping secrets from men whose lives were on the line, and that made me no different than any natural-born officer.

I went to my company office and found the orders Moffat had left for me. They came directly from Major Terry Burton, our battalion commander.

Leaning back in my chair, I picked the orders up off the desk and read. Burton had not attended the briefing at the Science Lab, but he knew the score. These were orders for every platoon in our regiment to provide three men to protect the Hen House. That was the name we gave the compound in which the officers kept their wives and families. These were the kinds of orders you gave when you needed to dig in and hold your position.

I listed Herrington, Skittles, and Philips. I chose Herrington because of all the men in my platoon, he was the one who pushed himself the hardest. He needed a break. I sent Skittles because I liked the kid, and I thought he would have better odds protecting the Hen House than on the front line. As for Philips, this was my chance to do something with him before he got himself killed. Muttering to myself about this being Philips's lucky day, I keyed the new roster into the computer and forwarded it to Base Command.

When they returned from their night out, Philips, Herrington, and Skittles would find new orders waiting for them on their racks. They would fly out to the Hen House first thing in the morning.

As I sat at the duty desk, I considered all that had happened that day. I felt tired and hungry, so I went to the mess and ate a good dinner. Then I returned to my quarters and climbed into bed.

23

We held the funeral at 0600 the following morning.

The Army guarded the city while the Marines buried their dead. More than three hundred thousand Marines—enlisted men in white combat armor, officers in dress uniforms—assembled in rows as straight as razor blades, standing still as grave markers as they waited for the honored to arrive. We used a city park with four baseball diamonds, two soccer fields, and a long stretch of rolling pasture for our assembly. The Corps of Engineers removed the fences and goals from the various fields to create a large enough contiguous space to accommodate us all.

We stood at attention, facing an enormous stage on which sat General Glade, the highest-ranking Marine on New Copenhagen, General Morris Newcastle, the Army commander who had made such an ass of himself at the briefing in the Science Lab, and General James Hill, representing the Air Force. Along with the generals sat twenty-five civilians in dark suits—five turned out to be U.A. senators who had flown in to oversee the battle preparations, five were local politicians, and the other fifteen were their bodyguards.

"Ten-hut!"

We snapped to attention.

An honor guard marched in bearing flags—the flag of the Unified Authority, the banner of the Orion Arm, the flag of New Copenhagen, the ceremonial flag of the Confederate Arms, and the red-and-gold standard of the Unified Authority Marine Corps.

A horse came forward pulling an antique caisson bearing the flag-draped coffin of a single unknown Marine. This man would be buried here. Should we survive this battle, a monument would follow. The other eighty thousand fallen were on their way to an industrial-strength crematory, likely a glass factory or some other location with an oven and an assembly line. The horse hung its head as it dragged the caisson. Steam formed around the horse's nose when it exhaled. The wheels of the wagon cut a groove through the soggy grass and snow.

Three columns of servicemen carrying antique bolt-action rifles marched behind the caisson. The Marine honor guard marched on the right, the Air Force marched on the left, and the Army honor guard formed the column in the middle.

Next came the pledges, the oaths, and the prayers, followed by the speeches. One by one, they all stood up and spoke... every last self-important man on that specking stage except for the bodyguards. The generals took precisely five minutes each. The politicians took ten or fifteen. The entire service took three hours.

I heard the speeches via the interLink, each voice rolling around in my helmet like a song you can't tune out. From the opening bugle to the closing remarks, I heard it all as clearly as if I had been sitting on the stand.

Snow started to fall. Heavy inch-wide flakes drifted down from the sky, first in a scattered dusting, then in a heavy bombardment.

After the speeches came a twenty-one-gun salute performed by the servicemen who marched behind with the caisson.

"Ready!" shouted the colonel leading the salute.

The men raised the antique rifles in perfect unison.

"Aim!"

They fixed their sights on the same invisible target.

"Fire!"

Twenty-one rifles fired as one, shattering the perfect silence. The horse drawing the caisson started, but it did not buck.

"Ready!"

The men snapped the bolts back and loaded another round.

"Aim!"

They raised their rifles.

"Fire!"

They fired again, then repeated the process one last time.

The bugler blew "Taps." I could not hear that music without thinking of the men with whom I had served. I thought of Vince Lee, my first real friend. I thought about Fleet Admiral Bryce Klyber and Sergeant Tabor Shannon, both great men in their times. One was natural-born and died a hero, the other a Liberator and died heroically.

The color guard left, the politicians left, then the generals departed. The fighting men were the last to leave. It took half an hour for us to file off the field.

What was happening on Earth? I wondered. They could not know that eighty thousand men had died in a single day of battle, nor could they know the utter meaninglessness of those deaths. Hell, only a handful of men on this planet knew that we could not kill this enemy. Did anybody care what happened to a few thousand clones back on Earth? For all I knew, they were fighting for their lives as well.

Despite our spearhead role in the battle, my company had lost only twenty-three men. That may sound like a lot, but it was only one-sixth of our men. During the latter part of the battle, some companies lost entire platoons.

When I returned to the barracks after lunch, I saw the "holes"— the stripped racks and emptied lockers of men who had died. They left a temporary scar. By the end of the day, Base Command would rearrange the roster. The platoons with the heaviest losses would be disbanded, their men sent to other platoons to fill the holes. Since we lost so few men, we would receive survivors from some of those disbanded units. In the past, our commanders would have sent us new recruits fresh out of boot camp, but there were no new recruits left on New Copenhagen by this time. We were all veterans.

"It's not over yet, is it?" Sergeant Thomer came to meet me when he saw me enter the barracks.

"I don't see how this can end as long as they have that light field around the planet. We're still trapped. They're still out there..."

"Do you think they will send a bigger army next time, sir?" Thomer asked.

"Let's grab a cup of coffee," I said. Then, as we left the barracks, I told him the things I could not tell him in front of the other men. "As long as the Mudders have those light spheres, there's nothing stopping them from sending in more soldiers."

Thomer took a long, deep breath as he tried to still himself. We headed down to one of the hotel restaurants—in use as a mess hall. "They let you in on more about this than the rest of us, didn't they?"

"Probably," I said.

"But you can't talk about it."

"Probably not," I said.

"But it's bad," Thomer guessed.

"I'm not going to talk about it," I said. "But it isn't good." We entered the mess. The place was empty this late in the morning. In another hour, the early-lunch crowd would roll in—assuming we were not heading back out to the front. Only a few men waited in the cafeteria line. We stood alone by Coffee Machine Row, filling our mugs and speaking in the relative privacy.

"One of the guys, Boll maybe, thought the Mudders might take down the curtain if we hit them hard enough... You know, maybe drop the curtain so they can land more men. He figures the Navy has ships circling the planet and they'll drop off supplies and men once the curtain goes down," Thomer said. "Does that sound possible?"

Supplies. I had forgotten all about supplies. "The military can't afford to waste men or bullets," Admiral Brocius had said as he handed me his pistol, and he was right. How many rockets had the Army fired as they defended the Vista Street bunker? How many did they have left? This much I knew—during that last battle, we had lost one-fifth of our Marines.

"I would not know anything about that, Sergeant," I told Thomer. "I hope you are right, though. I hope we can get more men and supplies."

We went to sit down at a secluded table. "What about the rest of the men?" I asked. "How is your platoon holding up?"

"Most of them think we won," Thomer said.

"We did," I said.

"Won the war," Thomer clarified.

"Yeah, well, we certainly won the battle," I said.

"I don't get that feeling," Thomer said. "You know something, and I know better than to ask what it might be." He stared into my face, trying to read me.

"I need you to keep your suspicions to yourself," I said. "Troop morale is strong right now, let's keep it that way."

I finished my coffee. I drank it black, strong and hot. It tasted good, fairly fresh. As I started to leave, Thomer asked, "Some of the guys moved out this morning. I heard you signed them up for some kind of guard duty."

"Battalion command wanted a detail to guard the Hen House," I said. "I figured it might be a smart idea to send Philips with them... get him out of the line of fire until he gets his head straight."

Thomer placed his cup down on the counter and stared at me. He looked angry, maybe exasperated. "The compound for officers' families?" he asked. "Are you shitting me? Please tell me that you're joking."

"What's the problem?" I asked.

"A few years ago, Philips nearly got himself court-martialed for screwing around with some officer's wife. Officers' wives are his favorite brand of scrub."

"Shit," I said.

Thomer said nothing.

I thought about calling him back and sending a replacement but opted against it. Depressed as he was, scrub would probably be the last thing on his mind. At least that was what I told myself.

The Army continued repairing its bunkers and servicing its rocket launchers. Apparently the Avatars had broken through our lines somewhere near Vista Street. If the rumors were true, they shot so many holes into a small section of bunker that it caved in under its own weight.

Since we Marines were technically an invasion force, we had nothing to rebuild. Every company in the Marines had a platoon assigned to support ops, and they performed any rebuilding or refurbishing we needed done.

Except for the latrine scrubbers and potato peelers in the support platoon, the company had too little to do while we waited for the next attack. Some men spent their free time roving around Valhalla. I decided to go back out to the spheres, the place General Glade now called "Camp Avatar." I wasn't looking for a fight, per se, but I did want to leave the Avatars a housewarming present.

Before leaving, I needed to locate Ray Freeman to ask if he wanted to join me on this excursion. Unfortunately, I could not find him. I left messages at Base Command and the Science Lab then went to requisition some hardware.

Upon taking control of the property, the Marines converted the hotel's underground parking facility into an armory. Riding the elevator down reminded me of heading through a department store.

The sign on the first floor of the garage said, "Combat Armor and Small Arms." Second floor—"Rockets, Mortars, and Grenades." Third floor—"Motor Pool: Tanks, Jackals, Jeeps, ATVs, and Robots."

When I asked the supply officer on the third floor what I might find on the lower floors, he said, "You don't want to go down to the fourth." Then he leaned over his duty desk, and whispered, "There are enough nukes down there to fry this entire planet. We might lose this battle, but we are not going to lose the war, if you know what I mean."

"Aren't you worried about leaks?" I asked. The officer was wearing fatigues that offered no protection against radiation.

"Not me," he said. "What's the worst that can happen—I start shooting blanks? Sounds like a beni in my book. Those guys who designed the clones had it right from the start. 'Copulate, don't populate.' Heh. Words to live by."

I pretended to laugh. I, of course, was a clone. So was the duty officer, though the dolt would never so much as suspect it. With a mind like his, the death reflex was the least of this guy's worries.

"Look," I said, "I want to check out a Jackal and three trackers."

"The trackers are no problem, sir, but I'll need authorization before I can give you a Jackal," he said. "For anything bigger than a motorcycle, I need approval from Base Command."

A communications console sat on the desk. I reached toward it, paused, and asked, "Will General Glade do?"

"Sure," the duty officer said with a snide smile. "You just ring up your old pal J.P. Glade and get his approval."

I punched in the code, and Glade's assistant appeared on the screen. I asked to speak to the general—it never pays to aim low— and the aide sent me up the ladder to a captain, who passed me to a major, who sent me to one of the colonels who attended the briefing at the Science Lab.

"What is it, Harris?" he asked.

"I need to requisition some equipment, sir," I said.

"You're calling the general's line for a requisition?" the colonel sounded incredulous.

"Yes, sir," I said. "I'm down here in the Armory, and—"

"Put the duty officer on," the colonel snapped.

"Right here, sir," he said, his voice nearly cracking.

The colonel looked at the duty officer, and said, "What the hell is the matter with you, boy? Give the lieutenant anything he wants. You got that?" Then he ended the connection.

I drove out of the garage with a Jackal, three trackers, an M27, two particle-beam cannons, and three combat helmets. Anyone else would have spliced video cameras into the trackers, but I knew nothing about electronics. I broke things; I did not splice them.

Before leaving, I returned to my quarters to put on my armor. I found a message from Freeman on my communications console, so I called him back and told him what I had in mind. He said he wanted to come along. An hour later, Freeman showed up wearing his custom-made oversized combat armor, and we drove into the woods just north of town.

We drove in silence—Freeman observing everything we passed and me holding a silent conversation with myself. No surprise. I had learned years ago that time spent in the company of Ray Freeman was lonelier than time spent completely alone.

The Jackal handled just like a jeep, though it had a lot more power. It had built-in radar. A screen on the dashboard showed an overhead readout of the world around us. Remembering how the Avatars' light bolts had shot through these vehicles as if they were made of papier-mâché, I did not bother with the retractable armor. If we ran into aliens, the armor would not protect us.

"What do you think it will take to win this thing?" I finally asked. We had been driving for half an hour.

"What makes you think we can win?" Freeman asked.

"Do your scientist friends have any ideas?" I asked.

"Sweetwater thinks we can win, but he has no idea how," Freeman said.

"Who?"

"Dr. Sweetwater, he's the head of the Science Lab."

"Was he the guy who gave the briefing?" I asked.

"That was Dr. Breeze."

I programmed in the path our convoy had taken on the way to the battle. That got us deep into the woods, where we slowed down to a mere twenty miles per hour, just fast enough to present a difficult target should we run into trouble.

"Sweetwater thinks we might stop them from coming back if we can block their signal," Freeman said.

"Block their signal?" I said. "Then what happens?"

"Nothing happens," Freeman said. "The invasion gets unplugged."

"Wow, unplug an invading army. I like it. Can he really do that?" I asked.

Freeman did not answer my question.

We bounced over a stream. Trees shot by on either side of the Jackal. Our radar showed no signs of enemy vehicles or armies, just open woods and lots of trees. Of course, I had no idea if the radar could detect an Avatar. "Looks like we have the forest to ourselves," I said as I stopped the Jackal. According to my map, we were still a few hundred yards from the spheres.

The new snow had not yet settled to the ground. Hoarfrost coated the trees, and mostly frozen mud covered most of the ground. Freeman did a visual scan of the area and nodded. We parked and unpacked the equipment.

"Why did you bring these helmets?" Freeman asked, lifting one of the helmets, then tossing it back in the bay.

"Surveillance," I said.

"Isn't that why they make surveillance cameras?" Freeman asked. He carried all three trackers and both particle-beam cannons and the M27 in the crook of his left arm while keeping his particle-beam pistol at the ready in his right hand. He left the helmets for me.

I rolled the helmets into a rucksack and closed the back of the Jackal. "Security cameras work great if you know how to install them."

"They clip right on to the tracker. Where are you going to place the helmets?"

"I haven't thought about it," I said.

"You're an officer, you could have had a tech install them," Freeman said.

"This way I can watch what happens on the interLink. I registered the helmets up as members of my platoon."

Freeman shook his head.

"What's the matter?"

"You're setting this up so you can watch over the interLink? Limited range, unstable signal…"

Freeman was right. With the interLink's limited range, the Hotel Valhalla would be on the outer reach of good reception. "What kind of range would I get with a surveillance camera?" I asked.

"Unlimited," Freeman said. He wasn't being rude or snappy. For him, this was downright chatty.

"How do you access the signal?" I asked.

"Satellite telemetry," Freeman said.

"A satellite signal? Will it get through the curtain?"

Other men might have stopped to slap their forehead or curse. Ray Freeman kept walking. "No, it would not get through," Freeman finally said.

"I didn't think so," I said. "With the planet sleeved, you'd just get static."

"You might not get anything," Freeman said. He sounded distant now, his mind was on other things.

We crossed a particularly dense grove of trees, then the foliage thinned. The bright glare of one of the spheres showed above the light from the curtain. As we approached, though, I saw that the trees around the sphere had begun to wither. The area looked like it had been exposed to radiation or toxic chemicals. The needles in the pine trees had turned from emerald green to a sickly lime green color.

The row of trees closest to the portal took the worst of it. They had clearly died. Their rust-colored needles looked hard as nails, and their bark had faded nearly white. I got the feeling that the rigid branches would shatter like glass long before they would snap.

In a normal military facility, you would find guards. Even when armies launched an all-out assault, they kept guards around their camps. The Avatars did not leave guards, however. They really did not need them since they had nothing to steal and nothing to break. Hell, technically speaking, they had never even set foot on the planet.

Freeman placed two of the trackers on the ground, then started to plant the third a few feet from the sphere.

"Not there," I said, remembering how the sphere dilated as it generated troops. "It's too close. The sphere might spread over it."

Without saying a word, Freeman wrapped his hand around the shaft of the tracker and pulled it out of the ground. He stepped back twenty feet or so and drove it into the ground a second time.

I picked up one of the two trackers Freeman had laid in the mud. I would arm this one with the M27. I had a pretty good idea what would happen when it opened fire, but I needed to make sure. I carried the robotic sentry beyond the first row of trees, trees that were completely dead from exposure to the sphere. I considered leaving it here, then decided to take it back farther. There would be plenty of time to experiment with the effects of direct exposure to the spheres.

I went about thirty feet away from the clearing where the trees seemed to have suffered only mildly from the effects of the sphere. Turning to make sure that the tracker would have an unobstructed view of the target, I stabbed the shaft into the frozen soil.

"You want them grouped?" Freeman asked me.

"We'll call this one twelve o'clock. Place the others at four and eight," I said.

"That leaves one tracker where they'll find it," Freeman warned me.

"Yes," I agreed. "I don't think they'll notice it."

Freeman stabbed the last tracker into the ground.

We could not place the combat helmets on the tops of the tracking poles. The top was taken up by a motion-tracking sensor housed in a four-inch ball. We placed the helmets at the feet of the trackers, then I used optical commands to tap into each helmet and check its view of the sphere.

"So where are the Avatars right now?" I asked as we left the clearing.

"Probably in there," Freeman said, sparing once last glance back at the energy spheres.

"I wonder if they know we are out here?" I asked. When Freeman shrugged, I added, "You never know, maybe tachyons have eyes."

24

We did not hear from the Avatars for two more days. They returned on the morning of the third day.

The day began with Corporal Boll pulling the first watch duty. That meant that he spent three hours sitting in front of an interLink-compatible command console. The console had forty-five five-inch screens, enough to assign one to each member of the platoon. We only used three of those screens, one for each of the helmets we left by the spheres. At 0300 hours, Thomer sent a man to replace Boll. At 0600, a third man took over. The spheres came to life at 0637.

The alarm rang on the communications console beside my bed. When I answered, Thomer said, "Lieutenant Harris, you better get down here, sir."

"The Mudders?" I asked.

"The spheres are getting bigger," Thomer said.

I rolled out of bed and punched up Freeman. "Freeman," I said, "it's on."

"Can you record it?" he asked.

"Yeah," I said.

"I'll get there as quick as I can." By the sound of things, he'd left the hotel but had not gone very far. I did not have time to think about it.

Barely taking the time to throw on my uniform, I headed for the ballroom barracks. I passed Lieutenant Moffat in the hall. Definitely an aging athlete, Moffat had just come in from a long run in the cold. His face was pink, and his bristly hair was clumped with sweat. He looked winded but not exhausted. He wore the general-issue shorts and T-shirt of the Marines, his perspiration making the shirt adhere to his chest.

"Where are you going?" he asked in an accusing tone.

"Freeman and I left the Mudders a surprise by their base," I said. Personally, I preferred the term "Avatar," but Moffat was not among the elite group cleared to hear it. As far as he was concerned, the aliens were still "Mudders," and we were able to kill them.

"Who authorized that action?" Moffat asked. The man could not help himself, acting like a prick came naturally to him.

"General Newcastle, General Glade... Freeman pretty much has carte blanche around here," I said, trying to sound oblivious to the fact that I had gone over Moffat's head. Then I decided to offer an olive branch. "They're just beginning to arrive," I said. "Want to watch?"

"What did you leave there?" Moffat asked, interest edging his voice.

"I left a couple of helmets. We're watching ground zero over the interLink."

"Are you heading over to General Glade's office?"

"No, sir. This was strictly a personal experiment," I said. "We have a command console set up in the barracks."

"Nice, Harris. Very nice." Moffat used that line so often that it sounded worse than canned.

We took the elevator to the mezzanine and trotted into the Valkyrie Ballroom. By this time a crowd had formed around the console. Men in boxers and undershirts were pushing in for a look. Moffat and I cut through the crowd.

"What's going on?" I asked.

"The sphere is getting real big," Boll said. "We haven't seen any Mudders yet."

"Is that where the Mudders come from?" Moffat asked. His mouth formed a strange sneer, the kind of fascinated repulsion you might see on a little girl as she watched a spider eating its prey. "What are those things?"

"I'm guessing it's a broadcast device," I said, lying and not looking back to see if Moffat took the bait.

Avatars appeared. First they showed as gold-colored smudges. I held my breath. In another moment, the aliens would step out of their incubator, and the trackers would open fire. With any luck, the particle beams would shred them.

The first row of Avatars took shape and strode out of the sphere. Nothing happened. The trackers did not open fire.

"Whose idea was it to place helmets out there?" Moffat asked, his eyes riveted to the screen.

"My idea, sir." It took me a few seconds to answer. I was distracted. Why weren't the trackers firing? What was wrong with them?

"Having cameras around ground zero was a good idea, Harris. I'm surprised the Science Lab didn't come up with it," Moffat said.

"They did." Freeman's low rumbling voice rolled over us. "They placed radars and cameras out there four days ago, but the experiment failed."

"Satellite telemetry?" I asked, remembering the conversation we had as we placed the trackers.

Freeman did not answer. He did not need to answer. One thing about Ray Freeman, he only spoke when he saw the need. I looked away from the monitor just long enough for a quick glance at him. He stood just behind the crowd, towering over the rest of us. No expression showed on his dark face. His lips were pressed together, and his eyes were focused hard on the screens.

Around the console, Marines chattered back and forth as they watched; but I filtered out most of what they said. I concentrated instead on the three screens.

"Too bad you didn't stick some trackers out there as well—maybe you could have massacred those bastards as they climbed out of their shell," Moffat said. I heard lots of agreement among the men.

"We did," I said.

By this time, dozens of Avatars had emerged from the sphere, maybe even hundreds. The trackers should have opened fire.

"We did place trackers, trackers armed with particle-beam cannons," I said.

"Did you forget to switch them on or something?" Moffat asked. Like the rest of us, he did not look away from the screen as he spoke.

"They're not detecting motion," Freeman said.

"What is that supposed to mean?" Moffat asked. "I've seen trackers D-and-D a specking grasshopper from three hundred yards off." "D-and-D" was Marine-speak for "detect and destroy."

Freeman ignored Moffat.

"What are those things?" someone else asked.

"They're the Mudders," said Boll.

"They aren't anything like the bastards I saw," the first Marine said. He sounded confused, maybe even scared.

Then came the sirens signaling the call to quarters. "Suit up," Moffat shouted.

I, of course, had to run back to my room to get my armor. As I headed for the door, I heard Moffat shout, "Hey, Harris, not bad." He smiled and nodded his head. "Not bad."

25

As the Avatars left their spheres, they took substance, and the early-warning radars that the Corps of Engineers rigged in the forest read movements that our trackers missed. As the klaxons rang through the Hotel Valhalla, Base Command circulated the battle report. An estimated fifty thousand Mudders were headed toward town.

Freeman and I were not the only ones who came up with the idea of using trackers. Trying to find ways to whittle the aliens' numbers down before we met them, the Corps of Engineers placed a number of booby traps along the path that the aliens had used in their previous attacks. The Corps planted a small grove of trackers along the top of a ten-foot rise one mile in from the spheres.

Their trackers worked no better than the ones that Freeman and I left behind. The Avatars had not picked up enough substance for the Corps' sensors to detect them. A half mile later, however, they passed another bank of trackers. By this time enough tachyons had attached themselves to the Avatars for motion sensors to read their movements. They opened fire with particle-beam cannons and M27s, dropping hundreds of Avatars as they marched by. The aliens retaliated, cutting the robots down with their light rifles.

The Corps of Engineers had placed canisters of noxium gas in one secluded glade. As the Avatars entered, the Corps released the flesh-eating gas, but it had no effect on the aliens as they had no flesh. Any deer or rabbits unlucky enough to meander into that glade, however, would have been reduced to soup.

The Army began its first rocket barrage while the Avatars were still out in the forest. They hauled out the big guns this time, surface-to-surface rockets that combined explosive procession and incineration. By the time the Avatars finally reached the edge of town, their army was down to no more than twenty-three thousand, a force that our soldiers dispatched from the Vista Street bunker with small rockets and machine guns.

Two regiments of Marines were sent into the woods to flush out and finish any stragglers, but there were no stragglers. The Avatars pressed forward into the line of fire until every last one of them was dead or broken.

We only lost twelve hundred men during the third battle for Valhalla, but our armory was severely depleted.

The rank and file did not know it, but they were on a sinking ship. Enlisted men and officers alike went out to celebrate yet another easy victory, but those of us who knew the score did not participate. Our ship had struck an iceberg, but it was sinking so slowly that the passengers didn't realize it.

26

Sweetwater and Breeze...

Arthur Breeze, you will recall, stood a bony six feet four and could not have even weighed 150 pounds. His skull was the size of a watermelon, and his teeth would have fitted on a horse, but the rest of his body vanished in the lab coat that hung from his shoulders. The lenses on his glasses were a half-inch thick, a collage of greasy fingerprints, dandruff, and shed hairs. Some people might have described him as "forehead bald," but I think he stretched the term. If he was "forehead bald," his forehead extended clear up to the crown of his head. What hair he had was a disorganized swatch of filament-fine white strands that formed a saddle-shaped band around his head.

Breeze was not the chief scientist at the Science Lab, he was the chief briefing officer. It did not take long to see that Breeze's talents lent themselves more to science than presentations.

William Sweetwater, the top scientist at the lab, was a dwarf. He barely cleared the four-foot mark. He was too short to pass the height restrictions for a fast roller coaster in a theme park, not that he looked like the kind of man who went out for thrills.

He had long, stringy black hair that hung down every side of his globe-shaped head. He had a potbelly and massive shoulders, like an athlete gone to seed. He stood more than two feet smaller than Breeze and probably outweighed the man by twenty pounds.

Until the moment William Sweetwater opened his mouth, I believed Arthur Breeze was the smartest man in the galaxy. But when Sweetwater spoke, everyone with any sense would shut up and listen.

The briefing took place in the basement of the building. This time it was for generals and up, even their staffs had to wait outside. There were five generals on the planet—one from the Marines, three from the Army, and one very contrite general from the Air Force. Freeman attended as a consultant and invited me along for the ride.

"That was some shock you gave us, Harris." Sweetwater looked at me as he said this.

"Us," in this case, referred to Sweetwater alone. He generally spoke about himself in the plural. He had a high, crackly voice. "It never occurred to us to consider what effect the ion curtain might have on existing satellite communications."

Sweetwater waddled around the room handing each visitor a five-page document. "This is a list of computer and communications systems that rely on satellite communications. Since the systems were not destroyed, we never got emergency messages; the signals just sort of blipped out."

I scanned the list. There was the local mediaLink—the system that hosted current events, entertainment broadcasting, and a large portion of civilian messaging traffic. I saw an item on the list and smiled—the New Copenhagen Emergency Broadcast System relied on satellite transmissions.

"Most of these systems do not impact your operations," Breeze said. His voice was low. He had the dried-out voice of a very old man, though he could not have been older than forty. "As Dr. Sweetwater pointed out, we didn't even notice when they failed."

"Raymond brought it to our attention," Sweetwater said. I

got the feeling that Sweetwater genuinely liked Freeman. He and his team were lab-coat intellectuals, men of science, not action. Freeman, a mercenary whose knowledge of science only extended to areas in which it impacted his work, must have impressed them as smarter than a soldier and braver than a scientist.

"We have rerouted most of these systems," Sweetwater said. That "we" probably referred to his team of scientists and engineers. "Even the mediaLink is restored. Thanks to Dr. Breeze, the youth of New Copenhagen can once again watch mindless cartoons and sports shows."

Breeze blushed and smiled—an ugly sight with those big teeth of his.

Looking over the list, I saw that it included the facility that managed the planetwide sewage system. I hoped the temporary blackout had not caused backwash—at least not in range of Valhalla.

"Have you restored the signal from the Seismic Activity Station?" Freeman asked as he flipped through the list.

"You noticed that, did you?" Sweetwater asked. "That was the one that concerned us the most. We expected to hear something if there was any activity anywhere on the planet. Of course, with the satellite link broken, we didn't hear anything at all."

Sweetwater walked over to a lab stool that was nearly as tall as he was and, with some effort, climbed high enough to sit down on it. "Maybe it was a lucky coincidence that we lost that signal. When we reestablished it, we did a little extra poking around to see if we had missed anything. The settings on the equipment were pretty low. The seismic station was mostly used for surveying earthquakes and volcanic activity.

"Dr. Breeze found a way to reroute the signal through a ground network, then he boosted the sensitivity. What a good piece of work that turned out to be." Sweetwater turned and nodded to Breeze, who blushed a second time. "It turns out that there is a lot more going on around this planet than we previously thought."

Sweetwater hopped off the stool.

Either the university did not have money for cutting-edge

holographic displays, or Sweetwater preferred not to use them. The dwarf opened a cabinet and pulled out a two-foot-tall globe that looked enormous in his pudgy hands. The thing was half his size.

He placed the globe on a counter. Spinning the ball slowly, he got his bearings. "Marduck Mountains... okay..." he muttered. Then turning to his audience, he said, "This spot here is Valhalla." He gave the globe a half turn and placed his thumb on a new spot. "We have discovered significant underground activity in this region. We will provide precise coordinates in our report. As you can see, the activity is occurring on this equatorial line. We do not know who is causing the disturbance."

"If someone is digging on this planet, I think we can all guess who it might be," General Newcastle said.

Looking at General Morris Newcastle up close, I didn't like what I saw. He looked more like a cantankerous old man than a supreme commander, someone who bullied underlings and wore his power like a medal. Sweetwater spotted this as well. The difference between Sweetwater and Breeze was that while Breeze allowed Newcastle to intimidate him, Sweetwater had the smarts and the self-confidence to put the general in his place.

"If you know something that we don't, General Newcastle, feel free to enlighten us," Sweetwater snapped in a clear, impatient voice. The dwarf stood silent, a bored look on his face, as he waited for the Army general to reply.

"Well, it's obvious who's digging there. There are only two parties on this planet, us and the Avatars, and we sure as hell know that we aren't digging." Newcastle laughed. So did the other generals from the Army. They laughed alone.

"You may be right, General, but if you are, the Avatari seem more concerned about digging than beating your forces," Sweetwater said. That was the first time I heard the term "Avatari." I liked it. The term "avatar" referred to a virtual representation. "Avatari" was a name for an actual enemy, and it did not sound nearly as juvenile as "Mudders."

"What do you mean?" Newcastle asked, his face red with anger.

"If the seismic readings are accurate, we estimate that the Avatari have a force of five hundred thousand, maybe even one million laborers, working in their underground site around the clock. Based on the numbers, it seems pretty obvious that they place more emphasis on clearing this underground site than beating your forces."

Newcastle's round face turned so red I thought he might have swallowed his tongue. He muttered something that sounded like, "You little runt," then went silent. He stared down at Sweetwater, who, in turn, stared right back at him. Sweetwater met the general's glare with a heavy-lidded expression.

"Excuse me," General Glade interjected, "but do we know what the Avatari are digging for?"

"Frankly, we have no idea what they are looking for," Sweetwater answered. "In fact, sending some men to investigate their dig site would be a wise precaution."

Glade nodded, then looked over at me. "Harris, you up for that?"

"Now wait a..." General Newcastle began. "The Army..."

"I'll go with you," Freeman said. Newcastle fell silent.

"Sounds like it's settled," said Sweetwater. "Are there any questions?"

"Have you made any progress figuring out a way to kill these Avatari things?" Newcastle asked.

"It seems to me like you have a pretty good handle on that," Sweetwater said, absolutely no trace of malice in his voice. "From what Arthur tells us, you broke their line in three hours with minimal casualties."

"Are you aware of how many rockets we fired off?" General Newcastle asked. "If we keep using rockets at that rate, our supplies won't last the week."

"How low are we?" Hill, the Air Force general, asked.

"I'm down by a third on my STS supplies. I've got plenty of guns and grenades, and I'm doing all right on tanks. We'd be a lot better off if we could get your birds in the air," Newcastle said.

"I already told you, the interference we get from the ion curtain has my boys grounded," Hill said. "The flight computers in our fighters shut down at one thousand feet."

"Fly low," Newcastle said.

"Like you did with your gunships?" asked Hill.

"If your pilots can't fly, maybe we should put them on the front line," Newcastle said.

"Let's play nice, boys," Glade interrupted.

Newcastle exhaled deeply and nodded. "The way things are going now, it seems like the only way to beat the sons of bitches is to smother them with troops or throw fireworks at them. Combining the two doesn't work so well—we end up losing a whole bunch of both."

Glade shook his head. "I lost twenty percent of my troops last time I sent them in the forest. Two, three more battles like the one we had last week and I'll be hurting for men."

"We need another solution," Newcastle told Sweetwater. "How long before you can have something for us?"

"What are you looking for?" Sweetwater asked.

"You say these Avatari just rebuild themselves every time we kill them? Fine. How long will it take you to find a way to stop them from rebuilding themselves?"

Taking a moment to consider the question, Sweetwater climbed back on his stool. His eyes never falling away from General Newcastle's, he said, "We can't even begin to guess."

"Then what the hell good are you?" Newcastle shouted. "You might as well be up on the line."

"We're dealing with an entirely alien technology that we never even knew existed. For all we know, the laws of physics as we know them do not apply in their world."

"The existence of tachyons was just a theory until the aliens landed," added Arthur Breeze. "Our scientists did not have the technology to prove that they existed."

"We need time," Sweetwater said.

General Newcastle nodded and turned to the other generals. "We defend the Science Lab at all costs. If we're going to win this thing, the answers are going to come from here."

The other generals grumbled in agreement.

"So it comes down to men or matériel," General Glade said. "Which can we afford to give up first?"

"We burn through the men," Newcastle said. "I'll assign my white-haired privates to man the line for an attack or two. Time to thin the herd and conserve the rockets."

I heard echoes in my head. I imagined every antisynthetic officer under whom I had ever served making similar decisions about clones. I imagined Admiral Thurston sending two thousand cloned Marines to a planet named Little Man, not for a battle as they had been told, but simply as bait. And I thought of Admiral Brocius stranding sixty thousand clone Marines on the Mogat home world as the planet melted around them.

Hearing the cavalier way in which the generals treated men and matériel, I felt a familiar angry pang. They judged everything in terms of expendability. First they would sacrifice the old clones, then the young ones, then the rockets, and finally the expendable natural-borns. Sooner or later, everything became expendable to these men except themselves.

PART II
THE AVATARI

27

The mood around Valhalla remained exuberant. All anybody seemed to know was that we had beaten back the Mudders and that this latest victory was the easiest so far.

Freeman and I returned to the hotel in time to see a truck loaded with Marines in fatigues driving out of the parking lot. The men in the back of the truck carried M27s, but they looked more like a hunting party than Marines on a mission.

A second group of men with M27s waited by the hotel entrance. "Where are you going?" I asked a corporal.

"Dog hunting, sir," he replied.

"Dog hunting?"

"Yes, sir. You know all those strays you see around town? A couple of them up and bit somebody. Base Command is offering a fifty-dollar reward for every dog pelt we bring in."

Most of the men held open bottles of beer in one hand and M27s in the other. Just beyond them I saw another group of would-be hunters waiting for a truck, and another group beyond them. Soon the town might be filled with half-drunk Marines shooting stray dogs and guzzling beer.

At first I felt angry about the waste of bullets, then I realized that even if I collected every bullet shot at every dog, I might not have enough firepower to bring down a single Avatar. Somebody in the chain of command was thinking. Scanning the parking lot, I sensed the excitement. A few of the guys might accidentally shoot each other, but the costs would be minimal compared to morale value.

Freeman and I went to the mess hall.

We walked down the food line, selecting dishes. The choices would have made for a fine breakfast, lunch, or dinner. There was bacon, steak, biscuits, vegetables, fruits in sugar syrups, ham, hot cereal, and soup. The salad bar was closed, but the cooks had left out plates with chef and vegetable salads. With the sky bright all day long and men on alternating shifts, breakfast, lunch, and dinner all mixed into each other.

"Hunting dogs," Freeman said as he loaded up his plate. "Does that make sense to you?"

"Sure it does," I said. "We wouldn't want those dogs to bite anyone."

Freeman did not respond.

"It's not about killing dogs," I said. "Those men are too busy thinking about scoring a fifty-dollars bounty to worry about being stuck on a planet with an alien army. It's a damn good morale booster."

Freeman took five fried eggs, a T-bone steak, and a football-sized wad of green beans. He also took two glasses of milk and a glass of orange juice. I picked up a bacon cheeseburger, saw the way the heat lamps had shriveled the bun, and put it back in the bin. Instead, I chose a plate with dried-out fried chicken and petrified french fries.

We carried our trays to an empty corner of the mess and sat down. "When do you want to leave for the dig site?" I asked. "I can set up a chopper and a pilot." I picked up a piece of chicken and took a bite of it. The skin was greasy, the meat was dry, but the flavor was fine.

"I'll fly us," Freeman said. Using his fork, he cut one of his eggs into three nearly equal triangles. The yolk had apparently solidified under the heat lamps and barely ran.

"You can fly a helicopter?" I asked.

"We'll take a transport." Military transports, the flying kind, were short-range birds used mostly for shuttling troops to and from ships. They were big, clunky, unarmed beasts with thick shields and no weapons. I knew Freeman could fly transports; I'd ridden with him before.

"I never thought of that," I said. If we ran into the Avatari, a transport would have a better chance of surviving their light bolts than a helicopter. The bolts would pierce the shields and pass right through the fuselage, but it would take a lucky shot to bring a transport down.

"Will you need time to arrange the transport?" I asked. I drank my juice and water but only picked at the french fries. The grease from the chicken felt heavy in my stomach.

"I might need an hour or two," Freeman said. He looked tired.

"Sounds good," I said as I got up from the table. I picked up my tray and started for a busing station.

"And Harris, bring standard armor, not the white stuff," Freeman said. He was right. If New Copenhagen was anything like Earth, the lower hemisphere would be warmer when the upper hemi sphere was in winter. There would be no snow to blend in with, and we might very well go underground anyway. White armor would stand out; dark armor would blend in.

I went to my quarters to rest. Stripping down to my boxers, I climbed into bed and fell asleep quickly. That was part of life in the Marines, you slept when you could and stayed awake when you had to.

I dreamed of Hawaii. I dreamed of white sand beaches and Christina—the girl I left behind at Sad Sam's Palace. I remembered her name. Her name mattered in my dream.

* * *

The chimes from my communications console woke me from a deep sleep. I thought maybe I had overslept and Freeman was calling to wake me up. I generally woke myself up with good accuracy.

"Hello?" I asked.

"You're sleeping?" It was Moffat.

I groaned softly. "What time is it?"

"It's 0300," he said. Freeman and I had planned on leaving at 0400. As far as I was concerned, I still had forty-five minutes to sleep.

"The general's staff says you're out of action for the next few days," Moffat said.

"I have an assignment," I said.

"I don't suppose you would care to share some details with your company commander," Moffat said. He said this in jest. The fact was, Moffat didn't bother me so much anymore. He had a high opinion of himself, but what officer didn't? At least he'd led his men into battle when we went to meet the Avatari in the forest.

"I wish I could, sir," I said.

"I hear you've been out to visit the University of Valhalla." Moffat was fishing for clues and doing a good job of it.

"I'm taking an after-hours annex course," I said. "It's in advanced interpersonal relations."

"Must be a big class," Moffat said. "I understand General Glade is taking it, too."

"You might ask General Glade about the class, he's probably in a better position to share his opinions."

"Nice, Harris. Very nice," Moffat said. "So are you going in for an extended seminar today?"

"A field trip," I said.

"What kinds of field trips do you take in a class on interpersonal relations?" Moffat asked.

"Social calls, mostly. We visit new friends, try to learn their likes and dislikes. It's not a trip to the beach with Ava Gardner, but..."

"Oh, shit. I hope you're not another of those guys who walks around fantasizing about Ava all day," Moffat said.

"You don't think she's beautiful?" I asked. In truth, I didn't waste much time thinking about Ava or any other woman... well, maybe Christina and Marianne, Freeman's sister.

"I don't waste time thinking about clones," Moffat said. He considered his audience and retracted the statement. "Fantasizing about clones."

Deciding that he had fished as much information as he was going to get, Moffat turned to business. "Will we see your ass back on the duty roster soon?" Now he sounded positively officious.

"This could take a couple of days," I said.

"I expect you to report in for duty the moment you return to base," Moffat said.

I could not actually do that—anything I found would be classified. When I got back, I would report to General Glade, who would hear what I had to say, then send me to the Science Lab, where I would repeat everything for Sweetwater and Breeze. After that meeting, I'd probably need a few hours' rest.

"Aye, aye, sir," I said with conviction, almost as if I meant it.

The rear end of the transport slid open slowly, the hydraulic rods pulling aside six-inch-thick doors that might well have weighed two thousand pounds each.

Walking up the grated ramp reminded me a lot of entering the Vista Street bunker. I saw metal in every direction. The walls were metal. The floor was metal. The lights in the kettle shone down from metal casings. Only the bench that ran around the perimeter of the cabin was wood, and it was painted the dull dark gray of metal. There were no windows, just a ladder at the far side of the cabin that led up to the cockpit.

I once spent six weeks trapped in one of these birds with no one to talk to except Ray Freeman. I had a Bible on that flight. Faced with deciding between trying to strike up conversations with Freeman and reading the Bible, I read through the Old Testament of the Bible four times. I started that trip a devout atheist and finished it having formed a religion of my own.

Over the last year, I had given up on religion; but now, walking up the ramp with Freeman, I could feel stirrings of devotion in my soul. Ray would pilot the flight. He flew these birds as well as any air jockey.

"You coming up?" Freeman paused at the base of the ladder.

"Give me a minute. I want to look through our equipment."

Freeman nodded and climbed up to the cockpit two rungs at a time.

I was glad for an excuse to get away from Freeman; his intense silence wore me down. Something had caught my eye. Along with the particle-beam pistols, grenades, and the Jackal Freeman requisitioned for this trip, I saw a familiar sight—a case shaped like a tuba with the acronym S.C.O.O.T.E.R. running along its side.

The case was maybe three and a half feet tall. As I walked over for a closer look, the rear hatch of the kettle closed, its grinding metal yawn filling the cargo hold. I barely noticed. I had a ghost to deal with.

The acronym on the top of the case stood for Subautonomous Control Optical Observation Terrain Exploration Robot. *They really had to reach for that name,* I thought, but I knew why they had done it. The inventor of this unit called his prototype Scooter. I met the guy once. Back then, S.C.O.O.T.E.R. was a name, not an acronym. The bastard loved his little robot. He treated the thing like a pet.

The walls of the transport rumbled as it lifted from the ground. The sheer tonnage of these ships was ridiculous. They were flying hunks of iron, made for space travel, where aerodynamics meant nothing. In atmospheric conditions, they had the grace and elegance of a brick. They were built to carry troops and absorb punishment and did a good job of both.

I placed the case on its side and opened it. The S.C.O.O.T.E.R. was shaped like a hubcap, a smooth chrome ellipse, twelve inches across, with four independent wheels on the bottom. The remarkable thing about these little robots was the sense of self-preservation that had been programmed into their processing chips. At the moment, this little robot could not have had the slightest idea of what danger it was in; but once it was deployed, the programming would come in handy. Sergeant Tabor Shannon, my mentor and the finest Marine I had ever known, died because he underestimated the self-preservation programming in one of these little bastards.

I stared down at the S.C.O.O.T.E.R.'s outer shell, which was not the mirror it appeared to be but a well-crafted 360-degree lens. This little robot could slip into narrow spaces, map out enemy positions, and plan routes of attack. I placed this new S.C.O.O.T.E.R. back in its case and headed for the cockpit. The powerful engines of the transport filled the kettle with a soft sucking noise, and the handles along the sides of the ladder vibrated.

"What's our ETA?" I asked as I entered the cockpit. Looking through the windshield, I saw virginal forests of snowcapped trees, a vast carpet that swept on for miles and miles. With the ion curtain above us, there was not a trace of blue in the silvery sky. There were clouds, lots of clouds.

"Five hours, maybe," Freeman, ever the raconteur, responded. Where was a Bible when I needed one?

28

I headed up to the cockpit and watched in studied silence as we flew closer.

The aliens could have dug their mines on an open prairie or deep in the deserts, some sensible convenient place. Had they been after gold, they might have done it the old-fashioned way, panning silt in streams and rivers. Whatever they were here for, they had burrowed into the side of a mountain in the middle of a remote range.

"Ah shit," I said, as a nearly paralyzing sense of déjà vu spread through me. The setting for the Avatari Mining Company looked very familiar indeed. A few years back, the Unified Authority Marines tracked the Mogats to a burned-out planet called Hubble. Finding themselves trapped, the Mogats hid in a series of caverns that ran deep below the only mountains on the planet. Likewise, when we finally tracked the Believers to their home planet, it was a burned-out planet in which their cities were hidden deep below the surface. The only way to get to those cities was through shafts that had been carved into tall mountains.

"I'm beginning to see a pattern," I told Freeman.

The mountains formed a jagged wall of granite gray slopes and icy peaks. They looked like a giant fortress from the distance. The light from the ion curtain illuminated the various nooks and crevices that would otherwise have gone dark.

Some of the peaks disappeared above the clouds. I pointed to one and asked Freeman if it could possibly extend through the curtain. He shrugged his shoulders, and said, "Don't know." Hypothesis was the sport of scientists like Sweetwater and Breeze; Freeman felt no inclination to try his hand at it.

"If that peak goes higher than the ion curtain, we might be able to climb to the top and set up some sort of communications link," I said.

"You saw what happened to the bullets I shot through the sphere?" Freeman asked.

"Yeah," I said.

"And you want to risk hiking through that shit?" he asked.

I thought about that as we approached the coordinates William Sweetwater had provided. This took us deep into the mountains, flying low among ridges and saddles. Freeman circled around until he found the exact coordinates where the digging had been detected, then circled more until he found an opening along the face of the mountain. This took over an hour, and I began to wonder if the Avatari had found a hollow spot in some mountain and materialized inside. Finally, we found our doorway, a squared opening in the face of a mountain that was fifty feet tall and one hundred feet wide.

Designed to fly in space as well as in atmospheric conditions, our transport could perform vertical landings. We would not need a long runway with this bird, thank goodness, but we would need someplace sturdy enough to support three hundred metric tons—preferably a location with a strong granite base so that the landing gear would not dig in too deeply. After another fifteen minutes, Freeman found a solid shelf about a quarter of a mile from the opening, and we touched down.

"You know, they might have dug a gravity chute," I said, as we headed into the cargo hold to off-load our equipment.

The only time I had ever seen a gravity chute was on the Mogat home world. It was an enormous well that ran between the surface of the planet and the underground cities a few miles below. The damn thing worked like an elevator, using some weird convection that lifted outgoing ships to the surface and lowered incoming ships to the core.

"There won't be a chute," Freeman said.

"How can you be so sure?" I asked.

"The Avatari haven't had time to dig one," Freeman said.

"Maybe they dig really quickly," I said. I knew Freeman was right, but that did not mean I wanted to give in. The chute on the Mogat planet went several miles straight down.

Freeman only grunted.

We loaded a dozen trackers into the back of the Jackal along with guns, grenades, charges, cameras, and the S.C.O.O.T.E.R. We took rappel cords for scaling any vertical chutes we might encounter. The goal was to get in and out of the mines undetected, but that did not mean we would not go in ready to fight.

Jackals might handle foothills well, but the landscape around us was cliffs and peaks. Jeep-sized boulders stuck out of the ground. There were ruts and drop-offs, every obstruction except for trees. We were one hundred feet above the tree level, and the mountain was bare.

We were able to drive to a ridge forty or fifty feet below the entrance to the Avatari mine. Then we had to ditch our ride and haul the equipment by hand. I strapped three particle-beam cannons and three trackers to my back and started walking.

My load weighed damn near eighty pounds, and I had nothing to complain about. Freeman carried the S.C.O.O.T.E.R., two trackers, and a satchel filled with demolition gear. He probably lugged 150 pounds out of the Jackal in all.

"I thought we didn't want to blow anything up," I said, remembering Freeman's response when I asked about bringing more men.

"Not by accident," Freeman said.

We came to a sheer cliff, where we would need to scale the side of the mountain. I found a groove in which I could climb and stripped off the gear I was carrying. Big as he was, Freeman was more suited for combat than climbing, and our combat armor wouldn't make scaling the ridge any easier. Once I got to the top, I would throw down a cord. I would haul up our gear first, then Freeman could use the cord to come up.

It did not take long for me to get to the top. I shot a piton into the granite and tied our cord to it. After securing the cord, I found a solid foothold on the dry granite and tossed the cord down to Freeman. He sent up the satchel full of explosives first, then the S.C.O.O.T.E.R., the trackers, and the rifles. Next, Freeman attached the cord to his armor and started climbing.

"You know that this whole thing will have been a waste of time if there's a gravity chute inside that cave?" I called down to Freeman, using an interLink connection.

"Did you see a gravity chute on Hubble?" Freeman asked.

"No," I said.

"Then they don't build one on every planet." He grunted as he worked his way up the groove. He was breathing heavily. The man weighed over three hundred pounds; mountain climbing did not come easily for him.

"So it's a fifty-fifty chance," I said. Something about Freeman's obsessive silence made me more chatty, like I was trying to get on his nerves.

Freeman did not answer. A minute later, he reached the top of the cord and pulled himself up to the ledge. I was not there to offer him a hand. I had walked a few feet into the cave to have a look around.

"You see a gravity chute?" Freeman asked.

"Not exactly," I said. What I saw was a wide corridor carved out of solid rock. The entrance was so large, I thought I could run six lanes of traffic through it.

Ray Freeman had made a rare mistake when he said that the aliens had not had enough time to dig a gravity chute. He had underestimated them. Judging by this digging, they could have bored right through the center of New Copenhagen and popped up in the Hotel Valhalla pool had they wished.

Not that Freeman commented on the immense excavation when he saw it. He simply gazed down one side of the corridor, then the other, and said nothing. He knelt, unloaded his gear, and brought out the S.C.O.O.T.E.R.

"Ever used one of these?" Freeman asked.

"I've seen one in action," I said, "on Hubble."

Freeman placed the S.C.O.O.T.E.R. on the ground, then opened the top of the case to access the control panel. The panel included a four-inch screen with touch controls. They had improved the robot's design. Freeman could give it voice commands using the interLink.

"Right or left?" Freeman asked me. The tunnel branched out in both directions.

"Doesn't look like it matters," I said.

A moment later the little robot rumbled off to the left, faltering over divots and skirting around large rocks, its sensors sweeping the area for signs of danger. I think I would have preferred the S.C.O.O.T.E.R. to have more balls and less brains. It found a rut along the wall of the cavern in which it could both travel and hide. The rut was just big enough for the robot, but it was useless for Freeman and me.

The ambient light inside the tunnel was just as bright as it was outside. I got the feeling that the glowing tachyons of the ion curtain had found their way into the mountains.

"This could take a while," I said. "The S.C.O.O.T.E.R. I saw on Hubble was better at survival than reconnaissance."

Wanting to kill time, I picked up the trackers and began placing them. I did not get very far, however. Within a few minutes, the S.C.O.O.T.E.R. found the Avatari. But they weren't the Avatari we expected.

29

Freeman sat fiddling with the S.C.O.O.T.E.R.'s controls as I lugged three trackers up the hall to the right. About twenty yards in, I started passing arterial hallways that led down into the heart of the mountain. The halls were fairly uniform, about six feet from floor to ceiling and somewhere around twenty-five feet from wall to wall. I tried to imagine a platoon of eight-foot-tall Avatari soldiers running through these halls. It seemed impossible. I would need to hunch my back to fit in there, and Freeman would need to crouch. I had no idea how a bunch of animated statues like the Avatari would fit; those bastards had another foot on Freeman.

As I peered into one of the tunnels, something surprised me, at least it surprised me once I realized what I was seeing. The grand corridor might have been brightly lit with the stuff that made the ion curtain, but the ancillary tunnels were dark as night. I relayed this piece of intelligence back to Freeman, but he did not reply. He might have been too busy guiding the S.C.O.O.T.E.R., or more likely he had already seen this in the S.C.O.O.T.E.R.'s video feed.

Looking for the right place to set up my first tracker, I walked just deep enough into a tunnel for my visor to switch to night-for-day vision, then called back to Freeman. "Think I should set up trackers in this tunnel?" I said.

"You wouldn't want to go too far in there," Freeman said.

"Any particular reason?" I asked.

"Because it's full of giant spiders," Freeman said.

I leaned the tracker against the wall and trotted back to have a look at the control screen. I did not like what I saw.

No one would ever describe the creature we saw on the tiny black and white screen as a "Space Angel." Apparently the Avatari considered the humanoid form efficient for combat but not for mining. The creatures in these shafts looked like enormous spiders. They had eight multi-jointed legs. The two forelegs were shaped like a knife blade; the rear legs did not taper down to points. They were broad at the base—limbs made for mobility.

"I don't like the look of that," I said.

Freeman had switched to manual controls so that he could bypass the S.C.O.O.T.E.R.'s self-preservation programming. Using a joy-lever and dials, he guided the little robot toward the closest miner, then directly under its belly. Through the fish-eye lens, I watched as the spider-thing slashed at the granite floor with its forelegs. There must have been real power in those legs—they hacked through the rock as easily as a shovel digging in dry sand, showering the S.C.O.O.T.E.R. with rock and debris.

"Think that thing can cut through armor with those legs?" I asked.

Freeman, who seldom speculated on anything, said, "Yes."

Scary or not, these things would have been useless on an open battlefield where men with guns could pick them off before they got within striking range. I saw no sign of guns or projectile weapons on the creature. Twisting through mountain tunnels, however, this creepy, ground-hugging bastard would have an advantage.

"Let's kill the specker, grab its carcass, and get out of here," I said.

Without saying a word, Freeman had the S.C.O.O.T.E.R. spin so that the camera showed the cavern. The walls were covered with dark spots that seemed to quiver in place.

"Those aren't..." I started to say, but I knew they were. They were more spider-things. The S.C.O.O.T.E.R.'s camera only captured a small portion of the cavern, but I could see hundreds, maybe thousands, of spider-things wedged in together, slashing and scraping at the walls.

I wanted to make a joke about having seen enough and heading back to base. Instead, I said, "They don't seem very alert. If their soldiers are avatars of real aliens, these things might just be drones."

Freeman drove the S.C.O.O.T.E.R. out from under the spider-thing and guided it up a peak.

"Probably," I added.

Now that I could see much more of the cavern on the screen, I lost all sense of proportion. I might have been staring into a nothingness as vast as the skies. What I saw was an endless vault with rough-hewn walls on which crawled thousands and thousands of spider-things, and I knew I had only seen the tip of the iceberg. Even with the S.C.O.O.T.E.R.'s enhanced optics, the camera only captured a tiny sliver of that enormous hive.

"Got any bug spray?" I asked Freeman.

He switched S.C.O.O.T.E.R. to autopilot mode.

"You know it's just going to come running for safety now," I said as he stood up, went to our gear, and slung the satchel of demolition equipment over his shoulder.

Freeman tossed me a particle-beam cannon. "You take point," he said.

Ah shit, I thought, *we're going in.* "Do we want to set up the trackers before we go in?" I asked. "We might need to leave in a hurry."

"Good idea," he said, so we spent fifteen minutes placing our trackers along the main tunnel. If we did need to beat a fast retreat, we could start the trackers using controls in our helmets... if we made it that far.

That done, we started down the main corridor. I took a second gun slung over my shoulder. Creatures like these spider-things could probably snap a cannon in two with one swipe of their powerful legs. On the off chance that one of them broke my first cannon without cutting me in two along the way, having a second weapon would come in handy.

Then it came time to enter the ancillary tunnel that led down into the main cavern. I boosted the volume on the ambient noise and heard scraping and thumping, but it came from far away. I had point—not exactly a significant position with only two of us—but it meant that I would plan our route and lead the way. In a situation like this, it was all a crapshoot. At the end of the tunnel, we might run into an ambush—a horde of giant alien spider-things just waiting for us, or they might not even register us at all.

Were these avatars of thinking beings, or robotic drones, or maybe living, breathing, eating creatures? Did they sling webs?

Visions of spiderwebs with threads the size of nylon cables played in my mind. I imagined those creatures trapping us, tying us tightly, then eating us alive. In my mind, I saw spiders with bayonet-like mandibles. I tried to erase these thoughts, but they lingered as I bent my back and started down that tunnel.

The ground sloped down at a twenty-degree angle. The world around me went dark for less than a second, then my night-for-day lenses took over and I saw everything around me in black-and-blue-white images. My sense of depth, however, disappeared quickly.

The tunnel was clearly not natural. Though it was pitted with pick marks and inch-deep lines, the roof of the tunnel was flat and straight, as were the walls. The spider-things had hacked the tunnel out of a solid granite slab.

The ceiling had to be almost precisely six feet tall. Standing six-three with two extra inches for my helmet, I had to duck my head as I walked. Freeman, who quickly fell back behind me, could only get through by walking in a crouch.

"Maybe we can trap these things if we place charges around the entrance," I suggested.

"No," Freeman said.

"Any reason?" I asked.

"They just hollowed out this entire mountain, they would be able to dig themselves out."

"So why bring all the demolition gear if you're not going to use it?"

"We might find a generator or some central control," Freeman said.

I realized I was thinking survival, and he was talking strategy.

The tube curled down like a spiral stairwell in which the steps had washed away. As I continued down, I moved toward the wall for a closer look. The walls and ceiling were anything but smooth—though flat, they were pocked with yard-long grooves into which I could fit my hands.

"Any guesses on how many of those things can fit through here at once?" I asked. Before Freeman could respond, I had my answer.

"Incoming!" I yelled into the interLink.

I saw two front legs first. They were shaped like an ax handle and tapered down to ice-pick points. I flattened my back against the wall as hard as I possibly could, and aimed my particle-beam cannon. That was all that I could do.

"How many?" Freeman asked.

"Just one, so far," I said.

It rounded the corner and scuttled past me. There was nothing resembling flesh on this creature. It might have had an exoskeleton or it could have been all armor, but I saw no soft spots on its body. And it was big. The sharp arches of the spider-thing's forelegs came almost to my chest.

Behind those legs came a featureless, ball-shaped head. It had no eyes and, to my relief, no mouth. The spider-thing had a low-slung body that cleared the ground by no more than a foot. The damned thing thrust past me without so much as a sideways glance, leaving me shivering in its wake.

I watched it from the back as it continued up the slope and around the curve. Unlike the insectile forelegs, the short rear legs looked reptilian. The forelegs clawed at the ground, breaking the rock and hard-packed earth loose. The rear legs swept up the debris. I felt a strong impulse to give that thing a particle-beam enema but resisted.

"It's on its way toward you," I warned Freeman.

"I see it," he said.

"It walked right past me," I said. "It doesn't seem to care about visitors."

Moments later, Freeman let me know that the spider-thing passed him as well. We continued down the tunnel, then, all of a sudden, I found myself facing a cavern that stretched far beyond the limited range of my night-for-day lenses. Using optical commands, I initiated a sonar sweep and pinged the cavern to determine its size. I got no reading. Something in the cave either dampened or absorbed my ping.

The spider-things were everywhere, digging at the floor, clinging to the walls, digging at the ceiling. I watched one near me as it dug, scraping the granite with its front-most legs, pushing boulders out of its way with its outermost legs, then sweeping at the dirt and debris with its hind legs. The spider-thing had dug a shallow pit around itself. Most of the spider-things around the cavern had dug themselves into pits.

I stood on a ridge overlooking the scene. A path led on, winding down the steep slope of the cavern. We would need to follow that path. The spider-things used it, too. They also climbed the sides of the cavern. By stabbing their dagger legs into the granite wall, they moved adroitly along the rock. It did not matter to them if the wall sloped down at forty-five degrees or ninety, they moved with equal alacrity.

A shower of small rocks fell around me. When I looked up, I saw two of those spider-things almost directly over my head. They could have pounced on me if they had a mind to, but a mind was something they seemed to lack.

I scanned the area using heat vision. Like the Avatari soldiers, these creatures gave off no body heat. That did not mean they were avatars; real spiders do not generate body heat, either. Just then a rock the size of a grapefruit fell, narrowly missing my head.

Above me, one of those creatures had arranged itself so that its face stared straight down at me, but it paid me no attention. It slashed at the rocks around it with one of its legs, dislodging rock chips, gravel, and rocks the size of golf balls.

30

"That way," Freeman said as he paused beside me on the ridge at the end of the tunnel. He pointed toward a mound on the floor of the cavern. The cavern itself was dark, but there was a cave on the mound, with light pouring out of it. I tried to measure the distance to that cave using a sonar ping. Apparently the signal returned garbled but readable, as an icon appeared on my visor warning me that it was "repairing" the test results. A moment later a virtual beacon appeared over the cave along with a measurement of 1.2 miles.

A ninety-foot drop stood between us and the floor of the cavern. To get down to the floor, we would need to follow a trail that switched back and forth along a steep slope. The ridge on which we stood jutted out over the top of the slope, so I could not see what was just below us. Once we reached the cavern floor, though, the path to the distant cave looked dangerous. We would cross more than a mile of spider-thing-infested cavern floor. As I traced the route we would take, I saw five or six spider-things cut across the path.

"I don't suppose we can examine the cave from here?" I asked. When Freeman did not respond to my little joke, I followed up with, "Let's go."

Viewed through night-for-day lenses, the spider creatures looked just a shade lighter than absolute black against the nickel gray of the granite stone. Of course, seen through those lenses, everything was blue-gray, blue-white, or black with a hint of blue. Down along the floor of the cavern, the drones looked like animated patches of grass. There were thousands of them, maybe hundreds of thousands. Most of them dug within their own personal divots, but some were working so closely together that their legs became interlaced.

I reached over my shoulder and touched my backup cannon for reassurance, then started down the slope. The moment I stepped off our ledge, I found myself no more than a foot from one of the spider-things. It had carved a hole into the granite directly beneath the spot on which I had been standing. Taking a half step back, I aimed my rifle at the creature, but the busy little bastard ignored me. It rolled a two-foot boulder out of its hole, pivoted around, and crawled back the way it had come.

My Liberator's combat reflex had already begun. Testosterone and adrenaline flowed through my veins, leaving me calm and ready for violence at the same time. I liked it more than ever before, my thoughts taking on new clarity as a nearly electric tingle ran across my skin. The danger had already gone, but I welcomed the effects as the reflex lingered.

If I kill one of those things, do you think the others will know? I asked myself. Probably not, but I didn't want to risk it.

"If those things have any brains, they've spotted us by now," I told Freeman. "Maybe they know we're here, and they're just too scared to do anything about us."

He did not respond.

I looked back the way we had come and saw something that disturbed me. All of the spider-things in this cavern appeared to be the exact same size... all of them except one. This creature was twice the size of the others, a spider-thing the size of a small car that crawled more quickly than its fellows. I spotted it moving along the roof of the cavern. While most of the other spider-things remained fixed in their small holes, this creature crawled in a straight line along the wall of the cavern, heading in our direction.

It was still hundreds of feet away. It crawled toward us slowly but steadily, dwarfing the other spider-things around it, its sharp, front legs stepping, stabbing, and pulling.

"You didn't happen to see the big spider on the wall?" I asked.

"I saw it," Freeman said.

We risked attracting more attention to ourselves by running; but seeing that big creature coming after us, I sped to a jog as we worked our way down the slope along the zigzagging trail.

I rounded a bend and had to stop moving while a spider-thing strolled across the path. I looked at its forelegs. From the ground to the joint at the top of their arch, those legs were as long and wide as a grown man's crutches. The ends of its segmented legs were flat and smooth and sharp as swords. They had a dull shine as if they were made of metal or plastic.

As I waited for the spider-thing to crawl off the path, I looked back toward the roof of the cavern. The giant spider-thing I spotted earlier was still coming in our direction. It might have gained some ground on us, but it still had not yet reached the ridge from which we had come. It scuttled across the wall, working its legs like knitting needles as it clung to the rock.

"At least they don't spin webs," I said.

Freeman did not answer. He stood about fifteen feet behind me fiddling with a T-shaped instrument of some kind. At the moment, I would have preferred for him to have a grenade in his left hand and a particle-beam pistol in his right, but we had come to gather scientific data.

"We better get moving," I said. "If that thing catches up to us, we might be in trouble." The gargantuan spider-thing might not need to catch up to us, though. As long as it remained between us and our way out of the cavern, it was in control of the situation. Freeman seldom made mistakes, but he might have made a colossal error when he switched the S.C.O.O.T.E.R. to its self-preservation autopilot too soon.

We passed dozens of regular-sized spider-things as we wound our way down to the floor of the cavern. Sometimes I came so close to them that I could have reached out and grabbed their legs, but they showed no sign of noticing me.

I hazarded another look back at the big spider-thing and saw that it had made it past the entrance to the tunnel. It moved slowly, maybe even slower than we did; but we were walking back and forth along a twisting path. The giant spider-thing crawled straight down the steep slope, gaining ground on us.

As I spared just a moment to watch its casual gait, I decided that the Avatari had not placed it in these caverns as a guard. This one was no drone. It might be the avatar of an engineer or maybe a foreman who located problems and sorted them out. It probably took care of cave-ins, explosions, floods, and the occasional two-legged stranger that meandered into its lair.

It was still a hundred feet back, but moments earlier, it had been two hundred or three hundred feet away.

"What do we do if it catches up to us?" I asked Freeman. The drones might have been on autopilot, but that did not mean their guardian would be.

"We don't let it catch up to us," Freeman said. His voice was absolutely calm.

A spider-thing rolling a seven-foot boulder crossed the path a few feet ahead of me. It moved the boulder so easily it might have been pushing a gigantic ball of string instead of a ten-ton rock. The spider-thing paused, tapped the boulder with its legs to change the direction it rolled, then, with a nudge, started pushing again. During the moment that it stopped, I aimed my weapon at its head and tightened my finger across the trigger. I was on edge and ready to kill.

"If any more get in your way, kill them," Freeman told me. He did not need to tell me twice.

I reached the bottom of the slope and waited for Freeman. The cavern floor was low around the edges and bulged up toward the middle. Because of the convex curvature, I could no longer see the cave entrance that I had marked with my virtual beacon. I knew we were heading in the right direction; and, because I had marked it with a virtual beacon, a chip in my visor marked the distance—0.7 miles away. We would have reached the cave by now if we could have moved toward it in a straight line. But between us and that beacon, thousands of spider-things scratched at the granite floor. They did not seem to care about us, but we were going to need to dodge any of them between us and the cave. Traveling that 0.7 of a mile might take longer than a five-mile hike once we worked in our winding trail.

"Did they give you that meter at the Science Lab? What's it reading?" I asked Freeman.

"I don't know what it reads," Freeman said. He held the T-shaped device in his right hand. Lights flashed across the broad bar on its top. "I know it's taking air samples."

"Can it broadcast a signal to the lab?"

"No."

"What happens if we don't make it out of here?" I asked.

"There's a computer recording our results in the transport," Freeman said.

"So if we don't make it, they'll get along perfectly well without us. How does it feel to be expendable?" I asked, thinking that Freeman was now just as replaceable as a bullet or a rifle, or a clone.

"I'm a mercenary; I'm worse than expendable. The people who hire us want us to die once we finish our job—that way they don't have to pay us."

For the first time in my life, I had to entertain the notion that there might be someone lower on the social ladder than a clone. Try as I might, I could not come up with a smart comeback, so I concentrated on reaching the beacon.

Moving along the floor of the cavern proved less dangerous than I had expected—I simply had to thread my way around the pits in which the spider-things worked. Most of the drones had dug three- or four-foot-deep pits around themselves. They moved back and forth in their little cells, clawing at the rocky floor, then sweeping the debris out of their holes. I had no idea what became of the dirt and rocks they dislodged. Presumably this entire cavern had once been a solid mass of rock and earth. They must have disintegrated it or hauled it out somewhere.

The spider-things spun and clawed and tore great shards of rock out of the ground. I had the feeling that if I fell into one of these holes, the creature inside it might tear me in half without ever noticing.

We continued up the gentle slope toward the center of the cavern, where the mound with the brightly lit cave-within-a-cave rose out of the ground like a pimple. The constant scraping and tapping of the spider-things around me caused the ground to vibrate. When I slowed to wait for Freeman, I could feel that vibration through my boots.

But I did not have time to worry about the drones or the way the ground shook beneath my feet. Maintaining a quick jog, I skirted one spider-filled divot, then the next as I headed toward the cave. I did not know how far we had traveled at this point but, according to my visor, we had approximately a quarter of a mile to go. When I looked back toward the tunnel from which we had entered the cavern, I saw that we had put a little more distance between us and the guardian spider. It had either slowed down or was hanging back to see what we would do next.

I did not have time to figure the spider-thing out. We reached the mound with the cave, a steep cone with no trails leading up its twenty-foot slope. Light shone out of the cave at the top like a search beam from a lighthouse. The silver-white beam stabbed into the darkness of the cavern like a flame from a welding torch, its glow so bright that when I looked at it, my visor switched from night-for-day to tactical view.

Loose dirt and rock shavings covered the sides of the mound; I had to scramble to keep my footing as I climbed toward the cave. When I reached the mouth itself, I played it by the book. For all I knew, the guardian spider had slowed because it had a buddy waiting for us in the cave. Crouching low to the ground, my particle-beam cannon ready, I spun around the lip for a quick glance in, then spun back out for safety. I did another peek in, this time darting from one side of the entrance to the other. Certain that I had not seen anything dangerous, I stepped into the mouth of the cave and scanned for spider-things. Then I went back outside to look for Freeman.

As I left the cave, I came within inches of a drone crawling along the outside of the cave. Two knife-blade legs pawed at the wall a few inches from my head. The spider-thing lifted one of its legs, then stabbed it into the granite. As it pulled that leg back, I saw that it had stabbed a three-inch gash into the rock, dislodging chips and fist-sized rocks.

I had been so intent scanning the cave that I hadn't even noticed the specker. Had it been an avatar instead of a drone, it could have killed me. But it was only a drone. As I stepped away from it, it ignored me and continued digging.

"Careful on your way up," I told Freeman. "They're up here, too."

Below me, Freeman no longer bothered taking readings with the meter. He pulled a line of explosive charges from his satchel and stabbed one into the ground.

"You planting charges?" I asked.

"I've placed twenty of them so far," Freeman said.

"Didn't you say these spider-things would just dig themselves out?" I said.

"I'm marking a path," Freeman said.

"Like Hansel marking his path through the woods with breadcrumbs?" I asked. Freeman did not answer, leaving me to wonder if he had ever heard of Hansel and Gretel.

Waiting for Freeman to reach the cave, I searched the cavern for the big spider-thing. I scanned up and down the winding path along the ridge. Nothing. I looked around the cavern floor, nervous that this creature might have enough intelligence to flank us, and saw no sign of it.

"It's gone," I said. "There's no specking trace of the bastard."

Maybe it was assigned to a territory, I thought. But I did not like that idea because if that big spider had a territory it protected, that meant there had to be more of them around.

Maybe, a fatalistic voice said in my head, *it can camouflage itself.* I felt a numbing tingle deep in my gut and realized that I was scared. The effect of the combat reflex had tapered off, and cold fear had replaced it.

"It has to be out there," Freeman said.

"Stop it. You're scaring me," I said, hoping it sounded like a joke.

Freeman showed no signs of nervousness. He pulled out the T-shaped meter that Sweetwater had given him and did a sweep of the area. A drone climbed out of its pit and walked past him. Freeman drew his pistol and covered the beast as it scampered past, then said, "Let's get this over with."

Taking advantage of the light that spilled out of the cave, I used the tactical lens in my visor because it showed color—not that there was much color to see. The spider-things were a light shade of black, the granite was gray, the atmosphere was dark. Even with the light, I could not see more than a hundred yards ahead of me.

If that big spider-thing was trying to hide, I hoped using the tactical view would increase the odds of my spotting it. Just for a moment, I thought I saw something at the edge of the darkness, but it vanished. I switched back tonight-for-day and saw nothing. I tried every gadget in my helmet—heat vision, telescopic lenses, sonic location—but still nothing.

"It's out there somewhere," I reminded myself.

Freeman stopped to scan the area, and said, "I don't see anything."

"Me either," I agreed. We both knew that our inability to find the creature did not mean a thing.

Freeman walked toward the cave, and instructed, "Guard the entrance."

"Last time I did something like this, the guy I came with did not make it out," I observed.

"Thanks for the warning," said Freeman. I spared a look back and saw him disappear into the entrance.

Now I was alone in the dark. Well, not alone. There might have been a million spider-thing drones around me, and somewhere out there, the king of the spider-things lurked like a shadow. Could something like that have gone invisible? Why would the aliens program that into the creature unless they meant to use the thing for combat purposes? I flipped through the different lenses in my helmet and spotted thousands of drones digging, but I found no trace of that guardian spider-thing.

"If there are more of those big bastards out there, this could be a one-way trip," I told Freeman. Suddenly my nerves had me babbling. *Here we were, a clone and a mercenary. Could any duo be more expendable?* I asked myself, knowing I did not want to hear the answer.

"As long as we finish what we came to do," Freeman said.

"Which is?" I asked.

"We find out what the aliens are up to," Freeman said.

"And you think the answer is in this cave?" I asked. I still had my back to the brightly lit opening and my rifle ready as I kept a lookout for that spider-thing guardian. "You know, you never struck me as the self-sacrificing type," I told Freeman.

He did not respond, not that I expected him to.

As I stood looking out into the cavern, I meandered toward the entrance of the cave, forgetting about the drone that had sneaked up on me a few moments earlier, and the little bastard caught me off guard a second time. It lifted a questing leg, then slammed it into the rock wall, barely missing my head. I spun, jumped back, and fired my weapon, hitting that digger in what passed for its face. The creature collapsed. No spasms. No struggles. It rolled out of its hole on the outside wall of the cave and tumbled down to the foot of the mound, where hundreds of drones dug around it.

I must have yelled, which Freeman would have heard over our interLink connection. "What happened?"

"I just killed a drone," I said.

Out of the corner of my eye, I saw the guardian drop out of the darkness, landing above the mouth of the cave. It was not invisible, but it had camouflaged itself. Its color had blended in with the darkness, and now that it was on the nickel-colored rock, its color faded to gray.

Shooting from the hip, I fired three shots with my particle-beam cannon, hitting the guardian spider each time. It toppled from its perch. Unlike the drone I had just killed, the guardian did not die. It landed on its feet and came toward me raising a leg high into the air as if issuing a challenge.

I fired between the legs, hitting the underside of the giant spider's body. The creature convulsed, then came toward me again. It seemed weakened. The legs pawed at the ground as it pulled itself forward.

"I found the spider that was following us," I shouted to Freeman.

"Kill it," Freeman said. The man seldom spoke, and when he did, there were times he might have done better had he just remained silent.

Stretched out straight, the guardian's leg might have been twelve feet long. The creature stabbed one of its two giant forelegs into the ground and slashed in my direction with the other. The sharp tip sheared through the air in a slow, powerful arc. I dropped to the ground to avoid being sliced and fired my particle beam at the foreleg that the spider-thing was using to balance itself. The emerald green beam connected and a section of the spider-thing's leg dissolved. What ever bond held the particles in that knife-blade leg broke, and it fell apart and turned to powder.

Seemingly unaware that its leg had evaporated, the spider-thing tried to step forward using the disintegrated appendage. It fell, the remaining joints of the leg still pulling at the ground. Trying to right itself, the creature stabbed its other foreleg into the ground, and I shot that leg as well.

The spider-thing fell on its face as it pawed at the ground with the remains of its forelegs. The two forelegs were its longest legs and its only useful weapons. The next legs were not designed to reach forward, they were there for propulsion. I approached the spider-thing and shot its head, which dissolved as easily as the legs. This creature was made for mining, not combat; it broke apart instantly. Beneath its head, the guardian's body was hollow and full of light that faded quickly.

Wanting to make sure that there were no more camouflaged spiders waiting to pounce on me, I fired quick bursts along the wall above the cave. Some crags exploded, but nothing fell as I ran into the cave.

The light in the inner cave came from a string of energy spheres, spheres that looked just like the ones in the forest—a string of ten brighter-than-light pearls about ten feet in diameter. Seeing the spheres did not surprise me. These spider-things had to have been incubated somewhere; they were no more alive than the Avatari soldiers attacking Valhalla. What I did not expect to see was the stream of mud-colored gas leaking from the bottom of these spheres.

At first I thought that gas might have been the stuff we called distilled shit gas, a substance I had only seen on two other planets—Hubble and the Mogat home world. Distilled shit gas was corrosive gas that ate through just about anything soft, including bodysuits and flesh. Sweetwater and Breeze would have known the stuff by its scientific name, "extreme-hydrogenation elemental compound distillation," but we military types knew it for what it really was—distilled shit gas.

I could see that this stuff was not distilled shit gas, though it looked like a close cousin. The substance was so heavy it almost qualified as a liquid. The way it leaked out of the spheres and streamed along the floor of the cave, it looked more like spent sludgy motor oil. Fumes from the gas caused visible ripples in the air in the cave.

Freeman stood near the stream of sludgy gas, waving his sensor over it.

"What is that shit?" I asked.

"I don't know, but you wouldn't want to breathe it," Freeman said. "It's eating right through the ground."

I looked back at the mouth of the cave, wondering what we would do if an entire colony of spider-things attacked us. That probably would not happen, but I suspected there might be more of the big ones hiding out there.

"You might want to move in farther," Freeman said.

"What?" Then I saw that he had placed charges around the mouth of the cave. He gave me a moment to move to safety, then he set off the charges. The cave shook. The noise was so loud that I heard it through my helmet. Freeman, a master at demolitions, had set the charges so that the percussion of the explosion faced away from us; but when the dust cleared, a solid wall of boulders and debris blocked the entrance.

Specking great, I thought. *Now I'm stuck in a collapsed cave filled with primordial shit gas.* "Why did you do that?"

"I needed more time," Freeman said, as if explaining the obvious.

"Great, now you have all the specking time in the world. We're trapped in here," I said.

"If there are any more of the guardians out there, you will be able to spot them when they dig through that wall," Freeman said.

"Damn it, Freeman, you just buried us alive."

That's one way to protect yourself from giant alien spider-things, I thought. *Bury yourself alive so they can't specking get to you.* That was not what I said, however. What I told Freeman was, "Next time you start feeling expendable, can you take somebody else along for the ride?"

31

Freeman's pyrotechnic display reduced the front of the cave to a wall of rocks and boulders. I went to the wall and tried to push a large boulder aside. It did not budge. I tried another. It moved easily enough, so I pushed this way, then pulled that way. After about five minutes' work, I dislodged the rock from its cradle and rolled it to the floor. Other rocks shifted as that one rolled down the pile, and, for a moment, I feared that the wall of rocks might cave in.

I waited for the rocks to settle, then reached into the hole I had created and touched a long slab of granite. Even through my gloves, I could feel the vibration, something, maybe many somethings, was scratching at the rock on the other side.

One of the larger boulders shook and rolled down the mound. "The Avatari Search and Rescue squad is here," I said. Touching a rock and feeling the strong vibration, I added, "This wall isn't going to keep them out long."

"You're a Marine, shoot them," Freeman said. "You know the distilled shit gas on the Mogats' planet; this stuff is worse. If we stay here too long, the fumes will eat our armor."

At the mouth of the cave, a coffin-sized slab of granite slid out from the pile. Smaller rocks, some as small as grenades and some as large as combat helmets, rolled off the pile. The creatures on the other side of that wall did not care if they pulled the rocks away or pushed them in on us.

"Better hurry it up," I told Freeman.

A moment passed, and he said, "I've got what I need." He clipped the meter to his belt and brought out his particle-beam pistol.

The digging on the other side of the cave-in got louder. More rocks fell. Something hit the pile with so much force that it caused a slab of granite to shatter. As the pieces fell, I saw the foot-long point of a spider-thing's foreleg sticking through. The leg vanished in an avalanche of dust and rubble.

"Can those spiders go invisible?" Freeman asked.

"They camouflage themselves," I said.

The digging got louder. It took form. The amorphous tapping and rumbling solidified into the sound of knife-blade legs scratching and stabbing into stone. Rocks the size of car tires spilled from the pile that had once filled the front of the cave. All too soon that wall of debris stopped a full foot from the ceiling. Five feet of questing spider leg came slashing through that gap.

"Don't shoot them yet," I said, stating the obvious. "We need them to make the hole bigger." I could feel my heart thumping in my chest and the sound of my breath echoing in my helmet. The steam from my breath created a small patch of fog on the inside of my visor. It was nothing bad, though, nothing that would block my vision. Somewhere in my nervous system, the combat reflex began.

We backed toward the spheres, keeping our guns aimed at the mouth of the cave and a wary eye out to make sure we did not step in the gas. I would take my chances against a whole herd of spider-things before I would step in that. And then there were those spheres... Between the gas, the spheres, and the giant spider-things, this mission was heading south in a hurry.

I knelt, using a boulder as cover, and waited for the guardians to dig through. Freeman did not bother crouching or looking for cover. He stood erect, his particle-beam pistol raised and ready to fight.

A three-foot-round boulder wiggled, then dropped out of place from the top of the cave-in. It bowled down the slope and crashed into a wall. Dust flew, then the first bladelike leg quested through the hole. It slashed at the air, hooked a large tray of rock, and dragged it out of the way. The hole at the top was now large enough for us to wiggle through, though it would have been a tight fit for Freeman.

A section of rocks exploded in toward us, two-hundred-pound rocks flying through as if they were beach balls. I easily could have crawled through the gap the rocks left, but, fortunately, the spider-thing that made it did not fit. Its legs speared through the hole, flailing slowly in the air.

I had a clear shot right then but held my fire. Freeman followed my lead, aiming his gun and waiting.

Another spider-thing bashed a second gap through the rocks. "Not yet," I whispered to Freeman. "Let them do the work for us." The guardian digging the second hole hooked a slab and dragged it back through the hole, causing the top of the pile to sift down one side. "Just a little more... a little more, then we shoot."

Another spider-thing began a second hole, forcing its forelegs through the gap it had created. With those powerful hind legs pushing, it might have broken all the way through had I not killed it. I sprang to my feet firing my cannon as I dashed for the entrance. The green, glittering beam dissolved the legs, and I fired at the head behind them and kept firing until the head disappeared and the weight of the boulders finally crushed whatever was left.

Another spider-thing tried to crawl over the now-wide-open gap at the crest, but I got there first. I aimed over the back of a rock and fired, disintegrating legs and heads and bodies. Amazingly agile for his size, Freeman darted into a gap in the rocks below me. He fired several shots at a guardian spider, then jumped through the gap and appeared on the other side. Lying on the top of the cave-in, I swung my legs out over the other side of the rubble and slid down to join him. We had destroyed three guardian spiders, and the shells of their bodies lay around us like wreckage from a plane crash.

Now that I had left the well-lit harbor of the cave, with its spheres and gas, my visor switched to night-for-day lenses. If there were more guardian spiders out there, their camouflage would render them all but invisible to me through these lenses. "We better get out of here," I said to Freeman, and I started running.

And then the world fell apart around me and I was knocked to the ground.

The spider-thing might have sneaked up on me as I left the cave, or it could have dropped from the shadowy reaches of the top of the cavern. It did not land on top of me, but it struck me with one of its legs, and that was enough. The leg clubbed me across the back of my helmet and along my left shoulder.

All I knew was that I was lying facedown and barely conscious. The world had gone dark and silent. Even as my head cleared, the world around me remained dark, and I knew that the electronics in my armor had failed. With my visor on the blink, I could not see or hear the outside world. Without the interLink, I could not call Freeman for help.

I would not be able to find my way out of the caverns blind. If I removed my helmet, I'd inhale the fumes from the gas. Feeling around blind, I tried to find my particle-beam cannon and came up dry. I accepted that I was going to die, but that did not mean I would die empty-handed. I reached back for my spare rifle and discovered that it was gone as well.

Something closed around my shoulders and lifted me to my feet. At first I thought it might be one of the guardian spiders, but this thing did not slice me or squeeze me to death.

"Ray. Ray. My gear's gone dead!" I screamed it at the top of my lungs. My voice echoed loud inside my helmet. It did not matter that he wouldn't hear me, not at that moment. I did not know if he was still beside me, but I suspected he was already gone. He had helped me to my feet, and now he was running to safety.

If I had stopped to think about it, I should not have expected Freeman to come back for me at all. He was a mercenary, not a Marine. Marines have a code about leaving no one behind. Mercenaries, lone-wolf soldiers with no real allegiance, have no such code. But here he was, my friend, my former partner. Some part of me still hoping to survive this thing, I made the intergalactic sign of distress—I stumbled around like a man gone blind, groping in the darkness with my hands outstretched before me.

At any moment I would stumble into one of those spider-thing drones and get pulled apart, but I didn't care. I probably had more adrenaline and testosterone flowing through my veins than blood, the combat reflex was coming on so strong. I felt no fear. My thoughts were clear, and I knew I would die, but I was okay with that.

Freeman did not leave me. He grabbed my wrist and pulled me forward. I followed, stumbling and unsure about every step. I was completely useless. Now the clarity of my thoughts worked against me; I understood my helplessness all too well. For the first time in my life, the combat reflex only added to my frustration.

Freeman led me across the floor cavern, then slowed as we started the uphill slope at the end. I could feel contours in the ground beneath my feet. If I stepped too far, I could lose my balance and topple into a divot and under a drone. It would not see me, I would not see it, but I would die nonetheless.

Something scooped up my right foot, and I flew face-first, hitting Freeman in the back—at least I assumed it was Freeman—and landing on my stomach. It may have been a guardian trying to kill me, or a drone may have accidentally tripped me while digging its hole. I did not know, and I never did find out. A tense moment passed, then Freeman pulled me back to my feet.

We started up the ridge toward the entrance to the cavern. I could tell because we would run twenty or thirty paces in one direction, turn sharply, and switch back in the other direction, all the time headed uphill. At some point Freeman set off the explosive charges he had placed around the cavern earlier. The sound of the explosion penetrated my helmet in the form of a faint growl.

And then just when I thought it would never happen, we had reached the tunnel that led out of the mountain. Freeman set off an explosion meant to keep any spider-things from following us. The powerful blast pushed at our backs, and suddenly I felt fresh air on my face as Freeman pulled the helmet from my head.

"You okay?" Freeman asked. We were in the open, standing outside the caverns. I could only squint because of the glare coming from the silver-white sky.

He handed me my helmet. There was a crack in the armor along the back, and the visor looked smoke-stained, like glass pulled from a fire. I could tell something had burned the back of my head, and my right shoulder throbbed. My neck hurt, too. "Fine," I said, as I headed toward the ridge and the climb down to our ship.

Climbing down the cord to the ship, I knew that something was wrong with my shoulders, but I was glad enough to be alive. I kept reliving the moment when I thought I was blind and alone in that cave. As much as I told myself that I really didn't care, I wanted to survive. I didn't want some spider-thing to tear me in half. I didn't want to breathe the contaminated air. I wanted to make it out of that cavern.

"So what did we get for our trouble, Ray?" I asked. "We know they have giant spiders digging a big hole in the side of the mountain. That seems like a big waste of time."

"Remember that underground city on the Mogat planet?" Freeman asked. "It had to start somewhere."

"You think that's what they're doing here?" I asked.

"I want to know about the gas they were spreading."

32

"Damn, what happened to you... sir?" Private Skittles, just back from his tour of duty at the Hen House, added the "sir" as an afterthought.

I had barely stepped into the barracks, and Skittles was the first Marine I saw. I had a sling over my right shoulder. My collarbone was broken, but the military had good medical facilities in Valhalla. The doctors grafted the bones back together and mended them well. The collarbone smarted, but I barely noticed it compared to the throbbing of my dislocated right shoulder.

When it dropped on me from the ceiling, the guardian spider had struck with enough force to dislocate my shoulder and shatter my collarbone. It also gave me a severe concussion, but the combination of instinct, neural programming, and high doses of combat hormone in my blood had masked the effects of the concussion.

I also had burns on my scalp and shoulder. Toxic fumes had seeped through hairline cracks in my helmet and shoulder pads, charring my skin. The armor itself was a complete write-off.

"I had an accident," I said.

"No kidding," Skittles said. "I always figured you were indestructible. That theory's out the window."

"Thanks," I said, and excused myself. I saw someone else I needed to speak to. Sitting on his bunk, playing a happy tune on his harmonica, Sergeant Mark Philips looked downright perky. He had his back propped against the wall, and one of his legs dangled over the edge of the cot, swinging with the beat of the song.

He put down the harmonica, and said, "I'd salute you, sir, but you might hurt yourself returning the salute."

"How did you like guarding the Hen House?" I asked.

"It beats running through a forest filled with shit-colored aliens," Philips said. "How do I sign up for another tour?"

"Did you see any action?" I asked.

"Oh, I saw action," Philips said with a schoolboy grin.

It did not take a genius IQ to interpret that message. He had found his way into some officer's house. Thomer had been right about him.

The team of scientists and soldiers that designed the clones had wrestled with the idea of stripping out their sex drive. In the end, the officers overseeing the project argued that an army of eunuchs would be worthless in combat. Those officers were long dead, but maybe Philips had found his way into the bedroom of one of their descendants. If so, they deserved what they got.

I left the barracks, hoping to slip back to my quarters for some rest. The doctor had even given me some pills to help me sleep, but no one in his right mind would take sleeping pills this close to the front. Get luded before a fight, and you might find yourself asleep when the enemy comes knocking on your door.

I went to the elevator. Tired as I was, I lacked the concentration to tell my men from any other clones. Men walked by and saluted me. I nodded, not sure if they were from my company.

When I entered my billet, I found the room just as I had left it. My white combat armor sat on the table beside my neatly made bed. Even here, with no one inspecting my rack, I kept a tidy room. I turned off the lights and dropped onto my rack to rest.

Then I saw the red light flashing on the communications console.

The first message was from General Glade. "Harris, I just got a report from Sweetwater. You should have heard the dwarf bastard; he sounds like he's going to wet his pants. Report down here ASAP."

A summons from a general, I thought, as I drifted to sleep. Then came the second message.

"Speck! Speck! Where the hell did they send him? Harris, this is Moffat. Where the hell are you?"

The third message was Moffat again. "Damn it. Harris." He sounded insane with anger. "I want a list of the men you sent on guard duty. You got that? I want that list now."

The fourth message. "Harris? Did you authorize Sergeant Philips to guard the Hen House? That wife-specking son of a bitch! I'll see that that specker gets the firing squad. You got me?"

That woke me up.

General Glade met me at the door of his office. He let me in, told me to sit, then started pacing back and forth in front of his desk. "I heard you had a rough time of it," he said. "Did you get hurt?" He had nothing remotely resembling concern as he asked the question. Like any general, he was a man who routinely sent other men out to die. He could not do his job without caring more about the missions than the men he sent to do them.

I should have appreciated his feeble attempt at courtesy. He was, after all, a natural-born and a general.

"I'm fine, sir," I said. Hell, he could see that my arm was in a sling. I had a severely blackened eye. How the hell I got a black eye wearing a combat helmet was beyond me. A bald spot and a bandage marked the burn where the gas seeped into the back of the helmet.

"Good. Glad to hear it," he responded so quickly he nearly cut me off. "I heard your armor failed."

"My visor," I said.

"Breeze had his team take a look at it. They say it shorted out when the alien touched you, a complete system overload."

"Was there anything on the video record?" I asked.

"There is no record, Harris. Breeze says every circuit in your helmet fused. You would have been electrocuted if your armor had a higher ratio of metal to plastic." *Huuhhhhhh. Huhhhhh.* He cleared his throat, stopped pacing, stared down at me, and said, "I hate those specking scientists."

"Sweetwater and Breeze?" I asked.

"Yes, Sweetwater and Breeze." He snorted. He cleared his throat again. "I don't know why we bother with them. So far the only thing Dr. Sweetwater has been able to discover about the aliens is that they break instead of die." He laughed. "I'll tell you what, Harris, the Unified Authority Marines do not care if their enemies break, die, or give birth to triplets so long as they stop moving when they are shot in the head."

"Begging the general's pardon, but I don't see how we can possibly win this one with bullets and bombs," I said. "If we're going to survive, the only way we can do it is if the lab comes up with something."

General Glade stopped pacing finally and sat behind his desk. "You seem like a man who keeps confidences. I'll tell you a secret even the Army brass doesn't know."

For effect, Glade looked around the empty office to make sure no one was listening. "Sweetwater was the last man off Terraneau before the Angels sleeved it. The dwarf took off just as the ion curtain began to spread."

"That sounds like a lucky break," I said.

Glade sat up so quickly and so straight you would have thought someone had stung him with an electric prod. "Lucky break, my ass, Lieutenant. He's a coward. He turned and ran. Everyone else on the planet is dead... everyone but him."

I wanted to point out that (A) there had to be a pilot to fly him off the planet and (B) technically speaking, we did not know if anyone on that planet had died. For all we knew, some botanist had discovered a tachyon-eating rubber tree, and the entire population of Terraneau was alive and well and watering their gardens twice a day.

"I don't suspect Sweetwater would have contributed much to the battle if they had sent him in with an M27," I said.

Glade stopped. I suspect he was imagining William Sweetwater carrying an M27. He laughed, fought back more laughter, took a deep breath, and started laughing again. "I have this picture of the little bastard wearing a man-sized helmet." He laughed again.

I smiled to be politic but did not laugh.

"Harris, have you seen Lieutenant Moffat since you got back?" Glade asked.

"He left a couple of messages in my quarters," I said.

"Do you know what happened at the Hen House?"

"I have a pretty good idea."

"He's calling for a firing squad," Glade said. "Major Burton had to post a couple of MPs inside the barracks in case Moffat goes on a rampage. Philips isn't allowed out of the barracks, and Moffat isn't allowed in. That's no way to run a base."

"Philips was confined to barracks?" I asked.

"Sure he was," Glade said, "pending his court-martial hearing."

"The guy's got a set of stones on him," I said. "I ran into him on my way in."

"He wasn't out of…?"

"No, nothing like that. He was sitting on his rack playing his damn harmonica. You'd have thought he was on vacation. He asked me to sign him up for another tour of guard duty," I said.

General Glade changed the subject. "So you and Freeman infiltrated the Avatari dig. What the hell is going on down there? What did you see, Harris?"

"Spiders," I said. "Spiders the size of small trucks."

33

Ignoring my own best advice, I took one of those sleeping pills and went to bed after meeting with General Glade. I slept for sixteen hours. I dreamed of a planet with winter forests, steel gray lakes the size of small oceans, high mountains buried in snow, and beneath it all, a wretched hell filled with giant spiders. I dreamed of New Copenhagen, dreams that grew out of reality. I squirmed and rolled in my sleep, sweating so profusely that the sheets became drenched and clung to my skin. The medicine I had taken gave my imagination a vivid, hallucinatory quality so that the bumps and jerks I made in my sleep worked their way into the fabric of my dreams.

When I woke, my mouth was dry and the world seemed to spin around me. I heard loud ringing in my ears, but that had nothing to do with tranquilizers. The ringing was real. It was the steel shriek of the klaxons calling every man to arms. I recognized the pattern in the noise; this was a yellow alert.

I sat up and tried to clear my head. Outside my door, the hallway echoed with the rattle and thud of doors slamming and men readying for battle. As I slid from my bed, I felt a twinge in my arm and shoulder.

I would need to put on armor before heading out, I knew that, as did the doctor who had set my shoulder. He had given me medicine to "mask" the pain. I turned on a light in my room, fumbled around the table until I found the medicine, took the pill, then changed into my bodysuit. By the time I strapped on my chest plate, I felt no pain.

As I left my quarters, I detected a feeling of panic. Officers ran through the hall in a helter-skelter frenzy, bumping into each other, pushing each other, rushing in a dizzy flurry and not speaking. It was almost as if they shared a universal premonition of something bad, not just a battle, but a defeat.

With my head clearing, I came to realize why the brass had only issued a yellow alert. This was to be the old men's march. This was the battle in which the Army would thin its ranks and preserve its munitions, not so much a genocide as a chronocide. They were killing clones according to age.

General Newcastle would flood the battlefield with his white-haired soldiers, the clones Philips had labeled the "Prune Juice Brigade." The general's plan was to win the fight by overwhelming the Avatari with vastly superior numbers, knowing he would lose the majority of his troops.

"Harris, where are you?" Moffat's voice sounded stiff as he addressed me over the interLink. Unless somebody had let him know that I had slept most of the last twenty-four hours, he would probably think I was avoiding him.

"Just entering the mez now," I said as I spilled out of the stairwell and onto the second floor. "What is the situation?"

"From what I hear, the Army's taking point on this one. Major Burton says we're on deck. Base Command wants us suited up in case the Mudders break through."

I entered the hallway that passed the various ballrooms-turned-barracks. Walking past the Odin Ballroom, I peered in and saw hundreds of men in white armor standing at attention. I had gotten off to a late start.

Klaxons still blaring, officers ran from barracks to barracks checking on troop readiness. I entered the Valkyrie Ballroom and saw the Marines standing at attention.

"Nice of you to join us, Harris," Moffat said, as I came through the door. "I hear you've been goldbricking." He might not have been allowed in the barracks during off hours, but as we prepared for an attack, he took his place at the head of the company. Without replying, I walked around the ranks and stood beside Moffat. Moments later we received an order from Major Burton calling for the entire battalion to fall in.

General Morris Newcastle, commander of the combined armed forces stationed on New Copenhagen, left few things to chance. For this battle, he selected the two hundred fifty thousand oldest soldiers under his command and stationed them in the woods six miles west of town. He assigned fifty thousand younger troops to man the Vista Street bunker. Granted, I could have made a fortune selling canes and dentures to the old fellows in the forest, but Newcastle sent enough men into battle to give himself a five-to-one numerical advantage.

At 0412, with the sky as bright as noonday, the spheres dilated and fifty thousand Avatari troops entered the forest. They moved east, following the same route they had taken on their previous assaults. Cameras stationed along the way—by this time the Army, Marines, civilian militia, and Science Lab had all placed cameras—were broadcasting images of their march back to town.

More than an hour passed before the Avatari stepped into the Army's trap. Their path took them into a brilliantly prepared gauntlet that gave Newcastle's soldiers the high-ground advantage and better cover.

Over the last three days, the Corps of Engineers had given the forest a practical make over. They dug tight channels that led scores of Avatari into narrow trenches. Standing above those trenches our soldiers could safely lob grenades. The engineers built up earth-and-concrete palisades so steep and high that the Avatari could not possibly see soldiers hiding behind them. They built blinds in which entire brigades could hide, and they designated rallying points where men from broken platoons could gather and regroup. In war, redundancy is the mother of victory, and General Morris Newcastle had covered all his bases.

The breakdown was not tactical but strategic. The brass had decided to win this one with men, grenades, and bullets so that they could reserve the more valuable munitions for later. But even after all the preparation, Newcastle's old men were not up to the task. The first problem was the weapons. Particle-beam weapons were effective enough against Avatari, but our general-issue particle-beam pistols were designed for close-range combat. M27s were accurate at over a hundred yards, but against the Avatari, they had proven ineffective at any range.

At 0723, the Avatari marched into the kill zone. Instead of staying to the low ground as expected, they fanned out, forming a thousand-man picket line. They spread out along the high ground, the low ground, and on the steep slopes in between.

It was a crazy formation that left them wide open to a frontal attack, but it screwed the hell out of the Army's FOCPIG preparations. Moving forward with that wide a front line, the Avatari wrapped around our blinds and palisades, trapping Newcastle's old men's brigades inside. Then the Avatari opened fire with their light-bolt weapons, boring through earthworks, sandbags, and trenches. The Avatari rifles had twice the range of our particle-beam pistols. Avatari light bolts cut through trees, slammed through embankments, exploded boulders.

Forced out of their cover, our antique soldiers tried to execute a staged retreat—falling back, taking cover, wearing down the enemy; but they were too old to run and gun. They lacked the mobility needed for an ordered retreat.

The front line of eighty thousand men Newcastle sent to stall the aliens did not last the hour. The troops he sent to flank and attack from the rear were massacred. And then...

* * *

Certain that a force of two hundred fifty thousand men would hold off the enemy, somebody at the top had issued an order to service the rocket launchers along the Vista Street bunker. For this reason, the missile defenses sat partially assembled when nearly forty thousand Avatari entered the no-man's-land on the outskirts of the city.

Without the missiles protecting their position, the men in the bunker had no more protection against the Avatari advance than the men in the forest.

"In the trucks, now! Move it! Move it! Double time!" I growled. I had my helmet on, and my voice came ringing back into my ears so loud it made them numb.

Some of the men clambered into the trucks even as they slowly pulled away from the sidewalks. Thomer stood at the back of the truck helping the stragglers make it up. As they jumped onto the bumper, he grabbed their arms and hoisted them in.

Around the U-shaped hotel driveway, I saw Marines in full battle armor sprinting to keep up with trucks that had already left them behind. There was no need to rush, once the trucks left the hotel drive, they entered streets clogged by gridlock. The Valhalla was one of dozens of hotel/barracks in this part of town. Hundreds of transport trucks now streamed out of every hotel driveway. Without police managing the flash flood of traffic, the congestion was inevitable.

"Shit! Shit! Shit!" Major Burton said over a network that every officer in his battalion could hear. With the Army's inability to stop the Avatari outside the city, the situation had turned from routine to dire.

Attempting to find a way around the traffic jam, transport drivers tried side streets and alleys. A row of trucks pulled onto the sidewalk, plowing over mailboxes, signs, and benches. In the streets, the traffic crawled at no more than five miles per hour.

"Everybody out!" I shouted.

"Harris, what are you doing?" Moffat asked over the interLink.

"Out! Move it. Move it!" Men leaped from the truck.

"It's only a mile or two from here to Vista Street," I said. "We can run it faster than this."

Moffat did not respond. Behind us I saw other companies doing the same, off-loading Marines and ordering them to run. With the trucks moving at such a slow crawl, we easily outpaced them.

I heard mortar fire as we got closer. I expected to enter the shielded bunkers along Vista Street; but we never reached Vista, the retreat had already begun. We reached the front end of the traffic jam and ran into the tide of men in green fatigues filling the streets.

Up ahead, the Vista Street bunker looked as jagged as a saw blade. Entire sections of the bunker had collapsed, other sections stood in ruins, shot through with so many holes that I could see right through the walls to other side.

"Hold the street." Burton gave the potentially fatal command over a frequency that would reach every man in the battalion; and I repeated it to my company.

"Dig in. Find cover," I shouted. Cars, corners, Dumpsters, signs, mailboxes, anything was better than standing out in the open. The Avatari could shoot through any barrier, but at least a car or a bush would offer someplace to hide. There was not enough cover to go around; and behind us, Marines were arriving by the tens of thousands.

I had a brief moment in which I wondered if the Avatari would actually breach the bunker. Then came the explosion—a powerful, jarring force that ran the entire length of the street. Suddenly, all that remained of the Vista Street bunker were a few of its ribs—massive arching girders that stood as separate from each other as the goalposts on either end of a football field. Everything else turned to rubble so loose you could drive a jeep over it.

Beyond the bunker, the Avatari horde came slowly across the

charred landscape that had once been the outskirts of Valhalla. I took a step back and thudded into something. When I turned to look, I saw that I had backed into an unarmed rocket launcher, its panels still hanging open for maintenance.

"This is General James P. Glade. Men, we need to hold this position at all costs. I have tanks and helicopter gunboats on the way." His voice had a forced calm about it. There was none of his customary throat clearing, none of the wildness or swagger. He took the tone of a father explaining life to his young son.

"I ask you men to give everything now… everything. If you die here, you die a savior. If mankind survives this war, it will survive because of the sacrifices you make on this street on this day.

"I am sending in every Marine under my command, officers and enlisted men alike. Help is on its way, but you must hold this position until it arrives. Fight to the last man. Fight to your dying breath. Do you understand me, Marines? The future of everything you have ever known or cared about depends on you holding this street."

Now there's a cheerful message, I thought to myself as I watched the Avatari wade through the wreckage of the bunker. He was right, though. It wasn't the street that mattered, it was the defenses along the street. Our rocket launchers had proven themselves to be our best weapon against the Avatari, and most of the launchers were lined up along this street. The problem was, I didn't think we could hold.

The aliens were still too far away for us to hit them when the first squadron of gunboats floated overhead. There were ten of them, and each got off a couple of rockets, then the Avatari fired back, aiming those big rifles in the air. I watched three bolts cut through one of the gunboats like an ice pick stabbing through a balloon. Trails of smoke rose from the fuselage of the gunboat as it began a slow rotation along the wing, and the chopper dropped out of the sky. Less than a minute after they appeared in the skyline, all ten gunboats went down.

Most of my men had general-issue particle-beam pistols with

an effective range of approximately fifty feet. Soldiers with M27s opened fire while the Avatari were still hundreds of yards away. As the Avatari closed to within a hundred yards, our grenadiers began firing at them. Boll and Skittles moved to the front of the platoon and piped handheld rockets into the advancing Avatari. Boll, the more experienced Marine, punched holes in the Avatari line.

The Avatari blended into the charred landscape. They were dark, the color of mud made from volcanic soil. So much smoke rose around them that they sometimes disappeared from view, but they never wavered. They never hesitated. They moved ahead, a juggernaut. I thought to myself, *Where are the tanks?* But I already knew the answer—they were back at the hotels, trapped in the traffic jam.

The Avatari came closer and began returning fire. We were no match for them. Their bolts drilled us no matter where we hid. Cars, buildings, trees, nothing offered enough protection. Up the block from me, an Army sniper hid behind the ruins of a Targ, an antipersonnel tank. He would stand, aim quickly over the front end of the tank, fire an explosive round, then duck back behind the protection of the tank. He was a good sniper; I saw him hit and break three Avatari with three shots before the Avatari retaliated with a barrage of their own. Dozens of bolts bored through the tank, turning its armor into a sieve. Three or four of the bolts hit the sniper, tearing holes through his body. The wounds were seared dry; no blood leaked from the wounds as the man slumped to the ground with his rifle across his lap.

Seeing the sniper die even as he hid behind a tank, I realized we would never hold this street. The Avatari fired a fusillade of bolts in my direction, ripping into my men and ravaging our cover. The aliens continued to come toward us in their disorganized march. They stepped into range of our particle-beam weapons, and we returned their fire.

So many particle-beam weapons fired at once that it looked like the facade of reality had cracked, releasing a sparkling green river of light. Rays from the particle-beam pistols hit walls, windows, the remnants of jeeps abandoned along the street and the advancing Avatari. Everything the beams hit exploded, and still the Avatari drove us back. They had no fear. They felt no pain. They lost nothing when they were shot. Death, to them, was little more than an inconvenience.

I heard the pop of M27 fire and saw soldiers firing from the second-story windows of the building behind a rocket launcher. These were technicians; I could tell by the insignia on their fatigues. Once they realized the Avatari were coming, they must have quit working on the launchers and barricaded themselves. Four techs climbed out of a window and leaped onto the top of the rocket launcher. As three fiddled with cables, the fourth aimed a single tube by hand, flipped a switch, and fired a lone rocket.

Across the street, the Avatari continued pushing their way forward. The rocket shot out of the tube, leaving a slanted string of smoke so narrow it might have been drawn with a pen. It struck the ground, throwing dozens of Avatari into the air and shattering a twenty-foot swath of street.

The Avatari seemed not to notice. The brown-black giants continued flowing toward us, firing their deadly light bolts. Men dropped on either side of me. Frustrated by the short range of his particle-beam pistol, one Marine tossed it aside and pulled out his M27. A light bolt struck him square in the visor, searing through his head and helmet. Though he had to have died instantly, the Marine continued standing on the spot for two or three seconds before he fell.

We had no choice but to yield. The Avatari would take the street and capture the rocket launchers no matter what we did. I could see this clearly; my combat reflex was in full swing. I felt calm. I was a man at peace in a chaotic battle.

"Harris, close in around the launchers," Moffat yelled. "We need to hold the launchers."

He was wrong. The batteries were lost, and I saw no point in losing my company along with them. The last thing we should do was cluster together. That would enable the Avatari to kill several men with each shot. Up and down the street, Marines were already dropping a few at a time.

We still had a huge numerical advantage, but that advantage was fading. We needed to attack. I stepped onto the street. The men from my company instinctively followed me. One of my men stepped in front of me, and a bolt slashed him across the throat, vaporizing the bottom of his helmet and taking his chin with it. He fell face-first to the sidewalk.

His virtual dog tag still showed—Corporal Ted Robinson. He had been alive just a moment earlier and ready to follow me even before I'd issued an order. If I had told him to stay back, he would still be alive, but I had no time for regret.

I contacted Burton, the battalion commander, on a direct frequency, bypassing Moffat. "Major, we need to launch a counterattack."

"How many do you need?" Burton asked.

"All three companies," I said. "And we need to act fast."

Burton did not waste a moment considering my recommendation before issuing the order, telling the men to rally together at a virtual beacon he placed precisely where I stood. Our grenadiers held back, concentrating their fire, blasting a hole in the Avatari line.

What was left of our battalion formed behind me. Grenadiers firing over us, soldiers with M27s behind us, we rushed the enemy firing our pistols as we ran across the street and into their line.

I leaped a tangled barrier and flew over the curb onto the other side of the street. I could hear men coming up behind me but kept my eyes straight ahead. Bolts struck into the crowd around me, but almost all of the Avatari fire flew over our heads. A rocket struck in the direction I was headed, sending up a geyser of dirt, concrete, and flames. I could see dark shapes in the haze, towering figures that moved slowly. I fired. The moment I saw any movement in the haze, I fired, all the while hoping that the men behind me would not shoot me in the back.

Remembering how my armor shorted out when that spider-thing attacked me, I shouted, "Don't let them touch you!" over an open frequency. We were in close now; my warning may have come too late for some. Running forward in a crouch as fast as I could, I almost fell on my face when I stepped onto the layer of loose slag that had once been the bunkers.

An alien stepped in my way and stopped. It did not seem to notice me. I shot it in the leg. As it collapsed, I prepared to shoot it again, then saw that there was no need. A cloud of powder whooshed out around the body as it hit the ground. The thing was severely chipped and dented, probably scars first received as the Avatari massacred our old soldiers out in the forest. My shot to the leg was just the finishing offense.

Crouching beside the broken alien, I moved my pistol from one target to the next. Before I could get back to my feet, another wave of Avatari came. I fired three shots, and more Avatari fell. The battle seemed to swell around me. By charging in, our battalion had broken the Avatari line in this one spot, forcing it to collapse in on itself. Listening to the chatter on the interLink, I could tell that this place was one of the few spots that we had managed to hold. Along Vista Street, the Marines who had tried to hold their positions were now in full retreat. Batteries of rocket launchers had fallen into Avatari hands.

Through the smoke, haze, and dust, I saw green beams and silver-white bolts. Then I saw something new. Across the street, a building lit up. For just a moment it looked like the red bricks along its walls had turned to glass, revealing a bright light in its heart, then the building collapsed to its foundation. The destruction was so fast and so clean that it appeared as if the whole thing imploded.

I did not have time to think about what was happening behind me. Marines continued to charge into the gap we had created. We fanned into the enemy lines and spread behind them. The Avatari seemed more interested in bludgeoning their way across the street than stopping our charge.

One Avatari soldier aimed its rifle at the Marine beside me and fired. I managed to shove the man out of the way, and the bolt struck another Avatari, searing through the big alien the way it might pierce a tank or hill. The wounded Avatari turned stiff and fell.

I caught a quick glimpse of Philips and Thomer leading a squad deeper into the Avatari line. A flash of green struck near Philips, missing him by inches. Philips ran on without noticing. There were no Avatari where that particle beam hit, just men. As I looked back, I saw Moffat, his particle-beam pistol extended in Philips's direction.

"Moffat," I said.

He did not answer.

Three Avatari moved toward me. There was a flash. One of them fired at me. Running on instinct, I dived for the powdery ground, somersaulted, and came up firing. I hit two of the Avatari. Someone else hit the third. I never saw who.

There was a flash across the street, coming from the spot where we had begun our charge. I looked over in time to see another building take on that glassy appearance and collapse. The whole thing happened so quickly that the tint shields in my visor did not react before the flash had imprinted itself on my brain. A negative image of the collapse replayed inside my eyelids.

When the tint cleared from my visor, I saw dust and rubble and the twisted remains of the rocket launcher. I looked for enemies to shoot, but the only survivors around me were Marines.

This part of the battle had ended. We held our ground, but the Avatari had still managed to destroy the rocket launchers. We were screwed.

34

Before we suspected it was there, the noose had tightened around our necks.

To hear the other generals talk about it, the entire debacle was Newcastle's fault. I suppose it might have been his fault in a "the buck stops here" way, but he did everything by the book. He set his soldiers up with a specking five-to-one advantage. Granted, they were all old men, but there were so damn many of them.

The big mistake was authorizing the techs to work on the rocket launchers with the enemy on the way. In a show of no confidence and a play for power, the two Army generals under Newcastle authorized an investigation into the error. We were trapped on a planet, fighting an enemy we could not hurt, cut off from the rest of the galaxy, and the brass was still wrangling for power. I should have seen it coming; these men were career officers, not soldiers. They thought like politicians.

The investigation only took a day. The men in charge concluded that the rocket launchers were complex pieces of machinery that required routine maintenance after every battle—maintenance that generally required a minimum of four days to complete.

With the Avatari attacking every three days, finding a good time to disassemble and repair the batteries was pretty much out of the question. The investigators also discovered that Newcastle had nothing to do with the maintenance of the rocket launchers. The order to work on the batteries had come from Brigadier General Samuel Hauer, the tough little weasel who was number two in the Army chain of command. As Hauer was the one who called for the investigation in the first place, the matter was dropped. Hauer resigned his commission the following day.

Even after the investigation ended, whenever General Glade referred to this battle, he inevitably called it, "Newcastle's speckup." He also referred to the ruins along Vista Street as "Newcastle's sandbox."

I heard all of this secondhand. Generals like Glade and Newcastle did not invite me to their high-level meetings unless Sweetwater or Breeze asked for me by name.

I had it better than any of my men. At least I knew about the Science Lab. I knew that the government had assigned great minds to this planet. My men heard nothing about Sweetwater and Breeze. They heard about the infighting among the generals and saw the costs of incompetent command, but they heard nothing about the mines, the spider-things, or whatever discoveries the scientists might make. Not that it mattered. The generals distracted most of their men with bounties for dog pelts and other entertainment. And then there was the work. We had an embattled city to maintain.

I didn't allow myself to worry too much about incompetent leadership as I fell into the rhythm of life without the protection of Vista Street. Within hours of the battle, the brass placed all personnel on a new duty schedule. We had a twelve-hour work detail, followed by a four-hour shift in which we could do whatever we liked, then an eight-hour sleep period.

The brass enforced this new schedule with a vengeance. We could loaf around the base or slum around town during our off hours; but, to a man, anyone not present and accounted for during work shifts and lights-out would find himself in the brig.

* * *

I spent my first work detail driving into the forest with Philips, Thomer, and eight other men looking for survivors. I did not think we would find anyone with a pulse, but I was wrong.

It was a cold, miserable shift. By the clock, it was 2200 when we arrived on the spot. The time did not matter as far as daylight was concerned, not with the ion curtain smothering the planet in a blanket of light. But ion curtain or no ion curtain, Valhalla became colder at night. The rest of the men wore combat armor; the lucky bastards had climate-controlled bodysuits to keep them warm. My dislocated shoulder already hurt from the last time I'd put on my armor, so I came in fatigues with an interLink piece clipped to my ear.

We found our first bodies along the highway, just a scattering of men the Avatari had killed as they headed toward town. Once we went off road, we found large pockets where soldiers had died trying to make a stand. They were everywhere, and it quickly became obvious that once shot, no one survived. We found a few wounded who had fallen behind because of broken legs or other injuries.

Philips and Thomer took turns loading survivors into jeeps and chauffeuring them back to town, while the rest of us stayed back to "smart tag" the dead. Smart tagging meant painting a laser beacon onto the bodies. This was not about burying the dead; it was about accounting. By scanning the bodies with lasers, we cataloged how many had died.

Burial was not a high priority. Right now we had more important things to do. With any luck, the winter chill would keep the bodies from decomposing too quickly. Once the spring thaw began, we'd probably set the forest on fire to cremate the remains.

So there we were, bright ion curtain light dissolving anything even resembling a shadow under the thick canopy of trees. I was cold and wishing I had worn my armor, bad shoulder or no, when Phillips said, "There are a lot more humans than Mudders out here."

"I heard the Mudders evaporate after you kill 'em," Thomer said.

Part of me wanted to say, "At the Science Lab, they refer to it as degrading, but these creatures are not 'Mudders,' they are 'Avatari,' and they don't die, they break." I wanted to tell them the truth. They deserved to know what they were up against. Instead, I followed the party line and played dumb. I said, "Yeah, I heard that, too."

"How many do you think we've tagged so far, sir?" Thomer asked. He brushed aside the ferns and made a gagging noise as if he was about to vomit. Even Philips grimaced.

"Six of 'em down here," Philips said. "Hey, there's barbecued brain poking out of this guy's skull." Philips was faking the old bravado. That was a good sign. I found myself watching Philips constantly, looking for signs of him recovering from the shock of losing Huish and White in our first encounter with the Avatari.

He had not yet reverted back to the reckless, obnoxious Philips of old, but some of his former swagger had returned to him. I could push him more now, but I didn't dare mention Moffat or the Hen House.

"Okay, we got them," Thomer said, straightening up and dusting dirt from his armor. "Where now?"

I suggested we head over the rise.

"Are you guys heading into town after this?" Philips asked. He sounded hopeful. He was still restricted to the barracks, but I mentioned that I might ask Major Burton for permission to take him out with us.

"After this detail? Man, I want to get good and drunk," said Thomer, who seldom got drunk.

"How about you, Harris?" Philips asked. As a noncom addressing a superior officer, he was supposed to refer to me as "Lieutenant" or "sir," but under the current circumstances...

"I'm ready to tie on a good one," I admitted.

We crested the rise, and the massacre was suddenly laid out before us. Fatigue-clad bodies carpeted the ground ahead of us, and every last one of them had muddy white hair and brown eyes wide open and startled. They lay in intricate patterns like the pieces of a jigsaw puzzle poured out of a box.

"Lord." Thomer sighed.

"Shit," groaned Philips. "There must be a million of them down there."

I surveyed the scene. It was absolutely still. Even the wind had stopped, but not everything was silent.

"There's a live one," Thomer said. He pointed along the ridge that surrounded the clearing. There, sitting on the ridge, was an old soldier curled around an M27. He cradled it to his chest and rocked back and forth. His sobs carried across the forest floor.

"Go get the jeep," I told Philips. "We'd better run this guy back to town."

Thomer and I stepped over bodies and made our way around the rim of the clearing. When we came to the bottom of his hill, the old man turned and stared down at us. "The Liberator," he said, his voice drenched with disgust. "All of these men die, and the specking Liberator makes it out alive."

It was Glen Benson, the Liberator-hating old man who sat next to me on that flight to Mars. Even with all these men dead around him, this piece of shit could not let go of his prejudice. *All these men died, and this asshole walks off the field untouched,* I thought, then realized he had just said the exact same thing about me.

"What is your name, Corporal?" Thomer asked, stepping between me and Benson.

"Benson. Corporal Glen Benson."

"Are you hurt?" Thomer asked.

"Just my leg," Benson said. Now that he mentioned it, I saw that it was bent at an unnatural angle.

"We'll take you into town," Thomer said, as Philips came driving over the ridge, his jeep bouncing as it cleared ruts in the ground. He worked a miracle, managing to drive right up to us without running over any bodies.

"Thomer, why don't you drive Corporal Benson back to town," I said, trying to sound sympathetic.

Benson shook his head. "I'm staying here with my platoon."

"You're doing what with who?" Philips asked. There was no sympathy in his voice; he let his outrage show. "Listen here, you old specker, we ain't got time to argue. We have a war to fight."

"These men died…"

"Damn specking right they died. That's why they've got all them holes in them," Philips said.

"I belong with my platoon," Glen protested.

"You do? You planning on killing yourself, or are you just going to sit around crying and wait for the Mudders to come back?"

I thought Benson would either shoot Philips or put a bullet in his own fool head. Instead, he climbed to his feet, wincing at the pain and obviously unsteady. Thomer grabbed him by the shoulder and helped him walk to the jeep.

"Can I drive the old bastard in?" Philips asked loud enough for Benson to hear. He had clearly taken a liking to the old fool.

"Doesn't matter to me," Thomer said, as he arranged Benson in the back of the jeep.

As they drove away, Thomer muttered, "What an asshole."

I nodded, then asked, "Which one?"

Over the next two days, more than ten thousand survivors found their way back to Valhalla from the forest. The rest of the two hundred and fifty thousand troops were officially listed M.I.A., though everyone knew they were deader than Caesar's ghost. We lost another thirty-five thousand men when the Avatari rolled over the bunker. More than two hundred and seventy-five thousand men died in a single day.

It wasn't the loss of manpower that upset the balance of power. We lost twenty-five rocket launchers when the battle reached Vista Street. With only six hundred thousand men and no working missile defenses along the western edge of Valhalla, we could no longer enforce our perimeter.

From here on out, the Avatari would be able to wage their war in town.

35

There were seven of us—Thomer, Skittles, Boll, Herrington, Manning, Sharpes, and me. Manning and Sharpes were from another company in the battalion, but we could overlook that shortcoming. The numbers in our company were down after the battle for Vista Street.

I had hoped to get Philips off the shit list, so he could come with us, but no such luck. When I asked Major Burton, our battalion commander, to give Philips the night off, he had refused even to consider the idea.

I did not bother asking Burton if he wanted to come into town with us because he would have said no. He would not come to town with a pack of enlisted men. As an officer, I wasn't supposed to fraternize with the enlisted folk either, but I did not think my fellow officers would mind. They were natural-born, I was a clone. I might have received the bars but that did not make me part of their fraternity. Knowing that I would never be counted an equal in the loyal order of officers, I fraternized with the conscripts.

We borrowed a truck and drove to the bar and restaurant

district. The first time I went for a joyride downtown, trucks were reserved for officers and noncoms who could produce a requisition slip signed by an officer. This time, Corporal Manning said he could procure the truck. When I volunteered to sign for it, he said, "Don't sweat it, I took care of it."

Since he'd signed his life away on the truck, Manning got to drive. Herrington rode shotgun up front. The rest of us piled in the back and swapped stories as we drove up Carlson Avenue and into town. I listened to the conversations around me but did not join in.

I had become preoccupied with what I saw. We passed a park that the Corps of Engineers had turned into a city dump with a twenty-foot-tall mountain range of garbage. Birds swooped down from the sky to hop along the garbage and pick at it. Cat-sized rats scurried around the base of the garbage. Seeing the birds and the rats, I wondered how long it would take until those carrion feeders found their way to the dead soldiers in the forest.

We drove down streets along which new barricades were under construction. The brass planned to cordon these areas off. With the Vista Street bunker destroyed, these areas might soon become the new fronts.

Some places we passed showed new signs of urban decay. We drove by an L-shaped bank building in which the wind had blown huge piles of loose papers along the walls; they looked like snowdrifts. Vandals had painted signs on a couple of police stations in one part of town. Other areas of town were immaculate. We drove past a central park in which dozens of soldiers worked, picking up trash, raking leaves, and trimming hedges.

"I heard you went out on a tagging detail," Boll said.

"Yeah," Thomer answered.

"What was it like out there?"

"A lot of trees and shit," I said, breaking in and hoping to stop Thomer from saying anything that might hurt company morale. That was a direct order, by the way. Officers were told to keep their men from speculating about the situation for all the good it would do. Telling Marines not to discuss the battle was like ordering someone who has been shot in the gut to stop bleeding. Stuff leaks out, no matter what you do.

"Did you find dead soldiers?" Boll asked.

Technically, I was supposed to tell them to change the subject, but they would have just fired up the conversation again a little later.

"Are you kidding?" Thomer asked. "We found this one clearing where they were piled up on top of each other. It was all those old guys, thousands of them."

"Did you find any Mudders?" Boll asked.

"Not many. I bet we lost a hundred men for every one of theirs that we killed," Thomer said.

"I heard it wasn't that bad, someone told me we lost twenty-five of ours for every one of theirs." Boll said.

"Maybe," Thomer said. "I only saw one small piece of the battlefield."

"I heard somewhere that we lost about two hundred and fifty thousand men out there and they lost ten thousand. That's about twenty-five to one." Boll was not going to let the subject drop.

"That wasn't what I saw," Thomer said. "It was almost like they were throwing those old guys away... like they didn't care whether—"

"Thomer," I said, realizing that I had let the conversation go too long. Smarter and more alert than any clone I knew, Thomer had just strayed too close to the truth. Newcastle had thrown men away.

"Sir?" he asked, not sure why I had interrupted him.

"Did you ever bag any dogs?" I asked for lack of a better way to change the subject. "I heard you can earn a full month's pay for shooting a few strays."

Thomer looked confused.

"I got one," said Sharpes.

"I bagged eight of them," Skittles said. "And Moffat paid up on them, too. Two specking weeks' worth of pay in a single afternoon. Now if I just had something good to spend it on."

"I hear the locals opened a Tune and Lude," Sharpes said.

The term "Tune and Lude" referred to dance clubs where they played loud music and served up enormous amounts of alcohol. Some ran a steady trade in illegal drugs; but that did not concern me, the neural programming in military clones stopped them from abusing drugs. Most Tune and Ludes, respectable or otherwise, were tied in with some form of prostitution. Some even had built-in hotels that rented rooms by the hour.

"Are you kidding me?" Thomer asked. "All-male Tune and Ludes, that's kind of disgusting."

"No way," Sharpes replied. "They brought in scrub."

Thomer, ever the Boy Scout, shook his head. "That's not going to help us win this war."

"I don't know. A good wiggle always helps me stay focused," Sharpes quipped.

"I heard Philips managed to get hooked up while he was in the Hen House," Boll said.

Skittles, who went with Philips, burst into a fit of laughter. "He bagged Lieutenant Moffat's wife."

"It isn't funny," said Thomer.

He started to launch into a lecture on honor when Skittles said, "You haven't seen Moffat's wife."

"Was she pretty?" Boll asked.

"Pretty in two ways—pretty ugly and pretty likely to stay that way," Skittles said. "She's got a face like a bear and legs like a chicken. If I had a wife like her, I wouldn't know whether to kill her or cut off my wanger.

"It didn't stop Philips, though. That guy is crazy. Did you see his tattoo?"

Thomer smiled and nodded. "I saw it."

"His tattoo?" I asked.

Skittles laughed. "Yeah, he got a Lilly Moffat tattoo."

Everyone laughed except Thomer and me. "I think Moffat took a shot at Philips during the fighting on Vista Street," I said. That quieted them down.

"Are you serious?" Thomer asked.

"I can't prove it," I said. "He's called for a firing squad. One way or another, he wants Philips dead. Can't say that I blame him."

That killed the conversation, but that was okay. We had just pulled in to the entertainment district. Packs of men in uniforms lined the streets. In fact, downtown looked more crowded than I had ever seen it.

I thought about the barricaded streets we passed, and the parks used for trash dumps. Somebody was closing off entire sections of town, compressing the population into smaller neighborhoods to hide our losses. Not a bad idea. It might keep morale up for a while, until men started noticing that no one along the street had white hair and wrinkles.

As we moved through the streets, I heard the sound of music thumping and the ringing of feminine voices. Hundreds of soldiers and Marines were fighting their way into a little alley. At least a dozen girls in short dresses danced and mooned down on the soldiers from a balcony above.

"I guess you found your Tune and Lude," Thomer said.

Sharpes, Skittles, and Manning stopped to stare into the crowd. "You guys coming?" Skittles asked.

"Doesn't interest me," Herrington said. He was older than the other men, sort of a father figure.

"I think they're staying," said Boll.

I placed a hand on Manning's shoulder, and said, "Give me the truck keys if you're staying here."

"Oh," he said. He took one last longing look at the girls on the balcony and stayed with us. Not far from the Tune and Lude, we found an empty bar and claimed our table.

"Didn't you used to read a lot of philosophy?" Thomer asked me as we sat. We all ordered beers.

"I used to," I said. "Then I found religion."

The beers arrived moments later. With so many men dead and the Tune and Lude attracting most of the survivors, business could not have been good for this hole-in-the-wall.

"Religion?" Herrington asked. "I never thought of you as a religious man."

"I'm not," I said. "After we attacked the Mogats, I gave up on religion. Now I don't believe in anything."

Herrington saluted this with his beer.

"Doesn't that make you an atheist?" Boll asked.

"Atheists believe something," I said. "They believe that they know that there is no God. I don't even believe that I don't believe."

"Wow, that's kind of bleak," Thomer said.

"But you still came to fight. It sounds like you believe in the Unified Authority," Herrington said.

"I especially do not believe in the Unified Authority," I said. "I used to think it was God."

Boll downed a whole stein of beer, and said, "Careful, Lieutenant, you're confusing me."

36

Freeman gave me exactly twenty-four hours to rest up from the battle. The next day he called early enough to wake me from bed.

"How soon can you be down to the Army airfield?" he began.

"I'm doing well. Thanks, and how are you?" I said.

Silence.

"Give me an hour," I said, figuring I would shower, dress, grab a bite to eat, and head out. It would take me a few minutes to commandeer a jeep, and the airfield was fifteen minutes away.

"Thirty minutes," Freeman said. "Bring full armor."

"What's happening in thirty minutes?" I asked.

"We leave in thirty minutes," Freeman said as he cut the line.

After making sure the line was indeed dead, I said, "Pushy specker." I dressed in full combat armor, left immediately to find a jeep, and arrived a few minutes late. As I drove through the gate, I saw Freeman waiting for me in a big helicopter, the kind the Army generally used for transporting artillery. The blade over the chopper began to spin as I parked my ride, they were in such a rush.

"What are we doing today?" I asked as I approached the chopper.

"Dr. Sweetwater wants us to run some experiments," Freeman said.

I paused before climbing into the bird. "Experiments? We're not going back to those mines, are we?"

"No," said Freeman. "We're going out to the Avatari landing zone."

"In the forest?" I asked. When he said yes, I asked, "You planning on parachuting down? The trees around those spheres are too thick to land."

"Not anymore," Freeman said. "They moved them closer to town."

Against my better judgment, I climbed in the helicopter. Besides our pilot, we were the only ones along for the ride. The chopper lifted off and flew across the western edge of town. The ground below us looked burned over and pulverized. We flew over five miles of city buried under rubble. Fires still burned in some of the ruins. I saw frames and shells of buildings, but nothing stood over two stories tall.

"So you've been out here running errands for the Science Lab, I never knew you were so"—I paused and pretended to struggle for the right word—"so altruistic."

Freeman, who was not much for conversation, gave me a go-speck-yourself glare.

"You know this is going to flush your macho, I-only-care-about-myself reputation down the shitter once and for all," I said. "From here on out, people are going to expect you to stop for children in crosswalks and help little old ladies cross the street."

"How much are they paying you, Harris?" Freeman asked, his voice a low rumble and his eyes as dark as the anger behind them. "Last I heard, they pay lieutenants twenty-five hundred dollars per month."

"I get a combat bonus," I said.

"Five hundred per month?" Freeman asked.

"Yeah," I said. "Something like that."

"If we survive this, I get a 1.5-billion-dollar payday," Freeman said.

"That's a lot of money," I admitted. "We're still partners, right?" We had been partners nearly three years ago. That was during one of my stints away from the Marines.

Freeman did not respond.

"Okay," I said, "just remember my birthday."

"You're a clone. You weren't born," Freeman said.

"I was born; I just wasn't conceived—kinda like Jesus," I said.

The spheres were in a large clearing just a few miles out of town. I had passed through this very clearing my first day on New Copenhagen, on my way back to town with Philips and the remaining members of his fire team. There had been a tall radio tower in the center of the clearing, but the structure now lay twisted along the ground like the skeleton of a thousand-foot snake.

Twelve Avatari light spheres stood in a line across the clearing. I looked at the scene and asked, "How long have they been here?"

"They moved last night," Freeman said.

"The aliens moved the spheres here after the attack?" I asked. It did not make sense, but on the other hand, they were balls of light. It wasn't like they had to lift the spheres onto a truck and drive them here.

Dead bodies littered the floor of the clearing, old soldiers now twenty-four hours gone. I saw M27s and pistols in the mud. Off along one edge of the clearing was a pile of crates and equipment. Freeman must have been busy all morning; the pile included a full-sized steam shovel. "What is that for?" I asked, pointing at the steam shovel.

"An experiment," was all he would tell me.

The helicopter landed in the farthest corner of the clearing from the spheres, and there the pilot waited as we made a long day of it. Freeman began the experiments by having me toss a grenade into a sphere. The grenade exploded, the sphere seemed untouched. When we found shrapnel from the grenade, it was already coated with tachyons.

Freeman recorded everything as I fired lasers from all across the light spectrum into the sphere. The laser color made no difference, they all dissolved in the light of spheres. He planted several chemical bombs around the spheres. The bombs had no effect.

The highlight of the day came when Freeman climbed into the steam shovel and dumped a two-ton load of dirt on the spheres. "What the hell are you trying to do?" I asked.

"Bury it," he said as he poured a second load of dirt over the sphere.

"Bury it? You think you can make it go away by burying it?" I asked, barely able to stop from laughing.

It did not matter what Freeman thought, and I didn't know if burying the spheres was his idea in the first place. The uselessness of burying the sphere became apparent as the sphere rose to the top of the dirt like a bubble rising to the surface of water.

In all, the day seemed rather laughable. I started making jokes about the different experiments. As Freeman climbed out of the steam shovel, I asked, "Got a fire hydrant? Maybe we can wash the spheres away."

Freeman did not dignify my joke with a response. He radioed the pilot of the helicopter. On the other side of the clearing, the chopper's blades began to rotate. "Are we finished for the day?" I asked Freeman.

"One more thing," he said, opening a wooden crate that was about the size of a footlocker. Until that very moment, I had not noticed that particular crate; but now that I did, I did not like the look of it. The symbol on the side of it was a black circle with three yellow triangles in it—the symbol used to mark radioactive materials.

"Um, Ray, that looks a like nuke," I said.

Freeman said nothing as he opened the case.

"Are you planning on nuking the spheres?" I asked. Across the field, the blades over the helicopter were in full whirl.

"This is a dirty bomb," Freeman said. The unit looked like a computer. The bomb and all its components were stored inside a keyboard with a little three-inch display.

"That's great," I said, "but shouldn't we give burying the spheres another shot. I mean, that looked promising."

"Sweetwater made it small, just a half-kiloton device with maximum radiation yield."

That was small. When the bomb went off, it would only go off with the force of five hundred metric tons of TNT. Of course it did not matter how big the bomb was; the air around it would still heat up to over five hundred thousand degrees. The good news was that our combat armor would protect us from the radiation if we survived the heat and the shock wave.

"A dirty bomb," I said. "How nice. Well, as long as the radiation yield is high."

Freeman typed some code into the bomb and 10:00 appeared on the screen. The countdown began immediately.

Freeman stood and headed toward the helicopter. I followed, glancing back and seeing that the clock had counted down to 9:51.

The truth was that Freeman had played it more than safe. With the helicopter flying us to safety, he could have set the clock for three minutes, and we would have survived. With ten minutes, we could get in a game of chess before boarding. Still, I always found it hard to relax around nuclear bombs.

We boarded the helicopter and left the clearing, circling three hundred feet over the forest and nearly a mile away. I would have preferred to put more distance between us and the bomb, but Freeman said he'd worked everything out with Sweetwater, and I had confidence in both men. Besides, so long as the blast did not short out our electrical system, this bird was made to withstand a little radiation.

Below us, the forest looked like a frosted green carpet. There were no shadows or dark spots. In the distance, I could see the clearing. And then the explosion took place, a bright flash that rendered the rest of the clearing as bright as the line of spheres running across its diameter. Above the clearing, the flash of the bomb solidified into a shape like a golden jellyfish rising from the forest floor that cooled into smoke, then rose like a mushroom. The trees around the clearing leaned out, swayed back toward the explosion, then caught on fire. They burned like matches in a book. A layer of smoke formed around the body of the steam shovel. When the smoke evaporated, it left a blackened hulk in its wake.

"Guess we won't be going into that part of the forest anytime soon," I said. There must have been a few hundred dead soldiers around there, men killed during the old men's march. They were the lucky ones. Incineration had come much sooner for them than for those who died deeper in the forest.

As the smoke and ash cleared away, I could see the spheres sparkling against the silver, black, and orange background that had once been filled with trees. "Nothing hurts them," I said.

Freeman said nothing in return.

37

During duty hours, I played the role of the faithful lieutenant in the Marines. I located the dead on tagging duty and prepared what was left of my company for the next wave of the invasion. During off hours, I socialized with enlisted men. I pretended to know only what they knew, and I acted as if I thought we would survive this war. That was the life I lived as a normal Marine. I also had another life, however, one that made it hard to spend time with men who were not in the know. My second life was working with the Science Lab.

"We've examined the data Raymond and Lieutenant Harris collected," William Sweetwater said as he waddled across the laboratory floor. As he always did, Sweetwater spoke in a tough and hip way, as if he did not realize that he was a pudgy little dwarf with a scraggly beard and thick glasses.

"Roll the feed," Sweetwater said to Arthur Breeze.

On the ten-foot screen that hung from the ceiling, the Avatari mining operation appeared. The video feed started with what we saw the moment we entered the cavern, as captured by Ray Freeman's visor. I stood with my back to the camera looking out at the spider-things.

As Freeman entered the cavern, the camera panned around it, and there the feed froze, focusing on one of the spider-things.

"What the hell is that?" asked General Glade.

"We think they're drone workers. From what we can tell, they're not much more intelligent than a mechanical arm on an assembly line," Sweetwater said. "They appear to follow a simple digging protocol and show no signs of initiative or independent thought.

"This is interesting." He waddled over to the screen. "See, here Lieutenant Harris comes within a few inches of that drone."

On the screen, I am walking down the path as one of the drone pops out of a hole and walks right past me.

"A sentient being would have attacked Lieutenant Harris," Sweetwater said. "With those sharp forelegs, it could have cut him in half."

"Do we assume that they came to hollow out the mountain?" asked General Haight, the Army's new second-in-command. "Are they going to hollow the entire planet?"

"We've run a computer analysis of this cavern. If our estimates are correct, the cavern is 41.3 miles long. Assuming the mountain was solid when the Avatari arrived, we estimate that they have displaced approximately eight hundred cubic miles of mountain per week," said Arthur Breeze. Unlike Sweetwater, Breeze did not refer to himself alone when he said "we."

"It's all hypothetical, of course," he admitted. Tall, slightly built, and obviously insecure, Breeze tended to decorate his speech with more scientific terms than Sweetwater.

"Eight hundred miles per week?" General Haight asked. "That doesn't seem like much. I mean, at eight hundred miles per week, it could take them years to hollow out the planet."

"They don't need to hollow out the planet," Sweetwater said.

"We think they are just trying to make enough space to hold their catalyst."

Breeze leaned over the projector, and said, "William, perhaps we should show them the cave."

"Good idea," said Sweetwater.

On the screen, the cave in which Freeman and I had found the spheres appeared. Freeman entered first and examined the spheres and the gas leaking out of them. He pulled out the meter Sweetwater gave him and held it over the mud-colored gas.

"This is not the extreme-hydrogenation elemental compound distillation that was found in other Avatari settlements such as the Mogat home world and Hubble," Breeze announced.

Nobody responded.

"The military term is 'distilled shit gas,'" Sweetwater said.

"Oh, sure, that," the generals responded. They all knew about distilled shit gas.

"Raymond ran a number of tests on the gas, and we have been able to make some educated guesses about its properties," Breeze said.

"That is a gas? It looks like muddy water," General Glade observed.

"It is very dense; so dense, in fact, that it is on the border of the definition of both a gas and a liquid," admitted Breeze.

"That's what those things are after? They just want that mud stuff?" General Haight asked.

"Quite the opposite," Sweetwater said. "That is what they are pouring into the planet.

"We think they are seeding the planet." He waddled over to Breeze and handed him a data chip to place in the projector. When the picture resumed, it showed the same map of the galaxy that Brocius showed me back on Mars.

"We assume you are all familiar with this map?" Sweetwater asked. Then, without waiting for an answer, he approached the screen, and continued. "Arthur, can you close in on Hubble?"

The screen switched to a close-up view of Hubble, the burned-out cinder of a planet on which a colony of Mogats tried to make a stand.

"Oh, sorry; would you display the prenova image of the Templar System?" Sweetwater asked.

A moment later the image of a very crowded solar system

appeared. The system had three planets orbiting so close to its sun that the planets could not have been habitable. There was a fourth planet that had surface area covered by water, a fifth planet that resembled Earth, and seven more planets that looked too dark to provide productive habitation.

"This is the Templar System," said Sweetwater. "The fifth planet is about the same distance from its sun as our Earth is from Sol.

"About fifty thousand years ago, some event caused Templar to expand suddenly, then go supernova," Breeze said. "Please understand, gentlemen, that fifty thousand years is a very short amount of time in astronomical terms. In astronomy, we generally measure events by millions of years. In this case, a sun expanded and cooked everything around it in a matter of fifty thousand years.

"As you can see, the first three planets in this system vanished entirely. But this planet"—he pointed to the fifth planet again—"this planet survived after a fashion."

The screen now showed the familiar murky landscapes of Hubble.

"We sent a military force to this planet a few years back and found that everything on it was made of the extreme-hydrogenation elemental compound," Sweetwater said.

"Distilled shit gas?" one of the generals asked.

"That was not the only time we ever encountered that gas," Sweetwater said. "Arthur, will you please show us the Mogats' solar system?"

The screen showed a new solar system. Like the Templar System, this one had gone dark. "This is the planet on which the Mogats built their home world," Sweetwater said.

General Hill, from the Air Force, started to speak, but Sweetwater cut him off. "Their home world was nearly the exact same distance from its sun as Hubble was from Templar... as Earth is from Sol... as New Copenhagen is from Nigellus."

The generals remained silent. They stared at the screen, which once again showed the map with the Avatari movements across the galaxy. "We have come to the conclusion that the same solar positioning that makes planets productive for human habitation also makes them desirable to the Avatari," Sweetwater said. "That would explain why they have only sleeved the planets we have colonized or planned to colonize."

"Why would they pump distilled shit gas into a planet?" General Newcastle asked, now rejoining the discussion.

"It's not shit gas," said Sweetwater. "The stuff they're importing into New Copenhagen is something else that we think can be turned into shit gas. It's highly toxic. Direct contact with the gas would be fatal. A healthy man who breathed this gas would die in under a minute. A few traces of this gas seeped into Lieutenant Harris's helmet and left him with a second-degree burn."

"The toxicity level from this gas is extreme," Breeze added. "If you poured a single gallon of that gas into Valhalla Lake, you would contaminate the water. That would be a ratio of one part gas to 160 million parts water, and the water would be rendered unsalvageable."

"From what the data tell us, this gas will expand exponentially when superheated. That is why we are more concerned about what the Avatari are doing with the sun than we are concerned about their work in the mountains," said Sweetwater.

"To the sun?" Several of the generals asked this at the same time.

"Dr. Breeze," Sweetwater said with a nod.

Now that we had entered his specialty, Breeze took over the meeting. He paused to collect his thoughts and steel his confidence, then said, "I have not been able to experiment on the gas itself, of course, but from w-what I have been able to observe, this gas is a catalyst. Hypothetically, it has the ability to transmogrify everything around it into the same extreme-hydrogenation elemental compound distillation found on Hubble and the Mogat home world. Of course, before it can do that, it must be superheated."

"And how exactly do you expect the aliens to superheat the gas?" asked General Newcastle.

"By causing the nearest star to supernova," Breeze answered.

He showed no emotion as he said this, merely blinking as he saw the commotion his announcement had caused.

"You think they are going to blow up the sun?" General Newcastle asked, his voice cutting through the confusion.

"They do not want to cause Nigellus to explode, they want to make it expand until it is large enough to incinerate New Copenhagen," Breeze said.

"That is what they did to the stars in the Templar and Hadriean systems," added Sweetwater.

This caused even more commotion.

"You're telling us that it's not going to make any difference if we beat these bastards or not; our goose is still cooked?" asked General Haight, who was clearly struggling to make sense of this.

"As a worst-case scenario, yes, that seems to be the case," Sweetwater said.

"We're stuck on a planet with an alien army we can't kill. The sons of bitches are filling the mountains with enough toxic gas to poison the entire specking planet. Now you're telling us that they're getting ready to blow up the sun and incinerate the entire specking solar system. Sweetwater, you don't think this qualifies as a worst-case scenario?" asked General Haight.

"So it sounds like you're telling us we're all going to die," General Newcastle said.

The room went silent. Sweetwater and Breeze looked confused as to what they should say next. The generals stood in morbid silence. Everyone was running the same equations in their heads and coming up with the same bleak answers.

"They can't beat us in battle so they're going to fry the entire goddamned planet?" asked General Newcastle. "Is this some sort of a scorched-earth thing. If they can't have the specking planet, they'll make sure it isn't any good to anyone?"

"They don't appear to care whether we die or survive," Sweetwater said. He climbed back on his stool. "If anything, we get the feeling they would be happy to see us leave so they could get on with their work. The map they sent out, the one showing their movements... We've come to the conclusion that they're using the map as an eviction notice."

"How very humane of them," Newcastle muttered. Unlike Haight and some of the other generals, Morris Newcastle had a certain sarcastic wit. Now that he understood the extent of the crisis, he seemed more determined than the other generals to rise to the challenge. "What happens if we send a division into that pit and stop those bugs from digging?"

"Maybe we could bomb them," offered General Hill. "If we caused a cave-in, it might force them to start digging all over again."

"You know," Glade said, "maybe we should nuke the bastards just for good measure. We have some nuclear devices back at our camp." By "camp," he meant the Hotel Valhalla.

Glade's suggestion set off some nods of appreciation.

"I recommend against using a nuclear device," Breeze said. He pulled off his glasses and rubbed the lenses vigorously with a handkerchief from his pocket. "And I caution you against any action involving their dig."

More silence.

"Why is that?" Glade asked.

"Because it might cause the Avatari to step up the level of their attacks," Sweetwater said. "We believe that the dig is their main operation. They haven't come here to kill us. We're like mice to them, as long as we stay out of their way, they won't stop what they are doing and fumigate. We theorize that the attacks on Valhalla are only a safeguard to prevent us from disturbing their excavation."

"A safeguard? They killed three hundred thousand soldiers during their last attack," Newcastle said.

"We would hate to see what happened if they launched an all-out assault," Sweetwater said.

"They destroyed our perimeter defenses," Newcastle continued speaking over the scientist until Sweetwater said, "And that attack came on the heels of our sending men to investigate their excavation." The little scientist snapped the words, his rough edge more apparent than I had ever seen it.

"You think we made things worse by sending in spies?" Haight asked.

"It had to be done," said Glade.

"It most certainly did," agreed Sweetwater. "If Raymond and the lieutenant had not gone in, we would still be in the dark about their plans."

"I thought you said those things were like robots," said Newcastle. "Didn't you say they were drones?"

"Most of the workers in that cavern were drones," said Sweetwater. "There are larger creatures that seem to perform the role of a project foreman or a guard. We think the larger ones may be avatars instead of drones."

"And they spotted Harris?" Glade asked.

"There is no question that they spotted Raymond and the lieutenant," Sweetwater said.

"Well, that is just specking great," General Haight said.

"And you think the Avatari upped their attack because of it?" Newcastle asked, clearly placing a lot of weight on the scientists' opinions.

"It seems like a reasonable assumption," Breeze said. "Of course, I'm a physicist, not a xenopsychologist."

A conversation began among the generals. At first they whispered among themselves, but their voices continued to rise as they blamed each other and the scientists. As they continued to point fingers at each other and everyone except themselves and the aliens, what started as whispers became shouting. The generals shouted and swore like schoolkids.

"We need to try a nuclear solution," General Newcastle said, his voice rising above the din. "We can place a nuke out there and let them deal with that."

"We've tried it," Sweetwater said.

The room went quiet. "Tried what?" Newcastle asked.

"We deployed a small nuclear device," Sweetwater said. He looked around the room nervously. "We had Raymond and Lieutenant Harris place a low-yield nuclear bomb beside the spheres," Sweetwater answered. "It didn't impact them."

"You nuked them without telling us?" Newcastle asked. He sounded angry. Like so many officers I had known, he looked upon a show of initiative as a challenge to his authority.

"Look, General, we've tried burning them with fire, freezing them with liquid oxygen, corroding them with acid, distorting them with radio waves, and irradiating them with a small but dirty atomic device." Sweetwater looked over at Freeman and smiled. "Oh, and we tried burying one of the spheres under several tons of soil."

"You buried it?" Glade asked.

"Raymond and the lieutenant took a steam shovel out there."

I looked over at Freeman, who kept apart from everyone else in a solitary corner of the room. He stood there like a statue, maintaining a grim expression on his face. He was tall and dark, the shadow of a giant that had somehow turned solid. He felt no compulsion to speak and had no need for recognition or approval. At that moment I respected Ray Freeman more than any man I had ever met.

"What happened when you buried it?" General Glade asked.

"The soil falls through the sphere and is altered, then the sphere rises to the surface," Sweetwater said. "We didn't seriously think it would destroy the sphere, but we wanted to see what would happen."

"Maybe blowing up the mountain would slow their digging," General Hill said. Hill always seemed so much more reasonable than the other generals.

"I'm not convinced it would have any effect," Breeze said. "It won't stop the spheres from excreting more of that gas catalyst into the mountain."

"Unless you gentlemen can figure out a way to destroy their spheres," Sweetwater added, "they'll just keep on dumping gas."

"Damn it!" yelled Newcastle, and he slammed his pudgy fist down on a nearby desk. The sound echoed through the room. "Damn it!" he repeated. "Stop telling us what we can't do. Give us something we can use. How do we fight these bastards?"

Breeze started to say something, then looked over at Sweetwater as if seeking permission. The dwarf nodded. Having been given permission, Breeze spoke. "We might have just what you need. At least we believe we are on the edge of a breakthrough."

"What kind of a breakthrough?" Newcastle asked.

"One of our teams is on the verge of decoding their technology," Breeze said. "We may soon understand how they manipulate tachyons."

"Well, what goddamned good is that going to do us?" snarled Newcastle. "I don't want to understand these bastards. I want to shove my foot up their asses!"

None of the other generals joined Newcastle in his tirade, though they seemed curious about the discoveries.

"Are you telling us that we might be able to use the tachyons to attack them?" General Haight asked.

"We think we may be able to block them from using tachyons," Sweetwater said.

"What goddamned good is that?" Haight demanded.

"If they cannot use the tachyons, they can't hurt us," Sweetwater said. "They would come out of their spheres as energy, but without the tachyon shell forming around them, their energy bodies will simply evaporate." It was like a ray of hope had found its way into this dungeon-like Science Lab. Men who one minute earlier had stood around smoldering and staring at the ground suddenly looked up in surprise.

"Damn," General Haight said, sounding impressed.

"How soon? How soon will you know?" asked General Newcastle. He whispered the question as if almost afraid to hear the answer.

"It's still a week out, at the soonest," Sweetwater said, sounding swept up in the excitement.

The generals' spirits dropped so hard I could almost hear the thud. "A week? A week?" Haight complained. "We're down to fewer than six hundred thousand troops. We don't have any working rocket launchers. The wall around our outer perimeter is down.

"Do you have any idea what you are saying? Those Avatari bastards attack every three days. We're almost out of soldiers, and you want us to hold off two more attacks?"

"General, ev-ev-every man we have is w-working around the clock," Breeze said. "W-we need to run tests. It t-takes time to an-analyze the data and build off the results."

"Whatever you think you can do, you get it done in forty-eight hours! You got that, Sweetwater?" Newcastle demanded. Perhaps he wanted to show everyone that he was back in charge. If so, it backfired.

"Then make it yourself," William Sweetwater said in an unnaturally calm voice.

"What?" barked Newcastle. "What did you say?"

"If you think you and your soldiers can decode an alien technology in forty-eight hours, by all means, do it," Sweetwater said. General Newcastle stormed over to the stool on which Sweetwater sat, but the dwarf did not budge.

Staring down at the misshapen little scientist, Newcastle growled like a dog. "Work faster," he said.

"General, we started with nothing. We didn't even have the technology to prove the existence of tachyons two weeks ago, and now we are developing a primitive method for controlling them. One of our teams is about to hijack an alien technology that is far more advanced than our own. It's a miracle we have gotten this far this fast," Sweetwater said. He was in control, and he knew it. General Newcastle glared down at him, and Sweetwater flatly returned that gaze.

"And you expect us to protect your facility that entire time?" he asked.

"No, sir, not the entire week," Sweetwater said. "Only when we are under attack." I saw the twinkle in Sweetwater's dark eyes.

Newcastle mulled his options over, then said, "Gentlemen, we have our orders. We need to hold out for another week."

38

"Harris, we're moving camp."

Moffat met me as I entered the hotel. The work of moving had already begun. A line of trucks waited along the access road that led to the hotel loading dock. The Hotel Valhalla had taken on the aspect of a theatrical stage during a change of settings. Men in fatigues stripped down booths, carried racks, and pushed carts filled with supplies.

As Moffat spoke, I saw something that left me deeply disturbed—graffiti. Somebody had spray painted a stick-figure mural on one of the walls. The portrait showed five large figures gathered around a smaller figure. The Avatari were big and bulky, each of them holding one of those four-foot-long rifles. The human looked pathetic beside them, a man on his hands and knees. He wore what appeared to be combat armor. At least, he had armor covering his head and chest. From the waist down, the figure was naked with a little sliver of a penis dangling below his stomach.

The caption on the bottom of the drawing, written in the same red paint, was "MUDDERS GANG BANG!" Under the guy on his knees was one word—"Glade."

If the name under the guy on his knees had been Moffat instead of Glade, I would have had Philips arrested. Hell, I might have killed him myself.

Giving the mural a second glance, I realized that what I had taken as Avatari rifles had been intended to represent a portion of their anatomy. Aside from the disproportionate generosity that the artist had shown the enemy, this painting bothered me because military clones were supposedly incapable of doing something like this. In theory the capacity for vandalism and lawbreaking had been weeded out of them through neural programming; but as I looked around the lobby, I saw shattered mirrors, broken windows, wallpaper stripped from walls, and more graffiti. If clones had done this, what other parts of their programming had also become undone?

"Yeah, we have a specking Michelangelo on our hands," Moffat said, when he saw my gaze return to the graffiti. "The company is stripping down the Valkyrie Ballroom. I need you to make sure the move goes smoothly."

I wanted to tell Moffat that I saw him take a shot at Philips, but I decided to play it safe. Instead, I asked, "Where are we headed?"

"The University of Valhalla," Moffat said. "They want us settled in by 1900."

I checked my watch. It was 1130. That seemed generous. "Seven and a half hours just to move racks?" I asked.

"We should be so lucky," Moffat said. "Command wants this side of town FOCPIG-ready by 0000 hours. We've got mines to plant and traps to wire."

"What about the armory?" I asked. It would take days to move all of the weapons out of the underground garage. Finding and stocking another location would not go quickly either.

"We're leaving it."

"Everything?" I asked. "We've got nuclear bombs down there."

"Yeah, I know," Moffat said. "I asked Burton about that. He says our best bet is to stop the Mudders before they get here."

"So, am I helping with the move or FOCing the PIG?" I asked.

"You're supervising the move, then you're FOCing the PIG," Moffat said. "Once we get everything loaded on to the truck here, I want you to take one full platoon to help the ACOE work on a new DMZ." In plain speak, he wanted me to take the company out to help the Army Corps of Engineers set up a new "demilitarized" zone. In this case, the term "demilitarized zone" meant a highly militarized zone, indeed. Once the Corps of Engineers finished their work, there would not be a safe inch of land west of the hotel.

"Let me get my armor," I said.

"How's the shoulder?" Moffat asked.

"Better," I said. I saluted and caught an elevator to my room.

"You know, you guys don't need to guard me every specking minute of the day," Philips complained, as we rode out on the truck.

I leaned back into the canvas awning. I had my helmet off so I could enjoy the bracing feel of the cool air against my face.

"I'm not guarding you, Philips, I'm protecting you," I said.

"I don't want to be protected," Philips said. He was dressed in fatigues, the only man on the truck who had not put on armor. There was no rule that said we had to wear armor, but most Marines wanted all the protection they could get when they laid land mines. It seemed like a logical choice—at least it seemed logical to those of us who wanted to survive the detail.

"I like keeping an eye on you, Philips; you're entertaining. I've never watched anybody self-destruct before. It's kind of exciting."

"Go speck yourself, Harris."

I hated to pull rank, but I was an officer, and I could not allow him to show me disrespect in front of the men. "You are speaking to an officer," I said.

"Sorry. Go speck yourself, sir," he said.

"What happened to that famous Mark Philips sense of humor?" I asked.

"I left it back at the Hen House," Philips said.

"Not back on the battlefield?" I asked.

We drove past Vista Street, deep into the neighborhoods on the west edge of town. Men in battle armor and men in fatigues lay in piles along the road. Crews of soldiers worked to clear the streets of death and debris, moving the burned husks of tanks and trucks along with corpses. In a patch of grass by a tumbledown house, a group of soldiers gathered for a smoke and a chat.

"Huish grew up in the same orphanage as me," Philips said.

"Did you know him?" I asked.

"Are you specking kidding me? He was twenty-three years younger than me. I made corporal by the time he was three."

"I've read your record," I said. "You were probably busted back down to private again by the time he was four."

"I specked it all up, didn't I?" asked Philips. He shook his head. All of the old arrogance drained from his face. He looked physically tired and mentally exhausted.

"You mean at the Hen House? Yes, you specked up royally."

"You don't get it, Harris," Philips said.

"I don't get what?"

"I don't give a rat's ass about Moffat or what he does. Let him shoot me. I don't give a shit. Thomer says I deserve it. That's what you think, too."

I didn't know what to say, so I said nothing.

"I guess I deserve a good specking, but not because I boffed Moffat's wife." He laughed. "Hell, more guys have ridden her than the goddamned Broadcast Network. I'm surprised she managed to work me into her busy schedule."

"You're shitting me?" I asked.

"Would I shit you about something like that? I think she has a thing for clones. Half the men guarding the specking Hen House had a roll with her. I think Skittles might have. I was the only one who talked about it.

"He's doesn't give a rat's ass who sleeps with the old girl. He's just mad 'cause I didn't keep quiet about it."

Philips unbuttoned his shirt and showed me his upper arm.

"He's pissed about this," he said as he displayed the tattoo he'd had placed over the biceps on his right arm. It showed a naked woman, a modern Venus in a half shell with one hand cupped over a breast and the other covering her pelvis. The banner around the picture said "LILLY MOFFAT, COUNT ME IN."

"Shit, Philips," I said. "When did you get that?"

"I got this while I was at the Hen House. It was her idea. Harris, she hates Moffat; she offered to pay for the damn tattoo."

"Nice, Philips. Very nice," I said. Philips missed the irony in my choice of compliments. "How did Moffat hear about it?"

The truck slowed to a stop. We had come to a busy stretch in which teams of soldiers dragged heavy carts across the six-lane street.

The other men jumped from the truck. Philips stood to join them.

"How did Moffat find out about the tattoo?" I repeated. "Did she tell him about it?"

Philips shook his head. "Not likely. She's had so many guys since me, I bet she doesn't even remember my name. He saw it when I showed up for morning calisthenics. I came in a tank top."

"You what?" I asked.

Philips shrugged. "And I lined up front and center."

"Were you trying to get yourself shot?"

"And I started doing arm curls while he was counting out jumping jacks."

While the rest of the men gathered in front of the truck, I held Philips back for another moment. "You really do want to die, don't you?" I asked.

"You know what, Harris. I don't care what happens," Philips said. I looked into his eyes. The fight was gone. The mischief was gone as well. He looked tired.

Groaning deep in my gut, I let my friend go join the other men. There was no way both Philips and Moffat would survive this war. Sooner or later Moffat would find a way to kill Philips, and Philips would do nothing to protect himself, the stupid prick. There are a lot of ways to kill yourself. At least suicide by screwing was unique.

* * *

The mine-placer looked like an industrial vacuum cleaner. It had a twenty-foot telescoping hose with ribbing for flexibility. You could have rolled a tennis ball down the length of the hose, but a baseball would not fit.

The Corps of Engineers had painted foot-wide Xs all along the street. Our job was to roll the mine-placer to each location, press the nozzle over the axis of the X, and plant the mine. The mine-placer literally shot the explosive right through asphalt or concrete.

We worked in five-man teams. It was grueling work. The mine-placer sat on wheels, but fully loaded with fifty mines, the damned thing weighed about four hundred pounds. The Corps assigned us a stretch of posh neighborhood with a row of elm trees between the roads. Pushing that specking mine-placer up hills and over speed bumps damn near killed us. Once we got to the X, it took three men to hold the hose in place as it blasted the mines through the street. The blast struck with so much power that it bounced all three men in the air.

The blast both placed the mine and removed the painted X without cracking the pavement beneath. The only trace the mine-placer left was a clean spot of road where the mine now sat. As a kid I thought it was magic. It wasn't. First the Corps of Engineers had used a sonic device to create a hollow spot under the surface of the concrete. The mines were made of liquid chemicals, which the mine-placer broke into a vapor so fine that it could pass through concrete. When we fired it off, the mineplacer blasted the atomized chemicals with so much power that it forced them through concrete, where they mixed to create a volatile, pressure-sensitive bubble. The chemicals washed away paint, grease, dirt, and anything else that got in the way into the ground.

"You think these are strong enough to kill one of those Mudders?" Skittles asked. My crew included Herrington, Boll, Skittles, and Thorpe. Boll and Herrington, both veteran Marines with more years in the Corps than me, worked quietly. Thorpe and Skittles, both three-year men who had joined the year before the orphanages were destroyed, kept up an endless string of commentary.

About a hundred yards away, Thomer and Philips led another crew. Thomer had a calming influence on Philips. Philips would not do anything crazy with Thomer around.

"Charge is up!" Skittles called.

"Hold!" I shouted. Herrington, Boll, and I braced our weight against the nozzle, and Skittles pulled the trigger. The sound the mine-placer made was a hollow *thwoop* as it sent a jolt that traveled up our arms and into our shoulders. Boll and I pulled the hose away, and Herrington crouched and inspected the placement.

"Good," he said, and we moved on to the next X.

We stood a few feet away from the skeletal frame of one of the destroyed rocket launchers. The structure stood thirty feet tall, a charred skeleton of twisted rods and melted wires.

Around the grounds, soldiers and Marines placed traps of many descriptions. A team of soldiers strung hot-wire fences. Once they finished the fence, they would hook it up to an electrical circuit, and four thousand volts would surge through the wires. A fence like that could wipe out a whole platoon, but I doubted the Avatari would even notice it.

"What do you think?" Herrington asked, standing straight and stretching out his back. "This should give us an edge."

"The mines might slow them down," I said.

"It's going to come down to a firefight again, isn't it?" Boll asked.

If Skittles or some other lightweight asked that question, I might well have lied, but I would not lie to Boll or Herrington. They deserved better. "There's a lot going on that I can't tell you about," I said.

"It's bad?" Herrington asked.

"Yeah, it's bad," I agreed.

39

General Glade sent an aide to retrieve me from the DMZ. We were on our fourth load of mines. My arms were numb, and the muscles in my back felt like they were tied in a knot. I wanted to head back to base and take a nap, but no one was handing out furloughs.

"Lieutenant Harris, General Glade sent for you," the man said. He was wearing his Charlie-service khakis—a captain with a chestful of ribbons for typing and filing. If they gave out purple hearts for paper cuts, this guy would have one.

I sized the captain up in an instant and did not like what I saw. Let the world collapse around him, this guy's peach-fuzz blond hair would never grow beyond regulation length. I quickly dismissed all his ribbons as having been earned by typing above and beyond the call of duty.

"Captain…" I paused because I did not know the man's name.

The captain took a moment to figure out that I was waiting for his name. "Everley," he said.

"Captain Everley," I said.

"Charge is up!" Skittles yelled.

I called, "Hold!" and Skittles pulled the trigger. The recoil of the hose reverberated through my body. "Captain Everley, do you realize that you are standing in the middle of a minefield?"

The officer's smug smile evaporated from his face. He was an administrator who had stumbled into an area for fighting men.

"Excuse me, sir," Sergeant Herrington said, gently escorting Everley out of his way so he could inspect the mine. He climbed on all fours and ran a hand over our work. "It's good," he said.

"You see those Xs?" I asked, holding on to the hose with one hand and moving closer to Captain Everley.

"Are those mines?" he asked.

"No, Captain, those are the only places you can be sure do not have mines. We're laying mines under the Xs." Everley looked back. The path he had come on was still marked with Xs.

"I'm guessing between the Marines and the Army, we've laid at least ten thousand mines out here today. Each mine is calibrated to blow the legs off a Mudder," I said.

Everley swallowed and looked around the street.

"Charge is up!"

"Hold!" We shot another mine into the pavement.

"You tell General Glade that I'll head straight for Base Command when we finish up here. It should be another hour or two."

"But the—"

"And, Captain, watch your step on the way back. I figure that any mine that could blow the legs off a Mudder would send your balls at least a mile away."

"I always thought it would vaporize them," said Herrington.

"Yeah, that's what I thought, also, sir," Skittles piped in.

Everley nodded and left, hopping from X to X as if they were stepping-stones leading across a pond.

"A bit on the harsh side, wasn't that?" Boll asked me.

"You think so?" I asked. It was harsh, but I had a pretty good feeling why General Glade wanted to speak with me, and I didn't feel like playing along. We were coming down to the wire now. When things came down to the wire, the men at the top often turned to the men they sent out to die for absolution. They wanted us to know they were not making these decisions lightly, and they wanted to know that we understood. It was all bullshit.

Having bright daylight twenty-four hours per day wreaked havoc on my internal clock, but it had some advantages. We worked well past 2100 hours on a winter night, and the sky was always as bright as midday.

By the time we finished, my right shoulder hurt just about the same way it did after the doctor reset it. The small of my back ached from all of my leaning over the mine-placer. I stood on the truck as we rode out to our new barracks working my back and neck. No one spoke on that ride. They may not have known the particulars, but most military clones can sense the calm before the storm.

I found my billet and stripped out of my armor. I took a muscle relaxant and headed for the shower. I wanted to eat a large meal and crawl into bed, but that was not on the agenda. Instead, I called Base Command, and General Glade's staff sent Captain Everley to retrieve me.

"Do we have time for me to stop by the mess for a sandwich?" I asked.

"I'd get to General Glade's office as quickly as I could if I were you," Everley said. "He's still in a rage about this afternoon."

"What happened this afternoon?" I asked.

"You didn't specking report that's what happened," he said. "When a general invites you in for a chat, you drop everything and report."

"I see. You know what, I really need that sandwich," I said, remembering just how much I despised admirals and generals.

We were nearing the dormitory cafeteria. The food wouldn't be as good as the restaurants in the Valhalla Hotel, but this was our mess hall. I turned in and headed for the food line.

"Lieutenant, I must—" Captain Everley whined. I had sized

him up as an officious weakling the first time I saw him. He was a captain, and I was a lieutenant, but I was the one controlling the situation.

"Just a moment," I said.

"But General Glade—"

"Unless he has chow laid out, he's going to have to wait. I'll eat on the way, Captain. I have just come from ten hours of laying mines and I'm hungry." I selected two slices of bread and slathered them with mayo and mustard. I used tongs to take slices of ham, roast beef, and turkey. After laying lettuce, onions, and tomatoes across the pile, I closed the sandwich, stuffed half of it into my mouth, and said, "There. That didn't take so long," around the sandwich as I bit.

"Can we go now?" Everley asked. He was mad, and he showed it by pouting. *Real officer material,* I told myself.

I grabbed two cartons of milk. "Sure, I'm ready."

Everley did not speak to me again as we drove around the outside of the campus. Except for the abundance of armor and fatigues, it looked like business as usual around the University of Valhalla. It had the right number of warm bodies walking its yards, they just happened to be soldiers instead of students.

The Corps of Engineers was out in force erecting rocket launchers. It would take days to get them ready for combat. If we managed to keep the Avatari out of the campus during the first attack, the batteries would be ready in time for the second. I just hoped some of us would be around to arm them.

Newcastle had teams of soldiers placing machine-gun nests and barricades all over the school. Checking the skyline, I saw blinds for snipers on rooftops. I thought about the exploding bullets Freeman made for himself and wished we could all arm ourselves with bullets like that.

Using sandbags to redirect the water, the Army converted storm drains into pillboxes along the main drag. The muzzles of high-caliber machine guns peered from beneath culverts and behind drains.

We came to the administration building, a three-story brick-and-plaster affair with useless pillars and an ornamental balustrade along its flat roof. Squirrels jumped on the bare branches of the elm trees on either side of the entrance.

We parked the car, and Everley spoke for the first time since we had left the barracks. He said, "Shit," because he locked his keys and cap in the car. He tried the handle several times, then gave up. "Shit," he repeated.

"Lost your keys?" I asked as I came around the car.

"Forget it, Lieutenant," he said. He walked past me and headed into the building. I followed. We headed up the stairs to the third floor. General Glade had set up shop in the dean's office. Through the open door, I could see him sitting behind the desk, staring into space.

Everley knocked on the doorjamb, then peered in. "I've got him, sir."

Glade swiveled around and said something softly that I could not hear.

"Go on in," Everley said, stepping out of my way.

I walked in, stopped two feet from the desk, and saluted. The salute hurt; my right shoulder felt like it might never heal.

"Everley says you were too busy to talk this afternoon," Glade said. He sounded angry.

"I was laying mines," I explained. Now that I said it, the excuse sounded weak.

"I served under Bryce Klyber for fourteen years. Did you know that?"

Klyber was the officer who developed the Liberator cloning program. He did that as a young officer, more than fifty years ago. Until his untimely death, he watched over my career. He mentored me and protected me from Marines who would have gladly killed me simply for being a Liberator clone. Klyber was murdered by a fellow officer during the Mogat War.

"I did not know that, sir," I said.

"Just about every senior officer in the Navy or the Marines

served under Klyber at some time or another, Harris. If he liked you, you could count on a long and successful career. I was a captain when I reported for duty on the *Grant*."

The *Grant* was a fighter carrier in the Scutum-Crux Fleet, Klyber's old fleet.

"By the time they transferred me to Brocius's command in the Central Cygnus Fleet, I was a colonel. From captain to colonel in fourteen years; you could say that's a good rate of promotion."

I had actually made the jump from private to colonel in under five years, but that was another story. Since that time, Admiral Brocius had demoted me to sergeant, then repromoted me to lieutenant. At least Glade held on to his promotions.

"I hear you spent a lot of time with Klyber," Glade said. "The way I hear it, you were something of a son to him... as close to a son as he ever got, I suppose. He did create your kind.

"Me, Harris, I have three sons of my own. I'm not looking for a surrogate. As far as I'm concerned, you're a Marine who gets things done, and that earns you some leeway. You're efficient, I'll give you that, but you're not a real officer. Only natural-borns qualify as officers in my book, Lieutenant. You may be the last of your kind, but you are still a clone... just a clone. You got that?"

"Yes, sir," I said.

"When I send an officer, a natural-born officer, to call you in, you will show him proper respect. Do you understand me? You will specking well drop what you are doing, whatever you are doing, and report. Do you read me, Lieutenant?"

"Yes, sir."

"Why did it take Everley so specking long to get you this evening?" Glade asked.

"I stopped off for a sandwich," I said.

"Maybe I've been too lenient with you, Lieutenant," Glade said.

"There's no question about that, sir," I said.

"What the speck is that supposed to mean?" Glade asked.

"It means, sir, that I am ready to resign my commission. More than four hundred thousand clones have died out there without even knowing what they were up against. You don't like clones, sir; and I don't like the kind of antisynthetic asshole natural-borns they make into officers. If you want my commission, you go right ahead and take it... sir."

Granted, I pushed General Glade way too far, but I didn't care. That was what Mark Philips had said when I asked if he wanted to get himself killed. He looked me in the eye, and said, "I don't care anymore." Maybe you could communicate suicidal tendencies like a virus.

Glade must have thought I was bluffing. He said, "If you are tired of command, I can have you busted down to private."

"I wish you would," I said. "You might want to stand me in front of a firing squad while you're at it. The way things are going, General, you wouldn't even be shaving a week from my life."

"What's the matter with you, Harris?" Glade asked. "Are you trying to get busted down?"

"General, every time we head into battle, I watch good men die thinking they're in a fair fight. You might not consider clones human—"

"You've got me wrong—"

I interrupted the general's interruption. "If you don't mind, sir, I would be happier as an enlisted man. I'm sick of running errands for you and the Science Lab."

General Glade sat staring at me. He paused for just a moment, just a fraction of a second, then said, "But we need you."

40

The next time the Avatari came, we knew they were coming even before the first of their troops emerged from the spheres. Freeman had rigged a rudimentary early-warning system by placing photocell-powered sensors near the spheres. When the spheres dilated, the light they gave off powered up the cells and set off the alarms.

Cameras hidden along the path showed the army of glowing specters as it trudged toward town. As always, they did not march in formation. They showed no semblance of organization other than marching in the same direction. They looked like a parade of giant ghosts all cloned from the same pattern.

By the time they reached the outer limits of Valhalla, the Avatari had begun to take on substance. Their brown-black shells were covered with cracks through which yellow light glowed. They each had two arms, two legs, and a chest and shoulders that were far too broad for any man. The features on their faces were flat and impassive. They did not search the area for traps as they walked through the ruins of the first suburb.

They passed burned-out doorways and toppled walls of what had a few weeks earlier been a fashionable neighborhood.

Grenades and rockets had left the streets a patchwork of scrapes and holes. The Avatari walked past the scabby remains of once-manicured lawns. They trudged across homes that now existed only as cinder. Gaining weight as more and more tachyons adhered to their forms, the Avatari crushed glass and wood and fragments of brick under their feet.

Abandoned pets still roamed the streets. A fluffy white dog with mangy fur paused to watch them from a few yards ahead. It growled and ran away.

By the time they reached the DMZ, the Avatari had become as solid as our tanks and bullets and weighed nearly two thousand pounds, these walking statues of alien stone. Their weapons had already formed into chrome cylinders, and the light of the ion curtain reflected off the barrels of those guns like sunlight shining off mirrors.

They entered the minefield.

At this point, every man in Valhalla knew that nothing but massive trauma would stop the aliens. One of the bastards marched straight into the electric fencing and pushed right through it. Sparks popped in the air around it. It looked like a miniature fireworks display, and it went unnoticed. The alien avatar paid no attention to the electrical air show as it trampled the fence and continued.

The Army and Marines deployed every available man. With all of the casualties we'd taken, my company had compacted its three combat platoons into two, and now we sent our support platoon into battle as well. Other companies had fared worse than us. Some were down to a single platoon, and some platoons were down to a single squad.

I watched the video feed of the Avatari entering the demilitarized zone from inside my helmet in a small window on my visor.

"Ten minutes to showtime," Major Burton told the entire company over the interLink. Every man in the company heard Major Burton's announcement, but only commissioned officers had access to the video feed. Somebody had decided that ignorance equated to bliss for the enlisted ranks.

"Harris, report," Moffat demanded.

"The company is ready, sir," I said.

Thomer ran one of my combat platoons, and Philips ran the other. I no longer worried about how he would react in battle; it was between battles when his self-destructive tendencies showed. Once the fighting commenced, all of his horse shit stopped, and he cared only about achieving objectives and keeping his men alive.

Philips's virtual dog tag showed above his helmet—Name: Mark Philips, Rank: Sergeant, Serial Number: 59682136029. I didn't need the virtual tag to recognize him, even when he was hidden in combat armor. The casual but efficient way he handled his firearms, the trademark of a veteran Marine, gave him away. Philips fussed about his men like a mother bear, slapping Marines across their helmets to get their attention, bullying them into safer slots, shaking his head as he walked away from young Marines who made stupid mistakes.

Thomer, a far steadier platoon leader, trusted his men. He did not fuss over them, but when I listened in on his communications, I heard him giving plenty of direction. He was a natural leader. Had he been natural-born, he might have risen to general.

I had promoted Herrington so he could lead the support platoon in battle. They needed a leader with experience. He did not like his new responsibilities as a sergeant. Corporal Boll, Herrington's best friend, assisted with the platoon. As I listened in on Herrington's frequency, I caught him chatting with Boll.

"Hey, Trevor, you think these Mudders are ever going to send a bigger army? I mean, they keep dribbling in small numbers, and we keep mowing them down," Herrington said.

"Man, I know what you mean. It doesn't make sense. If they'd sent more men, they could have had us last time," said Boll. "I'll tell you what, though, those bastards are wearing us down."

"Tell me about it," Herrington said. "You seen Lieutenant Harris? The guy looks like the walking dead. We better keep an eye on the poor son of a bitch just in case."

"Darn straight I'm keeping an eye on Harris; he's the only

thing standing between us and that ass-wipe Moffat," Boll said.

"Stow the unnecessary chatter," I said over an open frequency that every man in the platoon would hear. "Let's keep the Link open."

"Think he heard us?" Boll asked.

"Not a chance. They always say that before the fighting starts," Herrington said.

"That goes double for you, Herrington," I said.

"Shit," said Herrington.

Boll did not respond.

The entire company save one member was stationed in the hotel district, hidden in a park. It was a small park, no more than five or six acres. Monolithic skyscrapers surrounded us on every side. When I looked back over my shoulder, I could see the outline of the Hotel Valhalla against the sky.

The only man not present was Lieutenant Moffat. He and several other company commanders sat in a conference several blocks away. Even now, with humanity's back to the wall, when push came to shove, the natural-borns were sending us out alone.

I dug the men in along the crest of a hill. The ground in front of us was a marsh. I could see the still surface of the water through canes and reeds, plants that had gone dormant for the winter. The sludgy water reflected the ionically charged sky above it, with the added effect of a rainbow streak caused by a minor oil slick.

"Lieutenant Harris, are you watching the feed?" Major Burton spoke to me over a direct link.

"Yes, sir," I said.

"Those bastards danced through four thousand volts like it wasn't there," Burton said.

"Yes, sir," I said. I wasn't really listening to him.

From my perch on this hill, I could see far enough down the street to spot the Avatari. At this distance, I needed telescopic lenses to make them out, but I could see them tramping forward. Thanks to the hot-spot-identifying sensors in my visor, I saw thousands of fire red dots marking the spot where mines had been laid on the street ahead as well.

Walking point, a yard or two ahead of its comrades, one of the Avatari stepped on a mine. With my visor zoomed in on the bastard, I enjoyed the carnage as much as I would have if I were only a couple of yards away. I watched its foot come down on the virtual dot that marked the location of very real explosives. I watched the ground burst. Dust, rock, concrete fragments, and who knew what else, shot up like a pillar. The explosion tore the alien's leg from the rest of its body and it flew twenty feet through the air. The remainder of the body flew backward, flipping through the air and smashing into the Avatari behind it.

A whoop of victory echoed across the city.

"At least they're not mine-proof," Burton said. On the video feed, I could see that maybe as many as a hundred Avatari had stepped on mines. The rest of their army paused and studied the field for a moment. This was the first time they had ever shown the slightest concern about their surroundings.

An alien stepped forward, pointed its rifle at the street ahead, and fired. Watching the feed on a small window in my visor, I saw several other Avatari doing the same thing. I expected the rifle to fire a bolt of light into the street, but it fired a long string of light instead. There was a silent moment in which I decided that nothing would happen, then the entire street vanished in a mass explosion.

Working frantically with the optical controls in my visor, I rewound the explosion and watched it in slow motion. In one frame the Avatari stood before a perfectly normal street. In the next frame, the surface of the street began to crack in a thousand different locations. In the next frame, pieces of concrete began to sprout in the air. And in the frame after that, a thousand individual geysers of smoke, dust, and rubble appeared. The force of their simultaneous explosion sent the entire street flying in the air, where it shattered, crumbled, and turned to dust.

The explosion reverberated through the city. The ground shook beneath me as if it might break open. The buildings between us and the Avatari shook. Windows exploded. The base of one of the buildings at the edge of the park caved in—a hundred-story cloud shredder, falling in on itself, flushing a flashflood of dust and debris in every direction.

"Lieutenant..." Thomer and Herrington both tried to contact me.

"Stay focused," I said over a platoon-wide frequency.

"Harris, they've disarmed the minefield," Moffat said over a company-wide frequency. He sounded so specking calm. "Prepare to attack."

The cloud of dust, dirt, and smoke washed across the space between the buildings like a river breaking through a dam. It flooded the open ground of the park, then splashed into us and moved beyond.

"What the hell was that?" Philips asked on the companywide frequency. The conscripts did not have access to the video feed, they were in the dark about what was happening up the street.

"Steady," I answered. "They detonated the mines."

"So we got them?" Skittles asked.

"As soon as the smoke clears, Harris, take your men and..." Moffat said.

We stared straight ahead into the haze. Night-for-day vision made no difference, we might as well have been buried in mud. Heat vision revealed fires and spent mines, but the Avatari gave off no heat signature.

"Glad we worked so hard laying those mines, eh?" Philips drawled over the interLink. "Got any ideas on what to do next?"

There was a second explosion. I saw nothing, but it stirred the cloud of dust around me.

"What was that?" Skittles asked.

"They must have detonated more mines," Thomer said.

"Steady," I said. Minutes passed. I could feel the tension. I could hear my men breathing heavily when I listened over the interLink. There was no chatter. The men were scared but ready to fight.

"Harris, take 'em out," Moffat yelled.

He was ordering us to commit suicide. We had no idea what waited on the other side of that smoke. If I had been a normal clone, my neural programming would have forced me to obey, but I was a Liberator. I ignored him. What I could not ignore was the combat hormone welling up in my blood. With that hormone in my blood, the moments of waiting before we attacked were like foreplay. I wanted to get to the real thing.

The dust in the air slowly thinned. I could make out the edges of buildings against the sky. I could see more than five feet ahead of me.

"Harris, attack," Moffat said. "That is an order."

I said nothing.

Anything more than ten feet ahead of me was still a blur of dust and smoke. Standing in the park felt like swimming underwater. I could not see anything beyond the reeds in the pond at the base of the hill.

"Harris, I gave you an order. Acknowledge."

Some of the dust had settled on the surface of the pond. It floated on the oil film.

I listened to my men chatter over the interLink. Skittles, too young of a Marine to be in such a desperate battle, sounded terrified as he asked his platoon leader, "Thomer, can you see them?"

"It's okay," Thomer said. "We're ready for them."

"I never thought it would be like this," Skittles said.

"Harris, I have given you a direct order. I order you to attack."

"Why don't you get your natural-born ass down here and lead the attack yourself?" I asked. He could send me to the brig for saying that, and I knew it. I had been through battles before, but this one seemed different. I was in a rage. Was this the beginning of a full-fledged Liberator meltdown? I wondered if that old asshole soldier on the trip to Mars had been right about me. I wondered if I could really go out of control, and I realized that I didn't much care.

"Watch yourself, Harris."

"You want to send us in alone?" I asked. "You're sending a single company against fifty thousand Mudders?"

Moffat didn't care about killing the Avatari; this was about Philips. He wanted Philips dead, and he planned on using the Avatari as his instrument of choice. He probably didn't give a shit if any of us clones made it out... if I died, so much the better. All of a sudden, the Avatari were no longer the enemy in my mind, Moffat was.

Then something happened. There was a flash so bright that I could see it through the dust and smoke. I turned back in time to see another building folding in on itself. The explosion made no detectable sound, but the crash of the building shook the ground.

"What the hell was that?" Philips asked.

"Shit, they're knocking down buildings!" one of my men yelled.

"Harris, this is your last warning. Get in there!" Moffat shouted.

Without saying a word, I left the hill. I started back toward the hotels... toward the officers' sanctuary from which Moffat was issuing orders.

"Lieutenant, where are you going?" Thomer asked as he saw me leave. I did not answer him. I was beyond speaking.

"Lieutenant, where are you going?" Thomer asked again.

"Harris, my console shows that you are moving away from the line. What the speck do you think you are specking doing?" Moffat yelled. "You and your men get your asses in there! That is an order!"

"Lieutenant Harris...?" Thomer asked. He fell in behind me, so did the rest of the company.

I stashed my particle-beam pistol—a good weapon for killing Avatari—in my armor and pulled out my M27.

"Lieutenant, what are you doing?" Thomer asked, sounding confused.

"I'm going to help Lieutenant Moffat earn his combat pay," I said.

41

A second building fell off in the background as I cut across the park. The big building fell so smoothly it seemed to sink into the ground. I looked down at my M27, wrapped my fingers around the grip, and ran my thumb along the barrel as I visualized committing murder. Thomer, Philips, and Herrington brought their platoons in behind me, but I paid them no attention. Nor did I pay any attention to Lieutenant Moffat's nonstop ranting over the interLink.

The system had broken down, exposing a new weakness. Moffat, a prick even by natural-born-officer standards, wanted to sacrifice an entire company because he had a grudge against a single clone. Like the Liberators before me, I had given in to bloodlust. I cared more about killing Moffat than killing the enemy.

"Sergeant Philips, take your men and return to the park," Moffat yelled. He said it over an open frequency, and every man in the company heard him. Philips ignored the order. He stayed behind me.

Officers sacrificing clones and Liberators going on a killing spree were nothing new, but a general-issue clone like Mark

Philips ignoring a direct order... the fabric of military discipline had come undone. Clones of Philips's make had autonomic obedience hardwired into their brains. For them, obeying orders was as deeply seated as their need to breathe.

"Harris, you are relieved of command," Moffat shouted. "Philips, you and your specking platoon get your specking asses out there. Do you specking hear me, Sergeant, I specking order you to specking engage the specking enemy. I order—"

"Philips, what are you doing?" I asked.

"We go where you go, Kap-y-tan," Philips said.

"Philips! Philips! Philips, you specking waste of DNA—" Moffat ranted like a maniac.

"I don't need a damn posse," I said.

"We're not your damn posse, sir," Philips said.

Seeing that the entire company had attached itself to me, Moffat ordered Thomer's platoon to fall back. Thomer did as he was told. Moffat issued the same command to Herrington, who also fell back. That was good. I did not want them in the middle of this.

"Lieutenant Harris," Thomer called.

"Shut up, Thomer," I responded without looking back. I holstered my M27. Whatever I did once I caught up to Moffat, I would do with my bare hands.

Another building fell, but I paid no attention to it. Somewhere behind me, a fourth building fell as the Avatari began demolishing everything around them. Why should they care what they destroyed or how much damage they caused? For them, a scorched earth was as good as any.

"Harris, what the speck do you think you are doing?" Moffat asked. He was a big man, a strong man... not one to be easily intimidated.

"Harris, are we going to kill an officer?" Philips asked. "Is that what we are going to do?"

"Get out of here," I growled at Philips. "This is between me and Moffat."

"Bullshit," Philips said. "I'm the one who slept with his ugly-ass wife. This is my specking court-martial."

"Go kill a Mudder," I said. He did not listen. He and his platoon trailed after me, my unwanted entourage.

Behind us, another building fell. It may have been the fifth or the fiftieth—I had lost count.

I accelerated to a jog, skirted around a park bench, then kicked a trash can out of my way. Trash sprayed through the air. A wine bottle hit the ground and spun in a circle. I was almost to the street, Philips and his platoon just a few feet behind me. Across the street, I saw dozens of officers huddling around a makeshift bunker. They were the second echelon. They would watch how the enemy attacked the men on point, then send reinforcements. Technically speaking, Moffat was on the front line; but for those of us on point, he looked to be a million miles away.

I was too enraged to hate the man. Hate takes thought, and my brain was strictly on survival mode—breathe, walk, kill: things I could do without thinking. Nothing mattered to me except killing Moffat and the testosterone-laced adrenaline running through my veins.

Moffat stood at the front of the pack. I saw his virtual tag—Name: Warren Moffat, Rank: Second Lieutenant, Serial Number: 61752248013. He stood in the open, staring straight at me, his arms crossed before his chest.

"Arrest that man," Moffat said over an open frequency that every Marine in Valhalla would hear.

The first Marine to reach me was Major Brad Warren, a good man from the command staff. He came slowly, his pistol held low but drawn. He clearly did not want to arrest me.

"Lieutenant," he said, starting to raise his weapon toward my chest. I grabbed his hand, twisted the gun back against the top of his wrist, and flipped him out of my way. Another Marine reached for me. I slapped my palm into his right shoulder while kicking the inseam of his knee. He spun and fell.

Suddenly a dozen guns pointed at me. Marines standing so

close I could reach them with my elbows pointed guns into my chest. Marines standing a few feet away pointed guns at my head. I grabbed one of the Marines by the top of his chest plate, but staggered when the butt of another Marine's pistol slammed into the unprotected area between my helmet and shoulder plate. By this time, my combat reflex had all but obliterated my thoughts. Feeling nothing but anger and a desire to kill whoever had just struck me, I threw the Marine I had grabbed to the ground and spun to see who had hit me.

"For God's sake, Harris, stop!" Philips shouted.

As I started to come to my senses, the hammer struck. I felt the blow, knew it had knocked my helmet from my head; but that was all I knew as I fell face-first to the street.

Since the U.A. Marines did not have a base on New Copenhagen before the war, they did not have a brig of their own. As he prepared for the Avatari invasion, General Glade commandeered a downtown police station to use as a holding pen for grunts who got drunk or caused problems. When I woke up, I found myself a guest of that facility.

I was alone, lying on the floor in a jail cell. After weeks spent cursing the twenty-four-hours-per-day illumination of the ion curtain, I now found myself in near blackness. The only light came from two "EXIT" signs a long way from my cell.

The dim lighting was a good thing because my head felt like someone had used it for a soccer ball. This was worse than a hangover. When I reached back and felt the spot where my skull and neck came together, the goose-egg-sized welt was wet to the touch.

I reached out and felt a cot just a few feet from where I lay on the cold floor. Using that cot like a crutch, I pulled myself up. Blood rushed to my head, so I sat and tried to get my bearings. I took a personal inventory. My name was Wayson Harris, I was a lieutenant in the Unified Authority Marines, and we were stationed on New Copenhagen where some motherspecking aliens were going to annihilate our army and bake the survivors. *Good,* I thought to myself, *no brain damage.* Would I bake in this very cell?

I did not have my helmet. The MPs must have confiscated it as they dragged me down here. I did not have a gun or a knife or even my combat boots. Had Moffat brought me down himself, he probably would have shot me. Had he come with the MPs that dropped me off, he would have left a knife or a rope, something I could use to commit suicide so that he would not need to come back and kill me himself. He sure as hell did not want me getting out of here alive. Fortunately, the MPs must have brought me down here, and they would have done everything by the book.

My brain felt like an open wound. Circles of white light popped behind my eyes as I lifted myself off the cot and stood. I listened for the sounds of battle and heard nothing. But that did not mean anything—from what I could tell, I was in the basement of the police station. A few minutes later an explosion gave the building a quick shake, and I knew the war was still on. So be it; there was nothing I could do. I climbed onto the rack and lay there. If the Avatari reached this building, they might cave it in. I'd be crushed like a bug, but that might be better than starving to death. If we lost the battle, I might just be down here as the planet fried. I should have shot Moffat—at least then I would have gone down with something to smile about.

The tremors continued. They were not constant, and I never got the feeling that the police station would come crumbling down on me, but every few minutes I felt another undeniably unnatural vibration.

I must have been down in that cell for hours, the twelve-hour muscle relaxant I took for my shoulder wore off. That gave me some perspective about how long I had been down there. It also hurt like hell. I tried to sleep but could not get over the anger. I thought about Moffat and dreamed up a hundred different ways to kill the son of bitch. I lay there in the semidarkness, staring up from my rack, when I realized that I did not care if the Avatari collapsed the building on top of me. *Let them,* I said to myself.

Lost in my thoughts, I did not notice when the vibrations stopped outside the station. They might have faded, or they might have stopped abruptly. At some point I realized that I had no idea when the vibrations had ceased.

No one came for me. Time ticked by slowly. At least I thought it passed slowly. Without a clock, I had no way to judge. *Maybe there's no one left to come for me,* I thought. *Maybe they are all dead.* I liked that idea; it meant I had outlived Moffat and Glade and Newcastle and the whole clone-hating cabal. I did not mind the idea of dying in this cell. Starving to death did not sound appealing, but I did not mind the idea of dying alone.

Time continued to drag on. I fell asleep. When I woke, I searched around the cell until I found the toilet that sat in the corner. I took a piss. I found the sink while I was on the head and washed my hands. I cupped my hands and took a drink. The water tasted rusty. The sink was small and shallow, but I thought it might be big enough for me to submerge my face and drown myself. The problem was, I would never be able to kill myself. The neural programming in Liberators did not allow us to commit suicide.

Shredding the mattress and using the material to hang myself seemed like the best option as I considered ways to shorten my stay in the jailbird hotel. If I didn't mind hanging naked, I could use the sheer material in my bodysuit to tie a noose. I could drag my rack against the bars of the cell, then tie one pant leg around my neck and the other around the bars. My neck would snap as I rolled from the rack. I knew from experience that necks snapped easily when you gave them the right sort of force. I knew I could not bring myself to do it, but it felt good to think of ways I could end this.

Feeling like I might just be able to pull it off, I slid my cot against the bars, and there I sat. This was not the first time I had contemplated suicide to avoid a slow death. The last time I found myself in a similar situation, I discovered that I could not go against the things that were hardwired in my head. So I kicked up my feet and lay back on my bed and waited to see what would happen next. Time passed, then I heard someone open a door.

I did not worry about a visit from the Avatari; they would not bother hunting stragglers. What did they care about stray humans running around the city?

It could have been Moffat, come to fix me once and for all. I hoped it was. I would try to goad him close to the cell, then I would tear out his throat. We could die down here together. I liked that idea. Then again, I was feeling drowsy and possibly a little deranged.

"Harris? You in here?" I recognized the voice. Major Terry Burton came in with an entourage of officers and MPs. The low glow of the "EXIT" signs reflected on their combat armor. They came to my cell and looked at me through the bars. "Comfortable?" Burton asked.

"I could use some chow," I said, making no effort to get up and salute.

"Don't mind us," Burton said. "By all means, go back to sleep if you like."

"Did we win?" I asked.

"That depends on your definition of winning," Burton said. "I understand you tried to attack a fellow officer. Is there anything I need to know about before I let you out?"

Burton put on a good face, but there was something forced about his causal tone.

"Is Moffat with you?" I asked.

"No," Burton said.

"Then I'll behave myself."

Burton turned toward one of his aides, and said, "Spring him." He stepped back, and a moment later the cell door slid open.

"General Glade wants to see you. Apparently he has something he wants to discuss with you."

"My court-martial?" I asked.

"Nope," Burton said. "He wouldn't have bothered sending me if he planned on throwing you right back in."

Burton and his men cleared away from the door as I stepped out, acting as if I had a fatal disease. "Your things are in a box upstairs," one of the junior officers said.

We took an elevator up three floors to the ground floor, and suddenly the building looked as bright as the sun. The light hurt my eyes, and I winced. "I see the ion curtain is still up," I mumbled.

Parts of the station looked vaguely familiar. I recognized some of the maps and pictures on the walls as I walked through the building. I realized that I must have lapsed in and out of lucidity as the MPs dragged me in to my cell. *Bastards,* I thought. Whoever it was that had knocked me out had fetched me one hell of a blow. But I didn't really care who dropped the hammer; he had just been doing Moffat's bidding. The war was between me and Moffat.

One of the men in armor pointed to the box that held my holster and personal effects. I found my boots and body gear, but my helmet and weapons were gone.

"My guns?" I asked.

"We'll hold the guns for safekeeping. You can have them back after your meeting with General Glade," Burton said.

"And my helmet?" I asked.

"Evidence," he said.

"I thought you said there wasn't going to be a court-martial," I said as I picked up my stuff.

"There's going to be an investigation," Burton said. "If it leads to a court-martial, I don't think the court-martial will be yours."

I thought about putting on my armor. Walking around town in my bodysuit was about the same thing as walking around in my underwear. But who was I trying to impress? I mean, this wasn't a uniform inspection, so I put on my boots and carried the rest of my things in the box.

"Lieutenant Moffat claims you tried to kill him," Burton said, as we headed for the door.

"The thought occurred to me," I said. "Did he happen to mention why I wanted to kill him?"

"He says he was baffled by it."

"Did you check the record in his helmet?" I asked.

Burton laughed. "Funny thing about that, his helmet appears to have malfunctioned. The record got erased during the battle." He stopped in front of the door to the street, and said, "Fair warning, Harris—Valhalla changed a bit while you were locked up."

"Changed?" I asked.

Burton pushed the door open.

It was as if by opening the door, Major Burton had transported me from New Copenhagen to the cities of Dresden or Hiroshima after the Second World War. Instead of looking at a city, I was staring into a desert with slag instead of sand. Except for the litter and the ruins, the world outside the station looked primordial.

"The battle was all but done by the time the Avatari reached this part of town," Burton said.

"How far are we from the demilitarized zone?" I asked.

If everything had gone as planned, we would have kept the Avatari pinned down in the demilitarized zone. From here I could only see a small sliver of town, but I could already tell that the plan had gone down the shitter.

"Harris, this is city center. The demilitarized zone ends eight miles away," Burton said.

I tried to grasp the concept that the Avatari could have bashed their way so far into town as Burton led me to his car. "You must be hungry," he said.

"Yeah, a bit," I admitted.

"You had water in your cell?" he asked.

"It tasted like shit," I said. "How long was I down there?"

"A day and a half," Burton said.

"A day and a half?" I asked, totally stunned. I thought maybe I was there for five or six hours.

"How hard did they hit us?"

"Pretty hard," Burton said. I could see that. If we drove to the right or left, we could not go more than a block before we ran into wreckage.

"How hard?" I asked.

330

"I think General Glade wants to handle your briefing, Harris. The truth is, I don't know much more than you. They aren't giving out numbers. I figure my battalion took a seventy percent casualty rate. We're down to forty-seven men." That was forty-seven men out of three hundred.

As we drove, I became more aware of just how damaged the city had become. We entered one area in which I saw the ruins of an ornate security gate. Beyond the gate lay the wreckage of a toppled building.

Burton asked, "Know where we are?"

"No," I said.

"Don't recognize it at all?"

The sign dangling from the twisted archway gave it away: "Welcome to the Hotel Valhalla." Having seen the sign, I recognized the horseshoe drive. *The hotel,* I thought. Then I understood the bigger picture. "What about the underground parking lot?" I asked.

"I knew you'd ask," Burton said. "I'm not in the loop on these things, but from what I have seen, it's a total loss.

"Harris, we took it in the ass when we had six hundred thousand men and so much ammunition we didn't know what to do with it. Now, if we're lucky, we might have one hundred thousand men left, and we're down to rocks and bullets for weapons.

"I hope General Glade has something up his sleeve that I don't know about, or else we're screwed."

42

Campus Drive looked pretty much the same as it did the first time General Glade brought me to a briefing in the Science Lab. The tree-lined walks, the rows of redbrick dormitories, the fountains, and everything else remained untouched by war. As we cut across campus, I saw the lab in the distance.

They held, I thought. Newcastle had said that everyone and everything was expendable except the Science Lab. We had lost hundreds of thousands of men and our entire armory, but the specking science building stood unmolested. We rolled on to dormitory row.

"General Glade left strict orders for you to have a quick shower and report to his office," Burton said.

"I haven't eaten in—"

Burton put up a hand. "He said you might say something along that line. He ordered a meal for you from the officers' mess.

"He also said to warn you not to keep him waiting."

So I followed orders. I walked straight through the barracks, heads turning as I passed.

"Lieutenant Harris?" Sergeant Thomer came out to meet

me. "Where were you?" he asked. "Herrington told me that Lieutenant Moffat threw you in the brig."

"Is that what he said?" I asked. "I don't have much time; what did I miss? How's your platoon?"

"There are only nine of us left in the platoon," Thomer paused. "They got Philips."

I stopped walking. "Did you see what happened?" That was an attempt at tact. What I meant was, "Did Moffat shoot him?"

Thomer understood immediately. "No," he said. "I lost track of him in the battle."

"Have you gone out after him?" I asked.

"No, sir. We've been confined to base." There it was, the neural programming that Philips had somehow managed to overcome. Given a direct order, this make of clone was supposed to obey without question. Philips was Thomer's closest friend. He'd been Thomer's guardian angel on the battlefield, and Thomer protected him everywhere else; but some officer gave orders for the clones to return to base, and the programming hardwired into Thomer's brain would not ignore a direct order. That was how it was supposed to work.

"Who gave the order?" I asked.

"Lieutenant Moffat," Thomer said.

"Moffat again?" I whispered. Now I wanted a look at Philips's body more than ever. He would be dead, no question about that, but I needed to know what killed him.

"The Mudders got Manning and Skittles. Boll and Herrington made it. I never saw anything like it before," Thomer said in a flat voice. "They just plowed through everything. They knocked down buildings whenever they came to anything more than a couple of stories tall. I hear the Army stationed a regiment in a parking garage. The Mudders knocked down the building, and the Army lost the entire regiment... an entire regiment destroyed with one shot."

I did not have time to talk, but there would be time later. "Thomer, take five men and find Philips," I said, specifically framing it as an order. "His virtual tags will still be up unless he was shot in the head. Do you know where he took his platoon?"

"What about Lieutenant Moffat?" Thomer asked.

"You just get your team together and head out," I said. "If you run into Moffat, tell him he can take it up with me directly."

Thomer smiled and saluted. "Aye, aye, sir," he said.

As he started to leave, I added, "If you find anyone with a pulse, you bring them back, but Philips is the one I want to see. Once you find him, head straight back to the barracks."

Thomer nodded and went out to piece together his hunting party.

I stood and watched as Thomer left, not really following him so much as staring into space. Philips was murdered only after I'd gotten myself thrown in the brig for no reason. What did I accomplish by going after Moffat now that Philips was dead? Maybe if I had controlled my temper, I could have kept him safe.

What would I do if Philips's armor had been blown apart? Bullets from M27s left small holes where they entered and jagged exit wounds, light bolts from Avatari rifles created distinctive tunnels through the entire body, but particle-beam fire would blow obliterated armor apart. One look at Philips's body and I would know who killed him.

And what if the armor had bullet holes? If Moffat had enough guts to face Philips, there might be a video record in Philips's helmet. Even if Moffat shot him from behind, a pompous ass like Moffat might have said something over the interLink before pulling the trigger. I could just see him saying, "Philips, this is for Lilly." I could also see him standing over Philips body, maybe kicking him a time or two for good measure.

Shaking my head to clear those thoughts, I went to my room, stripped out of my bodysuit, and grabbed a towel. I found the medicine for my shoulder and gave myself a double dose, then headed for the showers. What if I ran into Moffat in there, would I attack him or ignore him? It would be one or the other; talking was out of the question.

The officers' shower was empty. There might not have been many officers left, and those still alive may well have needed a drink more than a shower. By now every natural-born knew we could no longer win this war. Only the cowards who ran would survive the next battle. I thought about the deserters come judgment day—when the Avatari caused the sun to go supernova. Would the world suddenly melt around them, or would it happen gradually over centuries? Sweetwater had never said how long it would take for the sun to expand. Would it be a year or a hundred years or a thousand? General Haight made that comment about our geese being cooked whether we won or lost the war, not the scientists. What was a thousand years or a hundred thousand in terms of space? However long it took, I hoped the deserters would realize they had leaped out of the frying pan and into a hot fire indeed. Heroes and cowards, we'd all burn as one on that day.

Semper fi... or should I have said "semper fry"?

I stepped into the shower and turned on the water. Strands of water arced out of the showerhead. I made the water as hot as I could, felt it lightly burning my skin, watched steam rise into the air around me.

So what if we all died, what did it matter? What did death mean to a clone? Heaven and hell were the domain of natural-borns. At least there would be no more talk about "fighting for Earth" or "preserving the Unified Authority" or "making the galaxy safe for mankind." From here on out, the most anyone could hope for was to take a few Mudders down with them.

This strange enemy had changed the nature of war. My shoulder hurt, but the medicine had already begun its magic, and the hot water felt good.

I finished my shower and dressed. Then I went to Base Command and reported in. As I waited to see General Glade, I noticed other generals milling around the building. Newcastle and Haight argued in a nearby office. I did not see them, but I recognized their voices. Army command must have moved into this building as well; I noticed several aides in Army drab.

Huuuuh huuuh. "Lieutenant Harris." Glade had cleared his throat as he came to meet me.

I stood and saluted. He returned the salute.

"Has the Army moved in with you, sir?" I asked.

"It would appear so," Glade said. "They lost their headquarters in the fighting. Let's talk in my office." He turned and started back down the hall. I followed.

A small food cart had been placed in a corner of the office. On it sat trays with several kinds of meats, breads, and vegetables. He even had packets of mayonnaise and mustard.

"Help yourself," Glade said. As I reached for a plate, he added something that took me by surprise. "We fought that whole damn battle for nothing, yesterday; the Science Lab is useless."

"Useless?" I asked.

"Burton didn't tell you?" Glade asked.

I lowered my plate back and stepped away from the cart. "Tell me what, sir?" I asked.

"Arthur Breeze is missing."

"Missing? General, if there's one man on New Copenhagen who knows there's no place to run…" I said. Breeze was the one who figured out that the aliens planned to bake the planet.

Glade sat down behind his desk. "Not Breeze, he didn't run away. Sweetwater's the one who would have bolted. He's the coward."

"So what happened?" I asked.

"All we know at this point is that Breeze stole a private plane," Glade said. "We don't know where he went with it."

"Sweetwater doesn't know?" I asked.

"Apparently not," Glade said.

Bright light from the ion curtain poured in through the window behind Glade's desk. It illuminated the back of his bald, parakeet-shaped skull. The light seemed to form a silvery halo behind him as he sat, silently watching me.

"You don't think much of Sweetwater," I said as I went back to making my sandwich.

"No, I don't," Glade agreed. "The little runt ran out on Terraneau."

"Maybe he's more cut out to be a scientist than a soldier," I said as I selected two slices of bread.

"He better be, 'cause he's all we have now," Glade said. "Lieutenant, I'm not sure how much Major Burton actually knows about the last attack."

"He said it went badly," I said, "but he did not know any specifics."

"Here are the specifics, Harris," Glade said. "The armory was destroyed. All our weapons, all our ammunition—buried. The Avatari destroyed the Hotel Valhalla. Did you know that they got the Valhalla?"

"Major Burton took me by the hotel," I said.

Huuuuhh, Glade grunted, shaking his head and clearing his throat.

"They just about cleaned out the Army. Newcastle is down to about twenty thousand men. I have less than ten thousand Marines. I think the entire New Copenhagen militia was wiped out, but General Hill still has all of his pilots, for all of the good those grounded bastards do us.

"We lost it all protecting the specking scientists, then Breeze just ups and runs. Why did we listen to them?"

"We didn't have any choice, sir," I said.

"No, we did not." Glade reached up and rubbed his temples, then went on. "General Newcastle wants to bring in any civilians old enough to carry a gun. There's no point in bringing in more bodies, not with all of our guns buried under that hotel."

"It doesn't sound like more bodies would make much of a difference," I agreed.

"They fought a completely different battle this time, Harris. Did Burton tell you that? Did he tell you that they attacked on two fronts?"

"There were one hundred thousand this time?" I asked.

Glade shook his head. "The same damned fifty thousand, but

they attacked on two fronts. They sent half their men in from the east side of town, and we didn't have a single platoon in place to meet them. Not a single specking platoon.

"They always came in from the west. Why did they have to pick this battle to start thinking strategies?"

He sat and thought for a moment. "Five days ago we had too many men and too many weapons, and we couldn't decide which one we wanted to throw away first. Now look at us."

That wasn't exactly accurate, but I knew better than to correct the general. Five days ago we were trying to decide whether to throw men or munitions at the Avatari, but we already knew we had limited supplies of both.

"Sir, what about the rocket launchers?" I asked. "Wasn't the Army constructing them around campus?"

"Completed," Glade said, sounding more miserable and frustrated than ever. "The only problem is that we left the damned rockets in the armory for safekeeping."

Glade leaned back in his chair. The chair looked comfortable, but the general clearly took no comfort from it. "Do you know where that leaves us, Harris? That leaves us so far up shit creek we're practically to the kidneys."

Glade droned on about the battle, but I paid little attention. I felt like someone had drilled a hole in my head and poured thick oil into my brains. Thoughts came slowly. The world was coming to an end, and all I could do was hang on for the ride. I finished my sandwich in three bites.

Someone rapped at the door.

"Come in," Glade barked.

"Jim, we better get going to the lab; the dwarf is waiting on us."

"Oh yeah, I forgot about the briefing." Glade laughed. "We don't want to miss out on the latest bad news."

General Haight turned toward me and paused. "I heard you sat the last fight out, son."

"I got thrown in the brig," I said, still trying to figure out who "Jim" was. Moments passed before I realized that Jim was commanding-officer-talk for General James Ptolemeus Glade.

"I heard that, too," he said. "A firing squad would be too good for the bonehead who took you off the line."

I did not say anything though I felt the same way.

43

The war did not reach the hallowed steps of the Science Laboratory. Not a window was cracked, not a doorpost was nicked. Not so much as a blade of grass looked out of place on the lawn. The only bombardment this building had seen came from the flocks of pigeons that gathered along its ledge.

I stepped into the lab and saw a janitor mopping the floor. In a city littered with dead soldiers, a city in which most of the skyscrapers now lay in ruins, here stood a man in blue canvas coveralls swinging a mop back and forth over the gleaming white floor. After everything I had seen over the last two weeks, this simple janitor looked more alien to me than the Avatari.

The floor was wet and shiny. Reflections of the fluorescent light fixtures showed in the water. I stopped to stare at that janitor for just a moment. He looked up at me and gave me a nervous smile, then one of General Glade's officers asked, "You coming?" and we moved on toward the lab.

Military high command was and always will be a club for overaged boys. As officers are known to do, some of the ones leading this campaign came up with childish epithets for Arthur

Breeze and William Sweetwater after that first briefing. The names that caught on were "the Cadaver" and "the Dwarf." I once heard Newcastle make a joke about them having a "lesbian affair." By now, however, the joking had stopped.

The generals walked through the lobby in silence. They did not speak to each other. They did not speak to their aides. They walked up the steps, taking one stair at a time, heads down and faces devoid of emotion. They did not look defeated, but they did not look proud. Gone were the days of boasting and haughtiness.

We filed into the lab and formed our familiar circle. Ninety-five percent of the fighting men had died, but the ring of generals remained intact. Sweetwater sat waiting for us, looking agitated as he fiddled with some odd contraptions.

"I suppose we should get started," Sweetwater said, looking around the circle. "We might as well begin with the good news."

"Good news?" Newcastle repeated. He did not wear his former smirk. "There's good news?"

Sweetwater pressed a button on a portable communications console and played a recording of an audio signal. It was weak and filled with static. Then came a human voice. "This is Valhalla Station. Come in. Repeat, this is Valhalla Station. Come in."

The crackle of the static grew louder, then... "Valhalla Station, this is UAN *Thermopolis*. We read you, Valhalla Station." The static increased and the signal ended.

"What was that?" Newcastle asked.

"We were able to make a hole in the ion curtain," Sweetwater said. He had always struck me as brilliant and arrogant, maybe a man with a chip on his shoulder. Without Breeze around, he seemed awkward. He fumbled for words and answered questions in sentences instead of paragraphs.

"There are ships out there?" General Hill asked.

"During the moment that we penetrated the curtain, we detected six battleships orbiting the planet."

"Do we know if the Avatari have attacked Earth?" General Glade asked.

Sweetwater shook his head. "You just heard everything we have."

"That's it?" Newcastle asked. He shook his head, the disappointment showing on his face. "That is the good news— that you located six battleships orbiting the planet? They can't send down reinforcements, you weren't able to speak to them for more than a second, and you don't know if Earth even exists. That is the best news you have for us? We can't even call them back, and that's the *good* news?"

"No," Sweetwater said. "The good news is that we believe we have cracked the Avatari's tachyon-based technology. Give us a little more time and—"

"A little more time?" Of all people, this time it was mild-mannered General James Hill, the Air Force officer who could not even get his pilots in the air, who cracked. "We are down to thirty-five thousand troops. Did you know that? I am about to send highly trained pilots into ground battles... ground battles! We have given you time, and blood, and everything else you have asked for! If you don't have anything now, then, then... we're specked. We're really specked."

William Sweetwater, short, heavy, with shaggy black hair and thick glasses, hung his head and sighed. The sound of that sigh was long and weary.

"Do you or do you not have a weapon that we can use?" General Newcastle asked in a quiet voice.

"Arthur had an idea," Sweetwater confessed, "but that idea of his probably cost him his life."

A stifling three-second pause hung in the room.

"Goddamn! We've lost. We've lost, do you understand that?" General Newcastle shouted. "We're out of fighting solutions. So far the only thing you have given us is six useless battleships."

He turned to the other generals. "Gentlemen, the end of humanity came on our watch."

None of the other officers said anything.

"Arthur believed he found a way to stop the Avatari from assembling," Sweetwater said.

Another moment of silence followed, after which General Newcastle said in a voice so calm I could not believe it came from him, "Stop them from assembling? I... I don't understand."

"Tachyons are not like other kinds of particles, they do not bond together. They are in constant motion. We have never been able to prove their existence because they move faster than the speed of light and we would need an incredible amount of energy to cause them to stop. It must take even more energy to fuse them together, and that is why the Avatari degrade so quickly... it's not because you destroyed them but because so much energy has leaked out. They no longer have enough energy to keep the tachyons fused," Sweetwater said.

He typed something into a keyboard, and a video feed of the Avatari spheres appeared on a small screen near his seat. Near the spheres sat the dirty bomb Freeman had used to nuke the site. Sweetwater did not run the feed; he just left the image on the screen.

"Raymond and Lieutenant Harris made an important discovery the first day that the Avatari landed, but we did not have enough data to realize what they had found." Sweetwater held up a petri dish holding a layer of rust-colored dust. "This was once a bullet."

The generals crowded for a closer look. Finally, Newcastle asked, "What did you do to it?"

"We didn't do anything to it in the lab. This was one of the bullets that Raymond fired through the light spheres. Something in the spheres coated the bullet, changing its chemical makeup.

"We initially thought it was some form of radiation. Then we found out about the gas Raymond and Lieutenant Harris discovered in the Avatari mines. Arthur... Doctor Breeze checked the information Raymond gathered about that gas and compared it to this bullet to see if the gas might have caused the changes to this bullet and found a match.

"It appears that the spheres are made out of that gas. They're like a bubble of gas.

"Now watch this," Sweetwater said. He started the video feed. The dirty bomb exploded. I relived all of the disturbing images on the screen—the holocaust, the flash that looked like a golden jellyfish as it rose in the air. Sweetwater froze the image before the firestorm re-formed itself into a mushroom cloud.

The scene occurred so quickly at the time that it took place in my head as a single blur. Watching from the helicopter, I had only paid attention to the conflagration itself. Now, on the screen, I saw the spheres. In the moment of the explosion, they seemed to dim.

Sweetwater pointed to one of the spheres with his pen.

"It's getting darker," General Glade said. "The bomb made it weaker."

"That was what we assumed, too," Sweetwater said. The feed resumed. As wind pushed and tore the forest, and the flash fire turned trees to ash, the spheres went dark. Then came the smoke, and the spheres vanished entirely. By the time that the smoke cleared, the spheres were as bright as before but considerably smaller. I had not noticed it at the time because I had been so focused on the explosion and its apparent failure. Now, in the recording, I saw that the spheres could not have even been a full yard in diameter. And there was something else, too—shit gas. A layer of shit gas covered the ground. Now, viewing everything magnified and in slow motion, I saw that the shit gas formed a layer under the smoke.

"The nuclear explosion had a much greater effect than we initially thought. After careful analysis, Dr. Breeze discovered that the spheres had not become darker, they had become coated with tachyons. The bomb both heated or irradiated the gas in the spheres, charging it so that it temporarily attracted tachyons."

"Do you know if it was the heat or the radiation?" asked General Hill.

"No, we don't know," admitted Sweetwater. "But we will only need to run a few quick tests to find out. Once we know, we should be able to adjust the next explosion to maximize its impact."

"But how does this help us?" asked Newcastle.

"When the Avatari emerge from their spheres, they attract tachyons and bond them together the same way this bomb attracted the tachyons to the sphere. The Avatari bodies are composed of supercharged gas, which attracts tachyons like a magnet.

"If we supercharge a larger source of the gas—"

"Like the gas in the mines," interrupted General Hill.

"That radio message we picked up from the *Thermopolis* was received twenty seconds after Raymond and the lieutenant ran the nuclear test. By charging the spheres, they were able to poke a hole in the ion curtain," Sweetwater said.

"So you are saying that if we charge the gas in the mines, we can get out of here?" asked General Haight. The mood in the room had changed, suddenly the generals sounded excited as they chattered back and forth.

"No," said Sweetwater, and the room became quiet.

"First of all, gentlemen, understand that we are discussing an extreme amount of energy. If we could tap the energy it takes to create one Avatari soldier, we might have enough power to run a small city for a year," Sweetwater said. "Assuming we can generate enough energy and we can take that energy to a large enough source of the gas, we might be able to attract the tachyons before they attach themselves to the Avatari. That was what Breeze believed, and it appears he was right all along."

"How does that help us?" Newcastle asked.

"Because without the tachyons to create bodies and weapons, the Avatari aren't much of a threat," General Glade spoke slowly, a man figuring out the answer to a riddle.

"If it works, the next time the Avatari emerge, they will remain in their pure energy form," Sweetwater said, "as will their weapons. Without tachyons forming a protective shell around their core, they should dissipate into the atmosphere in a matter of minutes."

"In simple terms?" Newcastle asked.

"It's as simple as this… The Avatari as we see them are an energy impulse made solid by a layer of tachyons. If Arthur was right, we can block the tachyons from attaching themselves to the Avatari by attracting them to a larger source of supercharged gas—the caves. The key is creating enough energy to attract tachyons."

"So we need to break into the alien mines and detonate a device like the one you used on the spheres?" asked General Newcastle.

"No, sir, we are going to need something a great deal bigger than that little half-kiloton bomb we sent Raymond and the Lieutenant to explode. According to our calculations, we're going to need at minimum a twenty-five-megaton explosion in their caves. We assume you have a device that size."

Several of the generals groaned. Newcastle remained silent as the other generals complained among themselves. When the groaning stopped, he said, "That, Doctor, is going to be a problem. The Avatari just demolished our armory. We had nuclear weapons, but they're all buried now."

"Well, that does present a problem," said Sweetwater. He turned to me, and said, "Raymond will be back in a half hour. Do you think the two of you could dig out one of those bombs?"

"What's the point?" General Haight asked. "If we stop the aliens from coming back, we're still going to fry." This earned Haight a few appreciative nods.

Huhhhhh. Huhhh. "You know what, General Haight, given a choice, I think I would rather die in battle than get fried by an overheated sun," General Glade said.

"Hear, hear," said Newcastle. General Hill patted Glade on the back.

"The sun? The supernova? Gentlemen, I should have been more explicit from the start. We have learned a great deal about how the Avatari create a supernova by studying the reaction they caused in the Templar System. If the Avatari were to begin working on Nigellus, it would be at least twenty thousand years before it began to supernova and another ten thousand years before it incinerated this planet."

"Excuse me?" General Glade asked.

"Twenty thousand years," Sweetwater repeated.

"Twenty thousand years?" Newcastle asked. "You made it sound like it would happen immediately."

Sweetwater stifled a laugh. "I believe it was Dr. Breeze who discussed it with you. This is more his area of expertise."

"What are you saying about twenty thousand years?" General Hill asked.

"I understood what Arthur meant. It never occurred to me that... well, the destruction of the sun in the Templar System took place over a fifty thousand-year period. We've documented the entire cycle by observing it from different locations across the galaxy.

"From the far end of the galaxy, one hundred thousand light-years from Templar, the solar system is unchanged. From approximately eighty thousand light-years away, we can detect slight variations in the size of the sun."

"So much for the goose getting cooked," Glade said.

"For the immediate future, I suppose you are correct, but they are still saturating the planet with a highly toxic gas. The atmosphere is already permeated. If they continue pouring gas into this planet, we will die."

Freeman liberated a jeep when he got back to Valhalla, and we drove through the graveyard that had once been the capital city of New Copenhagen.

"You missed all the action," I said, as we pulled away from campus. Had he known, Freeman might have pointed out that I had spent most of the battle stretched out on a cot. Freeman being Freeman, however, said nothing.

"I heard that Dr. Breeze is missing," I said, still trying to drum up a conversation. We were driving on surprisingly safe roads—the Corps of Engineers had sent teams out to clear a path between the university campus and the hotel.

"I found him," Freeman said.

I smiled. "Maybe that's a good omen."

"He's dead," Freeman said.

"Oh," I said.

We drove the next two miles without a word. I took in the sights—dunes where skyscrapers and office buildings once stood; parks and alleys filled with bodies; dogs brazenly gnawing at the bodies of the servicemen who used to hunt them.

The engineers had cleared the roads all the way to the hotel, but with trucks, jeeps, and emergency-equipment vehicles blocking the driveway, we had to park our jeep along the street and walk to the ruins of the hotel. I climbed out for a look around. Wind rustled past. The mild winter was ending.

In the distance, I could see that the engineers had cleared the rubble and debris from the entrance to the garage. The arch of the garage opened like a man-made cave with a road vanishing into its darkened maw. From here, the whole thing looked untouched except that there was supposed to be a luxury hotel on top of it.

"So, do you like spelunking?" I asked Freeman.

He said nothing.

"At least there aren't any giant spiders mining the garage," I said, trying to sound optimistic.

"Just a couple of nuclear bombs," Freeman said.

"Well, yeah, there are the bombs... and all kinds of unexploded shells... and probably some chemical weapons." Engineers scurried about us, ignoring us, surveying the damage. There were engineers everywhere. They reminded me of ants walking about an anthill.

I saw a flashlight sitting on a table and decided to borrow it. As I took it toward the garage, I heard somebody yell, "Hey! Who took my flashlight?"

"Let's go have a look," I said to Freeman.

"I mean it! I want it back now!" yelled the guy at the table.

The concrete arch at the front of the garage did not have so much as a crack in it. Light from the ion curtain seeped in, through the open archway, and I could see everything around me quite clearly. The structural integrity seemed intact.

The ramp entered the garage as a four-lane highway, then, just after the ticket booths, it narrowed to two lanes of traffic as it dropped toward lower levels at an acute angle. Jagged glass teeth hung from the windows of the booths.

Beyond the booths, the light from the ion curtain faded, and I switched on the flashlight. Standing a few feet behind me, Freeman switched on the torch he had brought. The ramp spiraled down about twenty feet, then spilled into the first level of the garage—a cavernous expanse that had once been as wide as the hotel itself. It wasn't anymore, though; a solid wall of debris rose from the floor to the ceiling.

The air was colder down here. My breath turned to steam. I blew on my hands to warm them. When I paused to survey the area around me, I stomped my feet to keep them warm.

"Dead end," I said.

Ahead of us, little bubbles of light marked the places where engineers were conducting stress tests on caved-in areas. Their voices echoed softly.

"I bet they could dig this whole thing out," I said.

Freeman shook his head. "If they had a month."

"So we find another way in," I said. "Maybe we can tunnel our way in from outside."

I saw a trace of red mixed in with the concrete and rubble and went to have a closer look. From a distance it looked as if it might have been blood, but it was dry. When I shone my flashlight on it, I saw that it was a wedge of the red carpet that had once covered the lobby. Stepping over concrete boulders and splintered wood, I gave the carpet a tug. It frayed before I could pull it loose.

This far into the garage, the floor seemed strong, but that did not mean much. Deeper in it might have collapsed under the weight of everything that had toppled onto it. I did not see any bodies or blood. As far as I knew, every Marine was on the streets when the Hotel Valhalla came down.

I saw a metal bar sticking out of a mound of cement chunks and pulled on it. The bar did not budge. I gave it a harder yank. It did not come out, but it wobbled freely. As I pulled it again, a small avalanche cascaded down the pile of debris covering the bar. Plaster and concrete rolled down and struck the floor.

They expected Freeman and me to go rooting through this and come up with nuclear bombs? I didn't like the idea of hauling live nuclear weapons through a collapsed structure but didn't see any alternatives. Being crushed under a mountain of concrete did not seem any worse than being shot by an Avatari rifle. I might die faster. In the end, though, it wouldn't matter whether a million tons of hotel fell on our heads or an atomic bomb exploded in our faces or the Avatari shot us through the head with their specking light bolts, dead is dead.

"We're not getting in through here," Freeman said, his voice almost as soft as its echo in the underground vault. He turned to look for another route.

It's all just a matter of time, I thought. If I skipped the dig, the Avatari would kill us when they returned. I could drive into the forest and hide from the Avatari, but sooner or later the gunk they were dumping into the mountains would poison the air. Even if I found a way off the planet, I would have no place to go. The aliens had "sleeved" every habitable planet in the galaxy.

Go spelunking in a crumbling underground parking lot? Sure. What's the worry when you only have days to live?

Freeman drove me to the dormitory, then went on to the Science Lab. He said he would pick me up when the engineers found a way into the garage.

The clock was ticking. We needed to get into that underground garage, liberate at least one nuke, fly it to the alien dig site, and detonate it before the next battle. The Avatari returned every three days. I'd spent a day locked up in that cell, another eight hours had passed since Major Burton released me…

"It might take them all day to find a way into the garage," I said.

"If you don't hear from me in twelve hours, don't worry about it," Freeman said. He had a point.

* * *

Thomer met me as I entered the dormitory. He looked like every other clone, but I recognized him just the same. You do that when you live in a world of clones. You find ways to pull them out of the crowd.

"We found Philips," he said.

"You brought him back with you?" I asked.

Thomer nodded.

"Let's go have a look," I said, and followed Sergeant Thomer out of the building. He led me to a little parking lot behind the dorm. A single jeep sat in the lot, which was ringed by three-foot snowdrifts with surprisingly clean snow. A cold wind blew across the scene, making the bare branches rattle in the trees.

We approached the jeep. Thomer had laid Philips out in the back of the jeep, curling his knees against his chest so that he would fit. He'd left Philips covered under an Army blanket. I pulled back the blanket.

The man lying in the back of the jeep could have been any of the over one million clones flown to New Copenhagen to defend the planet. His helmet was removed, revealing a face with an ice blue tint to the skin. He had died with his mouth closed. Even Philips would have appreciated that irony.

Gone were the swagger and defiance that once made Sergeant Mark Philips stand out. The Japanese said that it was "the nail that stuck out that got beaten down." I suppose the indomitable Sergeant Philips had finally been beaten down. What remained was a body lying on its side in muddy combat armor. Had he been shot with a particle-beam weapon, his armor would have been in splinters or entirely gone.

"Where was he hit?" I asked.

"Shot through the chest," Thomer said.

I wrestled Philips's body onto its back, prepared to see bullet holes. I knew how I would react; I'd already rehearsed the scene in my head. I would turn without a word and march into the dorms. I would find Moffat and kill him, without ever speaking a word.

The wound was three inches across and ran right through the

center of Philips's chest. Except for the trail of white where his armor melted and drooled into the wound, the hole was clean— the work of an Avatari bolt.

"It doesn't matter who fired the shot," Thomer said, "Moffat killed him."

"Yes, he did," I said. The son of a bitch had intentionally sent Philips to die.

"Philips knew this was coming," Thomer said. He was trying to stay in control… good clones don't accuse natural-born officers. "This is what he wanted to happen."

"I suppose," I said.

"The moment they carted you away, Moffat sent Philips's platoon back out to the enemy line," Thomer, the closest the clone Marines had ever come to producing a Boy Scout, had to struggle to say these next words: "I'll shoot that bastard if I get a shot at him."

I'll shoot that bastard if I get a shot at him. The neural programming hardwired into Thomer's brain should not have allowed him to think such thoughts, let alone say them.

I did not know what to say. I went back into the dorms wondering how things had become so undone.

44

The excavation project commenced within the hour. It began with two crazed Army generals trying to show each other up. General Newcastle, still the highest-ranking officer on the planet, had his Corps of Engineers begin digging while General Haight, the up-and-comer, sent soldiers to all the local rescue stations to locate specialized equipment.

In the end, it was General James Ptolemeus Glade who stole the show. He was preordained to win the pissing match because the man going after the bombs wore a Marine's uniform. When Sweetwater asked me to go down, nobody volunteered to take my place.

I helped General Glade trump Newcastle and Haight a second time by telling him about S.C.O.O.T.E.R., the exploration robot Freeman and I had used to scout out the alien dig before we went in.

"Good idea," Glade said. "But unless those robots can dig their way out of a collapsed underground garage..."

"They didn't all go down with the armory, sir," I said. "Freeman got one out of the Science Lab."

Huhuhu. I could not tell if Glade had just cleared his throat or laughed. Maybe that sound came as a combination of the two.

"Damn, son," said Glade. "That's a good idea. I love showing that son of a bitch Newcastle who's got the real stones around here."

In the battle to show who had real stones, Haight came in last. Rather than showing up with specialized equipment, his detail arrived on the scene with sonic cannons, ropes, a collapsible platform, radio gear, hard hats, flashlights, hydraulic lifts, and other bric-a-brac that Newcastle's Corps of Engineers had brought from the start.

A few hours passed before the engineers cleared out enough of the garage for Freeman and me to attempt an entry. An hour before the garage was ready, Freeman called to tell me I was on deck.

"Aren't we both on deck?" I asked.

"You're on deck," he said.

"Where are you going?" I asked. I could not help feeling like I was about to do something really dangerous, and Freeman was skating off scot-free.

"I need to find Breeze," Freeman said.

"I thought you said he was dead," I said.

"Sweetwater needs the equipment he had on him."

"Where is he?" I asked.

"The Avatari mines."

"You're going into the mines?" Suddenly retrieving nuclear bombs from an unstable underground garage did not seem so bad.

"Only the entrance. Breeze didn't make it very far," Freeman said as he hung up.

So I called Major Burton and had Herrington assigned to my detail, then I dressed and went down to the street. While Newcastle's engineers finished their stress tests, Sergeant Herrington located a staff car and picked me up in front of the barracks. "Where to, sir?" he asked, as I climbed into the passenger's seat.

"The hotel," I said.

"The Hotel Valhalla?" Herrington asked. "The Mudders smashed it, sir. They knocked that place flat."

Looking into the sky, I almost mistook this for the early hours of a beautiful day. The sky had the white-paper look that it sometimes has on clear mornings as the sun rises over a cloudless atmosphere. There were clouds up in the silvery brightness and I realized it was midday.

"Do you still want to go back to the hotel?" Herrington asked.

"I do," I said. "We're excavating the armory."

"The armory?" Herrington asked. "Hot damn."

We drove across campus. Snowdrifts still leaned hard on a few of the buildings. The parks and greenbelts looked far too peaceful. Soldiers walked the pathways, and jeeps crossed the roads, but the place looked empty. This was a large campus, and the tens of thousands of defenders left to hold this ground did not provide enough warm bodies to replace the missing students.

"We aren't going to beat the Mudders, are we, sir?" Herrington asked.

I thought about telling him the truth. I could tell him that they were not "Mudders," in fact, they were not even living beings, just avatars of aliens who were far away and safe from assault. I thought about telling him that nothing we could do would matter in the end since the Avatari were pumping the planet full of chemicals.

"Sure we can win. The Science Lab has some ideas that could turn this thing around," was what I said. I did not believe a word of it. As for Herrington, he was a clone. When an officer gave him information, his neural programming was supposed to make him accept it.

"So there's a chance?" he asked.

We drove away from the campus and entered Valhalla, a city in ruins.

"We're Marines," I said. "There's always a fighting chance."

If we could get into the garage and retrieve a nuclear bomb, maybe we could stop the Avatari from forming. Maybe magnetizing the gas in the mines would suck a wide enough hole through the ion curtain for us to contact those ships circling the planet. Then what? How would we stop the Avatari from returning? Templar went supernova and fried Hubble fifty thousand years ago. If the Avatari were the ones who did it, they had a long and powerful history.

I had come to dislike driving the streets of Valhalla. Every toppled building spoke of our failure to defend it. The bodies were everywhere. The first time I saw packs of dogs or birds gathered around bodies, I wanted to shoot them. But seeing animals feeding on bodies no longer bothered me; I had seen too much of it.

The Avatari, a numerically insignificant enemy, had attacked us like a cancer. The truth was that we had gone the wrong way at every turn, and maybe we deserved to go extinct. For centuries the Unified Authority had relied heavily on naval power, leaving our ground tactics pretty much unchanged since the nineteenth century. Now that we faced an enemy who we could not stop in space, our ground attacks proved inadequate.

We'd had a nuclear solution all along, but we had stuck to conventional weapons until it was too late. First we threw away our numerical advantage, then we chucked our weapons, and now we found ourselves alone and unarmed.

"I'm not fishing for answers, sir, but have you talked to Thomer lately?" Herrington asked.

"Should we talk about something in particular?" I asked.

"He's pretty upset about Philips," Herrington said.

"They were best friends," I said.

"Thomer blames Lieutenant Moffat."

"So do I," I said.

"I'm worried he wants to go after the lieutenant," Herrington said. He slowed the car down, hoping to talk.

"Not Thomer," I said. "I don't think he has it in him."

"I've known Kelly for a while. He's not a big talker. If he's talking about getting even, I'd take it seriously, sir."

"It won't happen," I said. "Thomer won't kill Moffat. I'm sure of it."

"What makes you so sure?" Herrington asked.

We had drifted within a block or two of the hotel. I watched soldiers carrying rescue equipment into the garage. "Thomer's a clone; he can't murder a superior officer. It's not in his programming."

"Lieutenant, I grew up in an orphanage. I don't know if you knew that, sir. I grew up around clones, and I am here to tell you that I'm seeing them do a lot of things these days that go against their programming. It makes me nervous."

"Yeah," I agreed, "me too."

Captain Everley, Glade's aide, bustled me through the crowd. We walked down the ramp toward the garage passing fire trucks and smaller emergency vehicles. The thump of air compressors and the buzz of a dozen electrical generators created a smothering blanket of sound. Between the arc lights, the workmen, and the hot air that always accompanies officers, the temperature had gone up in the garage.

"Captain Baxter, this is Lieutenant Wayson Harris." Everley introduced me to a big man in Army fatigues.

I saluted. The captain returned the salute.

"Harris is leading the team," Everley said.

"So I hear," the captain answered, his lack of interest obvious in his voice. He turned to me. "How many men do you want to take down with us?" The captain reminded me of some of the guys I used to fight at Sad Sam's Palace—slender around the gut but with huge shoulders. He had scars on his face and a surly attitude. I had already forgotten his name.

"You're coming?" I asked. "I prefer to work with Marines."

"You got a problem with regular Army, Harris?" the captain asked. "This is your op, but I'm coming."

"I see," I said. I thought about what we would need to liberate a couple of nukes. If push came to shove, having a big, strong moron to absorb the radiation might come in handy. "We might be able to get away with only five men if the lower levels aren't too broken up. If the damage is too bad and we can find a route—"

"I can help you with that." A sheep in colonel's clothing trotted in to join our conversation. "You're Lieutenant Harris, is that right? You're the one leading the search team?" He reached to shake my hand. "John Young, Army Corps of Engineers."

Young had an Army uniform and a military haircut, but those were the only military things about him. He introduced himself like a civilian, smiling and expecting me to shake hands. I shook hands, but when Young—probably not a military man but a civilian engineer pressed into service during a time of emergency—reached to shake hands with Baxter, he came up dry.

"I hope you found us a way in," Baxter said. His tone of voice reflected his lack of respect for Young. "I'm looking forward to the workout." He flexed his shoulder as if limbering up for a fight.

"We've taken soundings and X-rays," Young said as he led me to a card table in a brightly lit corner of the garage. He sounded cheerful, like a man who is just happy to be of service. He also sounded like a man in the know. I suspected that Newcastle had confided in him, and he knew the truth about the Avatari.

Strings of lights hung along the ceiling in this corner of the garage. The blades of a seven-foot-tall fan lazily spun, circulating the warm air away from the table.

Generals Newcastle, Haight, and Glade huddled around the table. Young pushed his way among them, saying in a dismissive voice guaranteed to offend any commanding officer, "Make way, make way. Some of us have work to do.

"General Glade tells me you were the one who suggested we use that robot. That was a great suggestion."

Newcastle glared at Glade, who answered him with a smirk. Young spread a set of blueprints across the table. The drawing showed a side view of the garage. He then spread a second blueprint over the first. It showed separate top-down schematics of all seven levels of the garage. Young pointed to an uneven circle drawn around the top level.

"We're here." He drew an X. "This circle represents the collapsed area. As you can see, it takes up most of this level of the garage."

Young moved his finger down to the next level. The collapsed area on the second level was less than a third the size of the area on the upper level. "Whatever kind of weapon the Mudders are using, it only impacts structures on the surface of the ground. Using that S.C.O.O.T.E.R. robot, we were able to get a look at a few of the lower levels. From what I can tell, the structural integrity remains good."

Even though he called the aliens "Mudders," something about the way Young spoke made me think that he knew they were avatars. I could hear it in his voice. He must have known that the Army guys did not know and that it was privileged information.

"What about this damage zone?" I asked, pointing to the circled area on the second level.

"It's caved in there," Young said.

"But the structure is sound around the cave-in?" I asked.

"Sound? As in unharmed?" Young smiled. "Harris, a fifty-six-story hotel collapsed on top of this garage. Frankly, I am amazed how well it held up."

Young said that the damaged area on the third level was only a fraction of the size on the second. The fourth level, where they stored the nukes, was clear.

"Yeah, I got that it's solid. How do we get down there?" Baxter, my Army-appointed second-in-command, demanded.

"Okay, so this is the top level of the garage," said Young. He pointed to a square. "We cut a hole through the floor here. That's how we got the robot in. I suppose we could make the hole bigger if you want to drop down through it, Captain."

Baxter bent over the schematic. He nodded and grunted his approval.

"That's our best way in?" I asked.

Young laughed. "Personally, I'd take the stairs." He pointed to two wavy lines that snaked along the circled area on the map. "We cleared a path to the stairwell."

As I looked at the blueprint, I saw that the collapse line only approached the stairs on the top floor. "Can we take the stairs all the way down?"

"Yup," Young said.

"Depending on the size of a fifty-megaton nuke, it's going to be rough going carrying the bomb up the stairs," I said.

"You'd be surprised," Young said. "Your bomb is not that big, two men should be able to carry it without any problem. If you prefer, though, you could take the elevator." He pointed to a spot on the blueprint. Under his finger were the words, "Shaft is structurally sound."

"The elevator works?" I asked.

"We had to put new braces on the motor and some of the gears, but the shaft is fine."

"So what was all that bullshit about dropping through a hole in the floor?" Baxter asked.

"You said you were looking forward to the workout," Young said. "I thought you wanted the exercise."

"Asshole," Baxter said.

Young smiled.

45

I had a couple of hours to rest before we left on our mission to the mines. While I slept, Sweetwater and the techs at the Science Lab prepared the bomb we had retrieved, the ground crew readied the transport we would fly to the Avatari dig, and the remaining troops dug in to defend Valhalla. Fifty-eight hours had passed since the last time the Avatari came knocking. Sometime in the next fourteen hours, they would come back for their return engagement.

Thanks to John Young and the Corps of Engineers, we were well armed. We had rockets loaded into the launchers along Campus Drive. Our grenadiers had more grenades and shoulder-fired rockets than they could use in a month. We had so many mobile rocket launchers that our riflemen and automatic riflemen abandoned their weapons of record and took up rockets. For the first time in known history, Marine fire teams were made up of four grenadiers.

The Avatari had forced us into an advantageous battleground. Mostly flat and studded with heaps of rubble instead of buildings, the field would allow men with rockets and grenades clear shots at an advancing enemy. The last defenders of Valhalla would have good ground with lots of cover from which they could engage the Avatari from a distance, yield ground, and engage again. If they were lucky, they might wear the Avatari down.

In a few hours I would take a crew into the Avatari mine. Our objective would be to reach the gas deposits and detonate a fifty-megaton nuclear bomb. We hoped to set the nuke and beat a hasty retreat, but hopes are not as important as objectives to Marines. If everything went as expected, the bomb would blow, the gas would charge and attract tachyons, and it would punch a hole in the ion curtain. If Sweetwater was right, the bomb would change the gas in the caverns to shit gas. Basically, we were going the speck the aliens' plans.

For some reason I had the feeling things were not going to go smoothly. I sat in my quarters, the curtains drawn, the room nearly dark, as I wrestled with ghosts from my past and nervousness about my near future. I had a copy of the Bible, a book that I once misinterpreted and now no longer believed. Beside it sat a copy of the Space Bible, a book I once dismissed and now believed and despised. Originally titled *Man's True Place in the Universe: The Doctrines of Morgan Atkins*, the Space Bible told the implausible story of how scientists had encountered an alien they called a "Space Angel."

Someone threw open the door to my room with so much force that it left a dent in the wall. The crash made me jump.

"I hear you've been looking for me, Harris." First Lieutenant Warren Moffat stomped into my room, drunk off his ass, swaying as he stood there glaring down at me with heavily bloodshot eyes. "You think you're scary shit, don't you, clone?" He shut the door behind him.

"I haven't been looking for you," I said, which was true. I sort of hoped we would run into each other, but the thought of looking for Moffat had not occurred to me.

"You think you're something, don't you, Harris? The general's pet clone. I heard you were an admiral's pet, too. Frigging Liberator clone."

He had his M27 with him, strapped to his belt. Even drunk, a good Marine never forgets how to use his weapon. I did not consider Moffat a good Marine.

The civil thing would have been to tell him to go home. I, however, was not feeling civil. My combat reflex had already started; the warm sensation of testosterone and adrenaline flowing through my blood had begun. What I felt for Moffat was not anger, it was hate. I wanted to kill the man. My combat reflex filled me with clarity of thought and the desire to kill. I had never hated anyone before, but I hated this man. The reflex had never given me the desire to kill before, but it did now. Somewhere in the back of my mind, I was aware of all the things that had come undone—clones spraying graffiti, Thomer wanting to kill an officer, Philips ignoring orders, and now I was ready to give in to the Liberator bloodlust. Things come undone in the end.

I pushed away from my desk and stood up. "You carrying that gun for show, or are you planning to use it?" I asked.

"Look at you, the big Liberator!" Moffat laughed. He was just like Philips—a Marine in self-destruct mode who planned to use a fellow Marine as the instrument of his suicide. He had to know I would kill him. I could kill him sober, he'd be no trouble drunk. He stared me in the eyes, no fear showing on his face. His body vaguely swayed as he stood there.

"Go sleep it off, asshole," I said, knowing the message would only piss him off. I took a small step toward him. I did not want him to go sleep it off, I wanted him to reach for his gun. I took another step in his direction. The dorm room was small, and he was only a few feet away.

"Do you think winning this war will make you human? Do you think it's going to make you a natural-born? Specking synth," he said. And then he did it. He reached for his gun. It was just a twitch. He could not have possibly meant to draw it, but it was enough for me.

I swatted his hand from the grip of his M27 with my left hand and slammed the blade of my right into his throat. As he gasped for air, I grabbed him by the chin and the nape of his neck and snapped his head to the side. There was a soft click as the chain of bones that made up his neck twisted apart Moffat collapsed. That was death—your body goes limp, you piss and shit yourself, nothing more. No one-way ticket to heaven. As far as I could tell, Moffat's journey ended when his head bounced against the floor.

Killing Moffat did not bring Philips back, but it left me feeling slightly better about life. The only problem was that now that he was dead, now that the threat had passed, I felt an emotional vacuum forming. The hormone began to thin in my blood, and I didn't want it to go.

"What do you think now, hotshot?" I asked Moffat. He lay on the floor as lifeless as a puppet cut from its strings. "Where are your natural-born buddies now, asshole?" I kicked him.

Kicking Moffat's corpse was not as satisfying as snapping his neck. It was not even a close substitute, and I wanted to feel that first satisfaction again. At that moment, I needed something exciting to happen, and I would sacrifice anything to get it. If I could have, I would have resuscitated Moffat so I could kill him a second time.

Now I understood why cats play with mice instead of simply killing them. The moment of death comes so quickly; and once it's gone, what do you do? I could sense the heat draining from my blood, and I felt desperate to make it stay.

There was Captain Everley, Glade's officious aide. I didn't like him much, maybe I could go kill him. Maybe, if I killed him... But he was such a weakling. And then it came to me—*Baxter, the prick from the Army that I took into the garage... I could... I could...*

I looked down at Moffat and nudged the antisynthetic bastard with my toe. There was no question about what I had done this time—I had committed murder. I'd suckered the poor bastard into reaching for his gun and snapped his neck. I felt bad, but I did not feel bad for him. I felt bad because he was dead, and I wanted more of the hormone in my rapidly chilling veins.

"My God," I said. This was how the Liberators became what they were. This was why my kind were outlawed. I went to the communications console and sent a signal to Command. There would be repercussions from this killing. The man was in my room, he had booze in his blood and his gun in his hands, but he was a natural-born and I... I was a Liberator.

"Harris, shouldn't you be getting ready?" Captain Everley asked as he answered the call.

"You might want to send somebody to collect my company commander," I said. "We had a bit of a run-in."

"Should I send a doctor?"

"No, but a priest might be good."

"Oh, shit," Everley said. "What have you done, Harris? I better call General Glade."

46

"I heard about Lieutenant Moffat," Major Burton said, as I climbed into the jeep. He had suited up in combat armor, not the white armor we'd worn out in the open but the standard-issue dark stuff—the stuff we would wear as we entered the Avatari dig, the same armor I now wore. "Let's go," he said to the driver. A caravan of four trucks followed behind us.

"Think there's going to be an inquest?" I asked. I felt curious but not concerned.

"I'm not entirely sure there's going to be anyone alive to hold one," Burton answered. "Even if there is an inquest, I think you will come off clean. There were two men outside your room when he smashed the door in. They said they heard him yelling at you and you telling him to go home."

"Did they?" I asked. "Did they happen to mention why they didn't call for an MP?"

"Yes, they did," Burton said. "When they heard Moffat fall, they thought he had passed out."

Had I been thinking, I might not have said what I said next. "The bastard did me a favor when he came to my quarters; he saved me the trouble of looking for him."

"I'm going to pretend I didn't hear that," Burton said. "Lieutenant, you went a long way toward proving that the killing was not premeditated when you reported it right away; don't spoil it now."

"So there could still be trouble?" I asked.

"We have an impossible mission, and everyone agrees that you are the best man to lead it. If we make it out alive, I don't think anyone is going to ask about last night."

"What if we don't make it out?" I asked.

Burton smiled. "If you don't make it out, will you really give a shit what anyone thinks about you?"

That last comment might have been meant to make me feel better, but it didn't. No one gave a shit about me; I was a clone. We spent most of the drive in silence.

During that silence, Major Burton's entire demeanor changed. When he next spoke, he looked pale. "I'm scared, Harris. I'm so specking scared I think I'm going to be sick."

I wanted to give him the same advice a drill sergeant once gave me: "If you have a choice, wet yourself." We had a hose inside our armor that gathered urine. When you vomited, you inevitably left sawdust-colored stains on your chest plate.

I did not say that, however. Instead, I said, "You don't need to come with us, sir. An extra pair of hands won't make much of a difference." He didn't need to tell me how scared he felt, I could see it in his face and posture. Natural-born or not, he was a Marine at heart, and he would not back out. I felt a strange sympathy for the man. He had always been decent.

"Do you think we're going to survive this?" he asked.

"No," I said. "It's a one-way ticket."

"And you're okay with that?" Burton asked.

"I'd rather take a one-way trip than wait around to be slaughtered."

Burton swallowed. He nodded but said nothing.

As we approached the landing strip, I saw trucks and jeeps

parked around the buildings. All the top brass came to see us off. Now that the end was so near, the new competition among the generals was to see which one could portray himself as being more a man of the people. General Newcastle, who had previously preferred a limousine, had came in a staff-driven jeep, probably the first jeep he had ridden in years. General Haight drove himself in a simple town car. General Glade rode in the back of the troop carrier with the men from one of my platoons.

Burton and I waited in the jeep while he collected himself, the color slowly returning to his face.

Thomer approached us. He gave me a sharp salute, then asked, "Want me to get the gear loaded, sir?" He had a new energy to his step. I could not be sure, but I suspected that Thomer's new enthusiasm had something to do with the late Lieutenant Moffat.

"Load it," I said.

He saluted and left.

"You okay?" I asked Burton.

He drew in a long, deep breath, looked up, and met my eyes.

"You know what, Harris, you're better than any of them." He looked at the generals standing in their little cult, then back at me, and said, "You're tougher and smarter than all of them put together. Harris, you're the real Marine."

"Wear your helmet until you get into the transport," I said. "No one will be able to tell you were scared."

"Lieutenant Harris. Lieutenant Harris, thank God we caught you." William Sweetwater waddled to the front of the pack of generals as they came toward the jeep. He was so out of breath from outrunning those old men that he bent over to huff and puff after calling my name. Sweat pasted his long black hair to his pudgy face. "Harris, we're coming with you."

Now there was an irony—Major Terry Burton, a professional Marine, had just told me that the thought of heading into the Avatari caves left him so scared he wanted to puke; now here stood William Sweetwater, all of four-foot-eight and out of breath from outrunning generals, demanding in on the mission.

"You want to go into the caves?" I asked. I looked over at General Glade, the man who had once called Sweetwater a coward. Our eyes locked for a moment, then he looked away.

"There's a lot more to this than just blowing up a bomb down there," Sweetwater said. Blowing up a bomb was, of course, exactly what I expected to do. "There are going to be tests. We're going to need to calibrate the explosion. We're not trying to blow up Avatari, we're building a magnet for attracting tachyon particles. We need to—"

"Does this have to do with Dr. Breeze?" I asked.

Sweetwater knew exactly what I meant. I was suggesting that he was trying to go because his friend had died. I was suggesting he was unneeded baggage, and the dwarf scientist knew it. He froze like a thief caught in a spotlight, turned to face me head-on, and growled, "You're goddamned specking right this has to do with Arthur."

"Breeze is dead," I said. "You're not going to change that."

"We are aware of that," Sweetwater said in a cold voice. "That does not negate the fact that you will need someone to run final tests on the gas and calibrate the explosion for maximum effect."

"And you are the only man for the job?" I asked.

"The best man for the job," he said. He fumbled in his jacket and pulled out a very-small-caliber automatic pistol. "We also know how to use one of these," he said.

Still sitting beside me in the jeep, Major Burton could not stop himself from laughing as he looked at the little man holding the little pistol. "A tiny gun like that won't do you much good against the Mudders," Burton said.

"You'd need armor," I said. "The air is toxic."

"We are aware of that, we authorized your first visit and analyzed the results," said Sweetwater. He opened the little canvas bag that hung from his shoulder and dug out a rebreather and a pair of goggles that were wide enough to fit over his glasses.

"I'm not sure what that gas is going to do to your skin," I said. I was anxious to get moving. We were wasting time.

"These will get us into the site," Sweetwater said. "We don't expect to come back."

"Lieutenant Harris, is there a problem?" Newcastle asked. He and the other generals stood a few feet back from the jeep, waiting for Burton and me.

"Someone get this man a particle-beam pistol," I said.

"You'll take us?" Sweetwater looked near tears. Small, pudgy, and severely uncoordinated, this man had probably grown up being picked last for every group activity that did not involve science.

"You just keep up with us," I said, handing him a particle-beam pistol. "If you fall behind, you're on your own."

Sweetwater stowed that pistol in his bag so gently you would have thought I'd given him a faulty grenade. "Freeman is in that transport; go tell him you're coming along for the ride," I said, pointing to the only transport with an open ramp. He thanked me, picked up his bag, and waddled off.

"You sure you don't need more men?" Newcastle asked.

I had a quick vision of him foisting an entire platoon of muscle-headed Neanderthals like Captain Baxter on me. "I just picked up another new recruit," I said, pointing at Sweetwater.

"That gets us to forty-nine." We had forty-seven men in the company, plus Freeman, and now William Sweetwater.

"You're going to need an entire regiment at the very least," Newcastle said. "I can have more men—"

"I've been in those caves," I said. "The entrance is a bottleneck, and the route to our target area is a narrow path. The plan is to place the bomb by the gas and beat a hasty retreat. The last thing I need is a regiment of men clogging the works once that nuke is armed," I said. It was a lie. I didn't expect any of us to make it out alive, but that didn't matter, not much.

There was just a brief moment when I stopped and questioned why I was doing this. I wasn't doing it for love of humanity, and I sure as hell was not going into that mountain again because I wanted to save a bunch of crusty old bastards like these generals. Mostly I was going because I was programmed to go,

I supposed I never had much of a choice.

Thomer jogged over to join us. "The gear's loaded, sir. The rest of the company is on board."

I knew why Sergeant Kelly Thomer was going on this mission—neural programming. William Sweetwater was going because he had something to prove, even if it would cost him his life. I suppose he felt he had to prove it to himself more than to anyone else. Surely he didn't care what Newcastle and these generals thought about him.

So the soulless clones and the misfit scientist would die carrying out a mission while these privileged jackass generals waved us good-bye. Maybe that was all they were made to do, these high-powered officers. They were the human equivalent of S.C.O.O.TE.R. robots, practicing the self-preservation programming that was genetically hardwired into their brains. Newcastle's version of self-preservation involved sending men to their deaths.

And the programming in my brain made me fight. I wasn't fighting for humanity. Hell, I wasn't even fighting for myself, I was fighting simply because that was what I did. I fought.

"I have a flight to catch," I told Newcastle.

"Good luck, Lieutenant," General Glade said with a salute. He turned to Burton and saluted him as well.

"I don't need to tell you just how much is riding on your shoulders," General Newcastle said. He also saluted.

In the background, I heard the thunderous roar of a Tomcat formation. The jets passed over us seconds before the noise of their engines could catch up. They flew a few hundred yards above the ground, remaining well below cloud level. We all watched the five-jet formation bank and circle back over us.

One way or another, this would be the final battle. Flying too low over the city, the jets would be easy targets; but they'd have been even easier marks sitting on a runway. The troops protecting the city would fire every bullet, missile, and rocket they had; why spare the jets?

I returned the salute. "General, good luck to you," I said,

knowing that every man who remained in Valhalla might well be dead by the time I returned... if I returned.

"We'd better go," I said to Burton. We walked past the generals, who held their salutes as we passed.

"Still feeling sick?" I asked in a whisper.

"More embarrassed than sick," Burton admitted. "Seeing that little twerp scientist begging to go, I wanted to shoot myself."

"I know what you mean; the little bastard's got guts," I said, as we walked up the steel ramp and entered the transport. The major bobbed his head enthusiastically, then ran to the head, a hand over his mouth to keep the bile from spewing out of his mouth.

Watching Major Burton dash into the can, I hit the button that closed the big doors. Somewhere below my feet, gears whined as they drew the six-inch-thick doors together.

The transport was made to carry two platoons—a hundred men. It was half-full. Some of the men stood near the ladder at the far end of the cabin; most sat on the benches along the walls. The sound of the iron doors closing served as a call to attention. The men stood, turned to face me, and saluted.

I returned the salute and told them to sit. The transport's powerful engines flared to life outside. Inside the kettle, the sound of the engines was no more than a rumble, but outside those thick walls, they made a deafening roar.

Our nukes—we actually had two of them—sat in a couple of large crates near the rear of the cargo hold. As we took off, I sat on one of the crates with the nukes, a combination of bravado and Marine Corps humor. Across the cabin I saw William Sweetwater, a short, stout man with mangy long black hair, thick glasses, and a second chin that hung from his neck like a hammock. He sat alone in a corner staring at the floor, his hands clasped between his knees.

"Dr. Sweetwater!" I yelled louder than was necessary for him to hear me over the engines. Hearing his name, he looked up with an alert, startled expression. "Why don't we head up to the cockpit?" I called out.

Sweetwater hopped off the bench and shuffled across the deck. His head was just about even with the heads of the Marines sitting on the bench. Just as he reached me, the door to the can opened and Major Burton came out wiping his mouth.

"Major," I called out. "The doctor and I were just about to visit the pilot. Would you care to join us?"

Burton looked at the ladder leading up to the cockpit and shook his head. "I'm still getting my sea legs."

"Aye, sir," I said. I was in charge. The generals had put me in charge, and Major Burton accepted my authority, but I wanted to show respect to an officer who had come out to die with his men.

I let Sweetwater climb the ladder first. With his chubby body and short limbs, he looked like a koala bear climbing a tree. I waited until he reached the top, then I went up after him.

As we reached the cockpit door, Sweetwater paused. He forced himself to look me in the eye, like a kid caught stealing cookies, and said, "Um, we might have neglected to mention to Raymond that we were coming on this mission."

"I thought I told you to report to Freeman." It occurred to me that I was scolding one of the brightest men in the galaxy the way a mother scolds a misbehaving child.

Even more ironic, he answered in kind. "We're sorry, Lieutenant. It's just… What if Raymond said we couldn't come?" Somewhere in that stubby body still beat the heart of the schoolboy.

Fighting back the urge to laugh, I tried to sound angry as I said, "Well, we're stuck with you now, whether he likes it or not."

Sweetwater brightened, led the way into the cockpit, and called out, "Good afternoon, Raymond." Then he said, "Good Lord, Raymond, that can't be comfortable."

Freeman sat cramped behind the controls of the ship. The engineers who designed the cockpit did not have a seven-foot, 350-pound man in mind when they placed the pilot's chair a mere twenty-four inches away from the yoke. Freeman's knees did not fit into the cavity under the HUD, so he had to sit with his legs straddling the yoke, a comical sight.

Freeman looked back, nodded at me, then said, "Good afternoon, Doctor."

"How is our flight time looking?" Sweetwater asked. He really did behave like a nervous adolescent. He stood there nervously fidgeting, swinging his arms back and forth while rocking on his heels.

"We have a few hours ahead of us," Freeman said in a velvet rumble. "Are you going in with us, Dr. Sweetwater, or just coming along for the ride?"

"We thought we might go in and help place the device," Sweetwater said.

"Of course," said Freeman. "Doctor, perhaps Lieutenant Harris and I could have a word in private." Cold and distant as Ray Freeman was in most situations, he had a fondness for Sweetwater. I could see it in the way he gazed at the doctor, like a father watching his child.

Sweetwater's confidence sank like a rock. He looked nervous, sad, and desperate all at once. "We can help," he said. "We figured out about supercharging the gas before Arthur. You'll need us there, Raymond."

Freeman nodded, then the softness in his expression disappeared as he fixed his double-barrel gaze on me, and said, "Doctor, I'm sure we need your help, but may I have a word with Harris now?"

Sweetwater looked at me, and asked, "Should we wait outside?"

"Why don't you go down and wait with the other men," I said. Then I added, "This could get bloody." I said it under my breath, so that neither man would hear me.

"Right," Sweetwater said, heading out the bulkhead. "We'll just, um, be down in the cabin with everyone else." He stepped over the threshold and shot back one last highly insecure look, then headed down the ladder.

I launched a preemptive defense. "It doesn't matter whether he comes with us or hides in the galaxy's biggest fallout shelter; we either succeed, or he's a dead man."

Freeman nodded, but anger still showed in his eyes. "Does he have armor?" Freeman asked.

"No," I said.

"He's going to die a bad death," Freeman said. I saw something I had never seen in Freeman's face before—sympathy.

"We can leave him in the transport," I said. "He can try and direct us over the interLink."

Freeman shook his head. "He's right. We were either going to need him or Breeze to come with us. You just get us down there, Harris; I'll watch out for Sweetwater."

I stayed in the cockpit for most of the flight. When I finally came down, I found my Marines gathered around Sweetwater. He looked like a coach prepping his team before a big game.

"Oh, Lieutenant Harris, we were just explaining to your men about the nature of the Avatari miners."

"I see," I said.

"Is it true?" Thomer asked. "We never fought the real aliens, it was just their reflections all along?"

I sighed. I had come to brief the men, but Sweetwater had already handled most of the briefing. The problem was that while he had all the information, he would not know how to couch it so that it would motivate the men.

"Doctor, Freeman wants to talk to you," I said.

"What does Raymond want to discuss?" Sweetwater asked, sounding nervous.

"He's ponying the equipment," I said. "I think he wants to plan out his part of the mission with you."

Satisfied that Freeman would not leave him tied up in the transport, Sweetwater said, "Excellent idea. We really do need to plan out what to take and what to leave behind. Excuse us, gentlemen." And he waddled to the ladder and climbed to meet Freeman.

I looked at Major Burton and noticed the relaxed way in which he leaned back on the bench. It was dark in the kettle, so I could not be sure, but Burton did not look pale or sick. In fact, the entire company looked ready for action.

"Put on your helmets," I said. "Let's test the gear.

"Sound off, Marines," I said.

The fire teams answered to their team leaders. The team leaders reported to their squad leaders. Squad leaders sounded off for platoon leaders. Platoon leaders reported to Major Burton, who reported to me. With only forty-seven men, we had enough men for one full platoon with a little spare change, but we organized the men into two miniature platoons.

Major Burton told the men to remove their helmets, then came over and took his place behind me and to my right, and I began the mission briefing.

I'd seen many briefings during my stints with the Marines. They were generally conducted by officers who had nothing but disdain for clones. The officers often began by insulting our intelligence, then proceeded to play off our emotions to work us into a frenzy. The meetings were somewhere between a pep rally and an evangelical revival with homicidal overtones. This one would be different, I decided, I would show these men the respect they deserved.

I took a moment to arrange my thoughts. "Who knows what's in these crates?" I asked.

Herrington raised his hand. "Those would be our nukes."

"Yes, these would be two fifty-megaton nuclear devices," I said. "We have a matching set. Any of you ever set off a nuke in battle?" No one raised his hand. "No?

"Here's the drill. We are going to hike into a hollowed-out mountain that is filled to the gills with giant spiderlike creatures. Some are six feet tall and some are ten feet tall, any of them can tear a man in half without thinking twice about it, and your combat armor won't even add any challenge.

"If we can hoss these big bombs in there, we will fry those motherspeckers. These bombs will bring the whole damn cave down on top of them. These bombs will make the insides of those mountains so hot the rocks will melt and the dirt will turn to ash."

I could tell my briefing was not going over well. The men looked confused. They looked nervous.

"Are we planning on hanging around to watch that happen?" asked Private Peterson.

"No, Private, we are not," I said. "The plan is to deliver our little presents and beat it out of there rapid, quick, and pronto. I don't know about you, Peterson, but I plan on being halfway back to Valhalla before that big bang goes off.

"Any other questions?"

No one responded. They looked confused.

Burton laid a hand on my shoulder, and whispered, "May I, Lieutenant?"

"Be my guest," I said.

"Okay, Gyrenes!" he shouted in a voice that was several decibels louder than it needed to be. "You, Sergeant. What's your name?"

"Herrington, sir."

"So, Sergeant Herrington, can you tell me why we are taking a couple of nukes on this little joyride?" Burton asked. "What's so good about nukes?"

"They make a really loud bang, sir," Herrington said.

"Damn specking right it makes a big bang. Gyrene, you are specking officer material. You're a goddamned genius. Nukes make big, hot bangs. They make big, hot, radioactive bangs. Tell me, Herrington, what do you think about giving the specking Mudders a big, hot, radioactive bang?"

"I like it, sir."

"You say you like it? That's all? Shoving a nuke up these planet-stealing motherspeckers' asses is just okay with you. Is that what you just said?"

"Sir, no sir," Herrington yelled. I could hear Herrington's confidence building. He did not want to be treated with respect; he wanted to be cudgeled. "It makes me horny all over!"

Burton's disdainful approach made Herrington feel relaxed. It had the same effect on the entire company. Men sat up straight, they smiled. The verbal beating placed them in territory they knew.

"Just so you assholes know, I believe in the big bang theory," Burton said. "I believe we should shove something that makes a big bang up every one of our enemies' asses."

The funny thing was that giving the briefing, Burton's confidence also seemed to grow as he went on. Until this moment, I had never realized the yin and yang in the relationship between natural-born officers and general-issue clones. These boys did not want respect and honesty. They deserved the truth; but going into battle, what they really wanted to hear was assurance. Burton, an experienced officer, gave them what they needed instead of what they deserved.

"We reserve the really big bangs for the pecker speckers we hate the most. And let me tell you, Gyrenes, fifty-megatons is the biggest bang of them all. Now what does that tell you about Mudders?"

"We hate the speckers," yelled Thomer—mild-mannered Kelly Thomer, the Boy Scout.

"Damn straight, we goddamn hate those pecker speckers. There is no one and nothing we hate more than those speckers. I hate those bastards more than my wife's time of the month. Do you read me, you mean horn-dog sons of bitches?"

Burton sent the men into a frenzy. They didn't just respond, they ignited.

"Listen here, Gyrenes; these nukes are the second-worst weapon in this man's universe. You ugly sons of bitches are the specking worst. You are the cruelest, meanest, most lowdown, dirty weapon in the Unified specking Authority's arsenal."

As Burton put on his show, Sweetwater shambled down the ladder and came to stand next to me. He looked scared but determined. He glanced over at me, then mimicked my stance and posture—feet shoulder-width apart, hands clasped behind his back, chest out. The stance looked unnatural with his short, dumpy posture, thick glasses, and lank hair.

"We are going to shove you forty-seven sons of bitches so far down those speckers' throats that nothing else will ever fit. You got that, Gyrenes?"

"Sir, yes, sir!" the company shouted so loud that their voices frayed.

"Did you Gyrenes say something? I think I almost heard you. Think you peckerwoods can put enough voice into it so I can hear you?"

"Sir, yes, sir!" they screamed.

Burton took a step back, and whispered to me, "Tell them what you need to, but for God's sake, try to keep them warmed up."

I explained what we would do, and the briefing ended. The men went back to speaking among themselves, clearly more relaxed than before. As I headed toward the cockpit, Major Burton quietly whispered, "You Liberators may be killing machines, but you don't know shit about giving briefings."

Looking ahead through the windshield, I could see the serrated silhouette of the distant mountains. "I'm going to park us next to Breeze's plane," Freeman said. Sweetwater leaned over the copilot's seat for a look below. He did not speak a word.

"What's our ETA?" I asked.

"Ten minutes," Freeman said.

Outside the transport, the plains gave way to steppes and the steppes gave way to foothills. Soon we would cross the guardians of the mountains. I could imagine these granite giants framed by an orange sunset, as dark as shadows and as mysterious as the night. I could also imagine them turned to dunes of ash with Avatari spider-things creeping across them.

I looked out and saw something I had not seen for a couple of years, something I had hoped never to see again. A series of trenches crisscrossed the flat areas between some of the mountains. "Snake shafts," I said.

"Those weren't there last time you came," Freeman commented.

"No, they weren't," I said as I studied the network of trenches and troughs that the drones had dug. Until that moment, I had never put two and two together properly. Nobody knew what snake shafts were used for, but the common consensus was that it had something to do with smuggling. Now I understood all too well. The Avatari would cover the trenches without filling them in, and they would serve as a capillary system for harvesting shit gas from the planet.

As Freeman circled for a landing, Sweetwater and I returned to the kettle. I found most of the men in the cargo hold sitting in clusters, checking their weapons or simply talking. Burton stood at the rear staring at the crates with the nukes.

Sweetwater found a shadowy corner where he could be alone. He sat with his head down, examining his breathing mask.

"Doctor," I said in a soft voice, as if waking a sleeping child. "Dr. Sweetwater?"

"Lieutenant," he said. "Please tell us you're not giving another briefing."

"Ha, very funny," I said.

Sweetwater smiled. "So it's showtime."

"Yes, Doctor," I said.

"Call us William, Lieutenant."

"Freeman wanted me to warn you Dr. Breeze's body is just inside the caves. He also told me to warn you that the body is pretty messed up."

"Thanks for the warning," Sweetwater said.

"You really don't need to go in there," I said.

"You're wrong, Lieutenant," Sweetwater said, a new stiffness in his voice. "We do need to go in there. That is the very place we need to be."

47

The late Arthur Breeze must have been one hell of a pilot.

Freeman had a far easier time lowering our big bird than Breeze must have had landing his plane. Our ship weighed at least twenty times more than Breeze's craft, but transports had rockets for vertical landings. Breeze's light craft required a runway. The ridge on which he had landed was too short and too bumpy for a safe landing; and if he'd overshot the landing, he would have either crashed into the mountain or skidded off a cliff.

We touched down not more than a hundred feet from Breeze's ride. The loose ground settled unevenly beneath our skids, and forty-six Marines lunged for the crates with the nukes to make sure they didn't slide.

"You don't need to do that," I told them over the interLink. "You can toss those bad boys off the side of the mountain, and they won't go off. The specking Hotel Valhalla fell on them, and they didn't go off."

I heard some nervous laughter, and the men backed away from the crates.

I pulled off my helmet and looked down at Sweetwater; he

stood beside me waiting to exit the transport. "Maybe I should go out there first and check the air quality," I said.

"You're worried about us? Lieutenant, we're touched." The little bastard might have had a better facility with sarcasm than scientific terms. "We already agreed this was a one-way trip."

"Know what, Dr. Sweetwater? You'd make a hell of a Marine," I said.

"Really?" he asked.

"Yeah, well, except for the height requirement," I said.

He smiled. "That means something coming from a homicidal clone like you. We heard you killed your commanding officer last night."

"He had it coming," I said, only half-joking.

"What did he do?" Sweetwater asked.

"Asked too many questions," I said.

"Oh," said Sweetwater.

I thought about what we were heading into and decided this was not the time to hold back. "His name was Lieutenant Moffat," I said. "He was one of those antisynthetic types."

"Lieutenant, we just want you to know that we wholeheartedly support clone equality," Sweetwater volunteered.

"Equality among clones?" I asked. "Not all clones are created equal."

"How about equal treatment and opportunity for clones?" Sweetwater asked.

"Lieutenant Moffat sent one of my platoons out to get massacred because he had a problem with the platoon sergeant," I said. "I couldn't live with that."

"Someone said that he wanted to kill you, too," Sweetwater said.

"Yeah," I said. "I suppose he did. We'd better test our gear."

As I put on my helmet, he strapped on his rebreather and protective goggles.

"Can you hear us?" he asked.

His breathing gear did not have an interLink connection. We

could give him an earpiece for listening in, but he would not be able to speak to us without breaking the seal around his oxygen mask. He said something to me that my audio gear picked up as an ambient noise. Given more time, we could have found some way to make our combat armor fit him, but time was the thing we lacked. What he needed most was a helmet, but that big head of his was too wide to fit a standard-sized helmet.

Wondering what tortures the air inside those caves would perform on Sweetwater, I gave him the thumbs-up to show that I had heard him just fine. Then I hit the button to open the ramp, knowing I had just signed the little scientist's death sentence.

The kettle doors slid open, revealing Breeze's aircraft. Standing silently beside me, William Sweetwater stared at the plane that had brought his close friend to his death. He was breathing through the oxygen mask now, his breath fogging the clear plastic.

Maybe it was just my imagination, but I sensed death as I looked at the little six-seater plane. Breeze had left the hatch hanging open. Up here in the mountains, that opened door looked out of place. It reminded me of a porch light left on for a traveler who would never return.

Sergeant Thomer asked, "Lieutenant, should I have the men unpack the crates?" waking me from dour thoughts.

"I would appreciate it, Sergeant," I said.

"Aye, aye, sir," Thomer said.

"Major, we might as well send everybody out," I said.

I felt a certain level of helplessness looking across the kettle. Marines in dark combat armor moved around the shadowy cabin. Across the deck, Ray Freeman slid down the ladder from the cockpit with the alacrity of a spider on a web. They were a good crew, a game crew, men ready to put up a fight.

Sweetwater opened his canvas satchel and brought out a T-shaped environmental meter much like the one Freeman had used on our last trip into the mines. As the little scientist tested the air, Thomer and his men removed the nuclear devices from their crates.

Stripped from their crates, the nukes were distinctly unimpressive—neither especially heavy nor unreasonably large—two polished metal cylinders about one yard long and two feet in diameter with two sets of handles, one at either end. With some struggle, a single Marine could have lugged each device, but we assigned four to the task. They carried the devices like pallbearers around a casket.

Freeman, carrying a case in one hand and a particle-beam cannon in the other, came to the ramp. Sweetwater naturally gravitated toward the giant mercenary. He had been the eyes and hands of the Science Lab. When they ran field experiments, Sweetwater and Breeze had relied on Freeman to carry out their wishes.

"I don't know how long he's going to last," I told Freeman over a private line. "Did you check out his breathing gear? That oxygen mask isn't going to protect him. I've seen masks like that before; it's from a paramedic's emergency kit. The seal around his mask is not airtight."

"I know," Freeman whispered.

"He's going to breathe in fumes," I said. "Most of his face is exposed. You saw what that stuff does."

"I'll take care of him," Freeman said.

"We'll carry him as long as we can, but when he falls behind..."

"I'll take care of it," Freeman said. I knew better than to argue.

I took one last look around the kettle. The men stood ready to fight, but I sensed something brittle in their resolve. Burton stood at the head of the company, a man ready to take any risk because he feared losing control of the situation or possibly control of himself. The men fell into lines. William Sweetwater, who now held nothing more than a small penlight in his hands, kept himself apart from the Marines. He orbited around Freeman like a child keeping an eye on a protective parent in a crowd.

"Let's move out," I said, giving the order in an unnaturally quiet voice.

The bright ion curtain sky shone in through the open ramp as we marched out. It had rained recently. My boots sank a quarter of an inch in the mud-covered ground.

"It's 2100 hours," Burton said. "Maybe we'll see a night sky when we come back out. I'd be willing to nursemaid a nuke through a cave of gigantic alien spiders to see a real night sky."

"Did Sweetwater mention that most of those spiders are mindless drones that are no more dangerous than a footlocker as long as you stay out of their way?" I asked.

"Yup," Burton said.

"Did he mention that some of them are as big as jeeps?"

"The hunter spiders?" Burton asked.

"I think there are live aliens controlling the big ones," I said.

"Yeah, that's what Dr. Sweetwater said, that they're avatars, just like the soldiers we've been fighting," Burton said.

"Yeah, avatars," I said, still stunned at how much more easily the men accepted the idea that they were fighting avatars than the generals had. "There aren't very many of the big ones."

"Good to know," Burton said.

We stood and watched as the men filed out of the transport. Thomer led the riflemen, each of them carrying particle-beam cannons—guns with slightly better range than our standard-issue particle-beam pistols. They also had rockets. Every man in the company carried rockets.

Next came Herrington and Boll, leading the team carrying the first of the nukes.

"Harris, you're not going to go berserk on us, are you? I mean, you're not going to get so hopped up on that combat hormone that you start killing us off, are you?" Burton asked over a private channel.

"If you have to die, wouldn't you rather be killed by one of your men?" I asked.

Burton turned and let the ranks walk past him until only Sweetwater, Freeman, and I remained in the ship. He raised his right hand as if preparing to salute me, then flipped me off.

Standing at the base of the ramp, Sweetwater saw Burton flip me the finger. He looked from Burton, then to me, then back to

Burton. "Does that mean the same thing to Marines that it means to scientists?" he shouted through his oxygen mask.

"I'm sure it does," I said.

"Trouble among the ranks?" he asked, then waddled off to stand nearer to Freeman.

Breeze had parked beside a different entrance than the one Freeman and I used. We would not need to scale the mountain to reach this one; it was level with the ridge.

"Get ready," I said over the open frequency, as we neared the entrance. The men lugging the nuclear devices pulled their pistols out of their holsters. The company grenadiers unstrapped rocket launchers, and the riflemen readied their particle-beam cannons. Seeing the other men with their weapons, Sweetwater pulled out the particle beam pistol I'd given him. He held it like an old-fashioned dueler—the barrel only inches from his nose, the muzzle aimed toward the sky.

"Last chance for you to turn back," I said to him through the speaker in my helmet. My respect for the diminutive scientist would not have changed if he'd soiled his pants and run back to the transport, but I knew he would not. Sweetwater turned toward me and pointed at the back of his hand. His skin was already turning an inflamed red as if he were having an allergic reaction. Given a little more time, blisters would form. The skin on his cheeks and forehead had a ruddy look as well.

"It's too late to turn back now," he yelled through the mask. He did not need to yell for me to hear him, but he did not know that.

"You took a reading before you left the ship. Did you know this was going to happen?" I asked.

He shrugged and walked away.

"Plucky little son of a bitch," I whispered to myself. That was heartfelt praise in Marine-ese. From where I stood, with their backs to me, Freeman and Sweetwater looked like a father-and-son act. Freeman, tall and broad, Sweetwater short and stubby. Sweetwater stayed in perfect sync with the big man. When Freeman turned left, so did Sweetwater.

Noticing Sweetwater's physical deterioration, Thomer fell back, and asked, "Is he going to be okay?"

"You mean Sweetwater?" I asked.

"Yeah, is he going to be all right?" Thomer asked.

"He's melting. The air out here is like acid."

Like the entrance Freeman and I used when we explored the mines, this entrance led to a foyer filled with light from the ion curtain. Burton and two of his riflemen led the way in. I entered next, followed by the teams carrying the bombs. Freeman and Sweetwater came next, with more riflemen and grenadiers bringing up the rear.

Burton hiked ahead, checked for enemies, then doubled back. "It looks clear this far in," Burton said.

"Did you see any openings along the walls?" I asked.

"I did," Burton said.

"The fun starts once we enter one of those openings," I said.

"Fair enough," Burton said. "Harris, do we really need two bombs? I could use four extra guns."

"We need them... both of them," I said.

"We're not just bringing the second in case we lose one?"

"Major, did you ever fly through Mars Spaceport on a busy day?" I asked.

"Sure, it's a real zoo," he said.

"Shoulder-to-shoulder crowds; you can't even swing your arms without hitting someone. That's about how crowded it was last time I stepped into those caverns—except instead of people with suitcases, you get drone spiders."

"You said they weren't any more dangerous than a footlocker," Burton said.

"I meant a footlocker with a forty thousand-volt charge. If one of those spiders so much as rubs against you, all the electronics in your armor go dead, then you either have to walk around blind or breathe whatever that lethal shit is in the air.

"I'm betting that we lose both bombs long before we reach the target area. This is one of those 'the fate of humanity is resting on us' moments, sir. Do you really want to cut the odds in half by leaving one of the nukes behind?"

Burton made a laughing noise, but it sounded short, sour, and forced. "So we're going to set off a nuclear bomb to save humanity? Did I ever mention that my parents left Earth and moved to the Norma Arm because they did not approve of all the violence?"

"They're probably dead now," I said. "Norma was one of the first arms to go."

A bat came flapping down from the ceiling. It was hit by green flashes from so many particle-beam cannons that all that was left was a fine, red mist and a few shreds of fur.

"Steady," I said over the open frequency, just glad that no one had fired a rocket at it.

"They probably are dead," Burton agreed. "Are you a praying man, Lieutenant Harris? I heard somewhere that you read the Bible."

"I stopped reading it," I said. "I lost my faith."

"I've never been much for religion, but I said a shitload of prayers on the flight over here."

"Yeah, well, if God is any good with a particle beam, we sure as hell could use him on our team right about now," I said. "We better move out, sir."

Major Burton gave the order to mount up, and we walked ahead. The ion light faded slightly as we moved deeper into the caves. Freeman led us toward the tunnel opening that would take us into the cavern.

"Breeze went in through this tube," Freeman said, as we came to the first opening. Under normal circumstances he would have communicated this over the interLink, but this time he used his external speaker so that Sweetwater would hear.

"Maybe we should go to the next one," I said over the open mike as well.

Sweetwater stared into the darkened doorway. "We want to see him," he said. It was hard to hear him, and I wondered how much of the gas his mask allowed in. The damage to his throat might have already begun.

"Okay, if you are sure," I said. Then I switched to a companywide channel on the interLink. "The angle is going to be like going down a spiral staircase. Got it? The tube is wide with a low ceiling. You men on point, no stopping until we get to the bottom, then fan out. I want the first men down to form a shield by the time the nukes make it through."

I heard a collective "Aye, aye, sir." Burton led the way in.

The tube was just as I remembered it, long and wide with a six-foot ceiling, deep scratches in the walls and ceiling. Like me, Burton had to duck his head to get through. Because their helmets added an inch to their height, the general-issue clones had to bow their heads, but Sweetwater could have skipped rope in there.

The light from the curtain faded out quickly. By the time we reached the second bend in the downward-spiraling tube, my visor had switched to night-for-day vision, and I saw the world around me in blue-white images. I listened to my men over the interLink. Some of them were breathing heavily, a sign of fear.

"Steady," I said. "There are two kinds of spiders in here, small ones and big ones. The small ones are drones. Don't bother shooting them, they won't know you are there. It's the big ones you have to worry about."

This was all review, of course, but Herrington asked, "How big are the big ones, sir?"

"What the speck!" Burton gasped.

"Hold," I told the men.

Burton had located a guardian spider. The damn thing had had to climb in here with its legs spread wide, and its girth left the tunnel half-filled. It remained perfectly still.

"Please tell me that is one of the big ones," Burton said.

"Stay here." I stepped past Burton and the men on point as I approached the guardian spider. It lay there absolutely still, just lurking there, blending into the darkness. I watched it for several seconds, then said, "It's dead."

As I approached, I saw that two of its legs had broken away. Its body was cracked and desiccated. The gash in its underbelly stretched from its head to its tail, and dust poured out of it.

Arthur Breeze had killed the creature that killed him. He sat against the far wall of the tunnel, his legs spread out before him. He held a standard-issue particle-beam pistol in his right hand. The spider-thing had slashed his white combat armor, breaking his chest plate and shattering his visor. I don't think I felt any special bond with Breeze; but looking at his corpse, I felt outrage. I spun my particle-beam cannon around and smashed the butt into the guardian spider's head. I hit it a second time. The hollow shell of the monster cracked under the force of that blow, and I hit it again and again.

"Harris, is it alive?" Burton sounded scared.

"Mother-specking son of a bitch!" I yelled. Spit was flying from my mouth into the microphone. I hit the spider again, and the uppermost ridge of its back and its exoskeleton crushed in on itself.

They had killed each other. Breeze probably died first, but he broke the spider. He would have fallen back and fired, but the spider-thing had still slashed him, nearly cutting off his head and channeling a deep, deep gash that ran from his neck to his thigh. Arthur Breeze's glasses lay on the ground along with the jigsaw puzzle of glass that had once been his visor. Beads of blood had dried on his snowy white armor, and a puddle of blood covered the floor.

His face had never been much to look at, but the only parts I now recognized were the big, square teeth that would have looked better matched in the mouth of a horse. The other features—the cheeks, the nose, the chin, and the forehead—had turned to sponge. The eyeballs had wilted so that they completely filled the sockets in which they sat.

The face lit up. Sweetwater stood beside me, shining his flashlight into his dead friend's face.

"Harris? Harris what the speck is going on?" Burton asked as he came over and joined us.

I ignored both Burton and Sweetwater, listening only to the echo of the insane scream I made inside my helmet. This was not just about Breeze, and I knew it. This was for Philips and Huish and White, and the nine hundred thousand clones who had died defending this goddamned planet. I spun and smashed my boot into the side of the dead spider. I kicked it as hard as I could, and the side of its body shattered. I felt something tug at my shoulder.

"It's not getting any deader," said Freeman.

Maybe it was the calmness in his voice or the weight of his hand on my shoulder, though more likely it was the way my combat reflex had sneaked up on me, but I whirled around and prepared to shoot Freeman. He was ready for me, though. As I came around and raised my gun, he shoved me hard, and I stumbled into the giant carcass. I fell on my ass angrier than ever, but before I could bring up my gun, the bastard had his particle-beam pistol pressed straight into my visor.

"You are going to get yourself killed," Freeman said, sounding so specking calm it made we want to piss myself. I was in a rage. I tried to bring up my cannon, and the bastard stepped on it. So there I sat, leaning against the shell of a guardian spider, my former partner pressing the muzzle of a particle-beam cannon against my helmet.

"Your combat reflex is taking over, Harris; this is why they killed off the other Liberators. You keep this up, and you're more likely to kill us than those aliens down there." Freeman tapped his cannon against my visor as he said this. Had he wanted to, he could have shattered the glass.

"You're the best man we have, but I will shoot you before I let you screw this job up."

Several things occurred to me at that moment. The first and most important was that even if I tried to kick his legs out or knocked his gun away, Freeman would shoot me without a moment's hesitation. The next thing that ran through my head was that I was exactly like the Liberators on Albatross Island—the ones who massacred helpless prisoners and guards. Freeman was right—once I finished off the spider, my blood in a boil, I would turn on anything I could kill.

With that thought came the beginnings of self-control. My muscles slowly loosened. I allowed my hands to drop palms down on my lap.

"You back in control of yourself?" Freeman asked.

The entire company, Sweetwater included, was staring down at me. Visors hid most of their faces; but I could see Sweetwater's expression, and he looked downright scared. I felt ashamed of myself. The funny thing was that as the reflex simmered, I felt all sorts of pains. I felt the last tremors in my shoulder and the vivid knot on the back of my head, and I felt small.

"Yeah," I said. "I'm back in control."

Anyone else would have helped me up. Not Freeman. He took a step back and kept his cannon trained on my face. I still had the last traces of rage, and I considered trying to shoot Freeman. Something in me liked the idea of shooting all of them, even Sweetwater. Then I took a deep breath, and the last traces of my rage evaporated.

I wanted to thank Freeman. I also wanted to apologize to him. Instead, I kept quiet.

"You okay, Harris?" Major Burton asked, as we started down the tunnel.

"Freeman was right," I said. "I'm surprised he didn't shoot me."

"If I were him, I wouldn't have shot you either. It was too much fun watching you beat the shit out of that dead bug," Burton said.

"Get specked," I said.

"After this is done, I hope to do just that," Burton said. "My wife's in the Hen House."

I laughed. It felt good. Then Sergeant Thomer said something for my ears only over a direct link. "Lieutenant, we better get moving. The guy from the lab is starting to melt."

48

"Holy shit, you could fit a whole city in this place," Major Burton radioed back when he reached the end of the tunnel. "This place is too big to be the inside of anything. It's like I'm looking across space."

A moment later, I stood out there beside him. The spider-things had hollowed out the mountain even more than I remembered, leaving a vast blackness in its place, a hollow vault that seemed to stretch on forever.

Giving the enormous vault a cursory scan, I had to agree. I could see for miles across the desert-like floor. I looked to find the cave-within-a-cave in which Freeman and I had found the spheres and the gas... that goddamned gas. It was gone.

The last time we were there, Freeman collapsed the entrance to the inner cave; but now the whole cave was gone, and the row of spheres shone in the darkness like a string of pearls. I did not even bother trying to count the glowing orbs; the string stretched on and on, and each of those damn orbs would have gas leaking from it—enough to saturate the planet.

"It looks like your spider drones are gone," Burton said. "The place is empty."

From this angle the cavern did look empty. I motioned back toward Breeze with an exaggerated nod so that Burton would see the motion, then I said, "That man back there did not slip and fall."

"No, he did not," Burton agreed.

So we turned and stared back down at the floor of the cavern. I do not know which lenses the major used, but I tried a combination of night-for-day and telescopic lenses, a bad combination under most circumstances. This time, though, it worked well enough. As I zoomed in, I saw movement hidden in the darkness. There were drones along the cavern floor; they had just dug deep pits around themselves.

I pointed this out to Burton, who followed suit, and said, "Shit. You're right, I see them."

By this time the rest of the company had caught up to us. Herrington and Boll, leading one of the teams carrying a nuke, sidled up to me. "So this is it?" Boll asked.

"This is it," I said.

"Where do we leave our packages?" Boll asked.

"See those lights out there, the spheres?"

"That's a long way out, sir," Boll pointed out.

"A long, dangerous way. Try zooming in on the floor down there," I said.

"I already have," Boll said. "Are they like the one that killed the guy back there?"

"No, those are the drones. They're the small ones. You saw how big the one in there was."

"Actually, sir, it was kind of hard to judge its size once you got through with it," Boll commented.

"Yeah, sorry. I guess I lost control," I said.

"Were you friends with that man in there?" Boll asked.

"Breeze? No, I barely knew him. He was one of the chief scientists at the lab."

"So he was friends with Dr. Sweetwater?" Boll asked. They all treated William Sweetwater like an old acquaintance. In the short time that I had mistakenly left the dwarf scientist unguarded, he had won them over.

"Yes, they were friends."

Freeman and Sweetwater waited in the shelter of the tunnel while the rest of us admired the size of the cavern. When I saw them, I radioed Freeman, and said, "I don't suppose we can detonate the bombs off from up here."

I watched them—Freeman kneeling to speak, Sweetwater considering the question. He pulled out the handheld meter, waved it in the air, then shined his penlight on it. He walked out to the ridge, squeezing between a couple of Marines, waved his meter in the air again, and shook his head.

Freeman bent down to see what the meter said. "We need to get closer."

"How close?" I asked.

Freeman and Sweetwater traded words. "Right up to the gas."

"Wonderful." I sighed though I had expected that answer all along.

Staring at the closest sphere, I could just make out the uneven carpet of gas bleeding out of it. Out of the side of my eye, I caught a glimpse of something moving along the cavern floor. I reacted instinctively. "Grenadiers forward. Rifles, cover the rear. Freeman, get Sweetwater back in the tunnel."

Just that quickly, the shooting began.

"Holy shit, there must be ten million of those bastards down there," said Herrington, the kind of Marine who normally downplayed the situation. That pretty much summed it up, though.

Eight of us remained on the ridge, including Herrington and Boll, who ran their nuke into the tunnel for safety, then came back out ready to fight. Below us, a small army of guardians and Avatari soldiers appeared out of nowhere. They poured out of trenches and climbed over dunes. Bolts of light seemed to generate out of thin air and fly at us. In the time it took me to hit my first target, three of my men went down.

Bolts of white light streaked through the dark air like fireworks. They were so bright against the darkness that they left echoes etched in my visor.

Out of the corner of my eye, I saw something fall. Memory and instinct taking over, I stepped forward, spun, and scanned the wall above us; but I saw nothing. The bastards knew how to camouflage themselves, but I had come prepared.

Dropping to the ground so that the Avatari soldiers coming along the floor of the cavern would not see me, I pulled one of the disposable flare pistols from my armor and fired an acetylene flare. The projectile moved at one-tenth the speed of a bullet, a packet of bright-burning chemical smoldering so hot that it melted anything it touched. The flare slammed into the granite fifty feet above my head, fusing itself to the rock and illuminating everything around it in white, blazing light.

With the light shining between the camouflaged spider-things and the granite wall, the spider-things showed up like islands of blackness. The guardian spiders did not have time to react before I tossed the empty flare gun, shouldered my particle-beam cannon, and hit all three of them.

"Boll, cover the walls," I shouted. Then I thought again. Assigning a grenadier to clear the walls would almost guarantee an avalanche. "Belay that order. Peterson, out here now. Watch the walls," I shouted as I pulled out another flare gun.

"The what?" he asked as he ran out.

"They're spiders, damn it. They're crawling up walls," I said, and then I fired another flare into the wall about one hundred feet up. The light exposed dozens of guardian spiders.

"Oh, shit," Peterson groaned and began firing. Burton and Mathis grabbed their cannons and joined him.

Still kneeling on the ground, I turned back to peer over the ledge. A hundred feet below us, dark shapes moved across the land. Closer in, a handful of Avatari soldiers stood firing in our direction.

"They're too far for rockets," Herrington said.

An Avatari soldier climbed over a ridge a few yards away, and

I picked it off with a shot from my cannon. A few stray bolts flew in my direction. In another moment, I would need to back up for cover, but first I took a second to study the lay of the land.

"Lieutenant, we can't stay here much longer," Herrington said. "They're coming."

I had already begun to have a combat reflex. I could feel the warmth in my blood, but I had control of my rage—my thoughts were clear. It was not about hate or even survival, this time I was fighting because I had an objective.

"Freeman, I need a sniper!" I yelled into my helmet.

Without saying a word, Freeman came lumbering out of the cave pulling his rifle from over his shoulder. He dropped face-first into a crawl and moved up beside me.

"I need that ridge cleared," I said, pointing toward an embankment. Even as I pointed, bolts flew out from behind it.

And then Freeman did something I did not mean for him to do—he pulled off his helmet. With one eye closed and the other pressed against the scope on his rifle, he sighted the aliens. Not wanting to inhale the shit in the air, he held his breath and fired several shots.

I tried to spot for Freeman as he hit enemies a thousand yards away. I saw the flash from the muzzle in peripheral vision, and one of the Avatari exploded. It looked out from behind a rock, and its head immediately burst. Another Avatari stood to fire at us. I caught the flash from Freeman's rifle, and its chest, head, and arms flew in different directions. Freeman hit four more, dropped his rifle, and slammed his helmet back in place over his head.

I started to say something to him over the interLink, but I heard him wheezing, heard a faint moan, a deep breath. Then he wrenched his helmet from his head again, raised his rifle, sighted in on his first target, and plugged four more Avatari before running out of bullets.

He threw on his helmet. Over our link, I could hear him sucking in air as he stuffed more bullets into the magazine.

"Can't you shoot that thing with your helmet on?" I asked.

Freeman did not answer, and the point became moot a moment later when Boll pulled out a big shoulder-fired rocket. The specking thing must have weighed thirty pounds, an aircraft-grade ordnance in a flimsy aluminum tube. Boll stood, fired, then dropped back down for cover. A moment later, the ridge the Avatari soldiers were using for cover dissolved in a bright flash.

I heard Boll laughing and cheering over an open channel on the interLink. "What the speck was that?" I asked.

"That, sir, was a thermite-tipped surface-to-air rocket," Boll said.

"Aren't thermite-tipped rockets illegal?" I asked.

"You brought a thermite-load down here?" Herrington asked, sounding incensed. "You'd have to be insane to strap one of those to your—"

"Lieutenant, those specking spiders are coming in behind us!" One of the riflemen in the tunnel interrupted the debate.

"Everyone out. Move! Move! Move!" I yelled. They were closing in on us, fighting more intelligently than ever before. Maybe they knew we were packing something dangerous, or maybe they just wanted to keep us out of their mines.

Boll and Herrington started back in to grab their nuke, but two of my riflemen had already replaced them. Freeman headed back for Sweetwater. There was an awkwardness to his movements. He walked with the overly solid movements of a man trying to cross a deck in stormy seas.

I dismissed it as unimportant. He'd probably burned his eyes when he took off his helmet, but I had no idea how badly. The fumes in the air may have hurt his equilibrium. I watched Sweetwater waddling toward Freeman and wondered how the little scientist had lasted this long. If a small whiff of the air had hobbled a giant like Freeman, what would it do to Sweetwater?

"Holy specking shit," yelled one of the men still in the tunnel. The opening flashed with the green of a particle-beam weapon.

"Get out of there!" I yelled.

The men with the nukes came out followed by riflemen, but there should have been more of them. I waited three seconds, then gave Herrington the order to "seal the cave." Anyone still in there had waited too long.

As we started down the ridge, Herrington piped a grenade into the tunnel. I cringed when I heard the explosion—it meant that we could no longer leave this hellhole the way we had come in.

49

Burton lost one of his riflemen, so I took a turn on point. That placed Burton, Peterson, and me on point, followed by another layer of riflemen, followed by the teams carrying the nukes. The grenadiers brought up the rear. Having handed off their nuke to two riflemen, Herrington and Boll took their places among the grenadiers.

Freeman and Sweetwater floated around our formation, sometimes meandering all the way to point to test the gas in the air, sometimes dropping back.

We did not bother with the switchback trail leading down ridge; instead we stormed down the slope, particle cannons out and blazing. We had come in with forty-nine men and were now down to forty-three, having just barely gotten our collective foot in the door. "You won't want to waste men or bullets," Admiral Brocius had warned me a million years ago when he handed me his pistol before briefing me on Mars. If only that bastard could be here to see just how right he had been.

Up ahead, a javelin-shaped foreleg came questing around a large boulder. I aimed my particle beam, waited for the head to appear, and fired. The shot hit one of the legs, and the spider-thing reared back on its hind legs. I charged toward it and fired again. The flash of my cannon lit up the creature's underside, and it dropped flat.

"Freeman, where are you?" I called out on the interLink.

There was an explosion behind me and just to my left. I instinctively dropped to one knee and spun just in time to see another guardian spider tip over and drop to the ground. The bastard's camouflage had fooled me. It was poised on a tall rock, and I had walked right below it as I attacked. The giant spider landed top down, its legs curled in, motionless on its back. That was the only time I had seen these things exhibit a truly spiderlike behavior.

I started to thank Freeman for pulling me out of that one, but that save came from Burton just a few yards away. "Speck!" he said, "I didn't see that thing until it was almost on you."

"They camouflage themselves," I said. I stared at the monster lying on its back and realized how close I had come. "Thank you... shit, that was close."

"Don't mention it," Burton said.

"Lieutenant, you've got two more heading your way at nine o'clock," Thomer called in over the interLink.

I turned, saw two spider-things working their way through a deep groove in the ground, and realized they were drones. They moved past us and continued on their way.

"Those are workers," I said. I watched them scurry away, both harmless and deadly. They could not attack because attacking was not in their programming, just as graffiti and lawlessness were not in the programming of the clones who had defaced the Hotel Valhalla, just like wanting to kill a superior officer was not in Thomer's programming.

I wanted to warn Freeman to watch the drones... maybe the aliens could change their programming. If the thousands of drones in this cavern suddenly rose and attacked...

"Freeman?" I called over the interLink. "Freeman?"

He did not respond.

"Thomer, where are Freeman and Sweetwater?"

A moment passed. "They're almost down the slope. The little bastard looks like he's burning up," Thomer said.

"Freeman," I said, creating a direct link. I heard the rasp of his breathing and realized that he had not responded because he could not respond. He must have inhaled some of the air when he removed his helmet. If he'd breathed even a trace of this gas, his throat would be seared.

I could see Freeman and Sweetwater threading their way toward me. In the blue-white world of night-for-day vision, they looked like a formation of shadows against chalky ground.

"We have to get Sweetwater out of here," Thomer said, naturally inclined to protect the people around him.

"He has a job to do, Thomer; just like everyone else," I said as I turned back to have a look at Sweetwater. I did not know what we could do for him, but we needed to keep him alive long enough to place the nukes, though I could not imagine how we could accomplish it.

Sweetwater's swollen face had puffed up badly. It was covered with blisters, and the skin was abnormally dark. His eyes had a glazed look. He might have been going into shock or he might have simply been dazed from pain. His ears, already covered with blisters, had a sponge-like texture. Liquid glistened on all of his exposed skin. At first I thought it was sweat, but I now realized it was fluid oozing out of the open sores.

"We've gotta keep moving," Herrington said over an open line. "There's a whole lot of company coming our way."

"Spiders or Avatari?" I asked.

"Spiders."

"Hold them off," I said. We could keep the guardian spiders at bay well enough with our guns as long as we did not allow them to get too close to us. The Avatari soldiers were another story, with those damned light-bolt rifles. They could pick us off, but they seemed scarce, just a guard or two. Perhaps the Avatari sent a small detachment to help guard this hellhole.

I signaled for Thomer to come.

"Freeman, they're closing in ahead of us. I need you up here." He did not answer, probably could not answer. I wondered how well he could breathe. As he and Thomer came to join me at the front of the party, I told Freeman, "I'm going to assign Sergeant Thomer to guard Sweetwater."

I heard a dry, painful sigh over the interLink, as Freeman brought down the particle-beam cannon he kept slung over his shoulder. He made an exaggerated nod and stood ready.

"Dr. Sweetwater," I said. I knelt beside him so that our eyes were nearly level. "Can you hear me?"

He looked at me and nodded. The sharpness returned to his eyes.

"Are we close enough to set off the bombs?" I asked, knowing the answer already.

He took a moment to consider this, then he opened his satchel and pointed to six metal tubes. "Need to take reading of the gas," he said in a whisper while shaking his head. The wet shreds of burst blister stretched the entire length of his throat. I wanted to shoot the little son of a bitch just to end his suffering.

"Can I run ahead and throw them in?" I asked.

He shook his head and held out that T-shaped meter of his.

"You need to run tests," I guessed, my heart sinking. We still had a mile-long hike ahead of us if we wanted to reach the gas. A light bolt soared over us, striking a large boulder and boring through it as swiftly as it flew through the air. Then the storm broke. The darkness took on a strobe effect as dozens of bolts struck all around us. We had stayed in one place too long, and the Avatari had homed in on us.

Freeman scooped Sweetwater up with one arm, his particle-beam cannon extended from the other, and ran for cover behind a boulder. Thomer ran behind them, shooting blind fire at the aliens to give Freeman cover.

"Major, close ranks around Sweetwater and the nukes..." I told Burton.

A few feet away from me, a man hid behind a boulder. Three

bolts seared through the rock, all of them missing him; but he panicked and jumped out from behind the cover. Bolts hit him in the leg, head, and chest, passing through him as cleanly as they had passed through the rock a moment earlier.

"Burton!" I yelled.

"On my way," Burton said.

To my left, a grenadier stood to fire a rocket. The bolt that killed him traveled straight up his extended arm and out through his shoulder, leaving only a shred of hollow armor behind. Had it been a bullet or even a laser, the man would have lived. He collapsed in convulsions, flopping around on the ground like a fish on a dock. I ended his suffering, firing a quick green burst from my cannon that exploded his helmet in a splash of blood and shreds of armor.

Sweetwater stared at me, a frantic mixture of shock and fear in his eyes.

"Looks like this is as far as we're going to get," Burton warned as he slid in beside me.

"Bullshit," I said. "Freeman, if this doesn't work, grab Sweetwater and make a run for the spheres." I rose to my feet, then spun so that my back was against a massive rock wall. I needed to clear a hole, just enough of a lane for us to get past this trap. If push came to shove, we'd detonate the nukes before reaching the gas, but only as a last resort. Prematurely detonating the nukes might not charge the gas, but it would do more than giving up and dying.

There were too many Avatari for us to fight our way through, and time was running out. In another five minutes, Sweetwater would die whether we got him close enough to calibrate the nuke or not.

Just when I thought we would never waltz out of the trap, I peered around the rock and saw something promising—aliens of a feather were flocking together. There may have been as many as a hundred Avatari soldiers out there, but they grouped together in a cluster. It might have been because they were not designed for underground combat, or it could have been because the aliens controlling those avatars were not used to this sort of firefight, but the soldiers massed in one small area were forcing the guardian spiders to handle the legwork.

"Boll, you got any more thermite tips?" I asked.

"Only legal loads from here on out," he answered.

"Shit," I said.

"I got one," Herrington said.

"You said I was insane for—" Boll said.

"You wanna point fingers or win this?" Herrington snapped. Then, in a calmer voice, he said, "Lieutenant, I have a thermite load to fire."

"Herrington, I'm placing a virtual beacon on the spot I need you to hit. Then I am going to break left and draw fire," I said. "Wait until you get a clear shot, then you light those bastards."

"Once you get clear of them?" Herrington asked.

"The moment you have the shot, you specking take it!" I said. As I said this, a barrage of light bolts splattered the ground around us. Two guardian spiders marched over a rock off in the distance. Freeman picked them off.

Crouching low and darting for cover, I tried to find a path that offered me cover as I circled around the Avatari. I sent messages as I ran, telling Burton and the rest of the company to move toward the spheres whether my plan worked or not. The clock was ticking; in the next few minutes every one of us might well die whether we succeeded or not.

Some sharp-eyed specker of an Avatari spotted me as I made my way toward a wall. A bolt missed my shoulder by inches. As I dived for cover in a trench, a bolt hit the rifle I kept strapped to my back. A few bolts flew over my head, then the attack simply stopped.

I peered out from the trench in time to see Ray Freeman stowing his particle-beam cannon. Freeman, murderous son of a bitch that he was, may have been the best man I had ever known.

I had already wasted seconds I could not afford. With Freeman as my guardian angel and trusting that none of the other Avatari had noticed me, I sprang from the trench and sprinted across open ground. At first I had a clear path, then one of the drone spider-things crawled out of a hole. I jumped left to avoid it, and the shooting began. Bolts flew through the air around me, not just one or two, but en masse. Four, maybe five bolts struck a rock ledge not more than twenty feet from me. The ledge exploded with such force that it threw me into a waist-deep hole.

Over the interLink, I heard Boll talking to Herrington.

"He makes a good distraction," Boll said.

"Shhh! I'm looking for my shot. I've waited my whole life to fire off one of these thermite jobs. It's kind of a life's ambition."

In order for Herrington to hit the target, I would need to distract the bastards. I placed my virtual beacon, then I sprang from cover. Bolts streaked around me, but they could not get a clear shot at me because I ran between rocks and stayed low to the ground. One bolt passed just a few inches from my face.

"Hey, there's the beacon," Herrington said.

"Fire the specking thing!" Boll shouted.

The flash Herrington's thermite rocket made seemed to make the world around me disappear. I had no idea if he had cleared the enemy stronghold, and I would need to go in to make sure the path was secure. As I lay facedown preparing to leap out, the dark form of a guardian appeared over the lip of the hole. It slashed at me with one of its forelegs, but I managed to jump out of its reach.

I couldn't kill the damned thing. If I shot and it fell on me, it would crush me under its bulk. If it touched me with its leg, my armor would short out, and I'd be blind.

The guardian lashed at me with a foreleg. I rolled to the other side of the hole and shot at the bastard's head. The spider reeled but did not fall, so I shot out its legs. The guardian fell backward, out of the hole. I did not waste time looking to see what happened to it.

"Cut your way through," I called over an open frequency. The message was mostly for Burton and Peterson—the men on point—but it was also meant for Boll and Herrington, our best grenadiers. I ran ahead until I had a clear view of the spot Herrington hit with that thermite rocket. I don't know how many Avatari had been there, but they were all gone now.

The grenadiers led our formation, with Burton and his riflemen coming up next. They had formed a tight circle around Sweetwater and the nukes. Even from a distance, I could see that Freeman was carrying William Sweetwater like a mother carrying a child.

Targeting guardians and drones, I cut across the ground between me and the rest of the company, leaping over holes and rocks, and skirting boulders. Somewhere in the distance, the Avatari regrouped and began shooting at us. Light bolts tore into two men behind me. As I turned to sight the aliens, I saw another of my riflemen fall.

My grenadiers went to work, firing rocket after rocket into the path to clear the way. The explosions cast a staccato of flashes across the bleak cavern. Their rockets exploded, sending twisting columns of smoke that rose from the ground and evaporated into the blackness.

In the flash from the rockets, I saw more guardians moving in the distance. "What the hell is it going to take to break through, damn it!" I yelled in frustration. I turned to look at the ridge to our rear and saw ten Avatari standing on an outcropping. Freeman cut down three of them. A dozen sparkling green beams demolished the others as the riflemen in the rear opened fire. The Avatari shot back at us, and I lost two more of my men.

The riflemen were falling back as the grenadiers forced their way ahead. "Stay together! Stay together!" I yelled.

Burton repeated the order.

Thomer fell back to help Freeman.

We found a twenty-foot rise that seemed to run the length of the cavern and climbed it. Along the crest of that rise I could see the light from the spheres as it traveled along its spine. We had to stick to the rise—the ground around us was buried under a layer of drones working so close together that their legs touched. The rise, though, left us as exposed as a can on a post in a shooting gallery.

"They're all around us!" one of my men screamed. That was our only warning that we had waded into the horde. The next moment guardian spiders started climbing up the sides of our path.

"They're coming in close," Herrington called over the interLink.

I barely had time to issue the order to switch to pistols before the guardian spiders began climbing the rise. Private Grossman, one of the men carrying the nukes, stood in the two o'clock position in our formation. When a guardian charged the circle from eleven o'clock, he and the three other men carrying the nuke shot it. He was still looking at the guardian they killed when another spider lashed out at him from the top of a twenty-foot shelf. His armor split, and he screamed in pain. The guardian slashed at him again and would have stabbed him clean through, but Herrington shot it.

Blind and scared, Grossman threw off his helmet. He inhaled a lungful of the poisoned air and dropped to one knee.

"Simmons..." I said. The man instinctively knew what I meant. He aimed his pistol at Grossman. "Sorry, pal," he whispered as he fired a single shot, which caused Grossman's head to explode. I did not know if being hit in the head by a particle beam was painless, but I was certain it beat the hell out of running around blind as the acid in the air melted you inside and out.

With only a hundred yards to go, the light from the spheres was so bright that my visor automatically switched to tactical view. Now I could see colors. I could see the black-gray spiders against the flat black rock.

A white bolt struck Thompson, the Marine walking next to me. He spun around and fell to the ground, lying there convulsing for a moment, then slumping into death. Another bolt struck Robison, one of the men lugging a nuke. It hit him in the head, and he fell dead and rolled down the hill. The other men handling that nuke lost their balance and slid after him, dragging the nuke in their wake.

"Cover me," Thomer shouted. He dropped on his ass and slid down the side of the rise. At least a half dozen of those spider-thing drones scurried along his path. I shot three; Burton might have hit five. We might have been down to two dozen men now. A bolt hit a man to my left a moment later, and we were down one more.

I spotted the Avatari trooper coming toward us, and fired.

"Boll, Herrington—cover our ass side," I shouted. "Use grenades, and don't worry about the trip home." The trip home was the last of our concerns. Herrington managed to pick off two Avatari a moment later. Boll took a bolt in the head and rolled into a hole with a drone. The giant spider-thing did not see him when it stabbed its leg through Boll's stomach and scratched at the ground flinging his corpse around like a rag. As it continued to dig, the spider-thing tore Corporal Boll in half.

"Get up here!" I yelled at Thomer, as he struggled to climb the side of the rise carrying the hundred-pound nuke. Bolts flew around us. Another grenadier fell.

I shouted for Freeman.

Ray came toward me, still carrying Sweetwater in the crook of his right arm. He dropped to one knee and reached for Thomer with his left. Instead of grabbing the big man's arm, Thomer handed him the nuke. He did not attempt to climb the hill. Instead, he turned, pulled out his pistol, and began shooting spider-things.

"What are you doing?" I asked.

"Get going," Thomer said. "I'll catch you on the way out."

"Sure," I said. "Catch you on the way out."

Three riflemen came forward and took the nuke. I was about to ask for a fourth man and realized these were the only ones I had left. We were down to twelve men—three men lugging one nuke and four lugging the other, Herrington watching the rear, Burton, Freeman, Sweetwater, and me.

We ran ahead as quickly as we could, stumbling along the top of the rise until we reached the spheres. A guardian sprang up to block our way, and I shot it. I shot it again and again because even though it was dead, it still blocked our path. The three men carrying the first of the nukes managed to snake their way around it, but the four-man team carrying the second bomb lost their footing and rolled down the side of the rise. They vanished into the darkness.

I could not go back to help them. Stray bolts flew through the air around us, and we had to move on. I did not see where they fell, and could not find so much as their virtual dog tags. Things were unraveling so quickly. By the time we reached the spheres, Burton was gone. Where we lost him, I had no idea.

Of the forty-nine of us that had left Valhalla that morning, only seven of us remained to place the bomb.

50

The line of spheres stretched out in both directions, an endless string of glowing balls simultaneously emitting crystalline white light and oozing brown sludge. The light from the spheres shone over the swampy puddle of the gas like overbright moonlight. The cave that had once covered the spheres had vanished, and only its footprint remained—a half-pipe trench partially filled by a layer of gas.

Still silent, Freeman carried Sweetwater to the outside edge of that trench and lowered him to the ground.

"Is he even alive?" Herrington asked me.

We got our answer when the scientist sank to his knees but remained vertical. Looking at the clock in my visor, I saw that only twenty minutes had passed since we had entered the Avatari dig. It didn't seem possible. It felt like the entire universe had changed in those twenty short minutes.

What was left of my company fanned out to form a perimeter while Freeman helped Sweetwater open his canvas bag and fish out equipment. I took my place along the perimeter, my back to the light, looking out into a darkness in which monsters lurked and stealing an occasional glance at Freeman and Sweetwater. One time I looked over my shoulder and caught a glimpse of Freeman dragging the scientist toward the spot where the gas came to the edge of the rocks. When I looked back again, I saw Freeman pulling some kind of cylinder out of Sweetwater's canvas bag. There were more cylinders on the ground, a whole pile of them. Freeman showed the cylinder he was holding to Sweetwater and the scientist shook his head.

Out in the distance, white bolts and green flashes were visible. One of my men was still alive out there, probably Thomer. A spider moved in the nearby shadows. Herrington raised a rocket to fire at it, but I hit it first with my particle-beam cannon.

"Nice shooting, sir," Herrington said.

Behind me, Freeman lay flat on his stomach and held one of the cylinders as far over the gas as he could. He brought the cylinder back and showed it to Sweetwater.

A bolt struck Private Ferris in the chest, and he crumpled. Herrington and I both returned fire, but the company was now down to six men. As I thought about it, for all intents and purposes, the magic number was five. Sweetwater could not possibly live much longer.

"Harrrisss." The voice whispering over the interLink sounded more like wind than someone speaking. "Harrrrisss." I would have dismissed the message as my imagination, but the name "Freeman" appeared on my visor.

I turned and saw both Freeman and Sweetwater staring in my direction. They had removed the nuclear device from its outer shell, and Sweetwater was sitting on the ground beside the disassembled bomb while Freeman knelt over him.

"Shoot anything that moves," I told Herrington and Grubb, the last of my grenadiers. I went and knelt beside Sweetwater.

Stripped from its shell, the bomb looked like a rock tumbler—a spherical canister with chrome piping and lots of wires. It had a little keypad, which Freeman must have used to program the explosion. Sweetwater could not have set the bomb; his fingers had swollen to the point of bursting.

The red LED above the keypad said *20:00*.

The goggles had done a fair job of protecting Sweetwater's eyes. The lids of his eyes were heavily swollen, and the whites of his eyes had mostly turned the color of blood, but he could see. Through the fog in his oxygen mask, I saw that blisters had formed on Sweetwater's lips around his mouth.

The scientist beckoned with both hands for me to come closer, so I bent down even lower until my helmet was practically against his face.

"What do you think, Harris? Would we have made a good Marine?" he asked.

"I still like you better as a scientist," I said. He chuckled, a painfully dry sound rising up from his throat.

"You'd make a shitty scientist, Lieutenant. You kill everything you see," Sweetwater croaked. Then he motioned me even closer. "The case... the case around the device. We've set the device to explode in twenty minutes. Put the bomb in the gas."

"The gas won't destroy the bomb?" I asked.

Sweetwater shook his head. "Not fast."

Even if the Avatari knew what we had and went looking for it, I doubted they would find the nuke in the gas. "You know, Sweetwater," I said. "I was wrong, you'd make a hell of a Marine."

Sweetwater coughed up something that looked like blood. "Run fast. Maybe you can make it out."

I wanted to tell him that we'd take him out with us, but I knew better, and so did he.

"The clock starts when you close the case. You better run fast," he said.

I toyed with the idea of simply setting the bomb off, then I looked at that clock again. If we made a mad dash and the aliens did not pin us in their cross fire, we could probably reach the transport in ten minutes, maybe less. A mile to the slope, a short uphill sprint, then out to the transport.

"The nuke's on a twenty-minute timer," I said on an open

frequency. "What do you think? Do we stay here, or make a break for it?"

"Think we can make it out?" Grubb asked.

"Maybe we should guard the bomb till it explodes. This whole thing is for nothing if the aliens disarm it," said Herrington.

"They won't," I said, "I'm throwing it into the gas."

"Well, in that case, I wouldn't mind collecting my back pay," Herrington said.

"Yeah, me too," I said.

I started to slide the inner mechanism of the nuke back in the sleeve, then stopped. Once I closed it, there would be no time to do anything but chuck the nuke in the gas and run, and there was something I needed to do.

A guardian spider dropped off a wall and landed on Private Neery. Herrington and Grubb shot the creature, but Neery was already dead.

Sweetwater lay on his stomach looking away from me toward the spheres. Sure that he could not see me, I slowly pulled out my pistol. The man had suffered too much. I wanted to end his suffering and seal the bomb, but I hesitated before pulling the trigger, and he turned and saw me.

He reached for me with the wad of raw meat that had once been his hand.

"Our gun," was all he said.

"You're an amazing man, Dr. Sweetwater," I said as I aimed my pistol at his head. I had not yet laid my finger across the trigger. I hated what I was about to do.

Freeman pushed my gun away. He dug through the scientist's canvas bag and pulled out Sweetwater's small-caliber pistol.

Freeman placed the gun in Sweetwater's hand, then gently closed the little scientist's fingers around the toy. Through the clear plastic of his oxygen mask, a faint smile formed across Sweetwater's bloodstained mouth.

"Turn us over," he called to Freeman, sounding like a sick child. Freeman carefully rolled him onto his stomach and stretched his arms out so that he looked like a soldier lying in wait. During their time alone in the cockpit, Sweetwater and Freeman must have discussed how the scientist wanted to die.

Herrington looked back over the scene, and said, "Good luck, Doc," on an open channel that everyone but Sweetwater could hear. "It's too bad they don't clone natural-borns; we could use an entire battalion of men like you."

As I started to slide the nuke into its sleeve, I saw Freeman gently pat Sweetwater on the back. The little pistol fell from his hand, and I knew William Sweetwater had died.

"Okay, boys, I'm going to start the timer. On my mark, start running and shooting, and don't stop till you've reached the transport," I said.

I heard a round of aye-ayes.

For a brief moment, it seemed like everything would work out, then the world around us suddenly became brighter. I turned and saw that the long line of spheres had begun to dilate; and worse, I saw the yellow outlines of Avatari soldiers inside each sphere.

Half-convinced the bomb would explode the moment I reassembled it, I shoved the inner mechanism back into its sleeve. The window on the outside of the outer cylinder showed that the clock had begun to count down the moment the innards snapped into place. I noted the time in my visor and sprang to my feet.

"Go!" I yelled.

Behind me, Avatari energy forms began marching out of the spheres. There must have been thousands of them, and there might have been tens of thousands more waiting to emerge. They were behind us, not between us and our way back to the transport, and they were slow. If we ran quickly, I thought we might still make it out.

Grabbing the handles on either end of the nuke, I hefted it off the ground, but I was weak from the march down here. I had trouble lifting the damn thing, and I had to wrestle it toward the gas. Less than a hundred feet away from me, more glowing yellow soldiers took form and emerged from the spheres—an army of creatures made of nothing but energy. Seeing the Avatari step into the knee-deep carpet of gas that surrounded the spheres, I had a moment's hope that the gas would dissolve them.

"Run!" I shouted, and dropped the armed nuke into the gas.

There were only four of us now. Grubb led the way, scrambling up the side of the ridge that led back across the cavern. Herrington followed, his pistol ready in case anything stepped in his way.

In the dark confines of the cavern, thousands of glowing beings poured out of the spheres behind us. They strolled across the layer of gas like a phosphorous tide, the light from their bodies spreading its glow through the gloom.

At the top of the ridge, Herrington stopped and turned to look back. "Harris, you better get moving. The whole specking Mudder Army's behind you."

A few yards ahead of me, Ray Freeman ran like an injured man, his back curled, his shoulders hunched and tight. He struggled to climb the loose slag along the ridge until I came up behind him and rammed him forward. It was a struggle—the man weighed at least 350 pounds, and he was weak, but we managed to reach the top together.

I hazarded a look back. Avatari soldiers continued pouring out of the spheres. They walked across the gas and moved in our direction, apparently unaware of the nuclear device I had left. In another minute or two, their rifles would become solid enough to shoot. We could outrun the Avatari but not their light bolts.

Herrington jogged back in my direction carrying a grenade launcher. He said something about slowing the bastards down, and I yelled, "Go! Just go!" At this stage, with their bodies still made of energy, a rocket would not hurt the Avatari, but it might damage the nuclear device.

I had only run a short way before I looked back and saw something that made the hormone-warmed blood freeze in my veins—the glowing front line of the Avatari had reached the spot where William Sweetwater's body lay on the ground as still as a rock. The light emanating from their bodies gave the ground around his corpse a golden glow.

I did not have time to process the images I had just seen; I could either push Freeman ahead or leave him behind. Left on his own, Freeman stumbled along as if he did not know where he was. The ground beneath us was loose and uneven, and the path was narrow and covered with rocks and slag. If he fell, I might not be able to get him up again, but I knew one thing—I would not leave this man behind.

Private Grubb lost his footing as he ran ahead of us. He tripped and flew face-first, but managed to land on the ridge. As he climbed to his feet, his right leg folded beneath him. He'd probably broken an ankle when he tripped. He stumbled, then rolled down the side of the rise, vanishing into a spider-thing's hole.

I fired a few blasts of particle beam in his general direction, but I could not wait to see if he made it out. Stopping for Grubb would mean sacrificing Freeman.

Freeman stumbled along at little better than a drunk man's run. *He's going to make it,* I told myself. I told myself this because it made me feel like I was in control, but the truth was that I didn't think Freeman's legs would hold out much longer. If he fell, I would stay and die with him.

Herrington pulled ahead of us by twenty, maybe even thirty, yards. Every few seconds, he'd pause, run in place for just a moment, and check back on us. When he reached the carcass of a guardian spider that we killed along the ridge, he stopped and lowered his gun. I thought he was waiting for us.

"Hey, asshole, get moving," I said.

Herrington fired his pistol into the darkness along the rise. Grabbing one of the dead guardian cablelike legs to keep himself up, he reached down the side of the slope, extending himself as far as he could. When he came back up the rise, Sergeant Thomer came with him.

By this time, Freeman and I were on his heels.

"Nice of you to join us," I told Thomer.

The other shoe dropped. The Avatari infantry began shooting.

We always knew that the Avatari's guns took on form more quickly than the avatars of the troopers. Silver-white bolts flew past us, sliding through the darkness at speeds just visible to the eye. Their aim was well wide of us, as if either their guns or their vision had not finished forming; but the message was clear—time had run out.

Still unaware of us, spiderlike drones toiled in their holes along our path. A guardian climbed on to the ridge ahead of us. Shooting his pistol as he ran, Herrington shot the thing so many times he dismembered it.

Had they been more fleet, the Avatari would have overtaken us, but speed had never figured into their battle plans. They won wars by attrition. Behind us, light flooded the cavern, not the silvery light of the ion curtain but the yellow glow of the onrushing tide of Avatari. Bolts flew through the air, ethereal dashes that flashed past us in a millisecond and vanished into the darkness. In the distance, more guardian spiders headed in our direction, but they were too far away to reach us.

Prodding Freeman from behind, I followed Thomer and Herrington to the final slope—the rise that would lead us out of the caverns. Only nine minutes had passed, nine minutes down and eleven minutes to go until the bomb performed whatever destructive magic Sweetwater had programmed into it. I hoped his magic would be strong enough.

The bolts were getting closer, striking the ground around us. A hailstorm struck just ahead of Herrington. He jumped back to avoid it, lost his balance, and slid back down on his stomach. Thomer made it to the top of the ridge, then dropped to the ground and began shooting to give us cover.

The next storm of bolts came so close that Thomer, Freeman, and I had to drop for cover. While we waited for a momentary hiccup in the steady stream of bolts, my eye flicked across the timer in my visor and I saw we now had only ten minutes to get away.

"Got any rockets left?" I asked Herrington.

"Nothing with a thermite tip," he said.

"The hell with thermite, give me anything that makes a specking bang," I shouted.

Herrington held up a grenade launcher. "It's all I've got left. I can—"

"Give it here," I said.

He did.

"Thomer, on my mark take Freeman and get out of here."

"I can—" Herrington began to argue.

"Shut it, asshole!" I yelled. "I'll be right behind you."

I stood and aimed the grenade at the spot on the ridge where the front-most Avatari were working their way around the dead guardian spider. "Now! Move!" I shouted.

The images I saw at that moment etched themselves in my mind's eye. Twenty or possibly thirty Avatari crowded around the dead spider. Their bodies had evolved to the point where the yellow light shone through cracks and crevices from behind a thin layer of tachyons. They had their rifles aimed, and I saw them fire bolts in the air, the flashes so bright they looked like holes in my memory.

The grenade struck the spider, igniting an explosion powerful enough to chew an entire section out of the rise. I did not wait to see if I hit them or if they could still follow us. Tossing the empty launcher aside, I sprinted straight up the ridge.

Above me, Thomer, Freeman, and Herrington fired a few particle-beam blasts, then darted into one of the tunnels. I followed. With eight minutes and five seconds left before the nuke exploded, the spiders and Avatari no longer mattered to us. We sprinted up the spiraling floor of the tunnel. My lungs and legs spent, I started to laugh when I flew around that final corner and saw the bright light at the end of the tunnel.

With seven minutes and twenty seconds remaining, we reached the outer entrance of the caves. Not until we left the cave did I realize that Freeman was our only pilot. There were only four of us now—Herrington, Thomer, Freeman, and me, and the Unified

Authority did not waste its taxpayers' money teaching piloting skills to simple combat Marines.

Every moment mattered. In another minute, fully formed Avatari troops would pour out of the cave like ants out of an anthill. They would be slow, but their weapons could tear through our transport. In five minutes a fifty-megaton nuclear bomb would explode, collapsing this mountain and hopefully attracting every specking tachyon on the planet. If Sweetwater had any other information about how the gas would react to a nuclear explosion, he took that secret with him to the grave.

We'd left the ramp of the transport open. Herrington ran in first, then Thomer. Freeman shambled in and stomped across the kettle, pulling himself up the ladder to the cockpit.

I hit the button to seal the rear ramp and headed toward the ladder to check in on Freeman. "Harness yourselves in, boys, it could be a bumpy ride," I told Herrington and Thomer as I climbed the ladder.

Freeman hunched behind the controls still wearing his helmet. His back was stiff and his shoulders hunched.

The transport's engines rumbled with just over two minutes to go when the craft lifted off the ground. We did not circle the mountain to get a good look at the explosion. Freeman took us straight up and straight away. We might have been a hundred miles away when the nuke finally went off.

They say you can hear a nuke from hundreds of miles away, but we never heard a thing. We flew at a speed faster than Mach 1, and the sound never caught up to us. Riding in the steel belly of the transport, we did not see the flash.

I shuttled between Thomer and Herrington in the kettle and Freeman in the cockpit. Time with Freeman was spent in silence. He did not remove his helmet, and he did not speak.

I was in the cockpit with Freeman when we reached Valhalla. The sky was dark, and lights sparkled in what was left of the city. The ion curtain had vanished, leaving a night sky in its place.

51

I spent the night in the hospital with Freeman.

Doctors spent six hours operating on his throat and lungs. When they finally wheeled him out of the operating room, his face was wrapped in bandages, and an oxygen vent was attached to his bed.

"He breathed in a vesicant," the doctor told me.

"A what?" I asked.

"He's got blisters in his throat and lungs," the doctor said. "Whatever he breathed, it burned a lot of tissue."

"Is he going to be okay?" I asked.

The doctor took a sharp breath, and said, "We tried to clean the toxins out of the blisters. If we got all of that stuff out, he should recover."

Two orderlies wheeled Ray down the hall to his room. I followed them down and watched as the doctor checked Freeman's vitals and chemical drips, then left.

Darkness never looked so good, I thought as I spread the blinds and peered out the hospital window. Streetlights blazed in the parking area below, stars showed in the sky, and in the distance, the first orange-and-pink streaks of sunrise pierced the horizon.

I dropped down in the seat beside Freeman's bed and fell asleep.

I woke the next morning in time to find some significant brass coming up the hall. One of the generals had come to look in on Freeman—General James Hill, from the Air Force.

"How is he doing, Lieutenant?" Hill asked as he entered the room.

Hill was younger than the other generals, and I had the feeling he was a great deal smarter than the other generals as well. He was the only officer who ever seemed to understand all of the scientific jargon used by the late doctors Sweetwater and Breeze. I sure as hell never fully understood them.

"They say he's going to live," I said. "He inhaled a vesicant." I tried to use the word as if I actually knew it.

"I thought he had combat armor," Hill said. He knew the word. "That should have protected him."

"He took his helmet off," I said.

Hill nodded. "That's right. I saw the video feed from your helmet."

My helmet... No wonder they didn't force me to stay for a debriefing. Once they downloaded the video from my helmet, they would know everything I knew.

Freeman lay before us, a mass of cotton and tubes. His massive chest expanded and contracted rhythmically under the sheet. Except for his chest, nothing on the bed moved, not his fingers, his eyes. The screen beside his bed showed steady vital signs.

"He was crazy to take off his helmet," I said.

"You were all insane," Hill said. "If any of you had acted sanely, we'd all be dead now."

I thought about Thomer jumping into a horde of spider drones to save the nuke. I remembered Boll and Herrington carrying thermite-tipped rockets strapped to their backs. They cared more about the mission than they did about themselves. If he lived, at least Freeman would walk away a billionaire. All Herrington and Thomer had to look forward to was a long life in the Marines.

"Did Sweetwater's plan work?" I asked. There was a night sky over Valhalla when we landed, so I knew that at least part of the plan had succeeded.

"Harris, Sweetwater and Breeze may have been the finest scientists of all time. Have you seen the sky? There's a sun in the sky. The ion curtain is gone, the tachyons are all stuck in that gas."

"Did you reach the battleships?"

"We've even sent messages to Earth," Hill said.

"What's to stop the Avatari from coming back?" I asked.

Hill shook his head. "They haven't come back yet. I suppose we know how to ruin their plans next time they do."

"They'll come back sooner or later," I said.

"We're going to take the war to them," Hill said.

"Take the war to them?" I asked.

"Apparently back on Earth they have some idea about which galaxy the Avatari are from. They're sending the Japanese fleet to explore the neighborhood."

I thought about this and fell silent. I was tired, and this new information left me dizzy. *Taking the war to them,* I thought. It had a nice sound to it.

Hill stood studying Freeman for several minutes, his hands clasped behind his back and a look of sympathy on his face. He watched Freeman's vital-signs readouts and stared into the bandaged face. Finally, he turned to me, and said, "Well, it was a pleasure serving with you, Lieutenant Harris. You lived up to everything I've ever heard about you."

We traded salutes, and the only general to visit Ray Freeman turned and walked away.

I stayed with Freeman for two more days. I watched his fingers twitch and his eyes roll as he dreamed. He woke briefly, then the doctors placed him in an induced coma, saying his body would heal more quickly if he was asleep. It was while he was in that coma that they grafted new skin on his face and throat. They rebuilt his eyes.

He would, they told me, leave the hospital as good as new.

But it would take time. Everything would be as good as new, but it would take time.

ACKNOWLEDGMENTS

While looking for the right name for his fictional spy, Ian Fleming poached the name James Bond from the author of the book *Birds of the West Indies*. I borrowed the name Wayson from a friend of mine named Wayson Okamoto, who was neither a bounty-hunting Marine nor a clone. Wayson was a microbiologist. He worked for the Board of Water Supply back in Honolulu.

I mention this only because Wayson Okamoto passed away in March 2007, and those of us who knew him will miss him deeply. The real Wayson and the one in my books resemble each other only in name. Wayson Okamoto was a kind and friendly person. He was a man who would quickly accept people into his circle of friends and someone you could always count on for a smile.

I attended the Nebula Awards in 2007. No, I was not a nominee, but that did not stop me from attending. Anne Sowards, my editor, invited me to join the Ace/Roc table during the banquet—a rare invitation for a freshman writer like me. During the banquet, I sat next to Joe Haldeman, author of *The Forever War*.

To date, *The Forever War* is my all-time favorite science fiction novel, so it should come as no surprise that I blubbered sycophantically upon meeting this pioneering author. Mr. Haldeman sat to my left, and Jack McDevitt, author of *Cauldron*, *Outbound*, and *A Talent for War*, sat to my right. On that particular night, Mr. McDevitt won the Nebula Award for his novel *Seeker*.

You know, it is a marvelous thing when you sit between two great masters and realize that they are friendly, interested, polite, down-to-earth people. Science fiction, and maybe writing in general, puts out a humbler breed of celebrity than most arts.

Anyway, I wanted to thank Anne and the editors at Ace for allowing me to join their table.

On to the business at hand.

As always, I wish to thank the lovely and talented Anne, for everything she has done to help me on this project. *The Clone Alliance*, the previous Wayson Harris novel, passed from manuscript to novel easily. *The Clone Elite*, which you now hold in your hands, required far more work. Thank you, Anne, Cam, and the rest of the crew for all of your overtime.

The first problem was that I ran into a bit of a literary detour while writing this book. The detour should have lasted eight weeks, instead it distracted me for six full months. The good news was that I had finished the first draft of the novel before hitting that detour. The bad news was that when I finally turned the first draft of *The Clone Elite* over to my readers, I did not receive the warm response I had hoped to get.

They all said the same thing—the first pages of the book were choppy, the middle seemed to fly by, then the book fell apart in the last lap. They all disagreed about the source of the problem. John Thorpe, the first one to read the book, wanted Harris to find true love with Marianne, Ray Freeman's sister. I thought that sounded good until Rachel Johnson pointed out that at the end of *Rogue Clone* Harris says he never speaks to Marianne again.

I originally killed Freeman at the end of this book. Rachel liked that a lot because, as she said, you cannot save humanity without sacrifices. Mark Adams and John (Thorpe) said absolutely not— not if I ever planned to write another Harris book. As of this moment, I have signed a contract for a new three-book series of Harris books. Book one is due out in 2009.

In the end, the repairs were done during rewrite; I hope you enjoyed the final results.

Thank you, Rachel Johnson, for spending so much time helping me get this book in shape.

As always, I turned to Lew Herrington when I needed advice about life in the Marines. And, as always, I did not turn to him nearly enough. I wish to apologize to the Marines for everything I have gotten wrong about their tactics and their culture.

I thank my agent, Richard Curtis, for help placing this book and for the sage professional advice he often gives.

Above all, though, as I close this series of adventures, I wish to thank those of you who have read these novels. Thank you for coming along for the ride.

Steven L. Kent
February 27, 2007

ABOUT THE AUTHOR

Steven L. Kent is an American author, best known for *The Clone Rebellion* series of military science fiction and his video game journalism. As a freelance journalist, he has written for *The Seattle Times*, *Parade*, *USA Today*, the *Chicago Tribune*, *MSNBC*, *The Japan Times*, and *The Los Angeles Times Syndicate*. He also wrote entries on video games for *Encarta* and the *Encyclopedia Americana*. For more about Kent, visit his official website www. SadSamsPalace.com.

**READ ON FOR AN EXCLUSIVE SHORT STORY
BY STEVEN L. KENT**

NOT WITHOUT HONOR

As he was known to do, Archie began the morning sermon with a scripture. "And whoever does not take his cross and come after me, cannot be my disciple," he quoted.

Sitting toward the front of the congregation, his teenage daughter Marianne heard these words and thought, *Oh shit. Here we go again.*

"So what is our cross? On what tree shall we be crucified?

"Can our cross be the planet on which we live? We live on a planet that yields her fruits grudgingly despite our labors. Is living on Sinai our cross? Life here is certainly burdensome."

Esther, Marianne's mother, sat to her left, looking serene and content, happy to float along with the tide of her husband's professions and words. Raymond, Marianne's younger brother, sat to her right, wearing a sardonic smile.

Archie's wife hung on his every word; his son considered him a lunatic.

Marianne sat between them, physically and spiritually.

"Sinai is a planet named after a desert. Are we here because God delivered us, or abandoned us? Perhaps God saw fit to bring us to this accursed planet as a trial of our faith. Is it possible that Sinai is our cross?"

As a member of a nomadic Neo-Baptist colony, Marianne had already lived on six planets in her seventeen years. The Unified Authority gave the Catholics and Muslims productive planets for their colonies. To the Neo-Baptists, the Unified Authority gave deserts and ultimatums.

Raymond stretched his legs straight, pressed his back against the old wooden pew, and leaned closer to his sister. "Is it possible that Archie is our cross?" he whispered.

She had to stifle a giggle. Raymond made her laugh, he always made her laugh.

"What about family?" asked Reverend Freeman. "Can our families be the cross we are asked to bear?"

The words bit deep. Though she worked in the fields all morning and taught school into the evening, Marianne never complained. Like her brother, she didn't share her father's beliefs, but his approval meant everything to her. She lived to make her father proud.

"Jesus Christ said, 'A prophet is not without honor, but in his own country, and among his own kin, and in his own house.' Words both true and bitter.

"Jesus's mother and brother watched as he died on the cross, but of his father we hear nothing. His extended family may not have nailed him to the cross or traded him for thirty pieces of silver, but they didn't welcome Jesus into their homes when he returned to Nazareth. His people ignored him and questioned his credentials. Were they not a cross he had to bear?"

"Sometimes his words hit me like they're made of wood," said Raymond.

Marianne shushed him, then asked, "What is that supposed to mean?"

"It means I'm bored to death," said Raymond.

Archie continued airing his laundry, cleansing his family of their sins by waving them over his congregation. As his sermon reached its crescendo, he said, "A father is not without honor except among his family and in his house. How can that be? And yet it is so."

Raymond leaned in so close to Marianne that his lips brushed the rim of her ear. "Dumb-asses don't get respect at home, either. A man can be a father and a dumb-ass at the same time. How can that be? And yet it is so."

Sinai was a Neo-Baptist colony with a population of three hundred and ninety-two people living in prefabricated cabins. It was a religious commune, though the people who belonged to it referred to themselves as a congregation and their commune as a kibbutz.

Everyone over the age of eight worked in the fields from six in the morning until three in the afternoon. While children and teachers attended school from four until eight, the rest of the colony cooked and cleaned, and then they all met for dinner, after which they retired to their cabins and went to bed.

On Sinai, the Sabbath truly was the day of rest.

Having never experienced life away from Sinai, few members of the congregation realized what a tough life they led. They were tenth-generation colonists; to them, knowledge of life away from dying fields and Spartan cabins was just another a sinful dream.

Raymond Freeman suspected life was better on other planets and shared his opinion freely, not that anyone listened. At fifteen, Raymond was six foot five. He worked hard in the fields and did well in school, but he was a big talker in a community that prized meekness, a free-thinker in world that valued obedience.

His father berated him, the people ignored him, and his sister feared for him. Raymond laughed at alienation. He taunted the other boys as he worked, challenging them to match his strength, daring them to silence his mouth.

During the spring, as the sun baked the fields so hot the seeds baked in their furrows, Raymond pulled pumpkin-sized rocks from the soil and threw them on a pile that grew taller every day. The other boys avoided him. They watched him from afar, fearful of his size and because they had tried to beat him down, and failed. Once, when he was fourteen and barely six feet tall, three boys had jumped Raymond as he worked. They were three of the biggest boys in the community, old enough to start families of their own. They surrounded him as he worked alone in the fields. When the fight ended, he left them where they fell and returned to picking rocks.

Raymond Freeman was the serpent that had entered their garden. He was the nail that stuck out and needed to be pounded down.

Most days, Raymond picked between two and three hundred pounds of rock out of the fields. He picked out the big rocks, then the others came and gleaned the smaller stones he left behind.

While the others went to the church building for lunch, Raymond sat on a pile of rocks and waited for his mother to bring him food and water. The sun heated the rocks and the warmth soothed the muscles in his thighs and the small of his back.

Following her husband's lead, Esther seldom spoke to her son. She handed him a cup and filled it with water which he guzzled quickly, then, silently, she filled the cup again.

Esther looked past him, staring into the endless flatlands that were Sinai. The ground and the horizon formed an unwaveringly straight line. No clouds lingered in the powder-blue sky and the wind carried not so much as the promise of moisture.

Raymond drank a third cup of water and then a fourth.

Esther handed her son a sandwich and waited as he devoured the meal. Though he was bigger than the others and worked harder in the field, the laws of the kibbutz allowed him no more food than anyone else. The laws and byways were unequivocal.

When Raymond finished his sandwich, Esther poured him a final glass of water and left, not having uttered a word to her son. The breeze whipped up dust and grains of sand that caught in his hair and nipped at the back of his neck.

By the time the others returned from their lunch, Freeman had pulled a half-dozen rocks. On other worlds, farmers used ultrasonic plow heads that made boulders crumble into gravel. The Neo-Baptists used no such machines.

They believed that man earns his bread by the sweat of his brow. By the sweat of Raymond's brow, the Neo-Baptists prepared their fields and planted wheat and corn.

Like her brother, Marianne worked in the fields during the day. At seventeen, she had blossomed into womanhood, her long wavy hair bleached brown by the sun, her body solid but curvaceous. She had big bones and wide shoulders and thighs as solid as a man's, but her face was lovely and her eyes were soft.

Archie had said that a prophet was not without honor except in his home. Marianne was not without admirers except in her home. The only men on Sinai who never dreamed about Marianne were her father and her brother.

Young men brought her gifts and older boys invented reasons they needed to chat with her. Older men fantasized about her and tried to convince themselves that they might still have a chance. Women feared her because they knew she could have any man on the planet.

Like Raymond, Marianne dreamed of leaving Sinai. It wasn't just Sinai, it was the commune and communal living that she hoped to leave behind.

Together they formed a snare, coiled tight and ready to explode.

There was the reverend, the father, the king—the man who ruled his home, his planet, and his commune; there was the son—bitter and boastful, resentful of the people amongst whom he lived; and there was the peace-making daughter—the self-sacrificial lamb, beautiful and splendid and so alone.

And into that mix came a naïve visitor, a man ignorant of authority, offensive to the offended, and the kind of man who wouldn't notice a trap until it was sprung.

* * *

The freighter arrived on a Wednesday afternoon.

The Sinai congregation couldn't sustain itself. The colonists placed acres of moisture traps around the desert, plastic sheets that harvested water from the ground in the form of condensation, but the traps didn't produce enough water to keep the congregation alive, let alone their crops.

So the colonists relied on the charity of the Church. Rather than allow their experiment to fail, the elders of the Neo-Baptist Church sustained Sinai with contributions.

The freighter orbited the planet while three transports ferried the supplies. They hauled filters for the desalinization plant that strained farming and drinking water from the sea. They brought crates of food and seeds for planting. They brought medicine and Bibles and clothing.

The transports were long, sleek, and diamond shaped. Rocs that seemed to drop out of the sun and glide down like shadows landed between the congregation and its fields.

Like military transports, these cargo ships only opened aft. They landed, their rear hatches split, and cargo handlers staged their crates while the men of the congregation hauled them to the church building.

The pilots didn't join in the work. They were young and skilled and too proud to tote supplies. They emerged from their ships and strolled while others lifted. They didn't speak to the workers or the colonists. They were officers in a Mercantile Marine corps. They were grand lords, and they separated themselves and watched as others toiled.

Had there been a shady hill or a stream where they could picnic, the three pilots would have sat and rested. This was spring, the rock picking season. In another two months, what wheat and corn survived long enough to break the soil would appear. At that moment, the only plants on Sinai lived deep beneath the sea.

The pilots paid little attention to the colonists. They ignored the men who helped with the cargo and the boys working out in the fields. They didn't thank the women who brought them water and sandwiches to eat.

And then Marianne arrived to hand them apples.

"Will you look at her," one of the pilots muttered to the man beside him.

"Not the prettiest flower I've ever seen," said the second.

"Maybe not," said the first, "but far too pretty a flower to waste away in a desert." He sat up and watched her. As she approached, he asked, "What's your name?"

Marianne smiled at the man, gave him his apple, and didn't answer. The colonists didn't trust outsiders. One of the reasons so few abandoned the congregation was their shared paranoia about the worlds their families had left behind.

"Let me guess... Miriam? Bethany? Hope? Charity? Faith? Chastity?" the pilot pressed.

Marianne smiled all the more. She handed fruit to the other pilots. Embarrassed, she walked away.

The pilot followed. By Unified Authority standards he was tall, six foot two, but a runt by the measure of the men on Sinai. The old man who stepped in front of him had four inches on the pilot. He wasn't old really, probably in his late forties or early fifties, but the sun had parched his skin to leather and his eyes had yellowed. He was mostly bald except for the half-moon of hair between his ears.

"Can I help you?" he asked in a soft voice with a thunderous crash that reminded the pilot of a waterfall.

"I was just..."

"Following my daughter," said the old man.

"Your daughter?" asked the pilot.

"My girl."

Now that he had stopped, the pilot noticed men staring at him. A line of boys stood at the edge field, watching. The men who had come to help with the cargo had stopped to watch as well.

The pilot put up his hands in surrender. "I think I'll just go sit with my friends."

Archie nodded. He pulled a chair from inside the building and leaned it against the outer wall. There he sat, watching as the pilot returned to his friends.

"That girl was nearly big as you," one of the pilots said when he rejoined them.

"See the guy sitting by the door there?" asked the first pilot.

"The one that shot you down?"

"Yeah, him. That's her dad."

"Really? Well, he may have saved your life. When those guys saw you walking after her, they stopped hauling cargo," said the third pilot, the oldest of the three. He pointed to the men by the transports, then added, "So did the boys in the fields."

"So what if I want to talk to her?" asked the first pilot. "I'm not going to take her away from them. I didn't try anything. What does it mean to them?"

"Don't you get it, moron?" said the third pilot. He was a small white-haired man in his fifties. "You're an outsider. We're all outsiders. They don't trust us. You're a wolf and they saw you following one of their sheep across their pasture."

The girl stepped out of the building and spoke to her father. Watching from a few hundred yards away, the pilot imagined that they were talking about him. The girl looked his way and so did her father.

"Oh Lord, they're really going at it. You didn't say anything stupid..." the older pilot said.

"I asked her what her name was," said the pilot. "Just her specking name."

Of the three hundred and ninety-two colonists of Sinai, there were five young Turks, each of whom saw himself as a prince in the kingdom. As the pilots sat and watched Marianne argue with her father, Hop and Phineas Eliasson, Boam Solomon, and the two Allred brothers approached them from behind.

Being between the ages of eighteen and twenty-one, the young Turks justified their every impulse and action in their minds. They could lie and make themselves feel good about it. They could bully a lone boy in the fields, and sleep at night. Now they saw outsiders trespassing on Sinai's most sacred treasure and they mistook murder for mischief in their heads.

Hop Eliasson shouted, "You! You have no business here!"

When the pilot turned around to see who had yelled at him, Hop hit him so hard that his legs went limp and he fell. Blood trickled from his nose and his split upper lip. Hop kicked him across the chest for good measure. When the second pilot yelled for Hop to leave, the other Turks attacked.

Hundreds of yards away, Archie Freeman saw the commotion.

"Hey!" he yelled in his thunderous preacher's voice, but he was too far away.

The young Turks spent their days working the fields. They had the stamina and strength and fearless conviction of youth, and they had grown accustomed to air that baked their lungs. The pilots were smaller and weaker. Boam Solomon grabbed the old one by his collar, threw him to the ground and kicked at his head. Hoping to protect his brother, Phineas Eliasson grabbed the last of the pilots by the hair.

"You! All of you, stop!" Archie's voice boomed through the air. Everyone heard him except the boys for whom it was meant.

Phineas Eliasson held his pilot by his throat and squeezed. He didn't worry about choking the man; instincts and paranoia and hormones had seized control of his brain.

The pilot felt the world spin. His chest and head burned. His knees went weak. He struggled to get free, thrashing as his arms went numb and his thoughts turned white and shapeless.

He had a knife.

As spots flashed and multiplied in his vision, his right hand brushed his pants and he realized his only hope of survival was the three-inch folding blade he kept in his pocket. Feeling like his head would explode at any moment, the pilot pulled the knife and flipped it open. He stuck it into the side of the giant... the boy.

It wasn't a fatal wound. The blade was three inches long and two inches had not gone in, but Phineas fell screaming and bleeding and holding the spot on the side of his ribs from which the blood bubbled. The fight became a riot as men and boys all threw in.

"Stop! Stop! Stop!" Archie Freeman shouted, but no one heard him. No one cared. Blood had been shed. The frenzy had begun.

And then the boy who everyone so feared stepped into the center of the frenzy. He was tall and strong, and above all, he was furious. When Hop Eliasson dashed toward the first pilot screaming at the top of his lungs, the boy threw Hop backwards to the ground. One of the Allred boys tried to hit the Goliath and then fell unconscious from a punch that landed with the resonance of axe cutting deep into a tree.

The boy grabbed Boam Solomon by the shoulder and twisted his head until he saw Phineas, lying in the dirt.

"Get him to the church!" the boy yelled. Boam obeyed.

Raymond turned to Archie. "Is this how you run things in your Garden of Eden?" he asked.

"Be quiet, son," growled the old man.

Raymond glared at his father and all the men around him.

"You, all of you, make me sick," he said. He turned to the old man and added, "You're not Jesus; you're not Moses; you aren't even Jonah inside the belly of the whale, old man.

"They don't have a Bible story for you. You're just a fool with a dying congregation."

Esther stepped forward, and the sound her hand made as it slapped across the Raymond's face rang out like a gunshot.

"Go away with these men, Raymond. You are not welcome here anymore," she said.

They stood and stared, the mother looking so angry, her unflinching eyes fixed on her son's. Raymond's shoulders fell. He turned to his father, but Archie Freeman looked away. And Marianne, beautiful Marianne who did everything her father told her, sobbed and hugged her excommunicated brother until her mother finally spoke.

"Step away from him, girl. He's not family no more."

That evening, Ray Freeman left Sinai on the freighter.

* * *

The following Sunday, Archie Freeman delivered a sermon about Cain, and Judas, and Satan, the son of the morning. He quoted the Fifth Commandment, "Honor your father and your mother that your days may be long in the land that the Lord your God is giving you."

The congregation rode along with his words. He was their strength, a man given to God who did not weaken in the face of temptation. He was the keystone that held their tribe together; he was the sure stake that held their camp in place.

Deep in his heart, Archie Freeman silently recited a verse that no one would hear, *"O my son Absalom! My son, my son Absalom! If only I had died instead of you—O Absalom, my son, my son!"*